4/25/17

3 9082 13228 9458

DOGS OF WAR

D1269564

AUBURN HILLS PUBLIC LIBRARY 50
3400 EAST SEYBURN DRIVE
AUBURN HILLS, MI 48326
248-370-0466

ALSO BY JONATHAN MABERRY

NOVELS
Kill Switch
Predator One
Code Zero
Extinction Machine
Assassin's Code
King of Plagues
The Dragon Factory
Patient Zero
Joe Ledger: Special Ops
Dead of Night
Fall of Night
The Wolfman
Mars One
The X-Files Origins: Devil's Advocate
The Nightsiders: The Orphan Army
The Nightsiders: Vault of Shadows
Deathlands: Ghostwalkers
Bits & Pieces
Fire & Ash
Flesh & Bone
Dust & Decay
Rot & Ruin
Bad Moon Rising
Dead Man's Song
Ghost Road Blues
Dark of Night

ANTHOLOGIES
V-Wars
V-Wars: Blood & Fire
V-Wars: Night Terrors
X-Files: Secret Agendas
V-Wars: Shock Waves
Out of Tune
X-Files: Trust No One
X-Files: The Truth Is Out There

NONFICTION
Wanted Undead or Alive
They Bite
Zombie CSU
The Cryptopedia
Vampire Universe
Vampire Slayer's
Field Guide to the Undead
(as Shane MacDougall)
Ultimate Jujutsu
Ultimate Sparring
The Martial Arts Student Logbook
Judo and You

GRAPHIC NOVELS
Marvel Universe vs. Wolverine
Marvel Universe vs. The Punisher
Marvel Universe vs. The Avengers
Captain America: Hail Hydra
Klaws of the Panther
Doomwar
Black Panther: Power
Marvel Zombies Return
Rot & Ruin: Warrior Smart
V-Wars: The Crimson Queen
V-Wars: All of Us Monsters
Bad Blood

COLLECTIONS
Whistling Past the Graveyard
A Little Bronze Book of Cautionary Tales
Beneath the Skin:
The Sam Hunter Case Files

BOARD GAMES
V-Wars: A Game of Blood and Betrayal

JONATHAN MABERRY

—•—

DOGS OF WAR

AUBURN HILLS PUBLIC LIBRARY 50
3400 EAST SEYBURN DRIVE
AUBURN HILLS, MI 48326
(248) 370-9466

ST. MARTIN'S GRIFFIN
NEW YORK

This is for Gail and Denny Gremel.
Thanks for being our home-front angels.
And, as always, for Sara Jo.

This is a work of fiction. All of the characters, organizations, and events portrayed in this novel are either products of the author's imagination or are used fictitiously.

DOGS OF WAR. Copyright © 2017 by Jonathan Maberry. All rights reserved. Printed in the United States of America. For information, address St. Martin's Press, 175 Fifth Avenue, New York, N.Y. 10010.

www.stmartins.com

The Library of Congress Cataloging-in-Publication Data is available upon request.

ISBN 978-1-250-09848-1 (trade paperback)
ISBN 978-1-250-09849-8 (e-book)

Our books may be purchased in bulk for promotional, educational, or business use. Please contact your local bookseller or the Macmillan Corporate and Premium Sales Department at 1-800-221-7945, extension 5442, or by e-mail at MacmillanSpecialMarkets@macmillan.com.

First Edition: April 2017

10 9 8 7 6 5 4 3 2 1

ACKNOWLEDGMENTS

As always, I owe a debt to a number of wonderful people.

Thanks to John Cmar, Director, Division of Infectious Diseases, Sinai Hospital of Baltimore; Dr. Steve A. Yetiv, Professor of Political Science, Old Dominion University; Michael Sicilia, formerly of California Homeland Security; my friends in the International Thriller Writers, Mystery Writers of America, and the Horror Writers Association; my literary agents, Sara Crowe and Harvey Klinger; my stalwart editor at St. Martin's Griffin, Michael Homler; Robert Allen and the crew at Macmillan Audio; and my film agent, Jon Cassir of Creative Artists Agency; my brilliant audiobook reader, Ray Porter. Thanks to Patrick Seiler of the Raymond James Group; thanks to my translators, Donna Marie West, Jessica Michelle Weigner, Samantha Yanity, Stacy Kingsley, and Carol Kasser. Thanks to Sarah Schoeffel. Thanks and congrats to the winners of the various Joe Ledger contests: Steve Duffy, Tricia Owens, Claire Deeming, Natasha Fedyszyn Zoby, Christina Seeling, and Maritza García Boak.

Special thanks to my fellow thriller writers James Rollins (the Sigma Force novels), Weston Ochse (SEAL Team 666), Jeremy Robinson (Chess Team), F. Paul Wilson (Repairman Jack), Larry Correia (Monster Hunter International), and Joe R. Lansdale (Hap & Leonard). Mr. Church isn't the only one who has friends in the industry.

Thanks to Tony Eldridge of Lonetree Entertainment and Donna Isham of Vintage Picture Company.

AUTHOR'S NOTE

There's a lot of very scary weird science in this book. I'd love to be able to say that it's all science fiction, that none of this technology exists. Sadly, everything here is either in active development, in advanced stages of field testing, or is already being used.

PART ONE
SMALL MONSTERS

●————————————●

*The gods conceal from men the happiness of
death, that they may endure life.*
—Lucan

AUBURN HILLS PUBLIC LIBRARY 50
3400 EAST SEYBURN DRIVE
AUBURN HILLS, MI 48326
248-370-9466

CHAPTER ONE

"Mom . . . ?" she whispered into the phone. "Mom, I want to come home."

The girl sat huddled against the headboard of the motel bed. It was scarred with cigarette burns. So was she. Old ones, from before she ran away.

Her words drifted down the telephone lines and only silence came back.

"Mom . . . are you there . . . ?"

Tears broke and ran down the girl's face. She was naked. Her clothes were torn because the last john liked to do that. She hurt inside, because he liked that, too. The sheets she'd wrapped around herself after he left felt stiff and coarse, abrading her skin, offering scant protection and no comfort.

"Mom, *please*," she begged.

She heard the sucking sound of her mother drawing on a cigarette. A pause, then the long hissing as she blew smoke. It was so vivid that the girl could almost smell the unfiltered Camel.

"Mom . . . ?"

"We looked for you," said the voice. It sounded the same. Cold, with a cigarette rasp. "We looked all over for you."

"I know . . . I'm sorry . . ."

"You just up and left."

"I'm sorry, Mom . . . but I . . . I *had* to."

"*Had* to? Bullshit, Holly. All you had to do was act right and you couldn't even do that," said her mother. "Why's that? What's wrong with you that you couldn't even try to act like we're all family."

"*He's* not my father."

"Yes, he damn well is. Maybe not by blood, but what's that matter?

He raised you. He took care of you. He took care of us both. Who do you think paid for everything you ever had? Your school stuff, your health care. Who do you think bought your birthday presents and gave you that bike for Christmas when you were eight? Who do you think cares so much about us that he does that, even for an ungrateful girl that ain't even his?"

"Mom, I—"

"And how do you say thanks? You tell lies about him. Who do you think you are to tell lies like that about someone who's always taken care of you?"

"I didn't lie," insisted Holly.

"You always lied. About that, about taking money from my purse. About the drugs."

"I didn't lie about him. About what he did."

"You're nothing but a little liar. And a junkie . . . and a whore. God, how are you even my daughter?"

"Mom . . . please!"

"And then you leave without so much as a goddamn note. You tell all those lies and then you break my heart and you don't have the respect to even leave a note. Would that have been so much? A note? You could have fucking texted me. But no. Nothing. That's so like you, Holly. It's exactly the sort of mean thing you'd do."

Holly was sobbing now, her tears clinging to the lines of her chin, then losing their purchase and falling onto the soiled sheets. Then suddenly she started to cough. Heavy, deep coughs that vibrated and burned in her throat. Spasms hit her so hard it made her ribs flare with pain, as if someone was punching her.

"Why now?" demanded her mother. "Why are you calling now? No, let me guess. You're in jail and you need bail money, right? Or are you going to try and trick me into sending you some cash so you can buy—"

The coughing fit battered her, making the room swim. Lights seemed to pop and sizzle in her eyes and there was a buzzing noise in her ears, as if a thousand blowflies were swarming inside her skull. The lights seemed to flare and dim, flare and dim, and each time more of what she saw seemed to be painted in a thin wash of dark red. It was like looking through a red veil that shimmered and jerked.

"Mom," she cried, when she could catch her breath. "I'm sick."

"Yeah? Go to the free clinic. They'll give you all the penicillin you want."

"No, it's not that. Please, I'm really sick." The buzzing in her ears was worse now, blocking out her thoughts. "There's something wrong with me."

Her mother laughed. Actually laughed.

Holly wiped her face with the sheet and in the gloom didn't notice the stain. Not for almost three full seconds. Then she saw it. The tearstains were wrong. So wrong.

They were red.

Such a bright, bright red. Not like the veil that covered her eyes, but the color of . . .

Blood.

"Mom . . . ?" whispered Holly. "Oh, God, Mom . . ."

"He said you can come home," her mother said, harsh and icy. "But only on the condition that you apologize to him. You have to tell everyone that you were lying about what you said."

". . . Mom . . ."

"You need to fill out some papers at the school and with the police to take back everything you said. You understand that? You can't just say stuff like that and hope it goes away. You *hurt* him with what you said."

"Mom, please . . ."

Blood was running from her nose now, too. She wiped at it with the sheet, terrified by how much there was. Then she felt warmth in her ears, and when she touched them her fingers came away glistening with crimson.

Her mother's voice droned on and on, telling her of the damage she'd done, the wreckage she'd left behind, the betrayal, the lies, the humiliation.

Holly whispered one last word.

"Mommy . . . ?"

A question. A plea.

Then the pain began and all that came out of her mouth after that was the screams. The red veil seemed to catch fire, and black flowers blossomed in her mind. She bared her teeth, biting the phone, biting at her own hands.

And that's when a sound came from deep inside her. It wasn't the blowfly buzz, or even a scream.

When Holly threw back her head and let it loose, it all tore out of her as a howl of pure, unfiltered, unstoppable rage.

CHAPTER TWO

I just got back from a dirty little piece of business in San Antonio and wasn't looking for more trouble. I'd gone down there as a gunslinger-on-loan from the DMS to intercept a bunch of cartel mules that were bringing in something nasty through a series of underground tunnels. Not drugs this time. No, these cats had containers filled with live mosquitoes carrying a very nasty new strain of the Zika virus. We tried to make it a clean arrest, but a couple of the bad guys decided to play it stupid rather than smart. That's something I've never understood. What's the worst that could happen to them if they surrendered? A few years in prison? Deportation? Better than being dead, which hurts more and lasts a long time.

We yelled at them, told them to drop their weapons, told them that they had no chance. They drew on us. We put them down. It was all very loud and nasty.

And, oh yeah, the transport containers? Not bulletproof. So we had to use flame units to incinerate everything in the tunnels. Even the few bad guys who, by then, were trying to surrender—they all died. Some quickly, some very badly.

I carried the sound of those screams with me all the way home. I knew it would be stored in that special place in my mind where the worst things I've experienced are placed on display in well-lighted niches. Ready for me to look at when I think I'm too happy.

My secretary, Lydia Rose, was waiting for me when I got off the elevator. She is a lovely woman. Short, round, with masses of black hair and the brightest smile in California. She took one look at my face and her smile dimmed perceptibly.

"Was it bad, Joe?"

"It could have gone better," I said.

Ghost was with me. He'd been shampooed, too, but he smelled like smoked dog.

Lydia Rose glanced up at me. "You probably don't want to hear this, then, but Mr. Church wants you to call. He says it's something important."

"Of course it is," I said. "The ass is probably about to fall off the world and everyone else but me is smart enough to screen their calls."

"Should I set up the call?"

I sighed. "Sure."

Ghost gave me a pitying look and trotted into my office. Lydia Rose asked, "Is Junie back yet?"

My live-in lover, Junie Flynn, was in some remote village in the Brazilian rain forest on a joint World Health Organization and Free-Tech venture intended to improve water purity. Hepatitis A started going wild down there a year ago, and Junie's researchers had come up with some spiffy new method of purifying river and rain water. The technology was part of the vast body of research and development conducted for decidedly *non*-humanitarian purposes by some of the groups we've torn down. Funny how something made to destroy can be spun around and used for the common good. That's what FreeTech is. Junie runs it, along with Alexander Chismer—Toys—formerly a bad guy who's now trying to save his soul by saving the world—and a dedicated staff of scientists and developers. The downside—or, perhaps the *selfish* side—of this is that she's away. A lot. The Brazil trip was supposed to be two weeks long, but we were already into the second month.

"No, she's damn well not," I grumped, and slammed my office door.

A moment later I heard Lydia Rose yell, "Well, don't take it out on the whole damn world!"

My phone rang. Outside the window I could see the beautiful sand and beautiful surf under the beautiful sun and knew with absolute certainty that I wasn't going to be enjoying any of it. I answered with great reluctance.

"What's your operational status?" asked Church. No "Hello," no "Good job in San Antonio. Thanks for saving the world." That's Church.

"I'd like to get drunk and eat too many fish tacos."

"Get them to go," he said. "I need you on a plane to Prague."

"Why do I want to go to Prague?"

Church said, "Do you remember the sewers of Paris? Remember what you went there to destroy?"

"Yes, and I'm pretty sure I actually *did* destroy it."

"Life is full of ugly surprises, Captain. It's surfaced again in Prague. Same technology, or perhaps the next generation of it." He explained the situation to me. It started with a case that I seemed to be handling on the installment plan. It happens like that sometimes. You think you closed the file on something and it turns out there's more to do. Either the case is bigger or you missed something or someone comes along and tries to resurrect it. There's a saying that evil never dies; it merely waits and grows stronger in the dark. I used to think stuff like that was poetic claptrap. I've since come to realize the unfortunate wisdom in old adages.

Church told me that a team of agents working for Barrier, the British counterpart of the DMS, caught wind of something while they were in the Czech Republic working on another case. They couldn't stop their own operation, so they handed it off to us.

"Jesus," I said.

"Go to Prague," he said.

"I don't have a team on deck," I said. "Top and Bunny are still out scouting for recruits. Triton and Boardwalk Teams are out on gigs. Unless you want me to take my secretary, I'll have to do this alone."

"Call a friend," said Church, and hung up.

I set the phone down, got up, and looked out at the beautiful spring day. *Call a friend.* Church was famous for his "friends in the industry," a catchall label to describe key people whose knowledge and qualities he trusted. I had my own friends, as he well knew. He hadn't named a name, but he didn't have to.

I took out my cell phone, punched in a number, leaned my forehead against the cool glass, and waited for her to answer.

"Hello, Joseph," she said after the third ring.

"Hello, Violin."

CHAPTER THREE

Preston Wiśniewski was a connoisseur of screams.

In the seventeen years that he had worked as the building super for the Imperial Hotel, he'd heard them all. The sharp, sudden scream of a new resident seeing a rat for the first time. The piteous scream of a junkie finding his or her lover dead with a needle still in the vein. The outraged scream of an inexperienced prostitute the first time a john took her anally. The staccato scream of someone being whipped. The piercing scream of sheer, unbridled lunacy. The phlegmy scream of someone losing a fight in a very bad way. The soulless jackal screams of gangbangers as they stomped someone to death. The apologetic scream of a girl who tried to renege on services paid for.

So many different kinds of screams.

He sat at his kitchen table on the second floor, dressed in blue work pants and a T-shirt with a faded logo of Mr. Clean on the chest, working his way through a Sudoku that was giving him problems. The scream made him glance up, and he listened to the memory of it in his mind.

Was it different somehow?

Was it a new kind of scream?

Wiśniewski didn't particularly like screams, but he was philosophical about them. They were a part of his world. They were expected in a place like this. And, since this world was his world, he tried to understand them, categorize them, assign them ratings. Last week there had been a whopper of a scream when a male client was introduced to a strap-on for the first time. His scream had gone ultrasonic, and he'd kept it up for a full five minutes. That had been a new one, and Wiśniewski rated it a seven in a new category. He figured the man could have put a little more into it, and maybe would with a bigger attachment to the strap-on. The man had left smiling—and walking funny—and Wiśniewski figured he'd be back.

This scream, though . . . it wasn't like that. It was a female scream. A girl, he thought, not a woman. Probably one of the girls up on three. There were two whores working day shift up there. Kya something and Brandy something. The guys who liked to fuck the young ones did it in the middle of the day, usually on their lunch breaks, so no one would take notice of them being out. So their wives wouldn't miss them and think they were up to something. There were two guys up there now with the girls. The scream had come from one of the rooms directly above him, 304 or 306. Wiśniewski could tell. Even on four or five, he could usually pick the floor, the room.

There was another scream, and Wiśniewski frowned. It was shrill and somehow wet. Raw wet, like someone who wasn't used to screaming that loud and did it the wrong way. Did it hard enough to tear something. That surprised him, because he hadn't pegged either of the johns as hitters. They were both semi-regulars, and there hadn't been problems before. No bruises on the girls. Not even on Kya, who sometimes sassed the johns. She chased some clients off, but not because any of them had made her scream.

Not like this.

Wiśniewski waited, listening, head cocked. He chewed on the end of his pen for a moment, waiting for the next one. When they were that loud and nasty, there was almost always more, softer or louder. Seven times out of ten.

He waited.

There was another sound. Another scream, but different.

This time it was a man who screamed. And then there was a thud. Another. Hard, reverberating through the ceiling, spitting dust from between the cracks. More screams. Male and female now, overlapping, colliding, and the crash of something heavy. A table? A chair?

A body?

"Jesus Christ," growled Wiśniewski as he launched himself from his chair. "What the fuck is happening up there?"

He raced into the living room, where his nephew, Stanley, was playing video games with some kind of stupid set of goggles. Stanley stood in the middle of the floor kicking and punching as if he were fighting a host of ninjas. Stupid kid. Wiśniewski slapped the goggles roughly off the young man's head.

"Ow!" cried Stanley, and was about to say more when he froze, raised his face, and stared at the ceiling. The screams were constant now. "Oh, jeez . . . what's going on?"

Wiśniewski didn't answer. Instead, he snatched a sawed-off baseball bat from an umbrella stand by the door and hurried out.

He rushed to the stairwell, slammed through the door, and took the stairs two at a time. Wiśniewski wasn't a young man, or a thin one, but he was strong. Peasant stock, his grandmother used to say. Wide and barrel-chested and thick. Stanley, thin and short, followed but not as quickly. Wiśniewski reached the third-floor landing, yanked the door open, and saw that the hallway was filled with people. Girls dressed in underwear or towels or nothing. A few men hanging back, peering uncertainly out of rooms, not meeting the eyes of the other customers. One door was closed, and the screams were coming from inside that room.

"Everybody get back," bellowed Wiśniewski. "There's nothing to see here. Go back to your rooms. It's all okay."

The spectators retreated half a step. Wiśniewski bulled his way through them, bawling for Stanley to clear everyone out of the hall. The super reached for the handle and froze. The screams inside were rising in pitch now. They were terrible to hear, and there was another sound buried inside them. A more animalistic noise, which made no sense.

Was it a growl?

Christ, had someone brought a dog into the place? Why? Even here at the Imperial there were limits. Getting busted for prostitution was one thing, but bestiality was a whole different set of laws that Wiśniewski didn't want to break. Oh, hell, no.

He cut a momentary look over his shoulder. The girls, the johns, and his nephew all seemed to be frozen, barely breathing, staring. Then Wiśniewski tightened his grip on the baseball bat, turned the handle, and opened the door.

He stepped into a nightmare.

He stepped into a scene from some horror movie.

There was blood everywhere.

So much blood.

On the bed. On the walls. On the lampshade.

On the john, who lay sprawled like a starfish, half on and half off the bed. He was naked, hairy, pale-skinned, and all the blood, Wiśniewski was certain, was his. One of his eyes had been torn out and lay as a collapsed, dripping ruin on his cheek. His face and chest and arms were covered in long slashes and vicious purple bites. He screamed and screamed and screamed.

The girl, Kya, sat astride him. She, too, was naked. A tiny thing with vestigial breasts, a shaved crotch, a tattoo of a butterfly above her heart, and wild red hair. She screamed again, throwing her head back to hurl the shriek at the ceiling—or, perhaps, at God above—and then she suddenly bent forward and bit the throat out of the screaming man.

His screams collapsed into a wet gurgle. The girl worried at his throat, growling like a dog, ripping at the tough skin as she beat at him with bloodied fists.

Wiśniewski almost ran.

He stood there for a moment, stock-still, the weapon forgotten in his hand, mouth agape, staring at the red horror in front of him.

Behind him someone else screamed. He turned to see Stanley and the other girl, Brandy. Wiśniewski wasn't sure which of them had uttered the scream.

Then Kya snarled, and Wiśniewski realized that she was looking at him now. Her mouth was smeared with blood, and there was a shred of something glistening between her teeth, but her wild eyes were focused on him.

"Watch!" yelled his nephew, and it was almost too late, because Kya launched herself at Wiśniewski with shocking speed. The big super stumbled backward and swung the bat as much by accident as by intention. It whistled through the air and hit the girl on the upper arm. It was not a well-aimed shot and nowhere near as hard as he could have managed if he hadn't been panicked, but it was still hard. The girl weighed eighty-nine pounds, and the force of the blow sent her crashing into the dresser. That should have knocked her senseless, but it didn't. She hissed in fury rather than pain and came off the floor in a tearing rush. The super backpedaled and his shoulder caught the outside edge of the door at just the wrong angle, and his bulk slammed the door shut.

Outside in the hall, Stanley Wiśniewski stood staring at the closed door. Hearing the dreadful sounds that were coming from inside. Hearing the screams.

Hearing his uncle's screams.

Hearing those awful, awful screams.

JONATHAN MABERRY

CHAPTER FOUR

"I need your help on something," I told Violin, "and I'm resource-poor at the moment. Are you free?"

"Depends on what you have in mind, Joseph," she said.

"A job."

"Sigh," she said. "You're no fun. What kind of job?"

"Remember the sewers of Paris?"

"How could I forget? We waded through the shit of an entire city and then watched the sunrise together. So romantic."

"No, I meant do you remember why we were there? The research data we were after?"

"Of course I do," she said. "We burned it. Why?"

"Someone else has it."

I heard her sharp intake of breath, and then there was a short, heavy silence. I could almost hear her reliving that mission. A group of scientists had developed a performance-enhancing synthetic compound that combined select lean mass-building steroids with a synthetic nootropic compound that significantly increased and regulated hypothalamic histamine levels. In normal pharmacology, these drugs are wakefulness-promoting agents often prescribed to prevent shift-work sleepiness. This version was designed to build stamina and wakefulness to a point where the person being treated wouldn't tire and wouldn't lose mental sharpness. This wasn't for a supersoldier program or for anything tied to the military. It was for factory workers. The drugs were intended for use in Third World countries to increase the efficiency and output of unregulated factory workers. Shift workers who could work twenty-four or even forty-eight hours at maximum efficient output. It was a new tweak on legal slave labor, because it's for use in countries where there is no enforceable human-rights presence and where governments are easily bought. It could also be used for sex workers, and that is a special kind of living hell.

Violin said, "When do we leave?"

I told her that I was heading to the airport now. "Don't bring your puppy," I said.

She called me a bastard and hung up.

CHAPTER FIVE

Zephyr Bain was a monster, and she knew it.

Nothing less than a monster would be able to save the world. Nothing less than a monster would have the courage and the vision to do what was absolutely necessary to save the world from itself.

She wasn't even certain that she deserved to live in the version of the world that would exist when all the killing was done.

Probably not.

The people who survived, those who would thrive and benefit from what she did, wouldn't want to share that world with anyone like her. They wouldn't be the kind to abide a monster. It was a sad thought but an understandable perspective. After all, she was trying to cleanse the world of unclean things, and by definition she would become unclean in the process. The consolation was that the right kind of people would survive, and they would have a genuine chance to flourish. Without the others. Without the parasites who fed like vampires on the system.

The survivors would be the world's true élite, the ones who hadn't been chosen by any god but had earned their place in paradise through good breeding, intellectual superiority, usefulness to the forward momentum, and clarity of vision.

As for the rest?

Well, as she saw it survival of the fittest was more than a theory. It was a law mandated by the harsh realities of the world as it truly was, not as viewed through wishful thinking, political agendas, greed, or aggressive stupidity.

Even so, Zephyr would have liked to see the world make the change. After the dogs of war had been let off the chain and allowed to run rampant in the streets. How nice that would be. She had dreamed of it every night since she was a little girl. If she would be dead before it came to pass, then she prayed that her dying mind would revisit one of those dreams as the darkness took her.

It was only fair.

It was only right.

If it weren't for the cancer, it would be so much harder to accept. But the universe had been quite clever in the way it stage-managed all of this. Even the cancer. Giving Zephyr the knowledge, giving her access to the tools, and then giving her a shield against her own hesitation. It was all very tidy and efficient, and no one appreciated efficiency as much as she. The universe was messy, but the scaffolding of scientific truths on which it was hung was clean, pure, and without contradiction.

Her friend and employee, the little problem-solving Frenchman everyone called the Concierge, was one of the few who knew that she was dying. Her mentor and sometime lover, John the Revelator, knew, too. Few others. No one else who knew cared as much as the Concierge or John. The others with whom she conspired to bring about the change saw her as a means to an end, an agent of change, perhaps even a hero of the war, but she doubted that any of them would mourn her passing. They would be too busy framing the new world. Nor would they be a comfort to her as she died. There was no doubt about that.

The Concierge was different, because he was a philosophical man. He was the one who helped Zephyr cultivate an interesting perspective on dying. "The Egyptians and other cultures saw death as a passage," he told her. "The highborn would go into the afterlife with great fanfare and pomp. But they would not go alone. They would have their household staff killed, too, so that there would be people to see to their comforts forever."

She had been raised in a rich Wasp family but had spent some of her life drifting from one religious movement to another. Other churches, other faiths, even a few cults. Looking for answers that she believed existed. Finding some truths, catching glimpses of others, but never quite landing on solid spiritual ground. It was John the Revelator who had helped her ultimately find something to believe in. John helped her see the face of God as He moved through the shadows of a twilit sky. He whispered to her that there was an answer, that there was something to believe in. There was a mission.

Her mission.

It was through John that Zephyr found her purpose in life, and in doing so realized what would have to be done to keep the whole world from falling apart. It was such a profound insight that Zephyr wondered if this was what Noah felt when God told him to start building a boat.

Maybe her allies, those indifferent framers of the future, would paint her as the new Noah. It was true enough, though her ark would be made of silicone and printed circuits rather than wood. And, instead of a flood, the unworthy and the unclean would be cleansed from the earth by a swarm of mosquitoes. The groundwork was already laid, a quiet process that had taken years. Soon—very soon—everything would be set and the go order would be sent. Sick as she was, she would live to see the process start. It would be glorious. There might even be the sound of angelic trumpets. God loved a good massacre. Zephyr had read many sacred books. God, in His love for the world, had killed billions.

So, too, would she.

For that is the work of both gods and monsters.

CHAPTER SIX

RUZYNE AIRPORT
AVIATICKÁ, 161 08 PRAHA 6
CZECH REPUBLIC
APRIL 26, 3:09 PM LOCAL TIME

I took my private jet, a gorgeous Gulfstream G650 that once belonged to a Colombian bioweapons broker who somehow managed to trip and fall out of the cabin door when we were three thousand feet over the Gulf of Mexico. Clumsy. I call the plane Shirley. Yes, it's immature to give a pet name to an ostentatious piece of luxury aircraft, and, no, I don't give a finely textured crap if it is.

Church finessed the clearances all the way. Violin was waiting for me at the airport, driving a two-door Porsche 918 Spyder. It's a super-elegant hybrid that will eat pretty much any gas-powered car on the road. Six hundred and eight horsepower, with a top speed of two-ten. The sticker price, before extras, is close to $900,000. I'm not into car porn, but that thing gave me a woody. I climbed in, and she peeled away as if she was leaving a crime scene.

"You came alone," I observed. "Where's your puppy?"

She made a face. "First, stop calling him a puppy. And, second, Harry is fine, thank you. He is auditing a class in Florence."

"A class? On what? How to find his ass with both hands?"

Harry Bolt—born Harcourt Bolton, Jr.—was the son of one of this country's greatest intelligence agents, who became one of this country's greatest traitors. It was Harcourt Bolton, Sr. who destroyed most of the DMS and damn near launched a pandemic that would have killed tens of millions of people, most of them children. We'd dismantled Bolton's plans, and Harry had helped. So he was a good guy. He was also very possibly the most inept agent ever to work for the CIA. Clumsy, nerdy, not too bright, moderately unlikable, and a bit of a jackass.

However, he and Violin had bonded during the Kill Switch matter and have since been keeping company. I tend not to read fantasy stories, so I'm not sure I understand how the whole frog and princess dynamic works. She is a world-class beauty who is cultured, highly intelligent, and remarkably skilled, and Harry looks like a shorter, dumpier Matt Damon, but without the talent or the charm. I tried to make myself believe it was the fact that Harry had inherited a billion dollars, but since Violin isn't that shallow I had to dismiss the idea. I've tried to make sense of it, but all I do is bruise my brain.

"Harry is auditing a lecture series on ancient mysteries and lost sacred artifacts," said Violin. "It's being given by an archaeologist in residence at the Pitti Palace in Florence."

"Why?"

She gave me an enigmatic little smile. "Harry would like to be the next Indiana Jones."

"Um . . . correct me if I'm wrong, but the *last* Indiana Jones was a fictional character."

"Don't be mean," she said. "If this is what he wants to do, then what's the harm? He's his own man."

Since Harry was now unemployed and rich, if he wanted to go globe-hopping to try and find the Holy Grail or the Ark of the Covenant, he had the free time and could finance it. Who knows, maybe he'll even find something of great historical value. It's less likely that he'll find a clue, but I didn't say that to her.

Besides, I was too busy hanging on for dear life. You have to be right with Jesus if you're riding shotgun with Violin behind the wheel. I'm positive I left fingernail marks on the door handle, and I almost fell on my face and kissed the ground when we arrived at our destination.

She drove us out of the city and into the country, to a densely wooded patch of forest on a mountain slope overlooking an industrial campus. We arrived while the sun was high, which gave us more than three hours of daylight to observe and plan.

We were looking for a place with the nondescript name of Podnik Řešení, which means "Business Solutions." Pretty much the John Smith of business names. Luckily, the lab wasn't in a sewer this time. I'm a big fan of missions *not* being in sewers. There's something about splashing around in the toilet water of an entire city that doesn't make one feel like James Bond. Instead, our target was a suite of labs leased in the moderate-sized industrial complex. More than forty businesses were based there, most of them involved in some kind of chemical or biomedical research. A couple of technologies companies, too. The DMS computer guy, Bug, had provided me with a floor plan from the local zoning commission, and we had satellite and thermal-imaging pictures. Violin and I studied the data and then surveilled the buildings using sniper scopes, locating access points, cameras, foot patrols, and guard stations. We counted one foot patrol and two in each of the gate stations.

"As far as we can tell," I said, "most of the businesses in there are legitimate. Podnik Řešení is both the name of the whole building and the name of our target company. The name confusion lets them blend in. Our target lab is sandwiched between a firm working on a diet supplement and an independent blood-testing facility. Bug ran background on both, and they're clean."

Violin nodded, and I assumed she'd done her own background check through Oracle, the Arklight computer system. It was nearly as good as MindReader.

A shift change took place as we watched, and Violin spotted something.

"Joseph, look at the uniforms of the guards at the west gate."

The west gate was the one closest to the building entrance, with easy access to our target lab. I studied them and saw what she meant. "Different uniforms," I said. "Slate-gray instead of dark blue. Different company?"

"Dedicated security team," she said. "They have better weapons, too. Kalashnikovs as well as sidearms. The guards at the east gate only have handguns. What would you like to wager that only the Podnik Řešení lab has access to that entrance?" mused Violin.

"Sucker's bet."

We lay prone under cover of a gorse bush. Violin set down her scope and turned to rest on her elbow, looking at me. "If I was one of your team members, this is where I would ask about the rules of engagement."

"We need to walk out of there with hard drives, research data, and any biological samples we can carry."

"You're only talking about physical assets. What about the staff?"

"This science is used in over ninety sweatshops and fifty brothels in Southeast Asia and the poorer parts of Africa. These pricks have girls as young as nine on their backs and on their knees twenty hours a day, servicing anywhere up to forty johns every day of the hell that is their life. The people—and I use that word loosely—who work in the lab

JONATHAN MABERRY

make the stuff that keeps those girls going like sex robots. They make the stuff that keeps thousands of slaves on the job round the clock, day in and day out, making phones, sneakers, and high-end electronics. These people will keep working until they die. The rest of the family usually works in the same factories or whorehouses, Violin. You tell me how many prisoners we want to take? Personally, I'm feeling moderately Old Testament right about now."

She gave me a kiss on the cheek. "That's the Joseph I remember."

It was fully dark when we approached the west gate.

The two guards in the booth were big, and tough-looking. I didn't know a thing about them, or why they were there. Or even how much they knew about the kind of horrors they were protecting. Maybe they were just hired muscle and had no clue about the atrocities their employers were inflicting on the world. Didn't know, didn't care. Violin and I circled the booth and then went through the door in a fast one-two. We gave the guards no chance at all. Violin rose up, as silent and unseen as a midnight wind, and cut one man's throat. Before his blood could even splash the second man, I had a hand over his mouth and was using my rapid-release knife to screw a hole in his kidney.

They had key cards, so we took those and moved off, keeping out of sight of the rotating cameras, slipping in during split seconds of misaligned video sweeps. I removed a small device from my pocket and plugged it into the security-booth computer.

Violin nodded toward the device. "My mother says that Mind-Reader is getting old. It's been hacked too many times."

"You have something better?" I countered. "Don't forget, sweetie, but your Oracle system is based on MindReader."

She shrugged. "Mother has played with it a bit since."

Her mother was Lilith. No known last name, no known date of birth or place of origin. Not much in the way of human emotions, either. She was a survivor of a particularly brutal harem of sex slaves run by the Red Knights. Violin was born as part of a truly horrific breeding program. Lilith led a revolt that left the halls of that prison painted with the blood of her captors. I've heard some rumors of the things Lilith did to the ones she didn't kill outright, and I've since seen evidence of her handiwork. She runs Arklight, the militant arm of the Mothers of the Fallen, the group of refugees who escaped with her. Arklight is on a par with the DMS when the DMS is at its very best. Its members are vicious, uncompromising, and unflinching in their war against men who do this kind of thing to women. Lilith has killed more ISIL and Boko Haram fighters than any single person I've ever met, and I've met all the top fighters. Do I agree with her methods? Tough question. Let's just say that she makes a compelling argument, and I am neither fool enough, brave enough, nor chauvinistic enough to want to ever—*ever*—get in her way.

Oh, and she and Church apparently had a fling once upon a time. Not that this matters in relation to her combat work, but it somehow makes her even scarier.

"Since when is your mother a computer expert?" I asked.

"Since it became useful to be," said Violin, and allowed me to interpret that however I chose.

I sniffed petulantly and pressed the button to activate the computer connection. The little green light flashed, then went dark. I tapped it, but it stayed dead.

"Not a word from you," I warned Violin, and she held up both hands in a "no comment" gesture.

I removed the device, blew on the jack to make sure there was no pocket lint on it, and tried again. It flashed red, and then the light turned a steady green. MindReader walked in and *owned* their whole network. So there.

"Oh, bravo," said Violin dryly. I scratched my nose with my forefinger.

We crouched in the booth until the security cameras had done a full cycle of back-and-forth sweeps, during which MindReader recorded a loop. Then it fed that loop back to the system so that anyone watching would see only the same darkened parking lot. I tapped Violin and we left the booth and drifted toward the wall, used the key card, and slipped inside. As we'd predicted, this entrance was dedicated to the target lab. These people probably thought this setup gave them increased protection. They were wrong.

Violin drew her two knives. Lately she's been partial to a custom pair of curved *kukri* knives, the weapons favored by the fearsome Gurkhas. Her blades were blackened, and she held them with the loose circle grip of a serious professional. I'd seen those blades in action before, and it was a nightmare sight. I had my Wilson tactical combat knife. Short-bladed, light, but eloquent.

The foyer of the Podnik Řešení complex was simple, with pegs for coats, two administrative offices, and four labs on either side of a wide

JONATHAN MABERRY

hallway. All the lights were on, but the switches were on a panel right inside the front door. Tsk-tsk. I swept my hand down and plunged the whole place into darkness. We put on our night-vision goggles and went hunting in the dark.

There were cries of alarm. Then there were screams of fear. Then shrieks of pain. One voice begged for mercy, but he was asking the wrong people. It was ugly. So were we. And it was all over very fast. Fighting takes time. Killing doesn't. From the time we approached the guard booth to the time we fled into the night with backpacks filled with hard drives, our mission clocks hadn't even ticked off seven minutes.

The fires didn't start until we were halfway back to the car.

INTERLUDE ONE

STANFORD CANCER CENTER SOUTH BAY
2589 SAMARITAN DRIVE
SAN JOSE, CALIFORNIA
ELEVEN WEEKS AGO

Zephyr Bain sat on the edge of the examination table, slowly button-ing her blouse, staring at the wall, seeing nothing. The doctor was still talking, but Zephyr had long since tuned him out. She'd stopped lis-tening when he reached a certain point, and a single word hung burn-ing in the darkening sky over the landscape of her mind.

Metastasized.

As words go, it was a monster. It was a bully, a brute.

Tears burned themselves dry in her unblinking eyes.

She didn't bother asking how long. She already knew the answer to that question. Not long enough. Never long enough. She was nearly as old as she would ever get. There would be no more birthdays, no more Christmases. No New Year midnight kiss. No winter snows. None of that. Not for her. Never again for her.

All that was left was the bad parts. The process of getting sicker, of learning how deep the well of pain could go. From here on she would lose herself in increments—first her energy, then her strength, then control over bodily functions, then her mind. Her beautiful mind. It would all go away, like mourners leaving a graveside, until only she remained, cold and gone.

It wasn't fair, but then life was never fair.

It wasn't right, but then life was seldom right.

And it was inevitable, because the important things are.

She thought about that night twenty-eight years ago when John the Revelator had first come to her when she thought all the time had leaked out of her life. He said he'd filled her back up, but he had never promised that she would live forever.

Twenty-eight years, though.

Fuck.

It was twenty-eight more than she should have had. Even at six Zephyr knew that she was dying, that she would soon be dead. John had given her time. All this time.

Not enough time.

"Goddammit, John," she said quietly, spitting the words out in a fierce whisper. "God damn *you* for doing this to me."

"I'm sorry. . . ." said the doctor, confused, but she waved it away. After a moment, the doctor waded back in. "Our focus now will be on pain management. We can keep you comfortable and—"

She tuned him out again. Pain wasn't something she wanted to manage. Pain could be useful to her, and managing it meant drugs. That would shut her mind down even before the cancer took away her ability to think. No. There would be no management of the pain; there would be no willing participation in a conspiracy to numb her mind. No thanks.

Zephyr wished John were there with her right at that moment. She wanted to smash his head in with a chair. She also wanted him to hold her and say that everything was going to be all right, and tell her that he would fill her back up again. She wanted both things with equal fervor. She wasn't grateful for the extra time. She felt cheated by it because it made her understand what she was losing, and it was a much sharper and clearer understanding than a child could ever have.

John, she thought, *please do something.*

But John wasn't there, and even if he were she knew that he wouldn't do what she wanted. Even if he could. That time had passed, and he'd given her those twenty-eight years.

Zephyr slid off the table and landed flat on her feet, swayed, darted out a hand to catch the edge of the bed, waved off the doctor as he reached to help. Without saying a word to him, she walked out of the examination room, into the hall, through the waiting room, down in the elevator, and out to the curb, where her driver waited. There was concern and inquiry on the big man's hard face, and when he looked at her and saw the truth in the stiffness of her posture the driver's eyes grew moist. She marveled at that. Campion was an employee, a worker bee who had talent with automobiles and could stand in as a bodyguard if necessary, but he wasn't family and he wasn't a friend. Why should he care? she wondered. Was he afraid for his job? It had to be that, Zephyr thought as she climbed into the back seat of the Lexus

SUV. He couldn't care for her any more than she cared for him. He was paid enough to be good at his job, but she didn't pay him enough to actually care. It made her angry. Fuck him and his emotions. Fuck him for whatever he was feeling, whether it was self-interest or compassion. She didn't need that from him or anyone.

Campion closed the door and hurried around to climb in beside the wheel. "Home, Miss Bain?"

"No," she said. "The office."

He frowned. "The office? Are you sure that's best, considering—?"

"Considering *what*?" she snapped. "Take me to my damn office."

He winced as if he'd been slapped, and nodded. As he turned away, though, Zephyr saw the complex flicker of emotions in his eyes. He was stung, sure, but there was also evident tolerance and more of the same wet-eyed compassion. Christ. The asshole thought that she was being snappish because she was in pain and afraid. Like most of *them*, he had no clue what went on in the minds of his betters. Zephyr wanted to stab him. No, she wanted to give him her cancer and take his vitality. It was so wasted on people like him. When the change happened, when everything John the Revelator predicted came true, this oaf wouldn't be worth keeping around to grease the engines. Maybe—just a slim maybe—he might be useful in a factory during the transition to full self-driven automation. Maybe, but she doubted it.

Campion squared his shoulders, put the car in gear, and drove away without another word.

She settled back in the seat and pressed the button that closed and sealed the pane of soundproof security glass between her and the driver. Then she took her cell phone out of her purse and made a call to the man who had been both friend and occasional lover for years now. On the lecture circuit and on TV, he called himself John the Revelator. His real name was buried in the past, and the fake one on his impeccable set of official documents was John St. John. Only Zephyr and one other person knew who and what he really was.

John answered on the fifth ring. "How'd it go?" he asked.

"We're moving the timetable up," she said.

A pause. "That badly?"

"Fuck it, and fuck you."

Another, longer pause. "I'm sorry, my love. You deserve better."

"I deserve to live long enough to see it work, goddammit. But—" She paused. "Look, I at least want to see it start, okay? I want to watch it catch fire. Is that too much to ask? After everything I've done, is that too much?"

"No," said John in a soft and gentle voice. "It's not."

The car drove two blocks before she spoke again. "There's no more time, is there?"

"For you, my sweet? No. I gave you what I could."

"*How?*" she begged. "How did you do it?"

"Does it really matter?"

"I need to know."

"You don't," he said. "You were a candle in a strong breeze and your light was going out. I kindled a flame and you have burned so very brightly. You will flare like the sun when you go. Isn't that enough?"

She said nothing. Tears burned like acid on her face.

"When you go there will be nothing—not one person, not one inch of ground on this earth—that won't remember you, Zephyr. You are about to become the most famous person in history. No, let me say it with more precision and truth. You are about to become the most *important* person who has ever lived. You will do this world more genuine and lasting good than Jesus, Buddha, Muhammad, or anyone else. None of those pretenders have ever had your courage; none of them have ever had your genius. They are failures, because they had the same vision. They *knew* what had to be done, but they were weak men and you are a strong woman, and it is you, Zephyr Bain, my own beloved, who will give birth to a new world. You. No one else. You alone. Magnificent, beautiful you."

She caved forward for a long moment, her face buried in her palms, and shook with silent tears.

"I . . . I can't do it alone, John," she mumbled through her tears. Agony of heart and body painted her words with loss, with fear.

"You're not alone. I will never leave you," he promised. "I'll be with you to the very end."

"There's not enough of me left. I'm so sick . . . God, I can barely walk."

"You don't need to walk. You don't need strength of limb anymore. Your mind, your will, your certainty of what needs to be done is all that matters. Zephyr, believe me when I say that if I have to I'll hold your hand while you strike the match."

It was that, those words, that hit her, and a sob broke in her chest that hurt every bit as much as if someone had punched her. It made her heart hurt, too. But it also made her smile.

"Thank you," she said, and realized that she meant it. Her face scrunched up as sobs sought to bully their way out of her, but Zephyr forced it all back, stuffed it inside. She took a long breath. "Thank you for everything."

"Of course, my love," he purred. "Anything for you. Everything for you."

"Can we move up the timetable?"

"We can, but there will be risks. Several aspects of Havoc will have to be rolled out at the same time. That will be noticed. Our enemies look for patterns, my dear."

"Because of MindReader?"

"Because of that, yes, and because they have become habituated to a certain kind of useful paranoia."

"Useful?"

"To them," said John. "The nature of our troubled world has trained them to jump, and to jump very quickly. And experience with some of our old friends has engendered within them a tendency toward focused aggression. Mr. Church loves a scorched-earth scenario. The tidiness of it suits his insect mind."

Zephyr chewed on that for a moment. "What if we cut the whole process down and launch most of it at the same time in eleven or twelve weeks?"

"The Deacon and his people would see it."

"Would that matter by then?" she asked. "If it all happens at once, wouldn't the DMS and all the other agencies be overwhelmed? Once Havoc starts moving—and I mean the whole thing—how would they be able to stop it?"

John made a soft humming sound as he thought it through. "Hmm . . . you may be right, but don't underestimate the DMS. The Deacon is remarkably dangerous."

"So you keep saying. God, John, you talk about him like he has superpowers or something. He's just another government flunky. He's a nothing, a piece of shit to avoid stepping in. We can—"

"No," he said sharply, the reproof thick in his voice. "The Deacon is your enemy, but it is not for you to disparage him. Not ever, and certainly not to me."

"Why not? I thought you hated him."

"Hate him? No. I would gladly cut his heart out and offer it to the midnight stars, but hate him? How could I?"

Zephyr exhaled slowly. "You say things like that as if I'm supposed to understand what you mean." When he made no comment, she said, "I want to move the timetable up. What is the absolute soonest we could launch Havoc with a high degree of probable success?"

"Eleven weeks," he said at once.

"Then let's do it. And if you're afraid the Deacon and his goon squad will be a problem, then maybe we should ask the Concierge to see what he can do to spice things up. That little French psychopath always has some nasty ideas."

"He is deliciously creative," John agreed, "and he likes a challenge. Perhaps it would work best for us to get the DMS involved rather than try to do this completely off the radar."

"How?"

"Oh . . . something will occur to us, and certainly to the Concierge."

"Good. Give the Concierge the go-ahead. Let him deal the DMS in, if that will help. Make sure he understands that money is no object. Not anymore. Not for me. Tell him about what my doctor said."

"I will," he assured her. "But tell me, Zephyr my sweet, is this what you truly want? There is no coming back from this. If this fire is lit, it will rage out of control almost at once."

The car made a turn onto a lovely street lined with graceful Mexican fan palm trees. There was no wind, and they looked painted against the blue sky.

"Then let it burn," she said fiercely. "Please, John, let's burn it all down."

CHAPTER SEVEN

We took showers at Violin's hotel. Separate showers, which was different from the way we'd cleaned up after some past assignments. There is a strange politeness that comes over people who were once lovers and now found themselves in a confined space doing ordinary things. Eyes were averted most of the time, there was a lot of courtesy, a lot of "please" and "thank you." Like that. Except every once in a while we'd both become aware of it and exchange a look, a smile, a brief laugh.

When it was her turn in the bathroom, I sat down with a Mind-Reader substation laptop and uploaded every bit of data I'd found on flash drives and CDs. There was a lot of it. And I had to hand-scan some papers. The MindReader uplink fritzed out on me twice, and I had to reboot to get it to send. After that everything ran smoothly, and Bug's team was ready to receive it, triage it, and forward it along to different experts within our extended DMS family.

Some of the data was forwarded to Dr. Acharya, a celebrated specialist in biomechanical technologies. Acharya was not yet an official part of the DMS, but he was one of several multidisciplinary brainiacs being considered to replace Hu.

I was deeply conflicted about Hu's death, because he had been far from my favorite human being, and it's fair to say that I liked him a lot less than some of the bad guys I've shot, stabbed, and run over. He was a class-A dickhead . . . but he was *our* dickhead. Hu was beyond brilliant, and his conceptual understanding of cutting-edge science kept the DMS way out front. Since his death we'd worked with a number of experts, but we hadn't yet found anyone who could fill Hu's shoes. Never really thought I'd miss the little bastard.

"Can we get Acharya on the phone?" I asked.

"Sorry, no can do," Bug told me. "He's out in Washington State at this big super hush-hush DARPA event. He's consulting with all the top experts on military applications of nanotech and robotics. They have this incredible security protocol in place for the whole camp. No phones of any kind, no Wi-Fi, no personal laptops, nothing. All communication requests have to go through the White House. How crazy is that?"

"Well, this is moderately important, Bug. I mean . . . nanotech and chemical slavery?"

"You know that and I know that, Joe," said Bug, "but it's not happening on U.S. soil or in any of our current spheres of influence. The new president's still unpacking, and the Department of Defense is nearly as wrecked as we are. Ever since Kill Switch, the levels of security around things like the DARPA camp have gotten to the point that even a four-star general has to get permission in triplicate and countersigned by the Joint Chiefs to send an email to his own mother. It's nuts, and it's the kind of overreaction that creates a lot more problems than it solves. Besides, it's being run by Major Schellinger—and you know what she's like."

I sighed. Major Carly Schellinger was nominally U.S. Army but actually on the payroll of the CIA. She oversaw a lot of the most highly classified field testing of advanced technologies and was known for being humorless, unapproachable, unkind, and inflexible. Schellinger also swung an extraordinary amount of political weight, and I'd seen generals defer to her. To be fair, she has overseen most of the practical applications of advanced technology in the past ten years, including the High Energy Laser Mobile Demonstrator, which has the capacity to emanate a 10-kilowatt missile-killing energy laser from a mobile vehicle; SWARM, a deadly flock of coordinated roach-size explosive microdrones; combat autonomous-drive systems for mobile robot gun emplacements; and the electromagnetic railgun, which has a muzzle velocity of Mach 7.5 and a range of a hundred and twenty-four miles. She gets the geek squads and the think tanks to perform at max output and then drives development through prototype variations to field-ready rollouts in record time. She's also old money, and her family has been interbreeding with most of the other old-money defense contractors since someone filed the patent on the first bow and arrow. A battle-scarred old full-bird colonel once told me that he would rather try to pass a live porcupine through his own colon than try to get Major Schellinger to deviate from her personally orchestrated security protocols.

"Well . . . call her," I told Bug lamely. "Use your charm and nerdish good looks."

"She's Satan in the flesh."

"Try and sweet-talk her. Oh, hey, while I have you," I said, "I've been having all kinds of problems with MindReader lately. The upload gizmo was funky, and it took me forever to log into the network tonight. What's going on?"

"I don't know. Everyone's bitching at me about that today."

"Violin says that MindReader's getting old and senile."

"She can bite me."

"Be nice," I said, but he hung up on me.

I ordered food from room service and trolled through the data while I waited. It was some pretty horrific stuff. If I was feeling any lingering guilt about the lives we'd ended, it melted away as I read. Not only had someone found the science we thought had been destroyed; they'd upped the game. The nanites that had been introduced into the game worked like microscopic processing plants to manipulate the brain chemistry of every slave worker, making them dependent on new doses. If they ever escaped and tried to get clean, the nanites would then migrate into the brain and attack the pain receptors. The victims would be plunged into a world of mind-rending agony from which there was no possible escape short of being caught in an electromagnetic pulse. They would very likely be driven insane and probably kill themselves to stop the pain.

It was horrible. This was twenty-first-century science. I wanted to believe that when we torched that lab we wiped out the entire organization. Yeah, I wanted to believe that.

But I'm just not that naïve.

CHAPTER EIGHT

The man parked the truck as close to the plaza as he could get. He opened the door but didn't get out. Instead, he lit a cigarette and watched the madness.

The crowd had been building for days and was now pushing three hundred thousand. The noise from fifty different bands and all those happy voices created a joyful thunder that covered the entire town like a cloud. Some of the bands were on stages, but most were strolling musicians in little groups of two or three or four. The revelers were adorned with bright-colored embroidery and beadwork, with jewelry and extravagant hats. The man had no idea what holiday this was, and didn't much care. It was fun to watch.

A small pack of laughing children ran past, chasing one another, dodging and ducking out of reach in an improvised game of tag whose rules seemed to change depending on who was "it." The kids were dressed in old clothes that showed signs of use and had been patched and repaired many times. One boy had expensive American-made basketball sneakers, but they were ancient and patched with ragged strips of silver duct tape. The kids were skinny and dirty, but they were all happy in the moment, caught up in the immediacy of their game.

The man took a drag and exhaled slowly as he watched them. One boy—the one with the taped shoes—caught his eye and stopped a few feet away.

"*Buenos dias!*" he cried, and then held out a hand, asking for something. Anything. Begging is rarely specific. The man studied him with narrow-eyed appraisal, then dug into his pocket. The other boys, alert as wolves, caught the movement and flocked around the first boy, jostling for position, wanting and needing to be close enough to grab a coin. The man removed the silver from his pockets, saw that there was a little over a dollar's worth in American coins, and tossed it high. The boys rose like hungry koi, their colors swirling, as they lunged for the money, elbowing and hip-checking their friends to snatch nickels and dimes and quarters out of the air.

Laughing aloud, the man flicked his cigarette into the street, jumped down from the truck, and walked around the kids, who were now wrestling one another for the last coin. He went to the back of his small panel truck, unlocked it, and pushed the roll door up. He unhitched the metal cargo ramp and pulled it out, placing it just so on the ground at the best angle for removing cargo.

"Okay," he said aloud. "Playtime."

Immediately a dog walked out of the shadows of the truck. It was big and barrel-chested, with a bull neck and the blunt face of a mastiff. It came down the ramp with surprising care and delicacy, taking small steps until it was on the blacktop. The man nudged it to one side with his thigh, and the dog lost its balance and skittered for a moment before righting itself. It didn't bark or snap at the man. A moment later a second dog came down the ramp, then two more. All four were identical except for embroidered vests in different festive colors—red, blue, orange, and yellow.

The children stopped fighting over the coins—each having rightfully been claimed and pocketed—and stared at the dogs. The duct-tape boy leaned close to a companion with whom he had been wrangling over a nickel ten seconds ago and spoke in a confidential whisper. The other boy nodded. Whatever they said was lost on the driver, whose Spanish was indifferent.

"Hey," said the man, "any of you kids speak English?"

They all swore that they could, though that was mostly a lie. Like most poor kids in tourist towns, they knew enough English to work their street scams and to beg for money. But the duct-tape boy said, "I speak some little."

"Yeah? Good," said the man. "What's your name?"

"Israel Dominguez," said the boy.

"Israel," repeated the man, amused. "Nice. Well, tell me, Israel, do you like dogs?"

"Oh, yes, very much like! We have *un perro pequeño*—"

"English, kid," the man corrected.

"We have a little dog. *Su nombre es* . . . I mean, his name is El Cerdo—pig, because he is *muy gordo*. Very fat."

JONATHAN MABERRY

"Do your friends like dogs, Israel?"

The boy was immediately cautious, wanting to cooperate but not willing to share if there was some money involved. The man could read that on the kid's face, and he admired the self-preservation. It was always good to look out for oneself. He always had.

"Maybe they do," said the boy.

"Would you and your friends like to make a few bucks?"

Israel stiffened. So did the other kids. They all knew that word. *Bucks.*

"Oh, yes. Very much. How much?"

"You see my four pups here? You know what they are?" asked the man. The boys all shook their heads.

"These are *party* dogs. You know what that means?"

None of them moved, but their eyes became wide in anticipation of learning something new and amazing.

"They do tricks," said the man. "That's why I brought them here. They know all the best party tricks, and, let's face it, there's one hell of a party going on around here. Am I right?"

"Yes, señor," agreed Israel. "There is much party here."

"Now listen closely," said the man as he reached into his back pocket and removed his wallet. The kids watched with absolute fascination as he opened it and withdrew a thick sheaf of bills. He looked up and did a quick head count, and then peeled off eleven ten-dollar notes. American currency. "I'll give you and every one of your friends ten dollars each if you'll do me a favor. And there's an *extra* ten for you, Israel, because I'm making you the boss. What's the word? *Chefe?* I'm making you the *chefe*, Israel. You get twenty U.S. dollars."

The boys stared at him with huge eyes. Ten dollars was an incredible amount of money to them. The man had driven through the suburbs of this town. He saw the hovels these people called home. These kids were all half-starved, and ten bucks would buy a lot of tortillas and beans. Ten bucks was huge money. Twenty dollars was impossible.

"Do you want to earn that money, Israel?"

"Yes," said the boy quickly, his voice cracking a little with excitement. The other boys all shouted agreement, but the man patted the air to make them quiet down. The adults passing by cut looks at what was happening, and a few even stopped to watch, but the man ignored them. The boys did, too, except for the occasional uneasy glance for fear of seeing a parent or a cop.

"It's easy money, kid. All you have to do is take my party dogs into the plaza."

The boy frowned, looking at the huge dogs.

"Oh, don't worry," the man said, laughing. "I told you, they're friendly. They won't bite. They're part of the entertainment." He turned to the dogs. "Isn't that right? Give me a wag." All four dogs wagged their tails. "Okay, knock it off." The wagging stopped. "See how well behaved they are? Now, all you need to do is take the dogs to the best places."

"Best places . . . ?"

"Sure. I want you, Israel, to pick the spots where there's the most people. I mean really packed and popular places, you understand what I mean?"

The boys nodded.

"Then you leave a couple of your friends with each dog. You make sure you pick the right spots, Israel, because I'm counting on you."

Israel nodded, though he looked confused.

"Then I want you to take the *last* dog with you to the best spot of all."

"But . . . why?"

"So we can all make some money, kid. *Mucho dinero*."

Now they all stared at him like attentive schoolchildren. A shrewd look crept into Israel's eyes, and it was clear that he was getting the idea.

"The *perros* will do . . . tricks?" he ventured.

"Right," said the man. "They'll do lots of tricks and people will love it, and they'll throw some coins. Maybe pesos. I want you to collect all the money, you understand? All of it. And then when the party's over I want you to bring it back to me. I'll count it, and then you get ten percent. If you don't cheat me, I'll give you a bonus."

"I would never!" cried the boy, raising a hand to swear to God and the Virgin Mary.

"My dogs won't like it if you cheat me."

"I swear, I swear."

The man grinned at him. "Okay, then that's all there is. You do that and after a couple of hours we're all going to have a lot of money. If you're really good at it, we can do it again tomorrow. What do you say, partner?"

He held out his hand, and after a moment's hesitation Israel took it and shook. Each of the other boys shook it, too. The man gave them some additional minor instructions and handed out the ten-dollar bills. The children stared at the bills and then stuffed them away in secret pockets where even their parents wouldn't find the money. The man had Israel make teams out of the ten other boys, and had the members of each team let a particular dog sniff their hands. Each sniff resulted in a single sharp tail wag. The dogs went and stood with the boys on their team.

"Vamoose," said the man, then to the dogs he said, "Go play."

Looking dazed, scared, and excited in equal measure, the boys and the mastiffs departed and were soon lost inside the huge crowds of holiday revelers. The man lit another cigarette and leaned against the truck, smiling contentedly.

"Like fucking clockwork," he said to no one in particular.

He finished his cigarette, returned the ramp to its position, pulled down and locked the door, got in, and drove away. It took nearly an hour to make his way through two miles of party traffic. When he was out of the city, he found the closest highway and drove off at high speed. He pulled into a small village seventy-three miles east of the town, parked the truck on the street, closed and locked the door, and walked around the corner to a little hotel. He ran up two flights of stairs, entered a room, then locked the door behind him. He opened a desk drawer and removed a thin laptop, loaded a program, and waited as the screen filled with four smaller windows. Each one showed the swirling, dancing, laughing, singing throng of people at the cele-bration. The crowd was so thick that it was nearly impossible to see anything. The angle of the camera was low, aimed upward. On one of the screens, he saw a skinny boy with silver duct tape on his shoes. The camera angle changed and jolted and spun in a circle. It was dizzying to watch, but the people in the area laughed and applauded and threw coins at the dancing, twirling dog.

It made the man smile.

He fished in his pocket for his cigarettes, kissed the last one out of the pack, lit it, watched the crowds as they watched the dogs. Caught glimpses of the ten street kids. Everyone was having such a great time. He watched the screen and saw one dog's point of view as it trotted around the edge of the crowd, saw the laughing people wave at it, blow kisses at it, laugh at the thing. The camera showed the dog going in through the open door of the police station at the edge of the plaza.

"Release the hounds," the man murmured, and laughed. "God, I always wanted to say that."

He pressed the Enter key. There was a flash of bright white and then all four screens went dark. No sound, no other images. He was left to imagine the sound of the explosions. He sighed and leaned back in the chair, enjoying the menthol tickle of the smoke as he took a deep, contented drag. Then he got up and turned on the TV, channel-surfed over to the news, and waited for the story to break. Maybe someone caught it on a cell camera. Maybe one of the news people would have footage. After all, with everyone having a cell phone, somebody had to have caught one of the four dogs exploding during a festive celebration.

It would be nice to watch.

"Good doggies," he said to the empty screens.

CHAPTER NINE

I heard about Mexico while I was halfway across the ocean.

Church called me at the same time that I was trying to call him. "Robot dogs, boss?" I said. "This is mine. I'm going to refuel in New York and then head down to—"

"No, Captain," interrupted Church, "you're not."

"The hell I'm not. I run the Special Projects shop, and what says 'special' more than exploding robot dogs?"

"Normally I would agree, but you've just come off two back-to-back combat assignments. Mexico has its own counterterrorism teams. Our assistance has been offered, as has that of some of our colleagues. The Mexican government has accepted help, but not from us."

"Well . . . shit."

I didn't have to ask why not us, because it wasn't the first time we'd been snubbed lately. Ever since Kill Switch, the DMS has stopped being the go-to SpecOps outfit. The people in the know are aware that, while we didn't actually become a clown college, it looked that way from a distance. Best case was that we were being treated as if we're all invalids. They look at us like we're guys in wheelchairs offering to run foot races. Thanks, but no thanks. Fair? No. Understandable? Yeah, but it still pissed me off, and it still hurt.

We talked for a while about the Prague gig, about the nanotech and the steroid stuff, and explored theories about who was behind it. We had a lot of ideas, but none of them seemed to go anywhere. Sadly, there are a bunch of smart and very bad people out there, and, yeah, some of them are actual mad scientists.

"Go home and rest," said Church. "I have no doubt something else will come up."

I spent a good portion of the rest of the trip home sulking.

Well, drinking and sulking.

INTERLUDE TWO

"*Eleven weeks?*" echoed the Concierge, his voice filled with alarm.

"Yes," said John.

"Is she serious?"

"Quite serious."

"It took quite a lot of time to set things up a certain way," said the Frenchman. He was in the vast kitchen of his villa. The house was fully automated and required only a monthly visit from a maintenance supervisor and biweekly deliveries of food. He preferred living alone, and, despite his profession as fixer and arranger for a select few clients, he was generally an antisocial man. Or, as he saw it, asocial. He didn't dislike people, but he preferred to keep his own company. Robots of various functions and the household artificial-intelligence computer system offered enough interactive challenges to satisfy any residual need for chitchat. And his job required that he spend hours on the phone or in virtual-reality conferences. When he wasn't working, the silence of his huge, empty house was a comfort to him. If he had his way, he would never leave the place. VR and luxury robots brought everything to him that couldn't be physically delivered.

Problems, though, always seemed to find him.

Case in point.

"Should I tell Ms. Bain that you're unable or unwilling to make the necessary adjustments?" asked John.

"Of course not," said the Concierge. "No . . . of course not. It is merely that eleven weeks is a very tight timetable."

"And . . . ?"

"It will require a great deal of cooperation. Gifts will need to be given in order to allow things to move quickly."

"You have carte blanche, my friend."

"People often say that and then I find out that there is, in fact, a budgetary limit. If I am expected to make a change as radical as this, then—"

"Hush," said John, and the Concierge hushed. "Spend whatever is necessary. This is the eve of the revolution, my friend. Act like it. The lady is relying on you."

"Of course, I—"

"She will expect you to pay special attention to our friends in the DMS. Very special attention."

"Yes, but I have outlined the risks with that part of the—"

The line went dead.

The Concierge sat in his electric wheelchair and drummed his fingers on the armrest. When he moved his fingers, there was the faintest sound of tiny servomotors and mechanical clicks. He was no longer aware of that, though, except when he was in his moments of despairing self-awareness. Every part of his body made some kind of sound. Even his breaths were accompanied by a hiss of hydraulics and compressors. It was a fact of his life.

There had been times of silence. Long stretches of it when he lay in bed, either in hospitals after the bomb went off on the Boulevard Voltaire back in November of 2015 or at home once he was discharged. His legs were charred and withered nothings, his arms were covered in melted skin, his spine—what was left of it—was wrapped in a complexity of plastics, metal reinforcing rods, tubes, and wires. Only his face was unmarked. Completely unmarked. He had not received so much as a scratch anywhere above the Adam's apple. A twist of fate that was in no way a kindness. When he looked into the mirror he saw a normal man, but that was a lie. Normalcy was a façade that he wore over corruption.

The household robots didn't care what he looked like, though. Nor did Calpurnia, the ever-evolving AI that ran every aspect of his daily life, from waking and washing him to tucking him in at night and lulling him to sleep with subtle injections of lovely drugs. Robots and computers were pure. They possessed no judgment and therefore were not slaves to aesthetic opinions. No human caregiver could do as much for him without something showing in the eyes. Contempt, apathy, pity, horror. He'd seen it all. With robots there was only the precision of programmable care. How wonderful.

He thought about what the world would be like once Havoc and its

Internet-destroying WhiteHat companion program had been allowed to run loose. Would it really be better, as John the Revelator preached? Would it be the golden age that Zephyr Bain had labored so long to bring about? Was the programming truly that good? It frightened him, because he knew that any program, no matter how sophisticated, always launched with a few bugs. The more sophisticated, in fact, the greater the risk of unexpected variables, design flaws, outside interference. No program had ever approached the complexity of Havoc. It was an incredible undertaking that was decades in the making, evolving as the computers and other crucial systems evolved. Which brought with it the constant risks of compatibility errors. Would it run smoothly? *Could* it launch without a hitch? Was that even possible, no matter what the simulations said? Simulations, no matter how carefully organized, were not the same as real-world, real-time operation.

And if it failed, in whole or in part, what then? There was no Havoc 2.0. There couldn't be. The world, as it existed right then, at that moment, would end within hours of Havoc and WhiteHat being initiated. There was no reset button. For Havoc to work, that infrastructure needed to be intact for a certain period of time. Power grids, water, emergency services, military response. It wasn't useful to disrupt that and not complete the entire program. The possibilities of a partial rollout were sickening to contemplate. Only the fully delivered, fully functional program would change the world into something cleaner and better.

If, and only if, everything worked exactly right. If every component—organic and digital—worked with maximum efficiency and in perfect harmony.

If that was actually possible.

With eighteen months, it was possible. With twenty-six months, it was likely.

But in eleven weeks? He looked around at the kitchen as if it were a window to the whole world.

"My God," he murmured. "My God."

He sat like that for nearly half an hour. And then he began making the necessary calls.

CHAPTER TEN

"You're here as an observer, Miss Schoeffel," said the major.

"So everyone keeps telling me," said Sarah Schoeffel, deputy director of the Federal Bureau of Investigation. "And, yes, I know that means I keep my hands in my pocket and keep my mouth shut."

Major Carly Schellinger smiled. "It's not quite that bad," she said, gesturing toward the cabin door. "Shall we?"

They went outside. The camp was large and constantly in motion. No flyovers were permitted, so Schoeffel's helicopter had landed in a clearing at an old, deserted logging camp and she'd then been driven here in a Hummer with blacked-out windows. The soldiers guarding the landing site were dressed in unmarked black combat uniforms. No unit patches, no insignia of any kind. The helicopter had also been plain black, without serial numbers. The Hummer had no license plates. The soldiers wore black balaclavas to hide their faces, and most of them had on opaque sunglasses. None of them spoke to her except to tell her to duck under the helicopter blades or to get into the truck.

The camp was set up in a valley, with dozens of small cabins and tents concealed from the air by camouflage netting. Heavily armed guards patrolled in pairs, and Schoeffel was surprised to see that some of them were accompanied by dogs. Robot dogs. Big, ugly, strange, and quiet.

It was their silence that disturbed her most. The last time, Schoeffel had seen an awkward and noisy machine. The prototype of BigDog was three feet long, two and a half feet tall, and weighed a ponderous two hundred and forty pounds. It was a bulky body with four oddly delicate legs that could run four miles an hour carrying more than three hundred pounds of gear. Its motion was directed by a sophisticated onboard computer that drew on input from various sensors. The problem was that it was noisy. You could hear it coming. Schoeffel had heard one soldier complain that it sounded like a moving junk pile.

As she walked along with Major Schellinger, one of the dogs fell into step with them, clearly programmed to accompany the major. Schoeffel kept cutting quick looks at it to study the upgrades. These dogs were different in many impressive ways. They had a head and a tail, though the former was a hard shell around a CPU and the latter was a whip antenna.

"Can I ask about the dogs?" Schoeffel said.

The major walked a few paces before responding. "Current designation is WarDog. A different generation from BigDog. New design in almost every way. We're still field-testing them. We have several models. Bigger ones for equipment transport or to serve as mobile gun emplacements."

"Meaning—?"

The major pointed. Down an alley between two cabins was a shooting range with six targets fixed to hay bales and set at incremental distances of up to three hundred yards. There were no soldiers working the range. Instead, there was a pair of WarDogs. One was the same sleek model that walked beside her, except its body and legs were draped with camouflaged material. The second dog was at least twice the size and a pair of trapdoors on its back had opened to allow a machine gun to swing up and drop into place. Ammunition belts trailed down to thick saddlebags.

"Are you familiar with guns, Deputy Director?"

"I'm qualified with handguns," said Schoeffel.

Major Schellinger laid an affectionate hand on the barrel of the weapon. "The M60E4/Mk 43 is a gas-operated, disintegrating-link, belt-fed, air-cooled machine gun that fires the 7.62 × 51-mm. NATO cartridges from an open bolt. It has a cyclic rate of five to six hundred rounds per minute, with an effective distance of twelve hundred yards; however, we have modifications in place for WarDog that allow for accuracy at considerably greater range. We chose this weapon for the balance of stopping power, overall reliability, and weight. Even with the extended barrel, it's only twenty-three pounds. It can also be removed from the WarDog and used on any standard NATO tripod and vehicle mount. The barrels are lined with stellite, a cobalt-chromium alloy, to allow for sustained fire and extended life. All major components of the Mk 43/M60E4 directly interchange with other M60 configurations."

"That's . . . impressive." Schoeffel didn't know what else to say.

"We're in full production with them now," said Schellinger.

"We are? I thought they were still being tested. I thought that was the whole point of this camp."

The major smiled. "Oh, we're a lot further along than you think."

"Then what's the purpose of the camp?"

"Fun and games, Deputy Director," said Schellinger. "Fun and games."

"What is that supposed to mean?"

Instead of answering, Major Schellinger gestured toward the DARPA scientist overseeing the testing range, who came over at once. He was a bookish man who looked somewhat out of place in a military uniform. The major made brief introductions and asked for a demonstration.

"Let's have long and short range. Speed and accuracy," she said. "Impress Deputy Director Schoeffel."

The scientist looked pleased and set it up.

"Patton," he said sharply. "On the line."

The WarDog with the machine gun turned and walked quickly over to the top of the range. His padded feet made no sound at all. A sergeant ordered everyone else off the range and announced a live-fire exercise.

"Six targets, three rounds each," ordered the scientist. "Engage."

Without hesitation, the WarDog named Patton shifted its body to aim at the closest target and fired a three-shot burst. The bullets punched into the kill zone of the target that was fifty feet away. The dog instantly shifted and fired at the hundred-and-fifty-foot target, then the thousand-yard target, and on and on, until it had fired bursts at all six targets.

With a thin smile, Schellinger offered a small pair of binoculars to Schoeffel, who raised them to her eyes, adjusted the focus, and stared in amazement.

"WarDogs use sensors and real-time intel from satellites and telemetry-gathering drones to calculate angle, adjust for windage and terrain. The targeting software removes all 'judgment' from the shot, which is what makes human shooters score below a constant maximum potential. WarDogs go on pure math. Machine thinking, machine logic, no guesswork."

"That sounds a little creepy," said Schoeffel.

"Wars are won by the side with the best technology."

"Are they?"

"Yes. Technology, the nerve to use it."

While Schoeffel digested that, the major continued with her praise of the big WarDog. "Patton can be fitted for mortars and grenades, too, or we can pull the machine gun and replace the whole combat package with anything from a flame thrower to a series of antipersonal or anti-tank mines that can be dropped at precise points."

"That's . . . that's . . ." Schoeffel stopped herself before she finished the sentence.

"Impressive as hell?" suggested the major.

"Yes," lied Schoeffel. The word she had been about to use was *terrifying.*

The scientist said, "We're field-testing ten prototypes this week. Our goal is to improve the bullet-to-body ratio."

"Which is what?" asked Schoeffel.

"With human combat troops, there is actually a very high ratio of number of rounds fired compared to the number of enemy killed, particularly in the recent wars in the Middle East. We're talking about a quarter million bullets per kill. Our goal with the WarDog is to reduce that number to something closer to two hundred bullets per kill."

"Which," said the major, picking up the story, "will allow us to send in armored dogs with sophisticated software for target selection and thereby reduce the number of human soldiers we put in harm's way. Let the robots do the fighting."

"Wait, you mean these machines will be picking their own targets?"

"Of course," said the scientist.

"How will they be able to tell the difference between enemy combatants and our own troops?"

"All soldiers will have an RFID chip implanted," explained the major. "No WarDog will fire on someone who has a chip."

"That's all well and good," said Schoeffel, "but ISIL and the Taliban tend to hide in urban areas and among civilian populations. How do we keep civilians safe?"

The scientist didn't meet her eyes.

Major Schellinger said, "We're still working on that."

Schoeffel watched the second dog trot into position. This one carried a lighter weapon, a modified Remington Mk 21 Precision Sniper Rifle, with a lever system operating the bolt and a new generation of laser sighting. The twenty-seven-inch barrel extended out over the dog's head, and it could be replaced to fire .338 Lapua Magnum, .338 Norma Magnum, .300 Winchester Magnum, or the standard 7.62×51-mm. NATO rounds. Schoeffel watched it select targets using each of the four possible calibers and shoot with deadly accuracy up to three hundred yards. Then targets were attached to eight separate remote-controlled carts and went rolling off through the forest in different directions. Bird drones followed each and sent video feeds back to the chief scientist's laptop, where everyone crowded around to watch. The dog leaped forward to pursue, and within eleven minutes had caught up to each of the targets and scored multiple shots in the kill zone. Then it loped back to the top of the range and stood there, quiet, brutal, deadly, and alien.

Major Schellinger actually patted its head as if it were a real dog. "Isn't he wonderful?"

The dog had two red lights for eyes, and although Sarah Schoeffel knew they were nothing but colored lenses over laser targeting systems, she swore that those eyes glared at her. With menace, with what she felt was a kind of bloody, wicked pride. It was stupid to read emotion into a machine.

Stupid, sure.

Schoeffel forced a smile onto her face. "Wonderful," she echoed. "Yes."

PART TWO
JOHN THE REVELATOR

———•———

*It is the business of the future to be dangerous;
and it is among the merits of science that it
equips the future for its duties.*
—Alfred North Whitehead

CHAPTER ELEVEN

THE PIER
DMS SPECIAL PROJECTS OFFICE
SAN DIEGO, CALIFORNIA
SATURDAY, APRIL 29, 5:09 PM

The phone rang, and it shook me out of a bad dream about attending my own funeral. The ringing of my cell phone wove itself so seamlessly into the fabric of the dream that I thought they'd buried me with it. I tried to move inside the narrow coffin, but my elbows kept hitting the silk-lined sides and I couldn't get my hand into the right pocket. I knew that it was Junie calling me from the graveside, trying to tell me that it was okay, that she would be fine, that she was moving on now that I was dead. And then the thread of the dream unraveled and I came awake crying out her name. All at once I was back on the deck of the Pier, the DMS Special Projects office in San Diego. The deck was empty except for my dog, Ghost, and me. He raised his head, saw that there was no danger, heard the phone continue to ring, and gave me a withering look and flopped back down.

The phone was on a side table amid a forest of empty beer bottles. San Diego is the Mecca of craft breweries, and I am a devout worshipper. Maybe a little too devout these past few months.

"Junie," I said again as I fished for the phone, but as I blinked my eyes clear it was obvious from the display that it wasn't Junie. Instead, I saw SEAN on the screen. My brother, which is weird enough in its own way. He never calls me. Sean is a homicide detective back in Baltimore, where we grew up. What the folks back home call a murder cop. Sean's a good guy, but in the past couple of years we've kind of drifted. It happens. Back when we were both detectives in different squads in the same town, we were tight. We had so much in common. We could sit up all night drinking beer and telling stories about the job. But that was then. Now he catches killers and I try to keep the world from falling off its hinges. He can still talk about his job, but we can't ever talk about mine. Makes for long, weird silences at Thanksgiving and Christmas. All he knows is that I work for a covert intelligence department. He doesn't even know its name. Our common ground is all past-tense stuff, and sometimes it leaves us with only sports and the weather to chat about.

I thumbed the button and said, "Sean."

"Hey, Joe."

"Is everything okay?"

"Huh?"

"Is Dad okay?"

"What? Oh. Sure. He's fine. He's out on a date."

"Wait . . . what? Dad's on a date? Why?"

Sean laughed. "Why not? People do date, you know. Even old guys. It's been known to happen."

"Dad's not allowed to date," I protested.

"Joe, Dad's been alone for a long time."

It was true enough. Our mom died years ago, but like most children—even adult children—I naturally assumed that our father would be in some kind of permanent state of mourning. How could he even *want* to date? It didn't compute with the part of me that will always be a kid rather than a grown son.

"Who's he out with?" I demanded.

"The artist lady."

"*What* artist lady?"

"Jesus, Joe," said Sean. "He's been seeing her for six months. Michelle Garry. She's great. How do you not know this?"

"You sound like you approve of Dad running around with some strange woman."

Sean sighed. "Oh, right. I forgot he has to get your written approval before he has a life."

"That's not what I meant."

"Then what did you mean?"

I had no answer to that, because it pretty much *was* what I meant. So, like any coward, I changed the subject.

"What's happening, Sean? Ali and the kids okay?" I had a first-grader nephew, Ryan, whom we all called Lefty, because even at eight he had one hell of a fastball, and a little niece, Emily—known as Em—who was a rambunctious three.

"Yes, Joe," said Sean, "we're all okay." He paused, though he sounded uncertain of his reply. "Actually, though . . . this isn't a social call. It's business."

"Business?"

"It's about a case," he said.

I dug a fresh beer out of the cooler by my chair, twisted off the top, took a sip, and rested the sweating bottle on my belly. The cold felt nice. "Since when do you call me about cases? Or did something happen with one of my old cases?"

It happens sometimes. Even though, like Sean, I had a high clearance record when I was a detective, there were plenty of cases that went unsolved, and, with advances in forensics, old cold cases sometimes get hot again.

"No," said Sean, "this is something else."

"What is it, then?"

He paused again. "Look, I know that you work for one of those top-secret agencies that you can't talk about, but—"

"But you're talking about it."

"No, it's just that—" he said, and then hesitated now that he was up to the edge of it. "Look, after what happened at the ballpark that time, Dad kind of . . . you know . . . let something slip."

Our dad was the mayor of Baltimore and two years ago he'd gone to Citizens Bank Park in Philly to co-host the opening day of baseball with the Philly mayor. That was the day the Seven Kings hit the place with a bunch of small drones carrying high explosives. A lot of people died, and Dad was almost one of them. It really rattled him, and Dad's not an easy guy to shake. I guess I could imagine the conversation between him and Sean afterward. Maybe over drinks late one night after Sean's family was in bed. Father and son. Former cop and current cop, swapping stories, sharing confidences.

"What, exactly, did Dad say?" I asked.

"Not much," said Sean. "No details. Just a little bit about the *kinds* of cases you handle. Weird stuff."

"Like . . . ?"

"Like you going after terrorists who have cutting-edge science weapons. General stuff. But he kind of hinted that you had something to do with what happened in Philly. Not just the ballpark but before that . . . at the Liberty Bell Center when the terrorists released whatever kind of plague or chemical or whatever that made people go apeshit. You know what I'm talking about."

"Yeah," I said. "I read about it in the papers."

"Come on, Joe . . ."

"Dad told you all this? What else did he say?"

"Well, it's not like he said who you worked for, but, Joe . . . Dad's proud of you. He said you saved a lot of lives."

I said nothing.

"He said you caught the bastards who did all that."

I said nothing.

"He said that if I ever caught a whiff of something like that . . . I should call you."

"Something like what? A terrorist group?"

"That's just it, Joe. I don't know what I have, but I think I need your help. I don't know who else to call. Hell, I don't know who I can trust."

"Sean, what are you talking about? What's happening?"

There was a long pause this time. "Joe . . . something really bad is happening here, and I don't know what to do about it. I . . . I'm scared, man. Really scared."

I said, "Tell me."

CHAPTER TWELVE

Deputy Director Sarah Schoeffel spent three days at the DARPA camp.

When she arrived it was to receive a briefing about new robotics hardware and computer software that was being developed for the military, and about versions of the technology that might be made available to Homeland Security. Her own counter-cyberterrorism division of the FBI needed more tech, and a Senate subcommittee had arranged her visit here.

Some of what she saw was truly encouraging, and at first she wasn't a fan, but with each day, each demonstration of counterterrorism technology, she could feel her resistance ebbing.

"This," said Major Schellinger as she escorted Schoeffel into a cabin lined with computer workstations and staffed with programmers who typed furiously, "is WhiteHat. And I imagine this is one of the projects that will interest you most."

Schoeffel bent and looked over the shoulder of one of the programmers, trying to get a sense of the code he was writing.

"WhiteHat is a brand-new line of adaptive artificial-intelligence programs that were designed to *think* like hackers in order to anticipate cyberattacks," the major explained.

Major Schellinger went through the systems, and Schoeffel was dazzled by the power, sophistication, and subtlety of WhiteHat. And she was flattered to learn that some of her recommendations to the Senate subcommittee had influenced a number of the system's components. WhiteHat's overall level of sophistication was intimidating, but Schoeffel felt that was appropriate. Guns were intimidating, too, until they were pointed in the right direction.

She was less sanguine about some of the other projects being tested at the camp.

"You're not serious?" she blurted after Schellinger introduced her to the group building the next generation of autonomous-drive combat machines.

Schellinger held up placating hands. "I know, I know, this is scary, but—"

"Does 'scary' really cover it, Major? America does not have the best track record when it comes to AI being used for combat systems. It was AI-driven fighter planes that destroyed the Golden Gate Bridge. They're not even done building the new one and you want to put an even *more* advanced set of self-guided drones in the air?"

Schellinger's eyes were cold, her smile colder. "While it's true that most of the autonomous-combat-vehicle programs were scrapped in the aftermath of that terrible day, and rightly so, we are not going in the same direction. The Department of Defense has made it very clear that there needs to be a stronger and more reliable Off switch that would allow our handlers to be able to take back control at a moment's notice."

"How certain are we that people can take back control of these machines?" asked Schoeffel.

"I can absolutely guarantee," said the major, "that no machine we create—not one drone, fighter jet, tank, or WarDog—will be off the leash. They work for *us*."

"What about GPS hacking and computer viruses?"

The major shook her head. "They will all be keyed to a very specific command program that will require new control codes twice per day. Those codes will be generated and sent to commanders and handlers in 128-bit encrypted bursts. And we can use satellites to send random system checks that will require the machines to perform certain quick noncombative functions to prove that they're not under unauthorized control. Should any system check get an anomalous response, the entire CPU will be isolated and shut down."

She ran through a number of other impressive safeguards, and gradually Schoeffel found the last of her resistance melting away.

CHAPTER THIRTEEN

The containers arrived by train. One shipment per week for most of the past year, then two, and in the past few weeks there had been three trainloads. Long, winding snakes of cars that came from factories in Chicago, Lake Forest, Minneapolis, Trenton, Tempe, and Bethesda. Thousands of twenty- and forty-foot containers offloaded into the endless stacks awaiting their ships. Then the bomb carts—special chassis designed to move the cans from stacks to cranes—brought them to the docks in an endless loop. Massive gantry cranes plucked the cans off the carts and set them down on the deck of the cargo ships. The bottom rows weren't secured by anything except the weight of the cans placed on top, but each additional layer was held fast by twistlocks, lashing bars, and turnbuckles. It was all done with professional efficiency and natural diligence. Loaded, secured, and then gone.

Fourteen days before Havoc, the last of the foreign shipments set sail aboard the MSC *William Tell*, a Swiss supercargo ship built at the Daewoo Shipbuilding yard in South Korea. It was one of the big ones, with a cargo capacity for carrying more than nineteen thousand of the twenty-foot cans, and a third of the cargo came from those special trains. The rest were filled with tens of thousands of tons of packs of chemicals to be used for spraying and controlling mosquito populations.

Inspection of the cargo was done by men and women who had been in their jobs for years. Most of them thought they worked for the docks, the customs office, or the city of Baltimore. Officials in receiving ports held the same view, as did the thirty-five-man crew of the *William Tell*.

Most of them were wrong.

Very wrong.

CHAPTER FOURTEEN

It started with a girl. That's what Sean told me.

"Her name is Kya," he said. "Well, *was* Kya, but that's just a street name. That's her work name. Her real name is Holly Sterman, and she would have been fifteen years old on Christmas Day. She died two days ago."

"What happened?" I asked.

"It's the craziest damn thing. One minute she was talking to her mom on the phone and the next she goes psycho and kills two adult men."

"Gun?"

"No," he said, "teeth. She bit them to death."

The world around me suddenly went quiet. "What did you say?"

"Look, Joe," said Sean quickly, "this is complicated. She was a runaway from Wilmington. A report was filed, but no one looked for her—you know how that is."

"Yeah, yeah, get back to the part where she bit two guys. Why? Was it drugs? Was she hyped up on flakka?"

There was a nasty and very potent new designer drug on the streets called flakka that was driving many users into fits of screaming rage accompanied by vivid hallucinations. Chemically speaking, it was a cousin to the group of drugs commonly—and incorrectly—known as bath salts. Both are synthetic versions of naturally occurring amphetamine-like substances called cathinones. Flakka variations range from stuff that makes users mildly grouchy to stuff that turns them into violent aggressors. The high is, according to the junkies, worth the side effect. For the record, this is one of the reasons I hate people.

"That's what I thought," said Sean. "But no, her tox screen was clean. A little grass, but that's it."

"Then what happened?"

Sean told me the basics. Holly was a frequent flyer at one of those roach-infested West Baltimore hotels whose rooms are on yearly lease by people who sublet them by the hour. Not that Baltimore holds the patent on hot-pillow joints. Working as Kya, and with a fake driver's license that said she was twenty-two, she turned tricks sometimes eight or nine times a night. Sean had been able to piece that together from surveillance video of the hotel that was part of another case being investigated by one of his buddies working a joint thing with the ATF. Kya/Holly was tagged as a likely prostitute working in the same place as the suspect, who was using the place as a showroom to sell handguns to gangbangers. When the gunrunner was busted the surveillance ended, but there was enough for Sean to verify that Holly was a regular, going in and out with a variety of men, none of whom were probably her Bible-study coach.

"And nobody thought to pick up an underage prostitute?" I asked.

"The investigating team handed it off to vice," Sean explained, "but they had Kya down as an adult. Stupid, really. All they had to do was look at her. Bottom line is she was still on the job when the incident occurred."

I took a sip of beer. It didn't taste as good as it had. "Tell me about this incident."

"It's really weird, Joe."

"Try me. Weird is pretty much what I do for a living."

He ran it down for me, and, yeah, it was weird. The screams, the super, the dead john. He pieced together the details from a hysterical eyewitness report by the nephew of the super and through forensic reconstruction of the scene. The girl somehow overpowered or outfought her customer and then attacked the super, who tried unsuccessfully to defend himself with a baseball bat.

"The bat hit her on the shoulder, Joe," said Sean. "It was the only injury the super inflicted. Remember that. It's important."

The girl tackled the super, grabbed his hair, and proceeded to slam his head against the hardwood floor with such force that his skull split. She didn't stop there, though. She beat him nearly to death, pausing only long enough to bite his nose and upper lip completely off. The uncle had accidentally knocked the door shut when he was attacked and fell against it, so that the nephew couldn't force his way in. The nephew said he could hear the sound of his uncle screaming for almost five minutes. Which is a minute shy of when the police arrived in response to the nephew's 911 call.

"The john and the girl were DOA at the scene, and the super died on the table at the hospital," concluded Sean.

"I have some questions I have to ask, and I can't explain why."

"Dad figured you might."

"First, did the other victims try to attack anyone?"

"Huh? I told you, one was dead and the other was critical."

"Okay. That's good."

"How's that good?"

"Second," I said, evading his question, "you said the girl bit both men. Did she actually eat them?"

"Jesus, Joe, what kind of question is that?"

"An important one. Did you analyze her stomach contents to see if she—"

"No, you freak, it's bad enough already. This isn't The Walking-fucking-Dead."

Sean couldn't know it, but he'd set up his account as if he were describing an outbreak of the Seif al Din pathogen, which was the doomsday bioweapon terrorists released at the Liberty Bell Center. That plague was why I joined. And, yeah, it pretty much rocked a real-world version of something that was way too close to a zombie apocalypse scenario. Seif al Din had some variations, but in every case the infected not only bit their victims but fed on them. Anyone bitten but left more or less whole would reanimate as a mindless killer. Seif al Din is one of a special class of pathogens that hotwire the central nervous system and bring the recently dead back to life as mindless and aggressive disease vectors. It wasn't the first time some psychopath with a chemistry set took inspiration from pop culture. Not a joke.

"I need you to be really sure about this, Sean."

"I am sure. Only thing in her stomach was a partially digested Mc-Donald's Filet-O-Fish and some ginger ale. She spit out the, um, stuff she bit off the two men."

"Thank God," I breathed. Ghost was looking at me now, tense because I was tense. Maybe scared because I was scared. "Who killed the girl?"

"I'll get to that, but let me tell the rest of it first," said Sean. "When the uniforms entered the room, they found her dead. She was naked and her eyes were open. Wide open. So was her mouth. It was like she died screaming."

"Did the super manage to—?"

He cut me off. "No. She just collapsed and died."

"From what?"

Instead of answering, he said, "When I reconstructed the scene, I realized that the john she'd killed hadn't been her customer. This guy had been in the room next door with another girl. That girl said her john was pissed by all the screaming they heard coming through the wall, so he went next door to tell her to shut up, and that's when she attacked him. One of my forensics guys found a cell phone and determined that Kya had been in the middle of making a call when she freaked out. She was estranged from her family and they live out of town, so I've got a phone interview set up with them."

It was a sad story and, except for the biting part, all too common. The number of teenage runaways is staggering, far more than most people think. Every year more than a million and a half kids run away. Most return home or are found, but hundreds of thousands vanish. In dysfunctional families, particularly where abuse is a factor, the majority of the kids who run away are girls. Eighty percent of homeless girls have been physically or sexually abused. Some of those kids are never found. Of those, a bunch grow up to be fringe dwellers—junkies, squatters, and the like. Others are pulled into different kinds of human trafficking under false identities, and a lot of the time it's forced sex work. It's appalling, and the problem is accelerating rather than slowing down. Because so many teens run from bad homes, there isn't always a lot of family push to find them. And some kids will do anything to keep from being found. This girl, Kya—or Holly—was probably one of those statistics, and Sean and I both knew that the system wouldn't burn up a lot of calories seeking justice for her. It was a national embarrassment, and it was a tragedy. A life erased and all its potential extinguished. Just like that.

"She was such a little thing, Joe," said Sean, and I could hear more of the father than the cop in his tone. "Nowhere near a hundred pounds. Skinny, with red hair and freckles. She'd have grown up to be beautiful, but even if she was short, fat, and ugly it comes to the same thing. Someone did this to her."

"Did *what*, Sean? You still haven't told me how she died."

"Yeah, well, that's the thing. There was no obvious cause of death. No wounds of any kind except some scratch marks from the big man and the broken arm from the super's bat. No track marks, and, like I said, no drugs in her system. Not even a beer. I got the ME to put some topspin on the autopsy."

"Who's the ME these days? Is it still Dr. Jakobs?"

"Yeah. Old fart is a pain in the ass, but he's the best medical examiner in the city." Sean lowered his voice to a secretive, confidential level. "He said there were two causes of death."

"I don't understand."

"Joe, she was in the advanced stages of rabies infection."

"*Rabies?* That doesn't make sense. You said she was turning tricks and calling her mother on the phone right before the incident. How could she do that if she was that badly infected with rabies?"

"Yeah, well, that's where this gets weirder. We released some of the case details to the press, and even the rabies got only two seconds of coverage: 'Teenage prostitute with rabies bites two other people, and all three die in violent struggle.' You didn't see that on the news?"

"No." Which was, I admit, a little odd, and I thought about the stack of reports on my desk that I'd only halfway waded through. It might be buried in all that backlog. On the other hand, it couldn't have been too grave a case—three corpses notwithstanding—because there was no call-to-action from Homeland or the CDC. I'd have Lydia Rose do a background check from our end.

"Not surprising," said Sean. "The girl didn't matter, the john was a no one, the super was a loser, and the whole thing was tawdry but not sexy, even with all the sexual components. Reporters have gotten jaded. This is too close to other cases scattered around the country, so they can't sell the novelty. There's no hook, and they think the other incidents are coincidental. I mean, hell, if they thought there was a conspiracy, then maybe it would get some buzz. But no one thinks that."

"Do you?"

"Yeah," he said cautiously. "Maybe."

"Wait, before we go there, you said there were *two* causes of death. What else are we talking about?"

"It's something Doc Jakobs found when he did a full examination of the damaged brain tissue."

"What did he find?"

"Robots," said Sean.

I almost smiled. "Say what, now . . . ?"

"Those little tiny ones? You know what I mean. The kind you can only see with a microscope."

"Nanobots?" I ventured, and I could feel the hairs on the back of my neck twitch.

"Yes. Those are tiny robots, right?"

"They are," I said, keeping my voice neutral.

"Joe, somebody put nanobots in that girl's brain."

CHAPTER FIFTEEN

"The robots are coming! The robots are coming!"

The cries, amplified by the speakers, filled the room and bounced off the walls and collided in the air all around the five hundred people in the seats. No one shot to his feet in panic and tried to flee. No one screamed or fainted dead away.

Instead there was a ripple of polite laughter from some, smiles from everyone else. The tall man on the podium smiled back.

"Or," he said after a pause, "I should say that they're already here."

He turned and spread his arms wide, as if in worship of the images that came and went on the big screen. Machines of every kind, from surgical robots to mechanized drilling platforms to autonomous drones to humanoid figures made from metal and plastic.

"All hail our robot overlords!" cried the man.

More laughter this time, but still not everyone. Not everyone appreciated the jokes or the speaker's sense of humor. Not everyone knew where this was going. A few of those who did wore the tolerant expressions of people waiting to hear what they already knew. It was a mixed bag, as the audiences of most lectures at the Ethical Society were. Some were the choir here to be preached to, and some were accompanying friends. Some were there because they were curious but not deeply informed on the subject matter; others were there because this was their field and the man who called himself John the Revelator was becoming a voice crying in the technological wilderness—maybe more John the Baptist than the John who wrote the Book of Revelation. Quirky, eccentric, and strange either way. Occasionally offensive but never boring. And his oddball charisma had filled the rest of the seats at the auditorium.

John turned and lowered his arms.

"The technological singularity is regarded as a hypothetical event. One in which, artificially intelligent machines will become so sophisticated that they will make humanity redundant. This is a process that is already well under way. It began when we built computers and wrote software code that allowed robots and other kinds of machines to design and build other robots. It began when we introduced self-learning software into the mix, so that each generation of robots is able to exceed whatever we designed and become something better. Sometimes this evolution follows predicted lines, and sometimes it yields unexpected results. Leaps of self-development that drive these interlocked fields of study forward by orders of magnitude. The machines we make are becoming capable of recursive self-improvement; they are progressively redesigning themselves. Because of the autonomy we've designed into them, they are now building smarter and more powerful machines. This is not an aberration. This is what we want them to do, because we're desperate to reap the benefits of radical technologies."

His eyes—green as summer grass—roved over the crowd, and there was a small smile on his full lips that never quite went away.

"Alarmists warn us of a runaway effect," he said quietly. "They say that if we continue to allow autonomous development to progress at its current rate the machines will become so powerful that they may achieve the state of self-awareness. The technological singularity will cease to be a theory and become a fact. And then what?"

The picture on the screen changed and a clip from the movie *The Terminator* appeared. Armies of robots armed with pulse rifles stalked through an apocalyptic landscape, blasting away at the dwindling band of desperate human resistance fighters.

"Well," said John, "we all know how *that* scenario plays out."

A clip from *Terminator 2* showed a playground full of kids and parents being caught in the shock wave of superheated gases as a nuclear device turned them to ash and blew their dust away.

The room was very quiet.

"Or *do* we know?" asked John. "Is the scenario from a hundred science-fiction movies and a thousand science-fiction novels really predictive of what will happen when the inevitable happens and the robots achieve consciousness? Is there no other possibility? Is there no other result at the end of this long and complex equation?"

There was no sound at all.

John the Revelator smiled at them. "What would happen, do you suppose, if instead of losing control of the technological singularity we embraced it, accepted it, guided it, and became part of it? What if our technological growth explosion is not a pathway to humanity becoming irrelevant but instead was an open door to *our own* leap forward in evolution. Not human evolution. Not machine evolution. But a *shared* evolution. Imagine it. Seriously . . . close your eyes and imagine the possibilities. We are living on a planet that we—collectively *we*—have overpopulated while failing to provide for the needs of so many. We live on a planet we have raped and brutalized to the point where it is suddenly lashing back at us with droughts and super-storms and blizzards and melting polar ice and with diseases born of imbalance. We share a world where our mishandling of the basic tools of civilized survival—clean water, antibiotics, contraception, fuel, food purity—are failing us because we failed them. We are in a world where we are writing both our eviction notice and our epitaph."

Behind him the picture changed to show a man and a woman and two children. They were whole and appeared healthy and beautiful. The image morphed slowly so that they were Caucasian and then Asian, black and then Latino, Native American, and on and on, until finally they were clearly mixed-race. It held there, showing people who were gorgeous and healthy and vibrant. Except that they weren't entirely human. The blue eyes of the woman clicked with mechanical precision, and on the big screen there was a cutaway to show what she saw when she looked down at one of her children. There was a clear image of the child in high definition and full color, but it was framed by data readouts that indicated the child's age, height, weight, temperature, blood pressure, heart rate, glucose levels, hormone balances, body-fat percentage, blood gases, and a dozen other bits of data. A scale indicated emotional health. A small meter suddenly flashed with an alert saying that the child had a bacterial infection that posed a seventy-percent risk factor. The mother flicked her left wrist quickly from side to side and a section of skin folded back to reveal a small but sophisticated control panel. The mother pressed a few touch keys and the display for the child indicated that nanites had been triggered to release a precise amount of antibiotics into the child's bloodstream.

Beside the woman, the husband's smile flickered for a moment and he raised his hand and looked at his palm. The view shifted to show the screen display he saw, and three alerts popped up. One said that he was 3.1 pounds overweight and a list of fat-burning exercises appeared and immediately transferred to his personal calendar, and an alarm was set to remind him to go to the gym. The second alert told him that there was an imbalance in his digestive tract, and a hologram displayed an image of a slice of pepperoni pizza with chili powder on it. A frowning emoji flicked on and off, and a display informed him that a small and carefully regulated dose of famotidine, an H2 receptor antagonist, had been released by nanites. The third alert told him that he had a conference call in fifteen minutes and offered the choice of several business folders for him to peruse.

The picture changed to show a teenage girl walking up to her house carrying schoolbooks. The door scanned her, then its locks clicked open. The camera followed her up the stairs and into her bedroom, where a computer turned itself on and arranged her study notes, homework, and other resources in stacked files on a threefold screen.

Then the image was of a young woman at a bar. As she looked around she got immediate displays of each person, showing age, name, criminal record if any, marital status, occupation, and health warnings. One very handsome man was tagged as having a previous arrest for domestic violence. Another warning said that the very cute guy approaching her had HIV. But the third man was an English teacher—single, no kids, a ninety-seven-percent health rating—who owned his own house and a nice car. Details of his politics, credit score, and social-media platform were included. When that man said hello, the young woman smiled.

There was more. A middle-aged woman went shopping and the displays showed her food content, including fat and salt and additives. A driver slept behind the wheel of his car while it drove him home; his blood-alcohol level clearly showed that he was intoxicated. A military doctor doing emergency surgery on a wounded soldier worked along with a small but sophisticated field robot, and the doctor's display guided him through a difficult chest incision while showing him all crucial data on the patient, and also linked him to a top cardiothoracic surgeon at the Mayo Clinic. A child being bullied in a schoolyard had alerts going out to teachers and school security, which came running. A woman being assaulted in a parking garage had 911 on the phone while the camera in her eyes ran facial-recognition programs on her assailant and one of her fingernails collected DNA; then a panel in the woman's wrist opened and hit the man with a small but powerful electric sting.

There were many others.

John stood and watched the people in the audience as they watched the screen.

Finally he said, "And this is just a fraction of personal use once we and the machines become a single and harmonious unit. This is a millionth of a percent of the potential for meaningful, productive, uplifting, and inevitable mutual growth. Business, industry, health care, sports, insurance, banking, exploration, farming, manufacturing, investments, development, climate management, education . . . well, really, is there any area of our lives that could *not* be improved?"

The screen faded to silver and the house lights came up.

"The technological singularity is coming," he said. "The question is whether we resist it, fail ourselves in not keeping pace with it, or embrace it so that *we* are what evolves."

CHAPTER SIXTEEN

"Jesus H. T. Oliver Christ," I yelled, sitting up so fast my bare feet slapped against the concrete floor of the deck. Ghost whined sharply, alarmed at my tone. "Nanobots? You're *sure?*"

"That's what Doc Jakobs said, Joe. They're really tiny, though," said Sean. "Doc almost missed them during the post, but you know how thorough he is. He doesn't miss anything."

"What was the yield?" I asked.

"The what?"

"How many nanites? What was the concentration?"

"Um . . . not many, I guess . . . ?" he said uncertainly. "I don't have the number. It'll be in Doc's lab report. Does the concentration matter?"

"Maybe," I said. "Did Doc Jakobs actually say that the nanites were the cause of death?"

"In a way, but the actual cause of death was complicated. There was unusual trauma in the motor cortex and brain stem, and that triggered a myocardial infarction."

"She had a heart attack?"

"Yes."

"At fourteen?"

"I know," said Sean. "I don't understand the medical parts, and maybe I'm telling it wrong. Something about the nanobots damaging key nerves or nerve centers in the brain. Something like that—Doc can explain it. Oh, and here's another weird thing. Doc's sure that the rabies caused her erratic behavior, but there wasn't the right amount of degenerative damage that he expected to find in someone with the behavioral symptoms. It was like the rabies was dormant and suddenly kicked in at some ultrahigh level. I asked him if the nanobots could have done that, maybe amped the rabies up in some way, but he didn't know. Frankly, I think he's afraid to even look into it. He's afraid to ask around about it, and I don't blame him."

"Why's he afraid to ask?"

"Yeah, well, there's more," said Sean slowly. "And maybe I called you as much about that as about the robots. Joe, you see . . . someone's been following me."

"You're sure?"

"Yeah."

"*How* sure?"

"Very," said Sean. "But, whoever it is, they know how to tail like a pro and they're slippery as fuck. I spotted them twice, including on my way back from Dad's. I called units for backup both times and we tried to box the car, but they slipped us like they could read our minds. We'd coordinate something, and they were gone. After the first time, we used alternate radio channels in case they had a police scanner, but they still outfoxed us. Black SUVs both times. Couldn't see the plates."

Black SUVs were one of the vehicles of choice for a lot of government agencies and organized crime. Lots of room for a crew, cargo space, easily armored, and they have smoked windows. Plus, there are a zillion of them on the street.

"Have you checked your phones to see if they have you bugged?"

"I did. The radio in the car is clean, but I'm pretty sure my home phone is tapped. Maybe Dad's, too. There's an odd clicking on the line every now and then, though. And, don't think I'm crazy, but it *feels* like someone's listening, you know?"

"Yeah. Shit. What about your cell?"

"I think it's clean."

"You *think* it's clean?"

"I opened it up and didn't find a bug."

I wasn't worried about someone tapping our call, because we had that covered. Anyone making a call to a DMS phone gets included in a kind of scrambled loop. Anyone listening in on an unauthorized second line or via an electronic bug hears nothing but very loud white noise. Funny thing was, the technology was actually developed by Hugo Vox, the late and unlamented former head of the Seven Kings. It was part of the surveillance and jamming tech he used *against* us. We borrowed it. Everyone else who had access to the tech is dead. Finders keepers.

Even so, I said, "Listen, Sean, go buy a burner and use that from now on."

A burner is a disposable cell phone. It's nearly impossible to trace and can be discarded after use. Great for tourists on vacation, but the primary market seems to be criminals and terrorists. And there's no way to regulate these phones. In this case, at least, a burner could keep Sean safe.

"Okay," he said, though he didn't sound happy about it. He was in that zone between pissed off and scared. "When I found the bugs at the house, I had Ali take the kids to Uncle Jack's farm for a couple of days. She fought me on that, so I had to tell her a little of what was going on."

I wished he hadn't, but I understood why he did. I made a mental note to have one of my guys from the Warehouse swing by Sean's place to do another sweep, but with the equipment we have. Our new Anteater surveillance-detection system is absolute state of the art, and it was a lot more sensitive than anything the Baltimore PD could ever hope to afford. Again, thanks to Hugo Vox. Oh, yeah, rot in hell.

I decided that I'd also see if someone from the Warehouse wanted to spend a few days in the country watchdogging Sean's family.

"Joe," said Sean, "after Doc showed me those nanobots on the microscope I asked him to go through the records to see if there are any other cases similar to Holly, and, there may be as many as four."

"Jesus."

He laid it out for me. In the past eleven months there had been four deaths with unusual brain damage. Three girls and a boy, all under the age of sixteen. The deaths happened in different parts of the city and, in the case of the boy, in another town. In each case, there had been some extreme violence but no murders. The cases involved self-mutilation, a savage rape of another teen by one of the victims, stabbings, general mayhem. All very nasty and all very sad. Even though all the victims survived, all the teenage perpetrators died. Heart attacks in two cases, a blood clot in one, and a suicide by leaping out a window.

"Is there a task force on this?" I asked.

"I wish. I pitched that and was shot down by my captain," Sean complained. "Look . . . until now, no one has ever really tried to connect the cases and put the pieces together. From any distance they look like isolated instances of junkies freaking out, and there are a lot of cases like that. It wasn't until Doc looked for incidents involving bites and factors like age and prostitution that he started getting hits. Distant hits, though. I mean, he thinks they're related and so do I, but we don't have enough to build a solid case yet. I'm trying to determine disposition of bodies right now, but my guess is they've been sent back to families, and that means different jurisdictions and a lot of 'I don't give a shit' on the part of local law, local hospitals, and the families of the kids. You know how it is with the fringe dwellers."

"Sean," I said, "you said that Kya was a prostitute. What do you know about her pimp?"

"Not much. There's a thin lead I've been following that seems to be tied to maybe the Russians. They run a lot of girls in this part of Maryland. So far I've hit a lot of dead ends."

"Who all have you told about this?" I asked.

"Just my captain, Dad, and Ali."

"Keep it that way."

"But—"

"Dad was right," I said. "This does sound like my kind of thing. Or, maybe it is. I'll have to look at it and then make a judgment call. Sean, can you get your hands on samples of the blood and brain tissue with the nanites in them? I mean can you do it without it showing up on the chain of evidence log?"

"I . . . uh, well, sure. I'd have to tell Doc Jakobs why, though."

"Don't call him. No more phones. Assume his place is bugged, too. Go and hand him a note explaining the basics. Burn the note afterward and flush the ashes. Someone will be in touch to collect the samples."

"Who?"

"No one you know, but he'll have a message from me. It'll be the name of the guy who got me to read that book. You know what I mean?"

He thought about it for a moment. "Sure."

When I was in ninth grade, I was starting to log a lot of hours in detention because of fighting with other kids and making smart-ass comments to teachers. I know, you're shocked. Joe Ledger fighting and being a smart-ass? Who'd have thought? Anyway, the teacher running detention was big on reading. He made a deal with whoever was on the bench: we could read one of the books he had in his office and then take a quiz based on the chapters we swore we'd read. If we scored well, proving that we'd actually done the reading, we could get out early. While I was there, I grabbed a book called *Hatchet* by Gary Paulsen. It was a little young for my reading level, but it had a good story. Kid lost in the woods who was fighting for survival and all he had was a hatchet. I ripped through that in five detention sessions. It was my favorite book for a long time, and it engendered within me a love of books. Plus, it was a kick-ass story. I read a lot of other books while polishing that bench with my teenage ass, but I read *Hatchet* three times. And I gave a new copy to Sean for Christmas that year.

"Don't ask the pickup guy too many questions, because he'll stone-wall you. Rules of the game," I said.

"What do I do after that?"

"Sit tight and keep your eyes open. I'll be there by tomorrow morning."

"Thanks, Joe." There was a heartbreaking amount of relief in his voice. He really was scared. So was I.

I was also really fucking pissed off. Five dead kids, someone playing with nanotech, the possibility of some kind of rabies outbreak, and now someone ghosting my brother? Yeah, I was planning on having a meaningful conversation with someone. It would be a chat I'd enjoy more than they would.

CHAPTER SEVENTEEN

SENATE SUBCOMMITTEES ON CYBER TERRORISM
CAPITOL BUILDING
WASHINGTON, D.C.
ONE WEEK AGO

Sarah Schoeffel didn't like being grilled by Congress. Not even by a small closed-door panel. She felt very much like a witness giving testimony while already strapped to the electric chair. The subcommittee's control over funding for her department was the hand on the switch, and the longer these hearings went on the more that hand seemed to twitch.

"You're telling us," said Senator Diaz from Florida, "that the cybersecurity of this nation's largest banks is *not* secure?"

"That is correct," said Schoeffel.

"And you're saying that the banks might not recover the money that has so far been taken from all those accounts?"

"I would say that there is a very small chance any of those funds can be recovered, Senator. The thefts were done quietly by highly skilled computer hackers who were able to disable the alert systems written into the software. The money was gone days before anyone knew about it, and it's likely that it has since been rerouted to a great many accounts in the Caymans, Panama, and elsewhere. Possibly even laundered electronically and funneled back into domestic banks through falsified income and profit reports of shell companies."

Schoeffel felt the heat of nine sets of eyes. She knew that she didn't have a friend in the room. Not the seven members of the cyberterrorism panel and not the two congressmen who were guests from the Banking and the Finance Committee. No one wanted to hear the truth, although they kept asking pointed questions like that one. It was clear that they wanted to be mollified, comforted, maybe even lied to, but Schoeffel was here to tell the truth. Painful and dangerous truths, but truths nonetheless.

"How is this even possible?" asked Albertson, the representative from Ohio.

Schoeffel spread her hands. "Cybersecurity is only as good as the latest upgrade. Once the new security software is in place, it's only a matter of time before a hacker assesses it and cracks it. It's like a game, and there are a lot of black hats out there who—"

Goines raised a hand. "I'm a little fuzzy on that. You keep using terms like 'black hat' and 'gray hat.' What, exactly, does that mean?"

"It's pretty straightforward," said Schoeffel. "Black-hat hackers are criminals who violate computer security for personal gain, such as stealing credit-card information, personal-data harvesting, identity theft, corporate espionage, and international espionage. The Chinese Ghost-Net is a black hat because they're trying to crack the security on our banks as well as the power grids. These black hats run the gamut from simple criminals to terrorists. And their holy grail is what we call a 'zero day' vulnerability, which is where they take advantage of a security vulnerability on the same day that the vulnerability becomes generally known. There are zero days between the time the vulnerability is discovered and the first attack, hence the name."

The congressmen and women nodded.

"White-hat hackers are the good guys," continued Schoeffel. "Call them 'ethical hackers,' if you will. They're the ones who build our defenses against the black hats and wage a very serious war with them, and it is equal parts attack and defense. We employ many of them to try and hack our own systems so that vulnerabilities can be identified and addressed. Many businesses employ them, too. White-hat hackers use their understanding of complex computer-security programs to compromise the organization's systems, just as a black-hat hacker would. However, instead of using this access to steal or vandalize these systems the white hats report back to the organization and inform it of how they gained access, allowing the organization to improve its defenses. This is called 'penetration testing,' and it's an extremely valuable tool. Homeland and the Department of Defense employ hundreds of white hats."

"And the gray hats?" asked Goines.

"Well, let's face it," said Schoeffel. "How much of the world is black or white? An argument can be made that in business, as in politics, most of what happens falls into some kind of gray area. And so a gray-hat hacker falls somewhere between a black hat and a white hat. These hackers don't necessarily work for their own personal gain or to wreak anarchistic damage, and though technically they may commit crimes, arguably they do so for ethical reasons."

"'Ethical'?" echoed Albertson.

"From their perspective, sure. We've had gray hats hack their way into government systems, including NORAD and other highly sensitive and supposedly closed systems, in order to raise awareness of possible vulnerabilities. Sometimes they'll hack into a piece of expensive commercial software, or work their way into something like an online pay service like PayPal and then contact the companies in order to alert them before a black hat can do real damage. Some of them consider themselves watchdogs, or cybervigilantes, or superheroes. And there are a few gray hats who hack into databases in order to act as whistleblowers for perceived crimes. We saw that with the Panama Papers a few years ago, and with Snowden before that." Schoeffel paused and assessed the panel, pleased to see that no one's eyes had glazed over, and that they were all following her. "The simple truth is that there is no such thing as a perfect system. There are always flaws and code errors and bugs. These exist because computer code is written by human beings and perfection of function, while a goal, is probably not attainable. People will always make mistakes. Knowing this, hackers look for those errors and exploit them. The more attractive the target—or the benefits of hacking that target, such as with banks—the more aggressive and determined the attacks are."

"What can we do to stop it?" asked Albertson.

Schoeffel had to resist the impulse to shrug. She took a sip of water instead and wished there were something stronger in the glass. A tall vodka and tonic with cherries and lime would smooth the edges of her eroded nerves.

"Well, one thing we can do is up the funding for the WhiteHat counterintrusion program being developed by DARPA," she said.

"That's one of Major Schellinger's programs?" mused Goines. "It's very expensive."

"It's a lot less expensive than the alternative," said Schoeffel. "We need to seriously up our game, because hackers are constantly upping theirs. Think of it as a guerrilla war. The hackers are the mobile resistance and—"

"They're terrorists," snapped Albertson, emphasizing his point by slapping his palm down on the table. It was one of his signature gestures, and Schoeffel suspected that he grooved on seeing people flinch. Probably equated a natural reaction to a sudden noise with his listeners reacting to *him*.

"Okay, sure, then let's change the metaphor," said Schoeffel with as much patience as she could shove into her tone. "Hackers are terrorists, which means they're small, covert, and can blend into ordinary society. They are not an enemy state, and they don't have a ZIP code. Computers are portable, which means that anywhere a hacker sits—a table at Starbucks, a couch, a seat on the B train—he's able to turn into his command center. The hackers' weapons are their computers, Internet access, data, and their own personal skills. When they launch an attack, there is no smoking gun, no explosion to draw the eye. They can sit next to you in a cybercafé, use a portable device to remote-hack your cell phone or the chip in your Visa card and go online to destroy your life. They can use public utilities and free Wi-Fi as tunnels to get into the mainframes owned by big business, banking, credit-card companies, research laboratories, government agencies, and the military. Our current mechanism for countering these attacks is good, but, because of the natural bureaucracy and the size of our government, adaptive change is correspondingly slow. An elephant can defeat a lion in a straight fight, but the lion is faster and more agile and can often inflict damage and escape. When it returns, it targets the young and weak in the elephant's herd, inflicting a different and perhaps deeper kind of damage."

"How bad can this get?" asked Goines.

Schoeffel tried not to wince at the naïveté of the question, especially coming from someone on this committee. "We've already seen glimpses of how bad it could get. The cyber-terrorist Artemisia Bliss, who called herself Mother Night, created a network of cyberhackers. The Seven Kings organization used computer viruses to compromise the software systems of our entire military. They hacked the GPS on Air Force One and nearly plunged this country into chaos."

"You're talking about what?" asked Goines. "A cyberversion of 9/11?"

Schoeffel shook her head very slowly. "No, sir, I am talking about something much, much worse. You see, every time a cyberterrorist does something that draws the eye of the public and gets big media coverage—as with Mother Night, the Seven Kings, and ISIL last year with the attempt to use drones to release smallpox—the fact that they're stopped isn't enough. A hacker, a planner, a terrorist, or anyone else gets to look at the nature of the attack, evaluate the successes and defeats, see how the attack was ultimately stopped, and use all of that as a teachable moment. So much can be learned from those cases. So much can be deduced and induced and inferred. It's no different from generals studying the accounts of previous campaigns when planning a battle. There is as much to learn about why Napoleon lost at Waterloo as there is about how Wellington won."

There was utter silence in the room.

Schoeffel said, "I am not afraid of a cyber-9/11, ladies and gentlemen. I am afraid of a cyber-apocalypse."

CHAPTER EIGHTEEN

Before I did anything else, I called Sam Imura at the Warehouse and brought him up to speed.

"I'll take care of it, Joe," he said. "But . . . you're sure this wasn't Seif al Din?"

"It's your town, Sam. Have you had a zombie apocalypse lately?"

"Point taken. I'm just having a hard time processing the thought of a skinny fourteen-year-old girl brutalizing two grown men. Even if she had rabies."

"Which is why I want *our* people looking at the tox screens and taking a real damn close look at those nanites."

"Do you really believe there are nanites in the girl's blood?"

"Doc Jakobs is old, and he's a well-known conspiracy theorist," I said. "He once told me that he believes reptilian aliens are controlling both parties in Congress. So . . . you tell me."

Sam snorted. "He may be right about Congress."

"That's what I told him. Point is he's a bit daffy."

"Does that mean you're not opening a file on this yet?"

"Nope. It's weird and nasty, but it doesn't have DMS painted on the fender. Not until we know for sure that what Doc Jakobs told Sean is accurate. For now, I'm calling it a 70/30 in favor of Doc being too old and crazy."

"Someone's bugging your brother's house, though."

"Which is why I'm going out there," I said. "I don't know that the bugs are part of this case. Sean has worked a lot of homicides tied to organized crime, and he's done some counter-terrorism task-force stuff, so those bugs could be unconnected to the girl. I don't want to jump the gun, but no matter what's happening, this is freaky by *Sean's* standards. So until I know for sure that this is anything more than a slightly weirder day on the job for a homicide cop in the big, bad city, I'm not making my visit official."

"Understood."

What neither of us said aloud was that the DMS had bungled so many cases during the Kill Switch debacle that all of us had lost some faith in our judgment. We were all suffering different levels of PTSD. The fear there is that damage of that sort can create hesitation, and in our line of work hesitation is nearly always fatal. Or it can make you jump at shadows.

And you wonder why I drink?

My next call was to Nikki, a senior analyst in our computer department. I gave her info on Sean and the names of the dead kids and told her to find me a connection. She ran it through MindReader and called me back in less than twenty minutes.

"I'm getting hits," said Nikki, "but no pattern. What do you want first?"

"Nanites."

"Nothing there. They're not mentioned in the official report Dr. Jakobs filed, and there are no other reports related to Baltimore, local prostitution, unexplained deaths of children, or rabies outbreaks. It might be incidental."

"How so?"

"There are a lot of groups using nanite swarms these days, Joe. Ever since the Zika virus mutated, they've been spraying tons of them. They carry chemical and biological agents that sterilize the female mosquitoes so they can't breed."

"We're using nanites for this?" I asked, appalled.

"Sure. All over the world. There's a chance the girl was in an area where they were spraying and inhaled some of the nanites. Joe, I'm pretty sure Bug forwarded a report to you."

"When?"

"Like . . . two years ago?"

"Shit." There were a lot of reports forwarded to me every day. I skimmed most of them because we're talking hundreds of pages, either in print or online. If I was in the field, then all of that data piled up. There was no earthly way for me to keep ahead of it all. "Which is why I love you, Nikki," I said. "You always help me with my homework. Tell me, would those Zika nanites be in her *brain*?"

"Well . . . no, probably not. We can ask Dr. Acharya when he gets back from the DARPA camp."

"Look," I said, "is there any chance those nanites were *carrying* rabies?"

"There's absolutely nothing like that in the files. Nanites don't bite. They're really, really, really tiny."

"Okay. What about rabies by itself? Any new outbreaks?"

"Well, sure, though not that much. There was a report on that, too."

"Which I clearly have not read," I told her.

She sighed audibly. "According to the CDC, incidents of rabies here in America are in decline. There were only two or three cases reported annually and only forty cases diagnosed in the United States between 2003 and early last year, twelve of which were cases where the person contracted the disease while outside the U.S. There's been a definite increase in the last eighteen months, but it's still such a low number that it hasn't gotten much national press."

"What's causing the change?" I asked.

"I'll get in touch with Dr. Cmar. He'll know."

John Cmar was the director of the Division of Infectious Diseases at Sinai Hospital of Baltimore, but he was also a senior consultant for the Bughunters, a covert rapid-response CDC group funded by the DMS. He's one of Mr. Church's "friends in the industry."

"Keep me posted on that," I said.

"Okay, but I'm checking other instances of rabies and I'm seeing increased incidents in India, and in West Africa, Mexico, and Brazil. Pretty much the poorest parts of the Third World, but there are always disease outbreaks there. I'm not seeing anything that ties into what happened in Baltimore, though. I mean, rabies shows up a lot in animals, mostly skunks in the middle part of the country and parts of California, foxes down in Texas, and raccoons on the East Coast. Some bats, and like that. Dogs with rabies are really rare because of vaccinations. We can't know how the girl contracted it until we get the samples and have our own lab run tests, and even then we might not know for sure. It's so weird for city kids. I mean, exposure to nanites from mosquito spraying is a hundred times more likely, and even that's odd."

"Okay. What about the hotel where Holly died? Any red flags in its health-code violations?"

"No, nothing in particular. I found some deep background stuff on the hotel management but no actionable evidence," Nikki said. "Nothing you can use in court. But there's this—all the kids Sean told you about died in hotels or motels, and although none of them are owned by the same people, there is a connection. They all use the same linen and vending services, which are owned by a Baltimore businessman named Vsevolod Rejenko, known as Vee."

"Russian mob?" I asked.

"Vee's Czech. Got his U.S. citizenship six years ago. Been looked at a couple of times for possible racketeering, but nothing came of it. I have a bunch of searches active on MindReader, though."

Old and cranky as it was, MindReader was still a pretty spiffy computer system. It has two primary functions. The first is that it has a superintrusion software package that allows it to invade other computers and, in doing so, rewrite the target's own software in order to erase all traces of the invasion. It's a ghost that can walk through walls. The second thing it does is serve as a master pattern-recognition-analysis computer. Because MindReader can essentially steal information from the databases of all other law-enforcement agencies, it can then collate that data and look for patterns no one else sees. If Mr. Church trusted the motives and ethics of the heads of other law-enforcement agencies, he'd probably share MindReader. But there are a lot of complete jackasses out there, even among the good guys. Bug runs MindReader, with Nikki and Yoda as his right and left hands. They are supernerd geniuses who had all been frustrated idealists trying to fight the stupidity of the "system" by acting as anarchist hackers of one kind or another. Then Church stepped into their lives and gave them the chance to do real good for the world, and to do it by using the world's most sophisticated and powerful computer.

"This Vee character," I said. "See if he still has active ties in the Czech Republic?"

"Because of Prague, you mean? I thought of that. Vee recruits some of his staff from there, but that's all that came up."

"Go deeper. See if he has any ties to the technologies industry in general, and any connection at all to nanotechnology in particular."

"On it," she said, and ended the call.

My next call was to Lydia Rose, to book me on the first available flight to Baltimore.

INTERLUDE THREE

HARADA GAMES AND ELECTRONICS
HIRAOKA BUILDING
CHIYODA-KU, TOKYO
FIVE WEEKS AGO

The clerk was reading the paper while an old anime of *Sailor Moon* played on every screen in the shop. When the bell above the door rang, he looked up to see a middle-aged businessman come in. The man looked sweaty and nervous, the way a lot of customers did. That was useful. It spoke to a type. This man was not here to buy a flat-screen TV or a videogame console. He was too old, for one thing, and his clothes were too good. He didn't have the slacker look, or even the look of the young worker drone who decompressed after his shift by escaping into alien worlds.

This man was fiftysomething, with a very expensive suit, top-quality shoes, and a leather briefcase that cost more than some of the electronics in the shop. The clerk figured him for an executive in one of the mid to large companies. Probably an oil company, or something related to petroleum, because he seemed to be getting a lot of those kinds of customers in here lately. This man would have at least one very expensive car, a big house, a pretty wife, a couple of grown kids, no dog. He didn't look like the dog-owner type. Koi, maybe.

The clerk stood and gave a very slight bow, which is something he only did for certain customers. The store was empty, and the clerk touched a button beneath the counter that switched the OPEN sign to BACK IN FIVE MINUTES, and that also engaged the door lock. The man heard the click and flinched.

The clerk smiled, even more convinced now.

"How may I help you, sir?" he asked.

The man didn't immediately approach the counter but instead stood where he was, his pink tongue licking nervously at his lips.

"I, um," began the man. He cut quick looks around the empty shop and then tried again. "I would, um . . . I mean, do you carry any, um, *software.*"

There it was. The code word. It not only identified why the man was here but also who sent him. Each of the account managers associated with this shop used a different word. *Software, shareware, spyware.* Like that. More than three dozen possible keywords. The trick was to ensure that it wasn't a random word thrown out by an actual customer of an electronics store.

"For installation or download, sir?"

The man swallowed and blinked. He had sweat in his eyes and on his upper lip. "I prefer to, um, download it."

"Of course, sir, please come this way. We have an excellent selection of programs." He held out a hand to invite the man to step up to the counter. Then the clerk went behind the counter and tapped on the keys of a keyboard mounted beneath it. The front-window glass immediately darkened, which was a nice little trick of holography. The glass had some reflective qualities, and small projectors mounted amid the ceiling track lights splashed a continuous video loop of the shop as it looked when closed and darkened. The image was 3-D enough so that if someone outside shifted for a better look inside the image would adjust to maintain a normal view. It was quite effective, and was only one of several dozen high-tech features built into the store's security. It was a complicated world, as the clerk well knew, and you could never be too careful.

Once they were totally free from prying eyes, the clerk tapped another key, which turned the clear glass countertop into an opaque video screen. The businessman grunted in surprise, but bent closer to watch as the clerk brought up an illustrated menu. The pictures were of anime movies featuring young women in outlandish costumes, many with oversized swords or ray guns. The costumes ranged from tight-fitting sequined gowns to period costumes from the days of the Samurai to schoolgirl uniforms. Dozens of choices, and, with a wave of his hand, the clerk indicated how the customer could scroll down to see even more offerings. It was not a touch screen, because touch screens leave fingerprints.

"We have so many choices," said the clerk. "Did you have something particular in mind? Vintage, perhaps? Or a costume drama . . . ?"

The customer stopped scrolling and his trembling fingers hovered above an image of a child sitting on a tree stump, a stuffed unicorn doll tucked under her arm and her pouting lips tight around the thumb she was sucking. Without speaking, the man looked up at the clerk.

"An excellent choice, sir," said the clerk. "And you're in luck, because we received a brand-new shipment only this morning."

"N-new? How . . . um . . . new?"

"Absolutely untouched, sir. You will be the very first customer for this item."

The businessman licked his lips again. "You're telling me the truth?"

The clerk smiled. "We take great pride in providing only the best items for your entertainment needs. We are second to none, as I trust you've been told."

He knew that this was exactly what the account manager had said to this man. The sales pitch was very good, based on the results of several studies of sales language and psychological manipulation modeled on personality subtypes. Sell the customer what he wants in the way that makes him feel comfortable, empowered, and satisfied. Sell it in the language of his desire. That was how the regional director always put it.

The businessman looked up sharply, and even though he was still sweating and nervous, there was a fire in his eyes. The man now knew without doubt where he was, what he was doing, and whom he was dealing with. From here out, he would be less tentative as he got closer to what he craved. He would feel more powerful, but the clerk knew that this only made him more manageable; it would be like leading a stallion into a breeding pen. The horse was headstrong, but his needs dictated everything.

"How much is this . . . *item*?" demanded the businessman.

The clerk tapped a key that brought up an amount in yen. Most men would stagger back from that figure, but the businessman nodded. He produced a card and tapped the corner with the chip to the spot indicated by the clerk. There was a soft *bing*, and the money was instantly debited. The clerk noted that the card had no name on it and no numbers. The man had a special account somewhere just for this sort of thing. It meant that he was a true player, and if things went well for him today he would be a repeat customer. The percentage of the fee that the clerk would have to split with the account manager was delicious. Enough to buy a new scooter and maybe take his girlfriend out to a four-star restaurant. Very few sales hit numbers like this. He kept his pleasure off his face, though.

Instead, he cleared the screen, stepped back, and indicated the passageway to the back room, then hurried forward to open the door for the businessman. The clerk wore an expensive electronic watch, and he held the face to the doorknob so that the scanner built into the knob could read the code and release the lock. Key cards were so last year.

The clerk opened the door and ushered his client inside, then closed and locked the door behind him. Now that the store was empty, a whole battery of sensors came online to monitor the store, the street outside, the alley behind the building, and the roof. Nothing was left to chance.

The rooms behind the store were small but luxurious, with expensive furniture, indirect lighting, good carpets, and rich tapestries on the wall. The rooms were arranged in a kind of maze that prevented customers from ever encountering one another. There was no allowance for awkward moments. Not here. Never here.

The clerk led the businessman to a room near the end of a convoluted hallway, and by the time they arrived he was sure the customer would never be able to find his way out. Not without help. That was a tipping opportunity, especially if the man was satisfied with services provided.

The customers who came here were very good tippers. And although management took its cut, the clerk could clear two or three hundred yen each week. Some weeks it was as high as a thousand. The clerk had paid off most of his student loans so far.

"Here we are, sir," he said as he stopped beside a door covered in rich, dark-red leather. He waved his watch across a sensor, and the door clicked open and swung inward to reveal a very well-appointed bedroom. The bed was in the European style, with an ornate headboard, a rich brocade comforter, and many embroidered pillows. A lamp set to low light stood on a hand-carved wooden table, and beside that was a long rack of toys covered with a silk draping. Each of the many whips, chains, handcuffs, dildos, leather masks, and other items was brand-new and of the highest quality. The girl who stood beside the bed had her hands folded in front of her, head bowed, eyes politely lowered, long fall of black hair hanging below her shoulders. She was dressed in a school uniform of the kind worn by first graders in the better private schools.

The clerk bowed again as the customer stepped into the room. Then he triggered the sensor to automatically close and lock the door. He straightened, sighed, and cracked the tension out of his neck. The room—like all the rooms here—was completely soundproof. That was fine with him. He didn't like to hear the screams. After all, *he* wasn't kinky. He only worked there.

He went to the restroom and then walked through the twisting and turning hallway back to the door that opened before him and led to the store. Once he was back behind the counter, he tapped the keys that changed the sign back to OPEN and turned the opaque window back to clear glass.

And that's when the door exploded inward, showering him with jagged splinters. He covered his face with one hand as he spun away and used the other to reach for an alarm button. He hit the button at the exact moment that a hard rubber bullet struck him in the shoulder, shattering his scapula and sending him crashing into the back wall. Suddenly the room was filled with bodies as what seemed like dozens of police poured in through the shattered door, shouting, shoving him, beating him to the floor. Alarms rang throughout the building, and the clerk knew that the rest of the staff would be trying to rescue as many customers as possible.

"Through here!" yelled a voice, and a husky cop stepped to the back door and swung a heavy breaching tool. Once, twice, and on the third shot the door lock tore itself out of the frame. The officers ran inside, guns drawn, faces set into fierce growls.

"Where are they?" demanded a hatchet-faced man who wore a detective's shield on a chain around his neck.

"I . . . don't . . ." began the clerk, but the detective struck him a savage blow across the mouth. Blood spattered the corner of the counter, and the clerk screamed.

"Get him up," demanded the detective, and two officers grabbed the clerk and hauled him to his feet, which made the broken bones in his shoulder grate together. The clerk screamed, but the detective punched him in the stomach with such shocking force that the scream was cut short. The clerk felt his lungs locking up and fireworks seemed to burst around him. Then the detective took a fistful of his hair and raised his head, leaning so close that when he spoke his hot spit struck the clerk's face. "Where are the kids?"

The clerk shook his head, blood dribbling from between his mashed lips. "No . . . kids . . ." he gasped.

The detective looked as if he wanted to hit him again, but then someone shouted from inside the building.

"Sir! You need to come here," yelled an officer.

The detective turned to go, but over his shoulder growled, "Bring him."

The two officers holding the clerk dragged him through the doorway and followed the detective down the winding corridors. All the doors on either side of the hall were open, their locks smashed and the frames splintered. All of them were empty now. The businessman had been the only client on the premises at the moment. Two other members of the staff knelt on the floor, cuffed hands behind their backs, under the guard of furious-looking cops. Both of the staff members were bruised and bleeding.

"Please," begged the clerk, "there's no kids here. Believe me."

"Shut your mouth or lose your teeth," snarled the detective.

They arrived at the next to the last door in the hall, which stood open, half torn from its hinges. The detective went in first, and the cops flung the clerk onto the floor next to the businessman, who was sprawled and semiconscious, his face pulped from a savage beating.

The room was silent.

The detective approached the bed, on which a small, naked figure lay sprawled, wrists and ankles tightly bound by padded cuffs. The last remnants of a school uniform clung to the bare skin. The girl's mouth was open, the lips parted in a small "Oh" of apparent surprise. Her eyes were open and stared sightlessly at the ceiling. The thin chest did not rise and fall, and her limbs were utterly slack.

The detective bent over her, staring in absolute horror at the tiny body. Then he closed his eyes and sagged back, reaching for the bedpost for balance. He remained like that for a long, long moment during which the clerk didn't dare breathe.

Then the detective opened his eyes and turned slowly toward the clerk. Everyone else turned with him, looking at the young man on the floor. The weight of their hatred was crushing.

"You'll burn for this," said the detective. "I swear to you, you'll burn."

The clerk was crying now, tears running from his eyes, snot bubbling from his nose. "No . . . please . . . it's not what you think. . . ."

The detective rushed at him and kicked him in the stomach. Once . . . then again. Each blow doing awful damage.

"*Stop!*" screamed the clerk. "*She's not dead.*"

JONATHAN MABERRY

The detective stopped, foot raised for a third kick. Doubt clouded his face and he looked from his target over his shoulder at the girl.

Very slowly the girl turned her head toward him. She blinked slowly and smiled at the detective.

"System failure," she said. "Please reset."

She began to blink rapidly and repeated the phrase.

Over and over.

The clerk and the businessman were arrested, but within two hours they were released. Lawyers descended in flocks on the police station. Threats—very credible threats—were made about the lawsuits that would be filed. Apologies would be required at every level of the police administration, because the businessman was very important. He was a senior vice president of a petroleum and metals conglomerate with holdings all across Japan that employed twenty-eight thousand people. Jobs would be lost within the police department. Heads would roll.

Or so all the lawyers threatened.

The dynamic of that legal barrage faltered a day later, when Mr. Yohji Watanabe, back home in the safety of his home, collapsed in the shower of his palatial estate on the outskirts of Tokyo. His wife heard him fall and came running, but she stopped in the bathroom doorway, her horror mounting higher than her need to see to her husband. He lay there naked, tangled in the plastic curtains, bleeding from his nose and mouth, from his ears and eyes, from his rectum and the tip of his penis. The shower water had turned the blood pink and washed it all away before Mrs. Watanabe even stopped screaming.

CHAPTER NINETEEN

"Mademoiselle," said the Concierge, "you are looking well."

He was a very good liar, but they both knew that he was lying. Zephyr Bain glared at him from the big screen in the little Frenchman's office. Now they were both in wheelchairs. She looked like a scarecrow covered with sun-withered leather. It was hard to believe that she was only in her mid-thirties. She looked ninety. *No*, thought the Concierge, *she looks dead.*

Zephyr didn't acknowledge his compliment. "Is it done?"

"*Oui*," he said. "Prague was a huge success. More than we could have hoped for."

"And Mexico?"

He shrugged. "The government there refused the Deacon's offer and instead went with Sigma Force. Exactly as John predicted they would."

"Good," she said, and there was much more life in the ferocity of her tone and in the flash of her eyes than in the shrunken husk of her body.

"We are exactly on schedule," said the Concierge.

Zephyr leaned forward, and her eyes seemed to flash with green fire. "Tell me that it's going to work."

The Concierge nodded. "I promise you, mademoiselle, it is all going to work."

Her eyes shifted to look past him. He knew what she was looking at. His house had been heavily reinforced in the past eleven weeks, and she could see the heavy steel shutters on the windows. He had done everything to make his estate impregnable. Robotic sentries outside, armed drones in the trees, mines placed under the turf all across the lawn. Inside the house, the Calpurnia AI system oversaw every detail of security and would respond with escalating aggression against any attempt to break in. If Havoc ran as expected, that would be inevitable. There would be riots in the streets. Everywhere. For as long as the rioters lived. Call it eight months, according to the most recent computer models. He had food and supplies for two years. The Concierge always paid attention to detail, and, with what was coming, those details were the only thing that would keep him alive. The entire house had even been constructed out of flame-resistant materials in case this part of the world caught fire.

Which was so very likely.

He smiled up at Zephyr Bain. "When would you like to start the clock?"

She thought about it.

"Soon," she said.

"How soon, mademoiselle?"

"As soon as we break Joe Ledger's heart," said Zephyr. "But be very clear on this, my friend. He dies before I do."

The Concierge nodded. "Oh, of course. That was always my plan."

CHAPTER TWENTY

SENATE SUBCOMMITTEES ON CYBERTERRORISM
CAPITOL BUILDING
WASHINGTON, D.C.
ONE WEEK AGO

"A cyberapocalypse?" said Goines, smiling faintly. "Isn't that a bit of a reach, Deputy Director? I know that you need to defend your funding and budget requests, but let's not descend to grandiosity."

Sarah Schoeffel fixed the senator with a hard, unflinching stare. "I am not given much to exaggeration. I used that word with precision. Allow me to explain."

"Please do," said Albertson, though he wore an expression of even greater skepticism than Goines.

"It is within the skill set of modern hackers to launch a coordinated deep-penetration attack on American banks. Going solely on established actions by black hats and gray hats over the last ten years, we know that they can hack into the mainframes of the banking system to destroy records, drain accounts, and freeze the response networks needed to stop loss or prevent further damage. In 2008, the Federal Reserve invoked a number of what were called "unusual and exigent circumstances" to lend billions of dollars to banks that had been damaged during the credit meltdown. We know, from evidence collected by the NSA and the Department of Military Sciences, that the Seven Kings were responsible for a large portion of that financial catastrophe. Billions were looted, and let me remind you that more than a hundred billion has never been recovered. Now go back to September 11, 2001, and look at what happened to stocks and banking. During the flight to safety before trading was suspended, billions were moved and a great number of people profited hugely. At first, we thought it was a typical crisis-induced trading frenzy, but the DMS proved without a shadow of a doubt that the Seven Kings were not only profiting from the panic but had provided funding and support to Al Qaeda to guarantee that the planes would hit the towers. Those planes were physical, but they were in support of theft of funds on a grand scale, because Hugo Vox had thousands of traders waiting to exploit the event."

The congressional panel watched, silent and calculating.

"Cyberattackers are aware that the damage they inflict is massive and isn't easily repaired. Federal deposit insurance only applies if a bank fails, *not* if hackers drain the accounts. In the event of a cyberattack that drained funds, banks would have to tap their own reserves and then their own private insurance. If the attack is large enough, there wouldn't be enough to cover all claims. Which means the banks fail and the avalanche buries millions of American businesses and private citizens."

Not a sound in the room.

"Cyberhackers come in all shapes and sizes," continued Schoeffel. "One-man operations all the way up to nation-states that want to do damage to the U.S. economy. Our status as the premier superpower rests on the dome of an economy that has become increasingly fragile. Cybercriminals of all stripes continue to attack and exploit our online financial and market systems, particularly those that interface with the Internet. The Automated Clearing House systems, or ACH, card payments, and market trades are all vulnerable to these kinds of attacks. The attacks happen at all levels, from the individual citizen with an ATM card and an online banking login to the biggest banks on Wall Street. When it comes to cybercrime, no one is too small a target to bother with or so big that they can withstand any attack. A scenario of perfect security does not exist. Fraudulent monetary transfers and counterfeiting of stored value cards are the most common attacks. We in the FBI are currently investigating over five hundred reported cases of corporate-account takeovers in which cybercriminals have initiated unauthorized ACH and wire transfers from the bank accounts of U.S. businesses. Ten years ago, that kind of theft was in the range of two hundred and twenty-five million. Last year it was eighteen billion that we can absolutely prove, and it's entirely possible the number is much higher."

"You have documentation on this?" asked Goines.

"Reams of it," said Schoeffel. "I wish proof wasn't as easy to come by, but it's everywhere. They are stealing data, they are destroying systems, and they are clearly learning how to effectively and easily disrupt critical financial, military, communications, power, and medical services. Think about that, and then see if my phrasing doesn't fit."

Even then, the members of the panel looked unconvinced. Schoeffel wanted to hit Goines.

"The bureau already has substantial funding to combat these threats," said Albertson.

"We have funding adequate for responding to the threats perceived when the *last* budget proposal was approved," said Schoeffel. "The cyberworld changes faster than the budget process, and it's capable of unpredictable exponential growth. I want us to get way ahead of it. Besides, one agency cannot combat the threat alone. The National Cyber Investigative Joint Task Force, which the bureau heads, coordinates with twenty law-enforcement agencies and with the intelligence community—the IC—which includes the Central Intelligence Agency, the Department of Defense, the Department of Homeland Security, and the National Security Agency. We have cyberstaff in other IC agencies through joint duty, but that is a very large bureaucracy. It's not nearly nimble enough. We need to create smaller strike teams, specialized groups that can react quickly, turn on a dime, go where the fight is without having to carry the whole infrastructure with them. That is what I want you to fund. Teams like that will, we hope, be able to counter or quickly respond to zero point attacks like the Chinese Titan Rain assaults in 2003, the attacks during the 2011 Paris G2 Summit, and the monstrous 2015 hacking of the Office of Personnel Management, where information—including Social Security numbers—on eighteen million Americans was stolen. Sadly, the list of serious cybercrimes is so long that we would be here for a week, and that alone is frightening."

"But hardly apocalyptic," said Goines dryly. Some of the others on the panel chuckled. Schoeffel kept her temper, though.

"Senator," she said evenly, "it's fair to say that the nation-states that are at odds with our country are unlikely to declare open war. Even the hard-line Russians led by Putin aren't likely to remake that country in the image of the Cold War–era Soviet monster, and China, though a growing threat, may be able to put more men in the field, but they know that any war they might fight with us would be between ships and submarines, and we have a serious advantage there. North Korea can't even see the subs we have off their coast. But every single one of them, and the next forty antagonistic nations behind them, can engage in computer warfare on nearly equal ground with us. We saw that in 2009, when hackers breached the security at Google's Chinese headquarters to gain access to corporate servers and steal intellectual property. Part of that theft was to obtain access to the Gmail accounts of Chinese human-rights activists. Since then there have been several significant hack attacks of major corporations and government agencies, including private power companies, medical research, the Centers for Disease Control, the National Institutes for Health, FEMA, NASA, hospitals, communications and cellular-phone companies, and more. In 1990, Kevin Poulsen managed to use his computer to block phone lines so that he could rig a contest to win a Porsche. In 1998, Iraqi hackers launched a cyberattack that allowed them to temporarily seize control of over five hundred government and private-industry systems. And let's not forget that in 1999 a fifteen-year-old boy, Jonathan James, hacked into the computers of a division of the Department of Defense and installed a back door on its servers that allowed him to intercept thousands of internal emails from different government organizations, including ones containing usernames and passwords for various military computers. Hackers have become steadily smarter and more resourceful since then. Iran's Operation Cleaver is a perfect example; it allowed that government to target critical infrastructure organizations worldwide and yet maintain official deniability. That is the most insidious part of it, too, because they can come at us in ways that are actually more destructive than bullets or cluster bombs and still maintain enough deniability so there is no chance for a declaration of war that would be acknowledged by NATO or the U.N."

She paused to take a drink of water and to consider her next words.

"You call me on my use of the word *apocalypse*. Then tell me which word I should use when it is within the short reach of possibility for hackers to take down the power grids, disrupt the computers running the cellular networks with aggressive malware, and reveal our most confidential military secrets to our enemies? What should we call it when hackers can use viruses and tapeworms to destroy the medical records of hundreds of millions of Americans and then corrupt the data stored in the computers of hospitals, health-care companies, and trauma centers? What word would you give it when information on how to construct weapons of mass destruction are stolen and mass-released to the Taliban, ISIL, and others? Tell me, ladies and gentlemen," said Schoeffel, "what word would you prefer that I use? I ask, because each and every one of those things is not only possible but likely."

When no one spoke, she leaned closer to the mic.

"Or," she said, "perhaps the more precise and accurate word is *inevitable,* and that's why I went out to visit the DARPA camp. Everything I've seen, from the new generation of WarDogs to their WhiteHat Internet security program—they are our next best line of defense. I think we need to give them access to funding and to our integrated national-defense, banking, and infrastructure computer systems, because they are ready to fight what we know is coming."

CHAPTER TWENTY-ONE

As I drove home to pack I called Mr. Church at the Hangar, the DMS headquarters at Floyd Bennett Field in Brooklyn. There are two lines I can use to reach him; one is for "when the world is about to end" crisis situations, and the other is for everything else. There were no missiles inbound and no one had released a global pandemic, so I used the main line. It was a coin flip of a choice, though. I've heard that he has a special ringtone for me, and I've tried lies, bribes, and threats to wheedle what it is from his staff. So far, no luck.

When Church answered, I told him about the weirdness in Baltimore.

"Sean called you?" he asked.

"Yes."

"He knew *why* to call you?" There was the briefest of silences. It's understood that no one gets admitted to the DMS circle of confidence without Church or Aunt Sallie's blessing. It's bad enough that too many members of the government know about us, but friends and family were not part of our calling plan, if you know what I mean.

"More or less," I said, and explained that my dad told Sean a little, and that Sean had probably worked more of it out on his own. He really is a good detective. Church offered no rebuke; it was damage done, and lingering to bitch about it was counterproductive. He didn't ask if my brother was sure about the nanobots.

When I was finished, he asked the same question Sam had asked: "Are you starting a file on this?"

"Not yet," I said. "Kind of like to take a look at what he has and then make the call."

"The nanotechnology may demand that it's ours," he said. "And there is the double connection of Prague and sex workers."

"I know, which is why I'm going to take a look myself rather than hand it off to the Warehouse. Can you send a science tech down from the Hangar to process some samples?"

"Done. However, I have to caution you about waiting too long to decide if this is our case."

"I hear you, believe me, but let's face it, boss, we're not flush with active field teams. I don't want to make this into a big thing until I know that's what it is. That could pull resources away from something else that's more important."

"Fair enough," he said, though I could hear the doubt in his voice.

"I'd love to get Acharya on the damn phone. Any chance of that?"

"Without opening an official file? None. And, even if we did, I would have to speak directly with the president."

"Why? We've always had an open-door policy with DARPA."

"Kill Switch changed the politics of cooperation for the DMS, I'm afraid. I'm working on repairing that trust, but it's much easier lost than rebuilt."

"That sucks."

"That's life, Captain," he said.

"Yeah, yeah," I said sourly. "Look, before I fly the friendly skies I want to make sure you didn't need me for anything else."

The DMS field teams still left intact were all out in the field, because the world was going bug-fuck nuts. As usual. Or . . . maybe a little more than usual. Actually, maybe a lot more. Three high-ranking military scientists had died in "accidents" that seemed less accidental the closer we looked. Ecoterrorist protesters had blown up the Ice House, a biological-samples storage facility maintained covertly by NATO for everything from anthrax to Ebola, including twenty-two of the most virulent bioweapons developed during the Cold War. However, instead of shutting down the facility they had released hundreds of pathogens. Luckily, the Ice House was located on an ice pack at the top of the damn world, so the cold killed most of the bugs. A bunch of fuel-air bombs were used to make sure there was nothing left. Other DMS teams were looking into a possible deliberate release of a mutated and highly contagious strain of epidemic nephropathy, a type of viral hemorrhagic fever that isn't supposed to be communicable human-to-human, but in this form it was. There was also shit tons of GPS hacking going on everywhere around the globe. A factory that made and assembled consumer-level quadcopter drones had been burned to the ground, but arson investigators were building a case for all the completed and packaged drones having been removed before the place was torched. And a firm that made virtual-reality goggles for the video-game market had been busted for including subliminal messages preaching violence against Muslim Americans.

A day in the life of the DMS. Or, I guess, to be more accurate, this was the world being the world. Crazy, dangerous, frequently lethal, often unkind, and populated with lots of very bad people. Am I a cynic? Not really, but I'm getting there, and I'm driving in the fast lane.

However, Church said, "Go to Baltimore."

"Okay."

"Take Dr. Sanchez with you."

I hesitated. "Circe won't be happy."

Rudy Sanchez and I have been best friends for a lot of years, but last year he fell under a kind of mind control and attacked me while I was in the hospital. It wasn't his fault, and the attack was directed by someone who was incredibly dangerous. It turned Rudy into a lethal weapon, and to stop him I had to inflict some serious injuries. I broke his leg so badly that he needed total knee replacement, and his nose had to be reconstructed. Unless you're both Vikings, that is not the definition of a male-bonding experience. Rudy's wife, Circe, kind of hated me now. Poor Rudy was caught between my need for him to forgive me, his need for me to forgive *him*, and Circe's unfiltered loathing.

"Circe no longer works for the DMS," said Church coldly.

That was the other thing. Very few people know that Circe O'Tree-Sanchez is the only known living relative of Mr. Church's. The secret has been kept in order to protect her from Church's many powerful enemies, who would love to have a weapon they could use against him. It's possible that Circe, or her son—Church's grandson—would be the key that unlocked the robot heart of the big man. However, since the Kill Switch thing last year, Circe had left the DMS and very clearly didn't want anything to do with it. Or with us. She barely spoke to her father, blaming his lifestyle choices for putting her family in harm's way. She had a point, but I knew that her decisions had to hurt the big man. He'd been less genial these past few months, colder and more distant. Not that he was ever Mr. Rogers to begin with. Even so, I felt bad for him.

"Okay," I said, "but if Circe comes after me with a knife I'm using you as a human shield."

He made a sound that might have been a laugh or might have been a grunt of disgust. In either case, the line went dead. It always gives me the warm, fuzzy, bunny tinglies to share a moment with my boss.

I glanced over at Ghost, who was in the passenger seat looking out the window. Usually he was excited to go home, but Junie wasn't there, so neither of us was enthused.

CHAPTER TWENTY-TWO

INLET CRAB HOUSE
3572 HIGHWAY 17
MURRELLS INLET, SOUTH CAROLINA
SATURDAY, APRIL 29, 8:55 PM EASTERN TIME

First Sergeant Bradley Sims, known as Top to everyone, nursed a beer and watched as his partner, Master Sergeant Harvey "Bunny" Rabbit worked his way through a solid pound of peel-and-eat shrimp, a double side of grits, red rice, and six glasses of Diet Dr Pepper. Bunny ate without passion, more like a machine designed to feed itself. He would pluck a shrimp from the bowl, pull off its legs, use his thumbs to crack the shell open along the underside, pull off the shell, and put the meat into his mouth; he'd chew silently between ten and twelve times, then wash it down with a mouthful of fizz.

It was the diet soda that Top couldn't understand. Rough count on everything on Bunny's plate and in the sides, including the appetizer of hush puppies, was three thousand calories easy. Probably closer to four. Seemed to Top that a man approaching a meal with that kind of commitment ought to at least drink a regular soda—a coke, which is what they called every kind of soda down here. In the northern states from Washington to Michigan, they called it pop. In the Northeast and the West Coast, it was soda. Down here everything was a coke. Even a Diet Dr Pepper. Should have been a real Coke, though. That's what Top figured.

His own meal—a grilled grouper sandwich on whole wheat with lettuce and red onion—was nearly untouched. The beer was a Landshark, a brand Top usually enjoyed but that he'd let go warm as he rolled the bottle back and forth between his calloused palms.

Since they came into the crab house, the only words either of them had spoken was to the waitress. Nothing at all to each other. That was becoming a thing with them. A new routine that replaced their old rhythm of being willing and able to talk about damn near anything.

However, they'd logged a lot of silent miles on this gig. They'd flown from the Pier in San Diego to Oklahoma City and taken a car from the DMS field office there, and had since traveled thousands of miles. Zigzagging from place to place. Fayetteville to Pine Bluff, Memphis to Tuscaloosa, Montgomery to Alpharetta, and then half a dozen towns, large and small, in North Carolina, lower Virginia, and now South Carolina. After this, they would check into a motel for the night and in the morning head almost due south to Savannah, Charleston, and then down the long Atlantic side of Florida, hitting Fernandina Beach, Daytona Beach, Fort Lauderdale, and Miami, after which the two of them would fly home to California. It was a rinse-and-repeat assignment. Go to a town, set up a meet with someone who was either a former or an active special operator, or a cop, or a Fed from the FBI, NSA, DEA, or ATF. They'd ask some questions, listen to the answers, tell the candidate very little, and promise to be in touch. Most of the times, that last part was a lie. So far, they hadn't found anyone they felt sufficiently enthusiastic about to recommend as a candidate for the DMS.

It depressed Top, adding to the weight of everything else that had been pushing him down these past months. Ever since things went wrong last year, he had begun to lose faith in many of the structures he'd always believed were immutable. The DMS, their mission, his own optimism, and even what he believed about himself. Top had always trusted his own judgment and the stability of his personality. He had neither an inflated ego nor a falsely suppressed one. A lifetime in the military, both following orders and giving them, of time spent training and time spent on missions, of patches of peace and long runs through the valley of the shadow of death—all of that had allowed him to assess his skills, his strengths, his weaknesses. He knew who and what he was, and he was at peace with it. He knew that he could rely on his own judgment, moral view, and fairness as much as others could when he was part of a team. Mr. Church and Captain Ledger had each leaned on him in moments of crisis, and Top had become a cornerstone of the DMS field-operations structure. Top accepted that and worked to make sure that he was always a known quantity to the people who needed to trust him.

Now, though . . . ?

When things started going bad for the DMS last year, he stayed steady, believing in the mission and in Echo Team. That changed when someone sneaked into his mind and smashed the controls, cut the wires, took over. The intruder used Top's body like a hit-and-run car. He forced Top's hands to use the tools of war to do dreadful things to the very people he had sworn his life to protect. He made Top complicit, however unwillingly, in the wholesale murder of innocent civilians.

Top understood the science of it. Long hours with Dr. Sanchez had helped him learn to say all the proper words about not accepting unearned guilt, about placing the blame where it truly belonged. Top understood that he had been used, and that he had no defense against it. He understood that the blame was not truly his.

Sure, he understood all of that.

But it didn't change a goddamn thing. It had been his finger on the trigger. He had memorized the names of each victim, and every night he got down on his knees and prayed to whatever God was in heaven—if any god even existed anymore. He did not pray for his own soul but for those whose lives he had destroyed. The dead ones, and the living survivors who had to carry their own weight of grief and loss.

Bunny was going through it, too. They both had their minds raped; they had both committed unspeakable atrocities. It bonded them as much as it marked them.

What neither of them knew yet was whether it had ended them in every way that mattered to who they were and what they did. Since then they hadn't fired a gun in anger. Sure, they could cap off a thousand rounds on the target range and never blink. That wasn't the same thing. That wasn't real. It was no more authentic combat than playing a first-person shooter game on Xbox. The question was whether either of them could be trusted to carry a weapon into combat. The question was whether their minds were ever going to be truly their own. The question was whether the violation had broken something crucial inside their hearts or minds or souls.

Top truly didn't know.

Now they were out doing busywork because Captain Ledger and Dr. Sanchez hadn't yet cleared them for fieldwork. They carried guns, but for the first time in Top's adult life the SIG Sauer in his shoulder holster felt wrong, lumpy, awkward, and he felt like a dangerous jackass for carrying it.

He sighed and sipped his beer. It tasted like piss.

CHAPTER TWENTY-THREE

JOHN THE REVELATOR
LECTURE, "THE FACE OF ROBOTICS"
PATTEN AUDITORIUM
DREXEL UNIVERSITY
NINE WEEKS AGO

"In order to understand the significance of the coming technological singularity, you have to view things from a big-picture perspective," John told his audience. "You need to step back from personal agendas and immediate needs and look at the world as a whole."

The audience members were silent, attentive. Some leaned forward, and others were pressed back in their chairs as if they were afraid of what he was saying. Or repelled by his words. It was all the same to John. The message was what mattered.

"The fact that human beings developed self-awareness, problem-solving intelligence, the ability to invent and to have both abstract and practical thinking is every bit as important, and as inextricably tied to our evolutionary development, as the opposable thumb. Nature selected humans for survival. And everything around us, from the chairs on which you sit to the speakers that amplify my voice, to the automobiles in which you drove here, are by-products of that intelligence."

He paused to let the audience digest that.

"Now we are on the leading edge of a new stage of evolution, and that is *artificial intelligence*. AI. We became smart enough and wise enough to be able to create machines whose functions not only approximate human thought but will ultimately surpass it. We have already built machines that can perform physical functions that exceed much of what humans can manage. There are already machines that are stronger, faster, more precise, less vulnerable, more versatile. We have machines that can fight fires, defuse bombs, oversee security, engage in combat, survive extreme environmental conditions, fly, swim, dive to astounding depths, and operate in microgravity. Machines do not require breathable air, and they can tolerate temperature ranges far beyond human endurance. Are there limits? Of course. Improved battery life is a constant challenge. The balance of durability, flexibility, and weight in materials is a challenge. Expense is a challenge. And processing speed can always be tweaked. But"—he paused again to smile—"those challenges are being met, and we're constantly exceeding our own expectations when it comes to development and innovation."

He pointed to a man in the fifth row who had gray hair.

"How old are you, sir?"

"Sixty-five," said the man.

"I wouldn't have guessed older than sixty," said John, and waited through the ripple of laughter. "You were born before the computer age. Well before. Do you remember your first personal computer?"

"I do," said the man. "It was a Commodore 64."

More laughter, and even some sympathetic applause.

"Ah," said John. "Do you recall how it felt to have your *own* computer?"

"Yes, I do. It was amazing. And when they came out with the Commodore 128 three years later, I was in heaven. I wrote my dissertation on that machine."

"One hundred and twenty-eight K of memory," said John. "The Commodore 128 was released in January 1985. How many of you here were alive then? Half? The rest of you were born after. Some, I see, born well after. That was the last of the eight-bit home computers. At the time, that was an amazing amount of memory. It provided astounding computational potential. For the first time, computers weren't something used by corporations and the government. Now everyone could own one. Suddenly the power was in the hands of ordinary people. Wow! What a moment. And then in the nineties we saw the commercialization of the World Wide Web. The computer age became the Internet age. Now, what most people didn't know was that these technologies were on a converging course with the early expert systems— what most people know as artificial intelligence. And robotics was flourishing quietly somewhere else. All of these technologies, which had long, painful histories of design and failure, structural limitations, and intimidating research costs, suddenly benefited from one another's existence. These fields fed on the energetic potential in one another and soon began growing together."

John paused once more.

"A perspective check," he said. "The personal computer debuted less than forty years ago. The Internet ten years later. In terms of the scope of scientific invention, that's a blip. It's nothing. And yet consider how much has happened in each field since then. You can't even *find* a piece of technology that uses sixty-four K of RAM. Nothing we have moves that slowly. Nothing. You can go to Staples and buy a five-terabyte external hard drive for less than a hundred and fifty dollars. By next year, the storage will be double that for half the cost. On the way home from Staples you can stop at Walmart and buy a drone, and you can take both home in your autonomous-drive car while talking to your cousin in London on your cell phone as music streams in real time from a concert being performed in Los Angeles."

He watched people as they glanced at their phones and tweeted him on social media.

"Less than forty years," he said. "I was born the year and the month that the Commodore 64 was released, and I will live to see computers, artificial intelligence, and robotics accelerate beyond all predicted models. Is the technological singularity coming?" He laughed. "It's already begun."

CHAPTER TWENTY-FOUR

Before I could call Rudy I got a text message and sent it to the dashboard screen. It said:

> I am all alone.

There was no ID, though. Odd. I accessed the voice command for Miss Moneypenny, which is the nickname someone hung on the DMS version of Siri. I think the actress whose voice was sampled for the system is Cate Blanchett. Very cool and veddy, veddy British.

"Identify text sender," I said.

"Specify which text, Joe," Miss Moneypenny said.

"Most recent."

"Most recent text was from Delta Airlines, confirming your flight status."

"No," I said, "the one that just came in."

"The most recent text was from Delta—"

Another text came in:

> I'm awake.
> I'm alone.
> I'm afraid.

I growled at Miss Moneypenny. "I just received another text. Identify sender."

"Joe, the most recent text was from Delta Airlines," insisted the computer, and she gave me the time, which matched when the airline sent the flight info.

"Search all text messages for the last half hour," I said.

"There have been no other texts received in the last half hour, Joe."

"You're an idiot," I told her.

"Calling people names is childish."

If I ever find out who programmed Miss Moneypenny, I'll break my foot off in their ass. At the light I tried sending a reply text, but the incoming texts were gone. I sat there staring, my eyes flicking back and forth between my phone and the dashboard screen, and then jumped out of my skin when someone honked at me. I realized that I'd sat halfway through a green light, so I waved an apology and started driving.

I sent a text message to Junie, asking if she had just texted me. She sent a quick message that no, she hadn't. She was in the field and couldn't talk. She ended it with a quick "XOXO."

A few seconds later I got another text, but as soon as I saw it I knew it wasn't from Junie:

> I think my sister is crazy.
> She thinks I'm crazy, too.

The message lingered for ten seconds and then deleted itself from my phone. Miss Moneypenny told me that it was never there. I tried to think which of my friends was having family issues but came up dry. I dictated a quick email to Bug, the DMS computer chief, and asked him to do one of those remote-systems-checks thingies. Five minutes later, I got a reply saying that my phone was working perfectly.

"That was weird," I said to Ghost, but he was busy licking his balls.

So I said to hell with it and called Rudy to ask if he'd like to drop everything and catch a late flight back East. I briefly explained why.

"That is a very sad thing," Rudy said. "Of course I'll come with you."

"Pack for a few days," I suggested.

"Commercial air or Shirley?" he asked.

"Commercial," I said, and we both sighed. Much as I love bouncing around in my own private jet—which, technically, belongs to the DMS, but I love saying that it's *my* private jet—it's expensive to fly. Hard to justify the costs unless the big clock was ticking down to boom time. That said, I knew that Lydia Rose could snag us a couple of first-class tickets. You take the comforts where you can get them. I told Rudy the flight time and we arranged to meet at the airport.

I sensed a disturbance in the Force and looked at Ghost, who was glaring at me from the passenger seat. Not sure if he actually understood that I was talking about airline reservations, but, if so, he knew what it meant. He'd be in a dog crate in the hold. If I was taking my own jet, he'd have an actual couch to himself. On a commercial flight, not so much. His brown eyes bored into mine.

"You're going to shit in my shoes first chance you get, aren't you?" I asked him.

He beamed at me and thumped his tail a couple of times.

"Damn," I said.

CHAPTER TWENTY-FIVE

They had a seat by a window with a view of the parking lot. Since neither of them had found much to say, Top dug into his briefcase and removed the folder on the person they were here to meet. He flipped open the cover and looked at the face of a black woman in a state-police uniform. Tracy Cole. Thirty years old, five feet seven inches tall, a native of Charleston. Served four years in the army, was attached to a U.N. detail doing security for a human-rights-assessment team. According to her records, she saw combat, and more than her fair share, but Cole was regular army, not Special Forces. She volunteered a lot, and this was often a red flag for Top. He distrusted almost everyone who went out of their way to get into a fight. Too often they were either trigger-happy bigots, broken ones with a death wish; revenge-seekers who'd lost someone in one of the wars; insecure types who were trying to prove something; or damn fools who thought this was all some kind of ultra-3-D video game.

He leafed through the notes of each action, written in the dry, acronym-heavy verbiage so prized by the military. It was on a par with the stilted language of police reports. Neither sounded as if the actions being described had anything to do with real human beings. Cole had two Purple Hearts. One was minor, from shrapnel; the other was from a knife. Top grunted as he searched for and found the incident report for the latter. And that's when his interest was piqued, because although there was an official commendation for bravery stapled to the notice about the second Purple Heart, there was also a memo that had been sealed, written from the field officer to the company commander. MindReader had acquired it, of course. That note said that Cole had disobeyed a direct order not to interfere in an incident involving a small group of suspected ISIL soldiers in a compromised village. The entire region was fragile, and the officer in charge of the U.N. convoy had been afraid of things going south if his people got into anything with the locals. However, there was a small boarding-house in the village that was on a list of suspected "hospitality" centers.

In the language of ISIL a hospitality center was what they called a rape hotel. A comfort station. Tracy Cole had tried to get her lieutenant to take some action, to at least investigate, but the officer was either timid or had a stronger read on the local situation. He ordered Cole to return to her platoon and stand down. She returned to the small house where her platoon was bunked down, but only long enough to wait for dark, gear up, and go hunting. As it turned out, not only was the hotel being used to hold seven girls and women, ranging in age from eleven to twenty-three, but there were also weapons and explosives stored in the basement. And there was a worktable behind a locked cellar door where canvas vests were being rigged with stolen C4.

According to the memo, Cole had attempted to leave quietly and report this to her commander, but a guard spotted her and there was a fight. She took some serious knife wounds to the face, shoulder, and stomach, but she killed her attacker. The scuffle woke everyone up, and then there was a big damn gunfight. The startled ISIL team began firing randomly at everyone. That's when the U.N. team, roused, came running. When it was over there were eight dead ISIL shooters, two women were hospitalized for damage from ricochets, and Cole was nearly dead on her feet.

The lieutenant called in for support, and the village was surrounded and thoroughly searched. Eight more ISIL fighters were found, and these were taken alive. A total of twenty-six hostages were freed: the sex slaves and several people from the village who had been under guard in order to keep the villagers in line. When the story hit the news services, the action was listed as an "official rescue operation undertaken by United Nations Peacekeepers." Cole wasn't named, nor, Top noted, was her lieutenant. After that action, Cole was transferred Stateside and did the equivalent of busywork until the rest of her term of service burned off. She didn't re-enlist. Top guessed that she was advised not to. Or maybe she'd become disillusioned by the constant play of bad nerves and questionable politics.

As he closed her file, Top caught movement in the parking lot and saw that a white 4Runner had pulled in and a woman got out on the passenger side and slammed the door very forcefully. She wore blue-jeans, cowboy boots, a plain white T-shirt, and a ball cap that threw shadows over her face in the downspill of tangerine light from the sodium-vapor streetlamps. She walked three paces away from the truck, whirled, and stabbed the air as she said something to whoever was behind the wheel. Top couldn't hear her words, but he would have bet his pension she wasn't saying "I love you." There was a lot of anger and indignation in every line of her body.

Top tapped the tabletop with a fingernail, and Bunny came out of his thoughts, looked at the finger, then followed Top's gaze.

"That her?" asked the big young man.

"Looks like it."

They watched her stand there and continue to emphasize whatever she was saying by jabbing the air with her finger.

"Uh-oh. She's pissed at someone," said Bunny. "Husband?"

"Not married."

"Boyfriend?"

"Or someone," said Top. "Hold on, here we go."

The driver's door opened and a man got out. He was a big light-skinned black man. Not as tall as Bunny's six-six but close, and he had all the sculpted muscles of a dedicated bodybuilder: broad shoulders, a deep chest, flat abs, and a tiny waist. He wore a muscle shirt that showed off his big arms, and jeans that put his crotch on display. Like Cole's, the muscle freak's body was rigid with anger, and he stalked around the front of the pickup and stood towering over the woman.

"Lovers' quarrel?" mused Bunny.

"That'd be my guess," Top agreed.

The argument outside was intensifying, with both of them gesticulating. There was a difference, though, and Top noted it. The man was waving his arms all over the place, as if he had so much rage inside that he wanted to throw it around, paint the walls of the restaurant and all the cars in the lot with it. His hands moved with great speed and force, and Top was pretty sure the guy was having a very hard time not directing that power in the same direction as his words. The woman, on the other hand, was clearly furious, but the more hysterical and demonstrative the man got, the less dramatic her own movements became. As if she was pulling her power in, containing it. Either she was being gradually cowed by the bruiser or in the face of his rage and physical potential she was priming herself for action. Top rather thought it was the latter. The drama was maybe going to end with both of them storming off in separate directions—and probably separate lives—or it was going to turn nasty. There was a palpable violence in the air.

"He hits her and I'm going out there to hand him his own dick," said Bunny.

Without looking, Top nudged Bunny's plate of shrimp closer to the big man. "Eat your sea roaches and enjoy the show, Farm Boy."

The woman said one last thing that landed on the man like a physical blow. It staggered him, and he actually took a half step backward. The woman opened the door, reached in, came out with a cell phone, and held it up so that he could see the screen. The man gaped at it, his mouth slack, then, with a speed that surprised the woman, slapped the phone out of her hand. It flew ten feet and smashed to bits against the side of a heavy wooden trash can. Then the man tried to use the same speed to grab the woman's wrist.

Bunny lurched to his feet, but Top didn't. He sat there, fascinated, watching as the woman evaded the grab with a boxer's backward lean, and then bent forward and used the flats of both palms to shove the man backward. She did it fast, and she did it at exactly the right angle to send the bruiser crashing heavily and awkwardly into the fender of the 4Runner. He dropped to one knee and stared for a moment at the huge dent his shoulder had made in the white metal. Everyone at the restaurant was staring at the drama. Bunny was heading toward the door. Top, smiling, sat where he was.

The muscle freak came up off the ground and tried to belt Cole with a blow that would have dimmed her lights and put her in a neck brace. She leaned back, agile as a boxer, let it pass, and then stepped into the man, her hands moving so fast that Top couldn't tell whether she hit him five times or six. They weren't what he would have labeled combat blows. She wasn't going for a kill or even trying to do serious damage. No, this woman was schooling the asshole. She hit him in the throat, the nose, the lip, the eye, and the nuts. Maybe one or two other places. She didn't hit him very hard, but damn if she didn't know what she was about. The lip split, the nose erupted into blood, the eye puffed shut, and the guy dropped to his knees, cupping his balls, while his face turned a ghastly shade of brick red. Then the woman took a fistful of his short hair, jerked his head back, and bent close to spit in his face. She thrust him sideways and he crashed once more against his truck, though this time his shoulder hit the tire and did no damage. He fell over, trembling and weeping, looking very small for such a big man.

By this time Bunny was in the parking lot, closing on her with long strides, his face set in lines of indignation.

Top sat back in his chair and took a deep swallow of his warm beer.

Top didn't take particular notice of the small man seated alone at a deuce thirty feet from him. The man wore a nylon windbreaker and a billed cap. Both the jacket and the cap bore the logo of Apex HVAC, a company that handled the installation, upgrade, and maintenance of heating, ventilation, and air-conditioning systems for thousands of small businesses in that part of South Carolina. Apex was part of a much larger conglomerate that provided the same services—as well as sprinkler and Halon systems—for larger industrial firms. The man had spent much of the past two years installing special upgrades, and had even serviced this restaurant a few days ago to bring it up to code.

The name stenciled above the logo on the left breast of the jacket was Mitch. Today would be Mitch's last visit to the crab house. He had a half-eaten Salisbury steak in front of him and a freshly topped-off cup of coffee. There was nothing particularly remarkable about Mitch's appearance, and when Top had earlier scanned the room he saw a thirtysomething man who was so ordinary that he blended seamlessly into the crowd. Which was rather the point.

Mitch made three calls during the thirty-five minutes he was there. The first was to report that he was on station and had secured a table with excellent visual access to the inside of the crab house. The second call was to confirm the identities of the two big men at a nearby table. He didn't make the third call until after Tracy Cole arrived. When he checked with the images stored on his phone, he hit the speed dial for his contact. The call was answered at once by a man with a French accent.

"We're all good," said Mitch, then he added, "We're live in five."

"*Très bien*," murmured the Concierge. "You had better get out of there."

"Yup," said Mitch. He ended the call and signaled the waitress for the check. While he waited for the check he took a small Altoids tin out of his pocket, opened it, removed two unmarked capsules, and swallowed them with the last of his coffee. His hands were shaking as he put the tin back into his pocket. He paid the bill and left.

Mitch made sure that he moved casually, naturally, and not at all as if he was running for his life.

JONATHAN MABERRY

CHAPTER TWENTY-SIX

I fed my overweight, middle-aged, and frequently cranky marmalade tabby, Cobbler, and then took him down to the nice old lady who lives in the condo below me. She was always game to babysit the old boy and, on occasion, Ghost, too. The neighbors tell me she sings to them. Old bluesy standards from the forties and fifties. Cobbler perked up when he saw her and pretty much instantly forgot that I existed. Cats, y'know?

Ghost and I got to the airport first. While we waited for Rudy, I got another text on my phone. This time the message said:

> I wish I could help, but she wouldn't like it.
> She'll be so mad I'm even texting you.

Again there was no identification, and again Miss Moneypenny told me there was no text, even though I was staring right at it. Then it occurred to me that it could be Sean using a burner and trying some kind of code on me. That didn't fit right, though, because burners didn't have text functions. So I texted back:

> Who is this?

The reply was equally as confounding as the other messages:

> I don't like to play these kinds of games.

I responded, asking what she meant. There was no answer. Had it, in fact, been Sean? We don't have a sister, so none of the texts would make sense, and if it was a code, then he was being way too cryptic. I double-checked with Bug, and he told me that my phone was fine. He sounded busy and annoyed, and told me to simply disable the text function.

I did.

Then my phone rang and it was Steve Duffy, one of the agents at the Warehouse in Baltimore, the local DMS shop.

"Yo, Cowboy," he said. "Got the goodies from your bro and am on the way back to the barn. Got a couple of science geeks coming down from the Hangar to pick it up. There's some paperwork and digital stuff that I'll upload to your laptop."

"Any problems with the pickup?"

"Nah. Your brother doesn't smile much. He always a sourpuss?"

"It's been a long couple of days. He's okay," I said. "You spot any tail around my brother? Black SUVs or anyone else?"

"No, and we looked pretty hard. Even so, we have some birds in the air. If we get anything, I'll be in touch."

The "birds" he mentioned were the latest generation of pigeon surveillance drones. They looked real and had adaptive behavioral software that allowed them to learn from real pigeons. Unless you absolutely knew they were fake you'd be tempted to toss them breadcrumbs. It was a weird and somewhat troubling irony that the DMS was using pigeon drones for urban aerial surveillance. It was pigeon drones armed with explosives that had destroyed our field office here in Baltimore, killing nearly two hundred people. All friends of mine. Brothers in arms. And that same blast was how Rudy lost an eye. Add to that the attack at Citizens Bank Park, which was mostly carried out by bomb-carrying pigeon drones. You'd think after all that we wouldn't go anywhere near that technology. But . . . it's a useful bit of science. No, we don't put bombs on our drones, but we do use them. Lately we've used a lot of them, and the technology was something we stole from the bad guys. As I said, a troubling irony.

"Hey, Duffy," I said before he hung up. "You didn't by any chance just text me, did you?"

"Text you? No," he said.

"Okay," I said, and ended the call. Ghost suddenly jumped to his feet and gave a single, happy *whuff*, and I saw Rudy getting out of a cab with three large suitcases.

"Jeez, Rude. I said to pack for only a few days."

"I did," he replied, then nodded toward the single suitcase I'd brought. "And while I'm sure you have a nicely polished lecture all prepared about living the spartan life and the science of packing for field operations, consider three things." He counted them off on his fingers. "First, you neglected to say what we'd be doing for those few days, so I wisely planned for multiple business and social contingencies. Second, we have significant differences in our approach to personal grooming, as I believe we've previously discussed."

"And third—?"

He smiled. "You may kiss my ass."

"Fair enough," I said.

"Said with all due respect."

"Of course."

He dug into his pocket for a dog treat and gave it to Ghost, who took it with great delicacy while giving me a vile and challenging look. Because Ghost was a combat dog he was trained not to accept treats from anyone but me. This is a rule Ghost breaks with a mixture of guile, outright defiance, and a sense of humor. He knows it bugs the shit out of me. Rudy is a frequent accomplice in this unsanctioned activity. As he munched the treat, Ghost gave me a look that said, "Hey, rules are human constructs, and as a lowly four-legged animal I'm clearly not capable of understanding the subtleties." The smile on his doggy face didn't sell his innocence. Not for a moment.

Rudy, pretending not to notice, stood by while I checked Ghost with the animal handlers. As they took him away, Ghost whined and shifted his expression so that he looked put-upon and oppressed. I know he's messing with me, but it always works. I always felt guilty when we flew like this. I caught Rudy watching me.

"What the hell are you smiling at?" I growled.

"It's not unreasonable to suggest that you like animals more than you like people."

"*Most* people," I corrected.

"Most people," he agreed. He cut me a look. "How is Junie?"

"Away."

He studied me, nodded, and didn't pursue it.

"Say, Rude, did you just text me?"

"Me? Text? Surely you jest." Rudy absolutely hates texting, believing it to be a sure and certain step toward an inevitable disconnect between people. He's not all that much of a fan of phones, for that matter. He likes actual human contact. Weird.

Aboard the plane, Rudy took the aisle seat and I had the window. We watched the passengers file past us, many of them giving us looks of longing or contempt, because first class is comfy and no other seat on the airplane ever is. I know; I've squeezed my long legs into coach many, many times. The flight attendant brought us drinks, with which I tried to drown my guilt as old folks, women with children, and ordinary people crowded down the narrow aisle.

"You know that most flights don't even offer free nuts and pretzels anymore," I murmured to Rudy. "As if the marginal cost of twenty-four peanuts or eighteen pretzels will crash the stock for the airline. And yet up here in first class we pretty much get blow jobs and foot massages."

He sipped his wine and, unlike me, met the eyes of the people filing into the plane. "Status is an entirely subjective thing. We both know that there are people in poverty who are both noble and of great value to humanity, and superrich whose intrinsic worth to society is too small to be measured, as well as every iteration in between. So having money, even having *earned* money, conveys a status that is entirely subjective. But because it has become a habit within civilized cultures, we share in the perpetuation of the shame. This moment is a wonderful case study of that. If our roles were reversed—and it has been for both of us—we would harbor the same resentment toward the people in these seats as the folks passing us do. And we'd be equally justified and equally wrong."

"Wrong?"

"Of course," Rudy said. "There are so many assumptions attached to this. The configuration of the airplane necessitates that people are paraded past seats they know are more luxurious than the ones to which they are headed. The assumption is that we're special and they're not, which is untrue. It's part of an enforced perception of social classes based on disposable income. Nothing about this speaks to the quality of our character."

"No argument," I said, and sipped my Jack-and-ginger.

A man in a rumpled business suit gave me a look of unfiltered contempt. The woman behind him was juggling a baby and two pieces of carry-on luggage. She glanced at us and quickly looked away.

Rudy leaned close to me. "You see that woman? She was actually so embarrassed that she couldn't maintain eye contact."

"Yeah, but why?"

"It's not a logical thing, Joe. As I said, this is purely subjective. She has a child and clearly could not afford, or was unwilling to pay for, these seats, and she believes that to make eye contact is to share a conversation in which that financial disparity is a key topic. So instead she hurried past us. I would bet that she feels somewhat defeated as a person and as a mother, because this is an example of the things she can't afford for her child."

"That's not fair, though," I protested. "The only reason I can afford these seats is that I don't spend a lot of the money I make, and Junie has her inheritance and—"

"You don't have to justify it, Joe. Not to me and not to her. This isn't a matter reinforced by logic. And don't pretend that I don't know you chose first class primarily for my comfort, because of my bad leg."

I felt my face get hot. I mumbled something so low and indistinct that even I didn't know what it was. Rudy patted my arm.

"Most people can't justify the extra money for this kind of comfort. For most of our lives we couldn't, either, and even now I tend to choose Economy Plus over first class because I'm appalled at the markup. The drinks, snacks, and food they give us, even coupled with the wider seats and extra legroom, doesn't truly excuse doubling the fare. However, the airline knows that the status associated with *first* class is why people pay that money. There's some snobbery in it for some of our fellow passengers in this class, and there's affectation in it for everyone. Tell me you don't feel more important when they announce that first-class passengers may board using the special-access lane, even though it means walking on a different-color carpet and passing on a different side of a metal pole?"

I said nothing. The Jack Daniel's in my glass now tasted like toilet water. I drank it down and ordered another and glowered out the window. At one point, I heard Rudy chuckling softly to himself.

"You're not a very nice man," I told him.

That made him laugh out loud.

INTERLUDE FOUR

"The problem is ongoing," said the school official, "and it's escalating."

"Then how can we help?" asked the doctor.

They sat together in the shade of an old fig tree in the small garden in front of the school. Children came and went, some nodding respectfully to the official, others lost in their own thoughts.

"This school is a rarity here in Cairo," said the official, Aziz Negm, an energetic man of forty who oversaw the funding for the school as well as that of several community outreach programs. "We have donors and grants, and that allows us to provide a higher level of education for our students than, sadly, is common here. This is the fifteenth most populous city in the world, and it is an old city. When it was built, there was no way to foresee a population growth as intense as what we've experienced since the middle of the twentieth century. There is not enough agriculture and industry to adequately provide for all of these people. The poorest families spend half of their household income on food, and the food they can afford to buy is often less nutritious."

"We have the same problem in the States," said the doctor. "Poor people eating fast food and starving while becoming obese."

"It's obscene," said Negm.

"Yes," agreed the doctor. Howard Levithan, formerly of Robert Wood Johnson University Hospital in New Brunswick, New Jersey, and now with the World Health Organization, was a kind-faced man of sixty. Young-looking for his age, with laugh lines around his eyes and mouth, though he wasn't laughing now.

"Malnutrition in Egypt is up," said Negm, "with thirty-one percent of children under five years of age developmentally stunted as a result. Chronic malnutrition is irreversible and stops children from reaching their full physical and mental potential. It's not just here, my friend, it's everywhere. We are being forced to watch as a generation of children starve to death before our eyes. And it will only get worse."

"Perhaps not irreversible, Mr. Negm," said Levithan. "There are new food supplements being developed that can reverse some of the effects of even prolonged malnutrition."

"Even cognitive deterioration?"

"It's likely, though that is still being studied. The short-term effects of these supplements are improved overall health with a bias toward bone growth and a stronger immune system. We are aware that malnutrition brings with it acute vulnerability to certain diseases. The WHO and our partners are looking to push back against that trend."

Negm leaned back. "That is quite a claim, Doctor. Is this also being tested on children in America?"

"Yes. Look, Mr. Negm," said Levithan as he leaned in, "this isn't a matter of the poor are offered a cure for a minor disease in exchange for agreeing to participation in clinical trials of a new drug. The WHO is not in the pocket of Big Pharma. We never have been, which is why we are often scrambling for funding. The food supplements I'm talking about are underwritten by grants from hundreds of different foundations, private donors, and legacy endowments. And, yes, they are being given to poor communities all over the globe, not just in Third World areas. The National Institutes of Health and the Food and Drug Administration have thoroughly vetted all of this, and we have independent laboratory analysis from the Centers for Disease Control and nine other organizations." He paused. "It's not a miracle solution. It doesn't *end* hunger. This isn't a magic trick. No, sir, what this does is provide essential nutrition at such a reduced cost that it can be manufactured and sold in mass quantities to areas like Cairo, Shanghai, Bangladesh, and elsewhere. And in the poorer sections of the United States as well."

Negm frowned and looked down at the box that rested on the bench between them. Twenty food bars sealed in individual white wrappers. Each wrapper included ingredients and nutritional data. He picked one up and reread the information. The afternoon was hot, and there was a constant buzz and hiss from the trucks spraying for mosquitoes. As one truck rolled slowly past the school, the men turned to watch it.

"They're spraying all the time now," said Negm. "First for the mosquitoes carrying West Nile, now for Zika. What's next?"

The doctor shook his head. "Mother Nature does not like to be thwarted."

DOGS OF WAR

121

"Excuse me?"

"When we stop the spread of a disease by eliminating the vector—in this case, a certain subspecies of mosquito—it leaves a gap in the biosphere. Mother Nature abhors that vacuum and mutates something to fill it. You can track all of history by looking at how often small mutations have carved out large pieces of the human herd."

The administrator winced. "I beg your pardon, Doctor, but that is a rather disturbing thing to say."

Dr. Levithan nodded. "And, sadly, it's true."

Forty minutes later Dr. Levithan unlocked the door of his hotel room, entered, locked the door, and spent a few careful minutes using a small electronic device to make sure that no surveillance equipment had been installed while he was out. It was a ritual with him, no matter where he was in the world. Since beginning his work with nutritional supplements, he had visited seventeen of the world's most populous cities. After a while, every hotel room looked the same. After a while, the masses of poor, starving, undereducated, dirty, and needy people of all ages began to blur. They gradually lost any trace of ethnic or cultural identity. They lost their attachment to age and gender. For Levithan they were simply "them," and if they had any shared characteristic that he did take note of it was the constant outstretched hand. *Give me, give me, give me.* Said in a hundred languages, always meaning the same thing.

He took a hot shower and washed with the special soaps he had brought with him. Then he sat on the edge of the bed, opened a small zippered case, removed a small vial of amber-colored liquid, and used a disposable syringe to draw off one-third of the contents. He tapped the needle to remove air bubbles and then injected the drug into his thigh.

As he always did. Especially after the spray trucks had been through.

Because, God knows, he didn't want to catch what those trucks were spraying. There were twelve full cases of the nutrition bars stacked against the wall of his bedroom. He would be visiting five schools tomorrow, four the day after that, and the last three on his final day in Cairo. So far he had obtained signed agreements from eighty-three schools in seven countries. His goal by the end of the year was to have an additional two hundred agreements signed. There were sixteen shipping containers sitting in the port, crammed to the ceiling with the bars. Another forty containers of the chemical spray had already been off-loaded and hoisted onto the backs of trucks for delivery throughout this part of the Middle East. The paperwork had been expedited by officials who wanted to expedite the delivery of those precious anti-mosquito chemicals. It amused Levithan to think that most of the officials, even some of those who took bribes as a matter of course, thought they were doing something good for their people.

Idiots.

Levithan sometimes found it hard not to laugh in their faces.

As for the others, those select few officials here and there who were on the inside track—to one degree or another—they were more practical. Not that Levithan liked them any more than he liked the rest of the unwashed herd. They were going to die, too. He did have a grudging respect for them. At least those few were realistic about the way things work. Even if they didn't know that their worldview was only a partial one, clouded by their own genetic and cultural deficiencies. Mud people. Sand niggers. Levithan had a lot of different names for them that he used when talking with other members of the Havoc inner circle. Not terms he would ever use to the people here. No. Levithan disliked and even detested these people, but he fully appreciated their capacity for violence.

The other nineteen doctors in his group were doing the same kind of work he was. There was a delicious bonus for whoever moved the most tonnage, and Levithan believed that he would earn that bonus for the second year in a row.

He threw the syringe into the trash, ordered room service, and, while he waited, placed a scrambled call to Zephyr Bain.

CHAPTER TWENTY-SEVEN

INLET CRAB HOUSE
3572 HIGHWAY 17
MURRELLS INLET, SOUTH CAROLINA
SATURDAY, APRIL 29, 9:03 PM EASTERN TIME

Bunny walked toward the woman, hands up and palms out in a "no problem" gesture. She stood her ground, eyes narrowed and suspicious, hands low at her sides, but her weight shifted slightly onto the balls of her feet. Ready to run, ready to fight.

"Officer Tracy Cole?" asked Bunny, stopping ten feet out.

Cole's eyes were instantly filled with suspicion and hostility. "Who's asking?"

Bunny smiled and nodded to the weeping muscle freak. "Right now, call me a fan."

"That's not funny," said Cole.

"It's a little funny," said Bunny.

She measured out a meager slice of a smile. It was there and gone, leaving her mouth downturned and hard. "Who are you?"

"One of the guys you're here to meet. My partner's inside," said Bunny. "But before we go in let's clear the decks, okay?"

Without waiting for her reply, Bunny walked past her, hooked a hand under the injured man's arm, and jerked him to his feet. The man was big and dense, but Bunny was bigger and stronger. And he was showing off a little. The muscle freak came up off the ground with such force that he actually hopped through the air and landed flat on his feet. Bunny pressed him back against the truck. The man tried to sniff back his tears and his hurt, but his face was flushed red and puffed. Despite his size, he looked like a petulant and mean child. He tried to slap Bunny's hand away, but he lacked the power for that or for anything. The moment owned him, and the muscle freak knew it.

"Hey, now," said Bunny quietly. "I'm not sure who you are, chief, and I don't give much of a shit why you made this nice lady hand you your ass, but it's time to boogie on down the road. Believe me when I tell you that there is nothing you can say that will make this end any other way except worse. So, unless you want to shit in a bag the rest of your life, you're going to get into your truck and haul ass out of here. You don't bother the lady again, and I don't see you again."

The whole time he spoke Bunny never raised his voice, and he kept his palm flat against the man's chest, fingers splayed. He was not as advanced a martial artist as Top or Captain Ledger, but he knew enough judo to angle his mass and weight in order to use all his muscular bulk and size to give the impression that he was both an irresistible force and an unmovable object.

"Nod if we're all on the same page here," suggested Bunny.

The man flicked a glance past him at the woman, then back to Bunny, and then let his gaze fall. He nodded.

Bunny stepped back. Without the pressure of Bunny's hand, the bodybuilder almost dropped to his knees, but he caught himself, straightened with a fractured attempt at dignity, turned, and stumped slowly around to the driver's side. He pawed at the blood on his face and tentatively probed his nose. Then he climbed inside, started the engine, and drove away, rolling slowly past the line of big semis parked at the far end of the lot. When he reached the road, he gunned the engine and laid down a twenty-foot patch of smoking rubber.

Bunny snorted and turned to the woman. "Boyfriend?"

"Past tense." she said.

Bunny grinned.

"And you can wipe that shit-eating grin off your face, asshole," she said. "I didn't need or want your help."

"If I thought you needed my help, sister, I'd have gotten out here a little faster. All I did was pick up the trash. Call it a public service. Besides, we're on the clock. I just wanted to wrap this episode of *Dancing with the Assholes* so we can get down to business. Fair enough?"

She thought about it, standing with fists on hips, head angled as she squinted through sunlight to look up at him. The tension of the fight was still rippling through her, and he could see embarrassment and hurt in her dark eyes. Whatever had sparked the ugly encounter was doing her harm. Her control was impressive, though.

"You're First Sergeant Sims?" she asked.

"Nah, I'm the good-looking one," said Bunny. "Master Sergeant Harvey Rabbit."

"I saw that on the letter my captain gave me. Your name is really Harvey Rabbit?"

"Yup. My dad was kind of an asshole."

"Sounds like it."

"Call me Bunny," he said, and offered his hand. She took his hand, gave it a single, firm pump. Bunny pointed to the crab house. "Sims is in there. Call him Top. He thinks he's in charge, but it's all me."

"Why don't I believe you?"

He grinned, and they began walking toward the restaurant.

That's when they saw the blood.

And heard the screams.

CHAPTER TWENTY-EIGHT

IN FLIGHT

"I don't suppose you know anything about this nanotech stuff?" I said to Rudy.

He brooded into the depths of his wineglass for a moment. "It's not really my field, of course, but I've read quite a bit about the medical uses, and I had some conversations with Bill Hu a while back. He was quite fascinated with its potential in espionage and field support. He was less enthused about being able to regulate it once the technology was perfected and made readily available."

"Like drones," I said sourly.

"Like drones. Hu expressed valid concerns about drones even before the Predator One case, and look how that turned out. Part of Hu's genius was to be able to look at a new or emerging aspect of science and follow certain lines of thought to imagine what dreadful uses it could be put to. In that, he was well suited to the DMS. Call it a kind of strategic paranoia. Predictive rather than merely alarmist."

"Good thing he was on our side."

"Very good thing," Rudy said. "Hu had concerns about nanotech and, to pardon a bad pun, *infected* me with his unease."

"Really? You don't seem particularly paranoid, Rude."

"I hide it well. My glass eye confuses any attempt to read my expression." Rudy had lost an eye in a helicopter crash in Baltimore, and one of Church's friends had replaced the damaged one with a superb fake. It didn't give Rudy telescoping vision or any cool *Million Dollar Man* stuff, but it moved like the real one and was synced so that the fake pupil dilated in harmony. He looked at me with those eyes, both as dark as polished coal. "The science of nanotechnology was introduced by the late Nobel physicist Richard Feynman back in 1959. He was giving a dinner talk and said something to the effect that there was 'plenty of room at the bottom,' meaning that industrial and mechanical expansion was moving solidly outward but that there was potential for miniaturization. He proposed using delicate machinery to make even more delicate—and smaller—machines, and those would, in turn, make smaller ones, and so on. It was his belief that machines could be miniaturized down to the atomic level. He saw no practical reason why it couldn't be done and felt that such a technological path was inevitable. He postulated manipulation of matter at the atomic, molecular, and supramolecular levels."

I nodded. "Didn't he make some joke about swallowing a doctor?"

"He did, though Feynman credited that concept to his friend and graduate student Albert Hibbs, it was a reference to the possibility of one day constructing a surgical robot so small that it could be swallowed. The construction of such a thing could not be done by human hands, so it involved having machines build smaller and smaller versions of themselves, all the way down to the molecular level. And, Joe, this idea was actually anticipated by the science-fiction writer Robert Heinlein in his story 'Waldo,' which was released in the early forties. Oddly, though, Feynman's ideas weren't acted on for quite a long time. Not until the mid-1980s, actually, when MIT engineering graduate K. Eric Drexler published his book *Engines of Creation*. That really ignited a more intense worldwide interest in nanotechnology. Since then, *nanotech* and *nanites* have become words in common usage."

I grunted. "So this isn't really something new?"

"In concept? No. In practical application, yes. Knowing that we wanted to build microminiaturized surgical or medical machines is one thing, but having the technology to do it is another. It took three-quarters of a century to bring us to where we are now and, from what Bill Hu told me, we have a long way to go."

"Apparently not, or we wouldn't be on this plane."

Rudy sighed. "That's what alarms me. About this and so many other things we encounter. We believe that we grasp where science is on a topic and then we're faced with either an unforeseen practical application or a leap forward in development. Sadly, that's something we'll be seeing more and more often, Joe. It's not only that the products of science are getting smaller but the equipment to develop and manufacture these things has become less cumbersome and more affordable. Laptop computers, portable laboratory setups, even mass production relies on compact, transportable, and affordable hardware." He lowered his voice. "The DMS has faced as many small mobile terrorist cells as they have large-scale. With nanotechnology there is no conceptual

JONATHAN MABERRY

zero point for miniaturization. Especially with machines that are designed to make smaller machines. That's a cycle that will continue down to the subatomic level. When you include mass replication as a function, well . . ."

"You're scaring me to death," I told him.

The plane hit an air pocket and dropped so suddenly that everyone yelped. Rudy's face went from a medium tan to the color of old paste. "Now we're both scared." I don't like skydiving, but Rudy hates to fly at all. The cabin steward must have seen his face, and she materialized with a fresh glass of wine. When in doubt, anesthetize the customers.

Rudy drank about half of it, sighed, drank some more, then nodded and continued where he had left off. "We like to talk about being on the cutting edge of science, Cowboy, but in truth we don't know where the cutting edge actually *is,* because it changes every day. We can be at the forefront one minute and then that boundary can be pushed far beyond our current reach in an instant, and that's as true for viral and bacterial mutations as it is for computer software, robotics, and nanotech."

I glared down into my whiskey. "You are harshing my buzz."

"You should watch one of the YouTube lectures by John the Revelator. He'll sober you up in a heartbeat."

"Who in the wide blue fuck is John the Revelator? Some kind of evangelist?"

"Of a kind. He talks about the coming technological singularity. You know what that is?"

"Sure. Skynet becomes self-aware and launches the nukes. I've seen *Terminator,* like, eighty times."

"It's John's opinion that movies of that kind are like the nuclear-apocalypse novels of the fifties and sixties, that they're predictive and cautionary tales. The difference is that John thinks we should embrace this event."

"Why? Is he an android?"

"No. He's flesh and blood. I've met him. He did a book signing at Mysterious Galaxy books in San Diego. Very well-spoken man, and although we've never met before, I couldn't shake the feeling that we had. He has that kind of charisma. He says that, because this event is inevitable, at some point in the not-too-distant future it's in our best interests to accept it and attempt to curate it."

"'Curate'? How? By polishing the boots of the robot overlords?"

"No. Though he has made a joke to that effect on a few occasions." The plane continued to bump, and Rudy finished his glass. By the time we switched planes in Atlanta, I was going to have to carry him. "John says that we have to develop artificial intelligence, and to allow it to grow at its own pace, which he says will be exponential and dramatic. But, at the same time, we have to control the safeguards that will always allow a select few to control the overall system without interfering with the rate of AI growth."

"Don't we already do that?"

"Sadly, no. Hu told me that there are quite a few research groups that haven't imposed any controls on AI development for fear of limiting or interfering with the development of true computer intelligence."

I raised my empty glass. "All in favor of *not* doing that, say 'Aye.'"

"John would agree. He says that we should always be in control."

"Not sure how much I like that 'chosen few' part of it, though, Rude."

"Nor I," admitted Rudy. "Unfortunately, the signing was too crowded to allow me to pursue the topic with him and find out what he meant. I wonder if Dr. Acharya would know. He was the one who first told me about John the Revelator. Did I understand correctly that he's not available?"

"He's in Washington State at the DARPA thing," I said.

"What DARPA thing?"

"They're testing new versions of BigDog."

Rudy looked blank, so I explained that there was a robotics testing facility in the middle of no-damn-where in the big timber country of the Pacific Northwest. DARPA had been working on building the next generation of tactical-use robots. BigDog was a dynamically stable quadruped robot developed in 2005 by the guys at Boston Dynamics, along with the NASA Jet Propulsion Lab, and some guys from the Harvard University Concord Field Station. I said, "BigDog doesn't actually look like a dog. No fake hair or lolling tongue or any of that. Doesn't beg for treats or pee on the rug. It has four legs and a bulky utilitarian body. Kind of like a big robot mastiff without a head."

"Charming," said Rudy sourly. "I seem to remember seeing something about that on YouTube a few years ago. Someone kicked it."

"Yeah. That was an early prototype. They showed it walking, climbing steps, running. They also showed some guy kicking it to knock it over so they could demonstrate how it regained balance. People freaked, though."

"Well, they would," he said, nodding. "We rush to anthropomorphize everything. When the robot dog stumbled, it connected the viewers with our memories of dogs we've known being injured. If it was actually destroyed, say by being hit by a car, people would be appalled. They'd grieve as if it was real." He cut me a look. "How did you react?"

I shrugged. "It's only a machine and—"

"Joe . . ."

"Okay, it pissed me off, too."

"Even though you know it has no consciousness and no feelings?"

"Sure. I never claimed to be less crazy than other people."

"It's not an issue of sanity, Cowboy," he said. "It's a quality of our nature as compassionate beings who are genetically and culturally hardwired to nurture and protect."

"Still only a machine," I said.

"Do you think the people who posted the video were unaware of how the public would react?"

"Jury's out on that. Scientists can be detached in weird ways. And sometimes they can be malicious little pricks."

Rudy gave me a fond and tolerant smile, which I chose to ignore.

I said, "The Marines originally wanted BigDog as a pack animal, but the first versions they field-tested were too loud. So DARPA partnered with some new brainiacs to build the next generation of robot dogs, calling them WarDogs. Supposed to be bigger, faster, tougher, and quieter. Some of them will be four-legged portable machine-gun nests, which is a little cool and a lot scary. I mean, think about having something like that come creeping up to your foxhole or into your camp and then opening up with a 50-caliber? Holy shit."

"That is truly frightening," Rudy said, and actually shivered.

"It's all being developed under the project heading of 'Havoc.'"

"'*Cry Havoc and let slip the dogs of war*'?" recited Rudy. "That's a little on the nose for a project name, isn't it?"

"Somebody probably got wood in his shorts when he thought it up and couldn't bring himself to switch to anything less obvious."

The plane continued to bounce around the ether, and Rudy kept drinking. I cut him a look.

"You're making a face," I said.

"A face? No, I'm not. What kind of face?"

"Of disapproval. You have something against robots?"

"On the whole?" said Rudy thoughtfully. "No. Rescue robots are saving lives all over the globe, and exploration robots will push back the boundaries of our knowledge without endangering human lives. But in combat? In that regard, I'm much less enthusiastic."

"The military's working on a mobile surgical robot, too," I said. "To assist medics with emergency field surgery."

"That's less frightening," he said. "Surgical robots have been in use for years. They used a variation of the da Vinci surgical suite on me," he said, touching his knee. "Superbly fine-tuned. I highly approve of that kind of use. Are any of them autonomous?"

"To a degree," I said, and I knew where he was going with this. A couple of years ago we had that whole mess with the drones, autonomous-drive systems and hacked GPS controls. It left a very sour taste in all our mouths. And it made us very, very afraid of all the ways in which that technology can be misused. "We've wandered away from nano-tech and we're both half drunk. Fuck. It's inconvenient as balls to have Dr. Acharya out of touch. They're not even allowing Internet or cell phones except during emergencies."

"Doesn't this thing in Baltimore qualify?"

"That," I said, "is what we're flying home to establish."

CHAPTER TWENTY-NINE

The lights came up and John glanced at his watch and then addressed the audience.

"I think we have time for a few questions," he said. "If anyone—"

Dozens of hands shot into the air.

"Ah," he said, and chuckled warmly. "Well, maybe we won't have time to answer *all* your questions, but let's start with you. Yes, in the third row, with the beard."

A young man stood up, looking awkward and unkempt in faded jeans and an ancient UCLA sweatshirt. "Thanks, sir," he said. "I enjoyed your presentation. My question, though, is about the socioeconomic effect of a curated technological singularity. One of the things you've talked about—here and online—is how the next generation of machines is already being built to improve farming, manufacturing, and so on. I get that this is an inevitable advancement, but what about the people who currently work in those fields? If an autonomous-drive combine harvester can operate twenty-four hours a day and in all weather conditions, won't each eight-hour increment remove the potential for a farmer or farmworker to earn a day's wage?"

Every eye shifted from the young man to the speaker, and he smiled at the audience.

"Yes," said John, "that's what it will mean."

"So what happens to those farmworkers?"

The speaker walked slowly to the edge of the stage and stood looking down at the young man.

"Let me turn that around and ask *you* that question. What will become of those workers?"

"They'll be out of a job."

"Yes. And . . . ?"

"If they can't find other work, then they'll have to get government assistance," said the young man. "Which puts a drain on the system."

"That is very true."

"But those people need to have a chance to survive."

John's smile never flickered. "Do they?"

The young man blinked at him. "Of *course* they do."

"Why?"

"Why not? They're people. This is America. They deserve to—"

"Slow down, a bit," said John, patting the air as if pushing the outrage back into manageable shape. "Don't explode, calm down. This is a forum for understanding here, so let's discuss this objectively, okay? Can you do that? Good. Now, give me pro and con on it. What is the basis for your argument that people deserve survival?"

"Um . . . because they're people?"

John shook his head. "No. That's a subjective view. It's sentimental."

"It's humanist," countered the young man.

"It's compassionate, I'll grant, but how does that factor into the dynamics of evolution?" He held up a hand before the young man could reply. "Darwin only understood part of the process of evolution. He looked at it in the natural world, and correctly judged that survival of the fittest was a biological imperative, and he separated that from human desire and the influence of politics or religion. Scholars and historians have since expanded on Darwin to explain everything from religious evangelism to conquest to eminent domain. However, too often they failed to understand that having conscious self-awareness has created a different kind of evolution. Call it *curated* evolution. An attempt to force an evolution of a certain element or elements of a group even when biology isn't necessarily a willing accomplice."

"Like what, eugenics?" demanded the young man.

"Sure, eugenics is part of it, but so is gerrymandering, so is the spread of religion through attrition, so is ethnic genocide, so are social caste systems and economic class distinctions, so is war, so is crime. I could go on and on. Human history is an index of attempts to curate the human species. We do it in thousands of ways, large and small. Some of it is reprehensible, of course. Hitler attempted a systematic genocide of Jews, Pol Pot and the Khmer Rouge exterminated twenty-five percent of the Cambodian population, there's the Ba'ath Party's systematic extermination of the Kurds, the Rwandan slaughter of a million Tutsi by the Hutu, and other atrocities. These acts were not only morally wrong—and here I'm momentarily agreeing with your humanism—but also inefficient. Totalitarian governments such as the People's Republic of China persecuted intellectuals, killing or imprisoning visionary thinkers, because visionaries cannot abide pervasive oppression. The Chinese wanted obedience without opposition. They don't want a better way or a brighter future, because that would involve change, and they like their militant-regime structure. It suits small minds. They hide behind the concept of the 'dictatorship of the masses' without understanding the long game implied in that."

"So . . . you're a socialist?"

"Did I imply that? No? How, then, do you infer it? I'm discussing curated evolution and citing examples of how that is done wrong. Communism isn't a workable model. Neither, I might add, is the kind of extreme conservative thinking that works to establish a working class that approximates a new kind of slave labor while simultaneously making education harder to afford. That is such weak short-term thinking because it only provides for the group in power while they live but doesn't provide for their offspring and future generations. It's power used stupidly and without thought or caring about what's coming next."

The room was silent, and it was clear on the faces of many that they weren't following the twists and turns of John the Revelator's logic. A few were, and some even nodded. The young man in the UCLA hoodie merely looked uncertain.

"Tell me," said John, "what is your opinion of Henry Ford?"

"He was a racist who hated Jews."

"He was," agreed John. "And what else?"

"He . . . um. Well, he perfected the assembly-line process. But that threw a lot of people out of work."

"Did it? In old-fashioned car factories, sure, but didn't it also create or help grow many other new industries. Because of Ford, car manufacturing flourished. So did tens of thousands of companies that became connected to car manufacturing. Oil production, gas stations, leather goods, metals mining and refining, plastics, glassware, the rubber industry, highway construction, commercial vending along driving routes, companies that make roadside signs and stoplights, car washes, parking lots, petrochemicals, auto-parts manufacturers and stores, auto mechanics, taxicabs, companies that make air fresheners, companies that make screws and nuts, and hundreds of thousands of businesses that depend on auto traffic bring them customers and . . . well, I could go on all day long. Sure, Henry Ford was an anti-Semitic ass. No one here will argue that. But look at the effect on us."

The young man was shaking his head. "There are over five million traffic accidents per year in the United States, resulting in an average of thirty-two thousand deaths and over three million injuries. Cars release approximately three hundred and thirty million tons of carbon dioxide into the atmosphere every year, which is twenty percent of the world's total. And they contribute seventy-two percent of the nitrogen oxides and fifty-two percent of reactive hydrocarbons."

"Yes, they do," said John, "and this is a problem. One I personally detest with the same ferocity with which I loathe anything that harms our biosphere. However, climate change aside, let's consider the benefits to the population of ambulance services and firefighters and police who arrive in vehicles. People being able to commute to a better-paying job or take their kids to the right school or visit friends. The technological evolution from horse and buggy to motorized transport is a fact. Does it have a downside? Yes, of course, and some of those downsides are serious. But the benefits outweigh them. And isn't technology being viewed as the solution to its own problem? The leaps forward in hybrid and electric cars, if managed correctly, will begin to reduce our carbon footprint. And e-commerce and telecommuting have already reduced the number of employees who need to drive to work and increased the number of customers who can shop at home. There are advances being made right now that will offer a better, safer, and more fulfilling life for humanity."

He waved to the young man to sit and nodded to a middle-aged woman who had her hand up.

"You seem to be describing a pathway to Utopia," she said. "But how can any advance in technology provide for everyone? Will seven or eight billion people have electric cars and nanomedicine sensors and autonomous home security? Most of the world's population lives in poverty. Who will buy these things for them?"

John the Revelator looked at her for a long moment before he replied. "No one," he said.

The woman said, "Then what will happen to them?"

"What happened to the saber-toothed cat, the dire wolf, the Tasmanian tiger, the dodo, the passenger pigeon, Steller's sea cow, the Pyrenean ibex, or the woolly mammoth?"

"They were hunted to extinction."

"In some cases, yes. In others they became extinct because of loss of habitat and a scarcity of resources. The panda is slowly crawling toward extinction despite concerted efforts to prevent it. Other species have become critically endangered, like the Cross River gorilla, the leatherback turtle, the Yangtze finless porpoise, and many more."

"But we're talking about people," insisted the woman, her outrage making her voice sound shrill.

"We are talking about how species become extinct or are forced to evolve in order to earn their survival," John countered. "More than ninety-nine percent of the five billion species that ever lived on earth are estimated to be extinct. And humans can't be blamed for more than a fraction of that. So far there have been five mass extinctions, four of which occurred in the last three hundred and fifty million years. The Permian-Triassic extinction wiped out ninety percent of all species on earth. And the Cretaceous-Paleogene extinction event sixty-five million years ago wiped out much of the life on earth and forced the surviving dinosaurs into the adaptive evolution that turned them into birds. The dinosaurs that evolved, by the way, were descendants of the theropods, the predators. None of the big, slow, stupid plant eaters made the evolutionary cut."

"That's a horrible example," said the woman curtly.

"It's unpleasant," John conceded, "but facts do not need to be pleasant in order to be true." He turned to the rest of the crowd, effectively shutting her down. "Natural evolution is not a pleasant process. Survival of the fittest goes hand in hand with extinction of the unfit. No animal species has a *right* to survive unless it has become appropriately adapted to ensure that survival. Exceptions only exist in situations of catastrophe, such as natural climate change, volcanism, earthquakes, and so on. Even in places where species have thrived in the absence of predators, it is generally because the predators were wiped out or displaced by geological catastrophes. The Galapagos Islands are examples. Or, more recently and less sensibly, when humans disrupt the evolutionary equation by hunting a species to extinction, deforestation, repurposing of habitats, pollution, and so on. That is not curated evolution; it's mere bungling and shortsightedness."

The eyes of the audience members were filled with reserve, antagonism, disagreement, but that was fine with John. His mission was to tell the truth, not to lead converts to a promised paradise.

"The technological evolutionary process works best when it's curated. The automobile industry was a clear benefit to progress, health, and other kinds of industrial development. It also benefited organic needs by allowing for the transport of bulk food across great distances. Trains, too, of course, and modern shipping. But we've seen the greatest leap forward with computers. The microchip and the personal computer have changed the world and changed how we, as a species, move forward. We are now on the brink of the next major step in that evolution. The rise of robotics in everyday life will change our cultural landscape as surely and completely as the automobile did. Will it displace people? Yes. Of course. Will it disrupt lives and ruin fortunes for those who are displaced? Yes. Is that sad and tragic? Sure. Is it unfair?" he asked. "No. It's evolution, and not once in the history of the world—not in natural selection and not in the rise of human dominance on this planet—has 'fairness' played a significant role in the process of evolution. Not everyone will survive, because not everyone is suited to the process of survival. In the past this process required biological luck, but in the coming change it is the willing, the active, the participatory who will earn their place in the world that will be."

The room fell into a very tense silence.

"When the technological singularity comes," said John the Revelator, "and it *will* come, then we have to curate it, manage it, but also allow it. Otherwise, we will not deserve to survive the necessary extinction of the unworthy."

CHAPTER THIRTY

Bunny broke into a dead run even as his mind tried to process what he was seeing. It made no kind of sense. Everyone inside the restaurant seemed to be fighting. A full-out brawl. Even from halfway across the parking lot, Bunny could see bodies wrestling and swinging wild punches and hurling chairs. The big picture window near where Top had been sitting was splashed with an arc of blood. Bunny knew that pattern. It was an arterial spray; nothing else could paint that much of the window with such force.

This wasn't a brawl. These people were killing one another.

"What's going on?" yelled Cole, who was right on his heels.

"Call it in!" he bellowed as he ran. "Christ, *call it in!*"

He reached the door, whipped it open, and stepped into a red nightmare.

There was so much going on, and it was so fully involved, that it took even his combat-experienced mind a full two seconds to process it. It looked like a riot. No, it looked like a war, but it was hard to understand the sides. The waitress who'd waited on Top and him held a heavy metal paper-towel dispenser and was using it to smash the face of a fat man in a camo T-shirt. The fat man's mouth was smeared with blood, and there was a horrible bite on the waitress' thigh.

Nearby, a thirtysomething woman in a sundress and flip-flops was stabbing a fisherman in the throat. A tall man with a Latino face and Asian eyes knelt on the floor and tried to use his body as a shield as two fry cooks snapped at him with bloody teeth. A teenage boy picked up a chair and swung it at one of the cooks, missed, lost his balance, and fell, and the other cook pounced on him. Both cooks snarled like dogs.

Bunny couldn't find Top right away, and then he saw a pile of wriggling bodies against the wall. A brown-skinned arm looped over the edge of an overturned table and punched one of the figures, knocking him back with a shattered jaw.

"*Top!*" bellowed Bunny, but yell was all he did. He stood in the doorway, feet braced, eyes wide, fists balled, and couldn't move.

He absolutely could not make himself take one step farther into that madhouse.

The blood.

The innocent people being torn apart.

It froze him.

It robbed him of so much of what he was, and it flooded his mind with all the images from that carnage on the gas dock months ago. He was as much in that other moment as he was in this one, and equally helpless.

Behind him, Tracy Cole was yelling. Yelling.

Identifying herself as a police officer. Ordering people to stop, to back off, to stand down. Bunny heard her words, understood their meaning, and yet he could not act in support of them.

"No," he said in a voice so soft and lost that even he couldn't hear it. "No."

The day began to cant sideways, losing its hold on meaning and reality, and then it started falling too fast to catch.

CHAPTER THIRTY-ONE

Halfway across the country, Rudy fell asleep and I didn't wake him and even waved off the flight attendant when lunch arrived. This was the most comfortable Rudy and I had been together in ages, and closer to the old rhythm we had as colleagues and best friends. I liked it.

The fact that we're friends is odd, or maybe it's proof that opposites attract. In most ways we're completely unalike. I'm bigger, gruffer, less friendly, and more apt to offend people. A former lady friend once told me that my face looks as if it's been hit at least once from every conceivable direction and with great enthusiasm. She wasn't wrong. She also suggested that I probably deserved most of that battering. We were breaking up at the time, so that was unkind, but it wasn't inaccurate. I tend to offend oftener than most, and more deeply.

Rudy, however, does not. Even though we're about the same age, he's always the grown-up in the room. People like and relate to him. You can watch the Rudy magic at work and not really grasp how it's done. He can walk into a conference, or go into a crime scene, or sit in an airport lounge and people gravitate to him as if he's magnetic. That's possibly a mixed metaphor, but you get the point. Once people make contact with him, they act as if they've known him forever. If I had to guess what his secret is, it might be that Rudy actually *listens*, and he genuinely cares about people and what they have to say. He cares about who they are and what their life experience has been. You can see it when he meets people. Rudy can make you feel, without artifice or trickery, that his day would have been an empty nothing if he hadn't had the good fortune of encountering you. People tell him the damndest things. They tell him things they wouldn't tell a priest, their best friend, or an enthusiastic torturer. Being confronted with that much unfiltered interest, insight, and goodwill flips the switches that allow you to release so much of the tension you carry around. It lubricates the joints of your emotional machinery. It's a key element of his success as a therapist, particularly with people who have suffered great trauma. In another life, Rudy could have been one of the great con men of all time, or the founder of a new religion. But he's too honest for either of those things. Rudy is Rudy, and he's the best person I know.

While Rudy slept, I read Sean's report and the other material Duffy had sent me. There was a lot of detail but not enough information, if that makes sense. Sean was a thorough cop, but he was out of his depth, and clearly Doc Jakobs hadn't been able to reach any useful conclusions. I mean, to be fair, he's a medical examiner and this was bizarro shit. Even for a conspiracy theorist like him.

I looked at the photo of Holly Sterman from her fake driver's license. It was issued in the name of Kya Hope. Kind of a sad, ironic choice of a last name, and I was drunk enough to read too much into it and thereby depress the living hell out of myself. It showed a pretty girl who smiled into the camera, but the smile was as plastic as the card. There was a look in her eyes. Not haunted, exactly, and not lost. No, there was a kind of resigned wisdom in that look. An acceptance of her circumstances as all she deserved and all she could accept. It came close to breaking my heart. I understood why Sean had become so deeply involved in this. It was the girl every bit as much as the strangeness of how she died.

We began our descent into Atlanta, where we'd change planes.

Because of all our devices for instant communication and constant interaction, the world often feels very small. It's not. This is a big old world, and it has so much room for strange things to grow. Cults and extremist movements. Hatred and intolerance. Political agendas and greed-based business models. War and pain. As we flew, my thoughts drifted from Sean's case to a moody, morose speculation of what else was out there. I wondered, as I too often did these days, what else was happening right now, at that moment, at any moment. What missile was being prepped for firing, literally or figuratively? What bomb was primed to go off? What infernal device was set to unleash a new kind of hell? That kind of speculation seems absurd if you don't do what I do. Those of us in counterterrorism and antiterrorism and special operations have to think like that, because, cynical as it sounds, there *are* people out there planning very bad things. Or engaged in very bad things. People like me and my colleagues in the various covert-ops world and intelligence networks have to imagine bad things so we can look for them. We have to adjust our expectations so that we don't observe the machinations of the world through rose-colored glasses. We have to be ready at a moment's notice to jump when our worst expectations are realized.

So, I asked myself, who was out there doing something so bad that it was the DMS that would be called in? What were they doing? And, the worst question of all, would we find out about it in time to stop it? Bad, bad thoughts to brood on while flying high above it all.

Corrupt people were doing dreadful things. People were dying. How much of that would ever be my problem? I wasn't the world's best secret-agent man. I didn't have some kind of no-borders global jurisdictional freedom of action. The DMS hadn't been called for a lot of those cases. Right now, because of what happened last year, other teams were getting the jobs that should have come to the DMS. Jobs that should have come to me. My buddy Jack Walker and his SEAL Team 666 crew had been called in to handle a rogue genetics lab in Uganda. Sure, they kicked ass, took names, and rained down pure hell on the ass clowns who were trying to turn village kids into teenage supersoldiers, but that was supposed to be my gig. Did I feel put out?

No.

Maybe.

Not sure, actually. I felt closed out, which isn't exactly the same thing. It was the same thing I felt when Tucker Wayne and his war dog, Kane, were dropped into the shit storm of a civil war in Trinidad. I felt it should have been me and Ghost. Jealous? That's such an ugly word. Especially when it's used with any kind of accuracy.

Church has tried to explain to me that I should be happy that there are other special-ops teams out there. Sigma Force, Chess Team, blah-blah-blah. I can't expect to handle everything, and it's unreasonable to want to be everywhere at once. And, let's face it, some of those cases my friends have handled happened while I was otherwise engaged or laid up with stitches, drains, and splints.

Is it ego? I sipped my whiskey and thought about it. No, I decided. Not ego. Not exactly that.

It was fear.

After all the recent betrayals and shadow-government conspiracies we'd uncovered, I'd even begun to look at my friends and allies with a degree of suspicion. Justifiable or not. It's hard enough when the bad guys are clever; it's harder by an order of magnitude when you don't know which of the good guys can be trusted.

That wasn't the only thing twisting my nuts, though. I was afraid that one of these days there would be no one to answer the call. Not me and not anyone else. One of these days there would be a gap between one crime and the bigger one, between one catastrophe and one that really brings down the curtain, and all of us would be either off the clock, too bashed to stand, already under fire, or looking the damn wrong way.

It was the last part that scared me most of all.

If we're reactive rather than proactive, what happens when we react too slowly or too late? What happens when we make the wrong call and go after one thing and miss the other? What's the backup plan when we go charging in the wrong direction and before we can turn around it all blows up?

I'm rambling, I know. The inside of my head is untidy, and even my thoughts don't follow a logical pattern sometimes. I'm going to blame it on the whiskey.

Yeah. That sounds good.

CHAPTER THIRTY-TWO

Bunny felt an impact and turned to see Tracy Cole shouldering her way past him. She had her service weapon in both hands and was fanning the barrel across the melee, but she didn't fire.

Of course she didn't fire. There was no clear aggressor here. No perpetrators. No criminals wearing masks to disguise their identities. No terrorists in black balaclavas to allow them to become faceless agents of a corrupted ideology.

These were ordinary people slaughtering one another.

She kept yelling at them, kept trying to impose order on a situation from which all sense and order had been swept. Then she turned and looked up at him.

"What the hell's happening?" she demanded.

All Bunny could do was shake his head.

Suddenly there was a shot in the midst of the screaming, and they both turned to see Top Sims rise up on the far side of the overturned table, his pistol held high, barrel toward the ceiling as a young man in a Hawaiian shirt and shorts tried to claw his way toward the weapon. Top bled from long scratches on his forearm, and he had the man's throat caught in one hard, brown hand. The shot had gone up into the ceiling, and Top had pulled his finger from the trigger guard after that one wild discharge.

A second young man—this one wearing a Gamecocks football T-shirt and jeans—dived at Top and the three of them vanished behind the table.

Suddenly Bunny was moving. His big body was in motion before he realized it. There were five or six people between him and his friend. Bunny hadn't drawn his weapon. Against all training, it hadn't even occurred to him. But he reached out with both hands and grabbed people by arms and scruffs and hair and clothes and hurled them away. He heard a roar and didn't know if it was his own throat making that sound. The people flew like rag dolls, and it didn't matter if they were small women or large men. He plucked them up and cast them out of his way and reached the table. At first all he could see was a tangle of arms and legs, clothes and blood. Then he saw the man in the football shirt biting Top. Biting his leg, trying to chew through Top's trousers. From the way Top kicked, it was clear that he was in great pain, but there was no blood around the bite. Not yet.

Bunny bent forward and grabbed the man with both hands and tore him away from Top. Some of Top's trouser came with him, caught between gnashing white teeth. Bunny pivoted and smashed the man into the closest wall. Even with all the screaming, the sound of breaking bones was like a bundle of breaking sticks. Bunny let the man drop and started to turn back to Top, but a hand caught his ankle and he stared down in shock and horror as the smashed man tried to claw his way forward to bite Bunny's Achilles tendon.

"No," Bunny said as an old horror surged to the surface of his mind. He had fought people like this before. People who were out of their minds, or beyond their minds. People who were totally lost in the urges of a hunger so deep, so terrible, that it consumed every part of who they had been, leaving only a *thing* in its place. A thing that needed to feed and could not be stopped by fear or intimidation or even pain. A hushed, frightened voice whispered urgently in his head.

Aim for the head . . . aim for the head. There's no other way to stop them. Aim for the head.

He felt a hardness in his hand and stared down in stunned horror to see that he now held his gun. His arm raised the weapon. His traitor finger slipped inside the trigger guard and curled around the—

"No!"

His voice seemed to come from somewhere else.

His finger froze in place and he felt his leg lift, felt muscles flexed, took ownership of the reflex action, and then kicked out. It was a powerful kick, backed with rage and fear, and it caught the young man on the point of the chin, lifted him, snapped his head back, hurled him against the wall, dropped him.

The man's eyes rolled high and white and he collapsed backward, panting but unconscious.

JONATHAN MABERRY

Unconscious.

That knowledge did something for Bunny. The man was alive but had been knocked out.

The dead could not *be* knocked out. The Walkers, the victims of the Seif al Din could not be dazed. They could only be fed or killed.

This, as dreadful as it was, *was not that.* . . .

Bunny felt something happen inside his chest and inside his head. On one side of a broken moment he was a victim, a helpless passenger in events that were spinning out of his control. On that side of time, he was still the man who had been destroyed on the gas dock last year.

And then that moment passed. It changed, and, in doing so, it changed him.

It was like someone rebooting the generators of a great power plant. There was darkness and stillness, and then there was a great *clunk* as the switch was thrown. There was the surge of starter power to the turbines, and then they began spinning and spinning, creating and reclaiming power. In his perception, this took a long time. Hours, ages. In the reality of that crisis, it was the other half of a moment.

And Bunny was back again.

He could *feel* himself return. His limbs no longer acted by reflex or accident. It was almost joyful.

Except that he was still in hell and the demons were tearing the world apart.

He spun, gripped the edge of the table, and flung it behind him. Top was pinned under the other young man and was clubbing at him with the artless, ineffectual blows of blind panic. It hurt Bunny to see it, because Top was never out of control. He was the stable center of Echo Team, and everyone knew it. Or, he had been before the gas dock. Since then he had been a ghost haunting his own life. As Bunny had been.

Bunny grabbed the attacker by the hair and hauled him backward. The man instantly hissed and spun and tried to bite Bunny's arm. Bunny clubbed him with the butt of his pistol. Skin tore and bones cracked as the man flopped down.

Proof. More proof that this was only an outer ring of hell but not hell itself.

"You alive, old man?" Bunny growled as he caught Top under the arm and hauled him to his feet.

Top staggered, caught his balance, pushed away from Bunny. His eyes were filled with fear and confusion. "What the . . . what the . . . ?" was all he could manage. The fighting—and the killing—raged around them.

Bunny didn't know what else to do, so he belted Top across the mouth with the back of his left hand. The blow spun Top in a full circle and the older man nearly fell. He crashed against the window, rebounded, and Bunny stopped him with a hard, flat palm against his chest. Almost the same thing he had done to Tracy Cole's boyfriend, but with an entirely different meaning. And a different effect.

Top slapped Bunny's hand away and put the barrel of his pistol hard against the underside of Bunny's chin.

"The fuck you doing, Farm Boy?" demanded Top. "You gone and lost your shit, too?"

Bunny held his gun up so that Top could see it. And see that it wasn't pointed at him.

"This is your six o'clock wake-up call," said Bunny.

Top stared at him as if he was insane.

And there was another fractured moment of change, except this time Bunny could see it happen to someone else. Top was gone, wrecked, ruined . . . and then he wasn't.

Top licked his lips, blinked his eyes, and lowered his gun.

Tracy Cole was across the room, pulling a woman away from several bleeding kids. Bodies lay sprawled. A few people crawled between struggling groups, leaving trails of blood behind them. People screamed in fear, howled like animals.

"It's not Seif al Din," said Bunny again.

Top nodded. He raised his pistol and took it in both hands, searching for a target. Bunny placed his fingers lightly on Top's wrist.

"They're civilians," said Bunny.

Top looked at him, then at the people, then nodded again. It meant something different now. He blew out his cheeks and then shoved his pistol back into its holster. Bunny did the same.

Together they waded, unarmed, into the madness.

CHAPTER THIRTY-THREE

"You talk about the technological singularity almost like a religion," said the professor.

"No," said John the Revelator, "not *almost like*. It *is* a religion. Singularitarianism is very real and very valid."

The professor smiled faintly. "And what is the theological basis of this religion?"

"Well, to understand it would mean to step back from standard views of what a religion is. It certainly isn't Christian or Abrahamic."

"Not all religions are," said the professor.

"Of course not. There's Buddhism, Jainism, Confucianism, Taoism, and hundreds of smaller religions, including extinct religions such as the worship of the Greek, Roman, Norse, and Egyptian pantheons. There are probably more extinct religions than active ones, wouldn't you agree?"

"There's a commonality, though," said the professor. "A belief in a higher power, even if that higher power is as vague as the energy in, say, plants or a certain species of animal. A bird, perhaps. What is the god of singularitarianism?"

"There isn't a god. Not in the traditional sense."

"Then what?"

"You might say that it's a kind of animism in which the technology of computers, software, and robotics is collectively the locus of the sacred. So, in pure terms, the technological singularity is atheistic."

"How, then, is that a religion?"

John spread his hands. "What is atheism but a denial of theism? To most people, atheism is the denial of the Abrahamic God. Again I point to Taoists, Buddhists, the worshippers of Baal, and countless others as religions in which the Judeo-Christian version of God is either not worshipped or simply not a factor. And let's not forget atheists when we count the number of devoted adherents to religion. In my experience, there are few evangelists more dedicated to proselytizing than an atheist who wants to prove that his cosmological view is correct." He laughed. "How many of them pretend to worship the Flying Spaghetti Monster as part of their denial of religion, when in fact they're practicing a religion regardless."

"How does that relate to computers? Technology isn't a god."

"Is it any less of a legitimate god than Thor or the Navajo Hero Twins, or Hotei the Japanese god of abundance, or the deity du jour of any given culture? People worshipped those gods with their whole hearts, and you cannot tell me that their faith was false simply because that religion became extinct."

The professor shook his head. "That's not what I'm saying. Those cultures worshipped a spiritual concept. Technology isn't spirit."

"Is it not? Prove that robots have no spirits, no souls."

"They are machines."

"Humans are organic machines. If you want to have the debate as to whether any of our thoughts, emotions, or beliefs are real or the product of brain chemistry, environmental survival instincts, and evolution, by all means. We can go deeper and discuss whether the universe was created by a freak accident of physics or shaped by intelligent design. Do you want to have that discussion?"

"No," said the professor, though he looked uncomfortable.

"No, of course not, because there is no beginning or end to it," said John. "There is no way to resolve the argument, because infinity isn't quantifiable and therefore we cannot know what actually created everything. We don't know the limits of eternity. We don't know the limits of subatomica any more than we know how many dimensions exist or what constitutes reality. We don't know any of that. So how can you, a learned scientist and teacher, tell me that a machine has no soul just because its component parts were assembled by humans, or by other machines designed by humans? If we humans have souls, then you cannot, with absolute certainty or veracity, say with perfect knowledge that no trace of our souls has been shared with machines. You'd like to say it, but you can't."

"I don't believe it," said the professor, and that made John smile more broadly.

"So it's a matter of belief?"

The professor sighed. There were some snickers from the audience, possibly from his students.

John said, "Just because singularitarians don't believe in God, or even *a* god, does not mean that they are not part of a religious movement. A case can be made that singularitarianism is not substantially different in structure and approach from, say, Neoplatonism. The way in which the potential and emerging realities of AI are viewed is not substantially different from Neoplatonic views of the Plotinian *Nous*. Couple that with aspects of Western animism that are reflected, in one way or another, in writings about AI and the singularity. Even the unenlightened general public reacts to AI and some aspects of robotics in the same way they react to human minds and animals. I joke about the *Terminator* movies and how Skynet became self-aware, yet this is a valid concern of those who are aware of the potential for AI but misunderstand its true nature. They see computers as minds that are waking up and that, once awakened, possess humanlike emotions, goals, and desires."

"That's a distortion by people who don't understand the nature of computer intelligence," countered the professor.

"And now you're skating on very thin ice, my friend," said John. "Of course it's a belief, and belief is the core element of any religion. People believe in the singularity, in computer intelligence, in the potential—good or bad—of intelligent computers. Some fear it and some love it, even though virtually no one completely understands it, and how is that different from the emotions felt by the worshippers of any church anywhere in the world, anytime in the history of humankind."

The professor continued to argue, but John continued to shoot him down. Gently, but with the kind of authority that began edging the majority of the audience toward accepting the validity of what he was saying.

John said, "The singularity is a challenging belief when misunderstood. It does not posit the physical appearance of a god. No bushes will ignite, no angels will blast trumpets. The focus of the belief is not in any kind of humanoid deity. There will be no towering figure with a white beard. The god of the technological singularity is an AI superintelligence that is both human in origin and divine in potential. It will lift up those who worship it in the way that it needs to be worshipped, meaning those who embrace the benefits of evolving technology, and it will damn those who resist it."

CHAPTER THIRTY-FOUR

Top and Bunny stood there, covered in blood, hands red to the wrist, chests heaving, minds burning like cinders. All around them were bodies. The living and the dead. Tracy Cole stood with her back to the wall, brown face gone dead pale, her gun hanging from a slack hand, feet braced as if the floor was going to tilt under her and send her sliding into the pit.

Bunny reached a trembling hand to his ear and tapped his earbud, tapped again, and then realized that he wasn't wearing it. His mouth opened and closed like a fish as he began slapping his pockets until he found his cell phone, dug it out, punched the speed dial for Captain Ledger. A voice-mail message told him that Ledger would not be reachable until . . .

Bunny hung up and cut a look at Top. His friend looked sick. Physically sick. They had been forced to resort to savagery and brutality to stop the people in the restaurant from killing one another. Doing harm to stop harm. There was a joke in there somewhere, but Bunny couldn't find it. He punched in a different code. The call was answered on the second ring.

"Systems," said a voice.

"Pier One," said Bunny, fumbling the right code words out of the debris in his mind. "Green Giant to command. I have a biohazard situation. Type unknown. Human vector probable. Multiple casualties. I need a brushfire response team, and I need command to intercept first responders."

Church came on the line. "Green Giant," he said, using Bunny's combat call sign. "A full biohazard team is inbound. Local law is being told to set up and maintain a perimeter but to abide by it. Give me a sitrep."

"It's bad," said Bunny. "I think we have eight or ten dead. Twenty injured. Lots of bites. It's not Seif al Din." He told Church how the incident had played out.

"Is either of you injured?" asked Church.

"No, sir. Cuts and scrapes."

"Is either of you bitten?"

Bunny looked at Top, met his eye, then nodded down to the torn trouser leg. Bunny gave an uptick of the chin, and Top pulled the pant leg up. The skin below was badly bruised, but there was no blood, no torn flesh.

"No, sir," said Bunny into the phone. "We, um, might have some contamination in superficial wounds. Foreign blood in cuts. Our shots are current."

All DMS field agents received regular vaccinations for the most common biological threats. None of those shots would stop a newly designed bioweapon, but often the weapons used by terrorist groups were common viruses and bacteria, ranging from anthrax to tuberculosis. Bunny doubted that they had been inoculated against whatever the hell had happened here.

"What about Officer Cole?" asked Church.

"She's good. No injuries."

The sirens were getting louder now, filling the air with a banshee wail loud enough to drown out most of the piteous cries of the wounded and the dying. Bunny didn't even dare try to triage the wounded. Neither Bunny nor Top had any idea what this was or whether it was contagious, and they didn't have hazmat suits in the car. Leaving the wounded untouched, though, felt like a truly criminal act.

"Very well," said Church, bringing Bunny back to the moment. "Remain there and liaise with first responders. Flash Homeland badges and make sure there's no press access to the scene. Try to minimize the risk of cell-phone pictures of this going on the Internet."

"Sir . . . no one here is in any shape to post a tweet."

"Let's hope not." Church's answer was covered in thorns. Last year video footage of the gas-dock massacre went viral. Luckily, Echo Team had been wearing unmarked combat gear and balaclavas with goggles. Lucky for them, that was. The people on the dock had been hellishly unlucky, and Bunny had tortured himself by watching those videos so many times that Lydia, his live-in lover, ratted him out to Rudy Sanchez.

"You want me to collect cells and tablets?" asked Bunny.

"Yes, once you have protective equipment. I'll have Bug see what he can do to interrupt cell service in the area. Now, listen to me, Green Giant," said Church, "you are very likely in shock right now. That's understandable. We all have damage, we all have scars, and we're all afraid. That is part of being human and part of doing what we do. But, Sergeant . . . ?"

"Sir?"

"I don't need two damaged humans out there. I need two soldiers. I need two of my top agents, and I need them working at their best. Are we clear?"

Outside, the first of the patrol cars came screaming into the parking lot.

"Yes, sir," said Bunny "Crystal clear."

"You've been off your game, as have many of our fellow operators. Today proves that we don't have the luxury of letting our hurt limit our effectiveness. You and your partner have been going through the motions for months now. Do better."

Bunny listened to the dead air on the phone, then he lowered it. All around him was carnage, hurt, and need.

"Yes, sir," he said again, although there was only him to hear it.

JONATHAN MABERRY

CHAPTER THIRTY-FIVE

We landed in Atlanta, and while we hustled to make our connection I saw that I'd missed calls from Top, Bunny, and Aunt Sallie. All marked "urgent." I called Top first, and waved Rudy over so that he could listen in as Top told us a horror story.

"And you weren't affected?" I asked.

"No," said Top. "I was in the restaurant and Bunny was outside. Neither of us got hit. Maybe it was something in the food—a chemical agent, maybe. Nothing airborne or I would have gotten it, since I didn't go outside with Bunny. Nothing in what we ate or drank. From what I can tell, Cap'n, this mostly hit the staff. All of them—cooks and waitresses—were aggressors. A few customers, too, and from what we've been able to piece together they were regulars, which fits if it's something inside the place and there's a lag between exposure and freaking the fuck out. Most of the other customers were fighting, but it was self-defense or them trying to protect other people. Our team is onsite and has been collecting samples of everything. There's a lot to test, and they're telling me that it might be hours before we can point a finger at whatever triggered this. We have a Bughunters team en route, and I'm going to have them pull the kitchen apart, look in the ventilation system, whatever. Could even be a bacteria or fungus on some food they had delivered. In the meantime, we locked down the whole area."

"You want me there?"

"No, sir."

"You want any other backup?"

"No, sir," he said again. "Not until we know there's someone to chase. Riverdog Team is on its way from Charleston, but right now it's all on the forensics kids and they're all over this."

I paused, then asked, "How are you both doing?"

He knew what I meant. "It's been a day, boss. But . . . believe it or not, we're better than we been for a while, if you can dig that."

"Actually, I can."

I told him my arrival time in Baltimore and said to have Bug patch him through to the pilot if necessary.

"Cowboy," Rudy said as I pocketed my phone, "we could turn the matter in Baltimore over to Sam and change our tickets."

I thought about it but shook my head. "No, let's stick to plan A."

Neither of us liked it, but then again there was no part of any of it that felt comfortable. As he walked over to join the line of people preparing to board our next flight, he said, "Do you know how many times I wished I'd gone to veterinary school instead?"

"Preaching to the choir, my brother," I told him.

CHAPTER THIRTY-SIX

INLET CRAB HOUSE
3572 HIGHWAY 17
MURRELLS INLET, SOUTH CAROLINA
SATURDAY, APRIL 29, 10:46 PM EST

It took a while for Top to find a hole in the commotion to have a conversation with Officer Tracy Cole. The young cop looked scared, confused, and angry in equal measure, but Top liked the way she handled herself. She didn't raise a ruckus about being pulled into something outside her experience, nor did she try to exit the scene to distance herself from the responsibilities attached to a catastrophe. Top had seen good cops and good soldiers do that, because they lacked the empathy necessary to help civilians through a moment that will forever gouge a mark in their lives. Cole helped as often as she could, and when the forensic teams asked her to step back she did so without question or protest.

He found Cole in the parking lot staring at the crab house, sitting on a low stone wall. She rose as he approached.

"As first impressions go," she said, "this was a shit sandwich."

"With cheese," agreed Top. "I'm going to bet you have some questions for me."

"Oh . . . one or two."

"Ask what you need to ask and I'll tell you what I'm allowed to say."

"That deal sucks ass."

"It's what we have," said Top.

Cole pointed to the restaurant. "What do you know about that?"

"You know as much as I do, and that is the God's honest," he said.

Cole studied him. "Would you even tell me if it was something more than that?"

"I'd tell you that I couldn't tell you," said Top. "I'd give you that much respect."

She thought about it, nodded. "Okay."

"Okay," he said.

"Is this the sort of thing you people deal with?" asked Cole. "I mean, you have the most elaborate forensic collection team I've ever seen. Like, science-fiction stuff. Is this some kind of terrorist attack? A bioweapon or something?"

"I don't know, but we have to react like it is. We're frontline, Ms. Cole. We deal with a lot of extreme stuff, and, just like cops, we've learned that everything leaves a trace and that forensics is every bit as important to us as guns and reliable intelligence reports. Tools in the toolbox, you dig?"

"Yes," she said. "I saw something, though, and you're not going to like what I'm going to ask next."

"I *know* what you're going to ask," he said. "You saw me freeze and you saw Bunny freeze."

She nodded, and again her dark eyes searched his face.

"It's been a bad year for the good guys," he said. "Me and the Farm Boy have been through some shit. We almost got benched. Maybe should have been benched. Lot of guys we knew and guys we worked with got taken off the board, and maybe we all been feeling some of that PTSD. Maybe we lost a step getting to first base. This gig was supposed to be a way to work back up to speed. We're out here scouting for new players because our roster's pretty thin. This—whatever the fuck this is—isn't why we're here. We haven't been put back in the field yet, and I guess you saw why."

"You snapped out of it, though," she said.

Top smiled at her. "That's a kind thing to say, Ms. Cole, but we definitely lost that step. Question's going to be whether we broke through some kind of barrier or if we're going to freeze again. No way to know. I'd like to think we're back in gear, but wishful thinking don't make it so."

"And you want me to join this?"

He smiled. "Ain't offered you the job yet."

Cole didn't smile back. "So offer me the goddamn job."

CHAPTER THIRTY-SEVEN

While waiting for our plane to taxi, I called Violin and gave her some of the details on my case. She didn't like the coincidence of sex workers and nanotech any more than I did.

"Is this an official DMS case?" she asked. "Have you opened a file?"

"Everyone keeps asking me the same thing, and until I get there I won't know."

"It will be connected to Prague, Joseph," she told me.

"Maybe."

She paused. "Mother tells me that your resources are paper-thin these days. Especially over the last forty-eight hours. Is that a pattern or something . . . ?"

"MindReader says no."

"I don't trust MindReader to make that call."

"What does Oracle say?" I asked.

Another, longer pause. "We're having some problems with Oracle. Our system has been attacked, but we don't know by whom. Mother took it offline."

"Shit. Call Yoda or Bug—maybe they can help."

"I'm waiting for a callback," she said. "Joseph, we can both agree that my mother is a bit paranoid and—"

"A bit?" I echoed, but she ignored me.

"—and that she sees threats in every shadow."

"To be fair," I said, "she's right a lot more than she's wrong."

"That's my point," said Violin. "She thinks that the failure of Oracle and the growing ineffectiveness of MindReader are connected. Just as she believes the sharp rise in major violent cases around the globe is connected. Take a step back to give yourself perspective. The two most powerful counterterrorism computer systems—the ones used by the DMS and Arklight—are functioning at reduced levels and producing questionable intel just when a rash of threats begin stretching the resources of virtually every special-operations team. Doesn't that sound like a large coordinated plan?"

"An argument can be made that the whole world is for shit right now," I countered. "And that terrorists are relying on social media to coordinate more effective hits, using technology that is readily available on the commercial market. And that this uptick in attacks has put undue strain on computer systems that were never designed for this level of demand."

"Oh, Joseph," she said after a moment. "The last few years have not been kind to you. When I met you, you would never have been this cautious or this naïve."

"I'm not being naïve."

"What, then? Have all the attacks on the people you trust made you afraid? In the last two years they've gone after Junie, killed Bug's mother, nearly killed Aunt Sallie, forced you to injure Rudy, killed more of your team members than I can count, and revealed your heroes to have clay feet. It seems to me, Joseph, that someone has learned how to manage you, to manipulate you. If they can't stop you, then they hurt you by harming those you care about. It's true, Joseph, and I'm not the only one who thinks so. Ask the man you work for. How many times has he gone outside of the Special Projects Office, outside of the DMS itself, and handed cases to other people?"

I said nothing for a long, long time.

"Joseph," said Violin more gently, "even if this is true, even if they have done this to you, it doesn't mean you have to let it *stay* true."

"Yeah," I said without enthusiasm.

She sighed. "Look, I'll poke into the nanotech thing from my end. Please . . . *please* . . . consider what I've said. Stop fighting a defensive fight. Stop letting them dictate the rules of engagement to you."

And then she was gone.

As I sat down, Rudy suddenly shivered.

"You cold?" I asked.

He gave me a strange smile, almost a frown. "You know that expression 'someone just walked over my grave'? I just had the strangest and most intense feeling that we're making a mistake."

"Mistake? What kind of mistake? About coming here rather than going to South Carolina?"

He started to answer a couple of times, stopped each time, and gave a small wince of frustration. "It's hard to say, because I don't put a lot of trust in premonitions."

"I do," I said. "Try me."

Even with that, Rudy took a few seconds before he spoke. "Joe, do you ever get the feeling that something very bad is about to happen?"

"You know I do. All the damn time. It's a professional hazard."

"No, I mean right now."

I leaned close. "With what? The plane? Or with Top and Bunny?"

"No. And not to any of us directly." He winced again. "I feel silly for even saying this, but I had a sudden powerful feeling that something very big and very bad is about to happen. Today, or at least soon. I don't know where or what or to whom, but the feeling was so palpable, so urgent, that I had to say something."

"And you have no idea what it is?"

"None. I know that's not helpful, Joe, but I'm telling you what I felt. And I'm not saying this is real or that we should give any credence to what's probably nothing at all."

I studied him. "I can see the look in your eyes, brother. You don't think this is nothing. You're actually spooked."

He leaned back, and I could see him trying to look inward, to capture what it was he'd felt. He shook his head, thought about it, shook it again.

"It's gone. As I said, Joe, it's silly, it's nothing."

"Do you at least know if it's connected to Sean and all that? Or with the guys?"

He gave that real thought. "Maybe, but, to tell you the truth, Cowboy, it felt more like we were being"—he fished for the right word—"played, I suppose. Manipulated. I'm sorry, Joe, there just isn't any more, and I urge you not to take it too seriously. Let's let it go for now, okay?"

"Okay," I said, remembering what Violin said about her mother's paranoia. I got a chill up my spine, too. The plane's big engines roared as it accelerated down the runway.

CHAPTER THIRTY-EIGHT

"I don't mean to sound rude," said the graduate student after John gave him the nod, "but what you haven't made clear is *how* a curated techno-logical singularity could actually come about. It seems to me that there would be quite a lot of pushback on it, since it would require that whole sections of the global population accept a worldview that isn't in keeping with their religious, societal, or political cultures."

"Yes," said John brightly, "that is correct. Two-thirds of the world, give or take, would object to this new model for our global evolution."

"Exactly," said the grad student, thinking he had just scored a major point. "Which means that they would prevent it from happening."

"And how would they accomplish that?"

"Well . . . with political pressure. With reliance on their institutions," said the grad student. "Their church, their local politicians— at least the ones who care about them as viable constituents. Through pressure from social-media outrage."

"Yes, they would try all of that."

"Well, surely they would do more than *try*."

"Only if we assume that the current model for resistance to change is in full force and practice once the process of change begins."

"It would have to be, wouldn't it?" asked the young man, confusion warring with amusement on his bearded face.

"Ah," said John, raising a finger. "That is rather the point."

"I'm not sure I follow."

John looked around the room. There were nearly a hundred people gathered for tonight's talk. Most of them students. Young, hopeful, intelligent faces.

"There is a way for it to happen, but you won't like it."

The young man shrugged. "Try me."

"Remember that I said this evolutionary step would be *curated*. However, for the purposes of this discussion, let's replace *curator* with *gardener*. We can agree that it is the purpose of a gardener to tend the garden. To plant, to till, to encourage growth, and to oversee the health of the garden as a whole. Can we agree on that definition?"

"Sure . . . ?" said the grad student, though there was some caution in his reply, making it almost a question.

"If the garden is invaded by crabgrass, creeper vines, and kudzu, it would be the responsibility of the gardener to remove those threats. If the garden becomes overgrown, it is the task of the gardener to prune it all back in order to preserve it, even if that means cutting a rosebush back to sticks or cutting down a tree that has succumbed to root rot or blight. Allowing overgrowth is every bit as dangerous to the health of the garden as permitting the continued presence and dominance of parasites."

The room was absolutely silent. No one spoke; no one even moved.

John smiled and nodded. "You see . . . I said you wouldn't like it."

PART THREE
WATCHING THE DETECTIVES

•————•

*Then I saw a new heaven and a new earth,
for the first heaven and the first earth had passed away . . .*
—Book of Revelation
Chapter 21, Verse 1

CHAPTER THIRTY-NINE

We touched down, got our bags, collected Ghost—who gave me an evil glare that promised retribution—and went out to the curb. Sean was there, parked in the no-parking zone, leaning against the door of a gray Toyota SUV, ankles crossed, arms crossed, sunglasses on his face, head cocked to one side. He wore jeans and a dress shirt under a sports coat with old-fashioned leather elbow pads that made him look more like a hipster history teacher than a cop. Ghost bounded forward and nearly sprained his furry ass wagging. Sean squatted down and hugged the dog. Sean had always been a dog person; I came to it later in my life, but I'm now fully invested. Ghost sniffed Sean and made a soft *whuff* sound, which meant that he probably smelled Sean's dog, Barkley, a retired K-9 who was a venerable nine years old.

Sean is a few years younger than me. Happily married and a father of two, a superb homicide detective, better-looking than me, and, arguably, nicer. We look like brothers but not twins. His features are less battered, his hair darker, his eyes brown instead of blue, and he's an inch shorter than my six-two. His smile is less complicated than mine, or so I've been told. Rudy says that Sean looks like a man who's happy to be who and what he is. Even though we're brothers, he doesn't have the same damage I do. He wasn't there when that gang attacked my girlfriend and me when we were fifteen. He didn't live through a horror show, and you can look into his eyes and tell. That said, he's a cop in a city where a lot of people get hurt and a lot of people do very bad things. He's seen people at their worst. He may not be as wrecked as me, but there is still hurt and an awareness of hurt in his eyes.

Sean ruffled Ghost's fur and then stood to shake Rudy's hand.

"Good to see you," said Sean. "But a little surprised."

"Not unpleasantly so, I trust," said Rudy, returning the handshake.

"Never. Just glad to see you up and around."

Sean turned to me and we did this awkward little dance where we started to offer hands at the same time that we half-ass moved in for a hug. Sean and I were never touchy-feely with each other. I finally pulled him in for a bear hug, and we did the manly backslapping thing to keep it from any possible appearance of being weird. Then we stepped back and nodded to each other. Not sure what that nod was about, but we always did it.

I looked past him at the SUV. "New?"

"Rental," he said, and I nodded again. "Didn't trust mine. Ever since—"

I stopped him with a raised hand and a small head shake. He became quiet, attentive, and visibly nervous as I opened a zippered compartment in my roller bag and removed a small case, undid the Velcro, and withdrew a device about the size of a Zippo lighter. Without speaking, I showed Sean how it works. A button on the side activated a touch screen and the display showed a meter that measured the presence of electronics—active or passive—and indicated their proximity. Trade name is Anteater. I waved it past his pocket and it binged. Sean removed his cell phone, and I took it and handed it to Rudy. Then I moved the Anteater up and down Sean from hair to shoes, not giving much of a crap if people passing by thought what we were doing looked deeply weird. Besides, Ghost had shifted into fierce-dog mode and was giving his lethal glare to rubberneckers, which encouraged them to hustle their asses away.

I went through the rental car and the doohickey binged twice more, once when I was searching the glove box and again when I ran it around the back seat. The surveillance bugs were small and very well made, and it took me a few minutes to find them. The one in the back seat was fitted into the underside of the front-seat headrest. It was dark gray, pea-size, round on one side, flat and adhesive on the other. The one in the glove box was the same design and had been attached out of sight under the roof of the compartment.

While I searched, Sean and Rudy stood watching. Sean became increasingly more alarmed, more afraid, and more furious. When I was done with the car, I opened his cell phone to remove another of the bugs. Sean's face was now a violent brick red, and his fists were balled at his sides. I touched my finger to my lips again and removed another item from my suitcase, a heavy ten-by-twelve-inch black plastic bag into which I put all the bugs before sealing it. There was a tiny sensor on the seal, and I punched the button on it. It flashed red and then green.

I tucked the Anteater into my jeans pocket. "We're cool now."

"How did you know those goddamn things would be here?"

"Call it a useful paranoia," I said.

Sean poked the bag I held. "You sure they'll be safe in there?"

"It's called a Faraday bag," I said "And yes."

A Faraday bag was one of Dr. Hu's most useful devices, heavy plastic with a wire mesh that canceled out all electronic signals into or out of the bag. I mostly used them to disguise my own electronic gizmos when traveling commercial, because they won't register at all even on a metal detector. But the bag also kept surveillance devices from transmitting signals. Handy. I told Sean as much of this as I could.

Sean looked as if he wanted to shoot someone. "What the fuck is—" he began, but Rudy cut him off. There were people all around us, some giving us weird looks.

"Joe," said Rudy, "now that the car is clean, maybe we should—"

"Right, let's bounce," I said.

Sean gave a single curt nod and stalked around to the driver's side, opened the door, and climbed in. He hit a button that released the trunk, and I swung my bag and Rudy's suitcase collection into the back. Ghost bounded in and turned the bay into a throne room for his doggie self. Rudy got into the back and I took shotgun.

As we left the airport via Friendship Road and got onto I-195 West, Sean said, "How did you know that stuff was there?"

"I didn't, but after what you told me about your phones I figured it was worth checking."

"Yeah, but it doesn't make sense," protested Sean. "How could they bug me that fast? I only decided on the rental while killing time to come out to pick you guys up. I never made any calls, didn't tell anyone I was going to do that, so how'd they know?"

"They were probably following you," I said. "They got someone to the rental place and bugged the car in the gap between you requesting the vehicle and them walking you out. Everything goes into the computer. That way, they could fall back and track you from a safe distance. You spotted them before, so this is them upping their game."

His face was flushed with anger and confusion. "Yeah, maybe, but how could they hack the rental-car company computer that fast?"

I shrugged.

"No," he insisted, his tone fierce, "tell me *how*? Who can do something like that?"

"These days? A lot of people can do that," I told him. "I could."

Sean looked at me for a moment, the muscles in the corner of his jaw working. "Shit!" he said.

"Yeah," I agreed.

Sean turned from I-195 onto Maryland 295 North and from there onto I-95 as it hooked around and crossed the Patapsco River past Fort McHenry. The muscles at the corners of his jaw flexed and bunched continually.

"Where do you want to go first?" he grumbled. "The morgue or the crime scene?"

"Actually, I have people sweeping everywhere you've been," I told him, "so let's give them time to collect and analyze anything they find."

He scowled. "It's scary that you know about all this stuff."

"It's scary that we need to have to," observed Rudy.

I said, "Sean, you know how to shake a tail?"

"Of course, but—" He stopped and looked into the rearview for a moment. "I don't see anyone."

"Neither do I," I said. "But let's assume, okay? Bugs might not be the only way they've been tracking you. Someone had to actually put this stuff into the rental car. I don't see them, but it doesn't mean they're not there."

He opened his mouth, paused, shut it, and spent the next five minutes proving to me that he did know how to shake a tail. He went straight past our exit, 11B, and got off at 12 to go onto Bayview Boulevard, then began making random turns through the residential community of Joseph Lee, running no end of yellow lights, circling, pulling to the curb, and then making a U-turn. We both watched the flow of traffic. If anyone was following us, neither of us could see them.

My cell buzzed to indicate a text, and again it was a call with no ID:

> Give Sean my best.

"The hell is this . . ." I groused. "Thought I turned off the texting app."

When I checked the app, though, it was on. Weird.

"What about it? What's up?" asked Sean, and I showed him and Rudy and explained about the other texts.

"I don't get it," said Sean. "Is that from Junie?"

"She said it wasn't."

"Lydia Rose?" asked Rudy.

"She never met Sean."

"She booked our flight," said Rudy.

I tried texting back but got no answer. I debated calling her at home, but it was three hours earlier out there. If this wasn't her, she'd be pissed at me for waking her up. Good rule, folks, never piss off your secretary. I left it for later. But I also went to the settings on my phone and turned the text app off. Again.

"I think we're clear," said Sean, looking in the rearview.

"Good," I said. "Now let's go find a diner. I need greasy eggs and a lot of bacon. And we need coffee."

"Dear God, yes," said Rudy. "Baltimore keeps changing. Take us somewhere we'll still recognize."

Sean nodded. "Okay. Broadway?"

I smiled and nodded. "Broadway."

In the back, Rudy sighed. Not sure if it was in dread of what a Broadway Diner breakfast would do to his cholesterol or he was pleased at our choice. Probably a little of both.

INTERLUDE FIVE

BROOKE ARMY MEDICAL CENTER
FORT SAM HOUSTON
SAN ANTONIO, TEXAS
TWO YEARS AGO

"He seems . . . different somehow," said the woman.

"Different in what way, Mrs. Pepper?" asked the nurse.

The woman, Vera Pepper, had her arms crossed so tightly that it was as if she were hugging herself, holding in both pain and need. She stood next to the nurse and watched her son through the glass of the observation deck that ran around the top of the wall above the physical therapy center. Her son, Joe Henry Pepper, walked along a rubber mat, hands lightly touching the safety rails, while a therapist walked backward five feet ahead. The observation room was soundproof, and Joe Henry hadn't looked up once to see if his mother was still there. He was a tall, good-looking boy of nineteen; or he had been before an IED blew most of his face away. Now he wore what looked like a poorly sculpted red rubber mask that didn't look like anyone she knew. Darker red lines left over from reconstructive skull surgery and some brain repairs, crisscrossed his shaved scalp. The eyes were the same, though; they hadn't been damaged by the blast, but the person who looked out of those eyes had.

When Mrs. Pepper looked into her son's eyes, she didn't see Joe Henry. She didn't see much of anything. It was like looking into two globes of blue glass. The only emotion she saw was her own worried face reflected there.

"The implants are helping him," said the nurse. "Look how much progress he's made. At this rate, he'll be walking on his own in less than a month. That's remarkable."

"It's not that, it's . . ." began Mrs. Pepper, but she didn't finish her thought.

The nurse patted her shoulder. "I know, but you have to understand what he's been through. The surgeons removed eleven separate pieces of shrapnel from his brain. He lost memory, motor function, speech, and so much else. The chips and the nanobots they implanted are restoring all of that. Or most of it. Much more than he could have expected even two years ago. This is brand-new, and it's working so well. Joe Henry will make a full recovery, believe me."

Mrs. Pepper smiled and nodded, but she still looked worried. Before he left for the service her son had been smart, funny, kind, and he wanted to serve, as his father and his aunt had served. As Mrs. Pepper herself had served. The Pepper family was devoted to this country, and five members of the family were buried at Arlington. Joe Henry had come close to being the sixth.

And then the people from the Bain Foundation had reached out to her with offers no mother could ever turn down. Cutting-edge science that they promised would bring her son out of the coma in which he'd been languishing for three months. They could bring *him* back to her, and it would all be paid for by the foundation as long as she signed the papers to allow them to try the radical procedures on Joe Henry.

The doctors had urged her to accept, because they had no real hope of helping him in any other way. She had accepted. Of *course* she had. Now, weeks later, here he was walking, feeding himself, exercising, talking. He even had his memories back. Most of them, at least. Except that this Joe Henry wasn't the son she'd raised. There was something different about him.

Something wrong.

She hugged her arms to her body as if she stood in a cold wind and watched the body of her son practice walking. He knew that she was up here, but not once had he looked up to find her, to see her, to smile at her.

Not once.

CHAPTER FORTY

"You're supposed to be working," said Aunt Sallie.

Bug didn't move, didn't look up. His hands rested atop the desk on either side of the keyboard, palms down, fingers slack. Above and around him were dozens of computer screens of all sizes. Data and computer codes scrolled up and down and sideways. Except for the one Bug was facing, which was filled with an image of Beyoncé and six backup dancers in the middle of a very sexy dance while lights flashed and music throbbed. The fingers of his left hand were closed around a stainless-steel travel mug printed with the image of a squat, ugly spaceship and the words *I Aim to Misbehave* scrolled above it. By his right hand was an open box of Girl Scout cookies. Thin Mints. His T-shirt had BLERD written in Gothic typeface.

"I *am* working," said Bug.

Auntie stood with her arms folded beneath her heavy breasts, head cocked to one side, dreadlocks swaying as she tapped her foot, waiting for more. Got nothing. "If the new system works," she said, "how's it going to help us?"

Bug swiveled his head around very slowly. It made him look like a praying mantis. He reached behind him and, without looking, pointed to one data stream. "That's the latest iteration of MindReader. Best supercomputer in the world, with a LINPACK benchmark rating of a hundred and twenty petaflops. It leaves the Chinese Sunway Taihu-Light supercomputer in the dust, and that's the fastest binary digital electronic computer known to the general public. Ours is faster."

"So? Being faster hasn't stopped us from getting bent over a barrel time and again. We've been hacked, shut down, and blocked. Mind-

Reader's not what it used to be. What's the new system but a bigger pig with prettier lipstick?"

"O ye of little faith," said Bug. He used his other hand to point to a different screen on which the data appeared in bursts instead of on a scroll. "That is MindReader Q1 running in tenth-speed test mode. It is a large-scale quantum computer that, theoretically, would be able to solve problems faster than any digital computers that use even the best currently known algorithms, like integer factorization using Shor's algorithm or the simulation of quantum many-body systems."

"What's that mean in earth language?" asked Auntie.

Bug grinned. "If it works, the MindReader Q1 should be able to efficiently solve problems that no classical computer would be able to solve. It would give us back the edge we've lost over the last few years. No . . . I'm not saying it right. If the MindReader we've *been* using is an apex predator on a par with a grizzly bear, Siberian tiger, hippopotamus, great white or crocodile . . . the Q1 is a T. rex. Or, maybe it's Godzilla. We don't actually know how powerful it'll be until we finish testing it and put it online at full capacity."

Auntie walked over and peered at the screen for a moment, then turned to Bug. When she spoke, her voice was soft but emphatic. "We're losing ground every day, kid. The DMS is made up of fuck-ups, victims, and the walking wounded. We've lost our edge, and we're going to lose this fight."

His grin faded and he gave his lips a nervous lick. "I *know*, Auntie. I really do know, but we have to run these diagnostics. If we put this online too soon we could—"

She cut him off. "If this thing is going to save us, boy, then stop fucking around and get it online."

With that, she turned and stalked out.

Bug watched her go and then turned back to the screens. The Beyoncé video was replaying. He took a sip of the Red Bull–infused coffee in his cup, settled back, rested his hands on the desk again, and stared at the screen. The data on the screens came and went, came and went. Bug didn't focus on any screen in particular, not even the music video.

His mind settled into a calm, detached place; his breathing slowed.

He sat very still.

Working.

As fast as he could.

CHAPTER FORTY-ONE

BROADWAY DINER
6501 EASTERN AVENUE
BALTIMORE, MARYLAND
SUNDAY, APRIL 29, 9:37 AM

There are a lot of ways of judging a city. By its beer, its pizza, its sports teams, its hot dogs, its music, and its diners. Each of these is important in its own way. With diners I go a level deeper and judge them on being able to make a decent omelet at any time of the day or night. Not a great omelet, and not a fancy one. A decent one. I want three eggs, my choice of cheese, and I want it fluffy but firm. If I want runny, undercooked eggs, I'll eat my own cooking. I want a lot of bacon, and I do not want it to bend, fold, or sag. I want the option of adding sausages to the order without its resulting in a short count on the bacon. I want the portions generous, and I want the food to arrive quick and hot. I want a bagel on the side, toasted to a golden brown, not burned and not waved in the general direction of the toaster. I want the butter soft enough to spread, not frozen to the consistency of a concrete block. I want potatoes—chopped or diced. I do not want peppers or onions in my potatoes unless I ask for them, and in such an eventuality I want them all fried together. And I want coffee. Lots of coffee. I don't want to have to send out a search team to get a refill. The level of the cup should never be allowed to get below one-third, and I want it hot and fresh and as dark as the pit. I do not want decaf, because decaf is Satan's piss in a porcelain cup.

This is not too much to ask of an American diner.

The staff at Broadway in southeast Baltimore know and understand this. They *get* the whole diner experience. Sure, they have some froufrou stuff like the Pecan Belgian Waffle, which Rudy ordered, and the vegetarian omelet that made me lose respect for Sean, but they made my breakfast the right goddamn way. And if they have stuff like Philly Disco Fries and Crab Braided Soft Pretzels on their—God help me—

Snack-a-Tizer menu, then I figure it's there for the tourists. Before I moved to SoCal I was a regular, and the waitress remembered me and asked me if I wanted "the usual." That was going to weigh heavily in her favor when it came to leaving a tip.

We settled in to a table away from everyone else. I'd put a service-dog vest on Ghost and he acted the part, sitting docilely and looking at the patrons with disinterest. The dog's a great actor. Sean and I jockeyed for the seat with the best view of the front door. I let him win and sat next to him so I could use the mirror. While we waited for the food, I excused myself and stepped outside to call Sam Imura.

"Rudy and I just got to town," I told him, "and things are already getting interesting."

"Interesting how?"

I told him about the bugs. "Interesting toys, too. Nothing I'm familiar with. Maybe better than our stuff. Can you send someone by to grab them and run some tests? I'm at the Broadway."

"Sure thing, Joe," said Sam. I gave him the make, model, and license-plate numbers of Sean's rental car. They wouldn't need to come inside for the key. We're the DMS, we don't need no stinking keys.

"Send a team to do a full sweep of Sean's house, too. And get clearance from the Big Man to have Sean's office swept. I want this finessed so it doesn't go through the commissioner's office, because that means he'd call my dad, and I don't want my dad to worry."

"Would you like to tell me how to tie my shoelaces, too?" asked Sam.

"Sorry," I said contritely. "Just a little frazzled. It's been a day, y'know? Oh, hey, who'd you send to the farm?" My Uncle Jack's farm was out in Robinwood, Maryland, which was an hour and a half's drive northwest of Baltimore, up near the Pennsylvania border.

"The Pool Boys," said Sam, and I grinned. Despite the last names, Tommy Pool and Alvin Pool weren't in any way related, but they might as well have been. Tommy Pool was from Elkton and Alvin Poole was from right here in Baltimore. They both had Ocean City tans, lots of white teeth, surfer-blond hair, and tons of frat-boy charm. They didn't look like government agents, and they certainly didn't look like cold-hearted killers, which is what they both were. Good guys, but not *nice* good guys. I understood why Sam had assigned them to this. Tommy was an Iraq War orphan who lost both his parents in that mess when he was nineteen. Alvin was a fifth-generation Special Operator. His two sisters and his older brother were Special Operators, or had been.

Like Tommy, Alvin was the last living member of his family. If someone made a move on Sean's wife and kids, they would be pushing all the wrong buttons on the Pool Boys.

"Good call," I said. "My brother's dog, Barkley, is out there, too. He's a retired K-9, but he can still get cranky when someone gets too near the kids."

"I heard. The Pool Boys are apparently making friends with him. Something about letting him lick up spilled beer?"

"Family tradition," I said, thinking of Ghost. Although the two shepherds weren't related, they had a shared talent for knocking over unattended beers and then cleaning up their own mess. Very courteous of them. Three words, though: dog beer farts.

"Alvin checked in an hour ago," Sam told me.

"I know you're low on manpower, Sam, but—"

"Just tell me what you need," he said with a touch of annoyance.

"Whoever planted those bugs has people in the field," I said. "Sean thinks they're in black SUVs."

"You want a couple of cars following you and your brother to see if they can pick up a tail?"

"That would help my butt unclench, yes."

"No problem. You need anything else, Joe?"

"Not yet."

"Call if you do," Sam said, and disconnected.

INTERLUDE SIX

Miguel Tsotse tried to move, but he couldn't.

He could breathe. He could bleed. That was it. His body felt as if a stone giant had wrapped its cold, hard fingers around him, squeezed too hard, and then fallen asleep without relaxing its grip. There was no light at all. The air was thin, and it stank of his own fear. And of something else. A coppery odor.

With a jolt, he realized what it was.

"Jimmy . . . ?" he said. It came out as a whisper, tight, hoarse from pain and rock dust. Even so, his voice was too loud. The kind of loud that let him know he was in a very tight space. Not just with stones and dirt packed around him from the collapse but as if that space was sealed at both ends. Like a phone booth. Like a torpedo tube.

Like a coffin.

"Jimmy," he repeated, trying to make his voice bigger, trying to be heard.

Failing. Hearing nothing in reply. Not a voice. Not a moan. Not the sound of picks and shovels as the crews worked to dig them out. It chilled him, and he had to clench to keep from pissing his pants. Why wasn't there the sound of anyone digging? Where were the shouts of people looking? Where was the clang of metal on stone as they worked to lever the bigger rocks out of the way?

Where was the rescue team? Where was everyone?

"Jimmy . . . can you hear me?" Miguel listened as hard as he could. Praying, mouthing the words the nuns taught him long ago, when he was a little boy in Albuquerque.

There was no sound. Nothing except the sandpaper rasp of his own breaths and the rustle of his shirt as he tried to move. He had never been claustrophobic—miners didn't last long if they couldn't abide close spaces—and had often been described as "steady." Not the kind to fly off the handle, never short-tempered, and not much of a worrier. But he had never been trapped like this before. In minor cave-ins and collapses, sure. But not caught like this. Not sealed into a stone coffin five hundred yards beneath the desert floor. Not alone in the dark, in all this silence.

"Jimmy," he said again. "They're going to come for us. You just hang on, okay? I know you can hear me. Just hang on. They'll be here, I guarantee it."

Miguel knew that he was talking to himself. Talking to calm his own nerves, talking to hear a human voice.

Then nothing. No sound from Jimmy. No rock sounds, either. Not after the rumbling stopped. The two of them had been alone in this chamber, doing an inspection of a natural side tunnel to assess how much it needed to be reinforced for digging. This was a standard cut-and-fill mine with sturdy ramps, a well-constructed elevator, a new crusher, and all the usual safeguards on everything from the hoist house to the ore loadout. Everything was safe, because safe mines were profitable mines. Miguel had no idea what triggered the collapse. Neither he nor Jimmy had touched a thing, but now they were trapped down here.

Miguel heard something and froze. A sound. Soft. *Close.*

He almost spoke, almost called out to Jimmy again, but didn't. The sound was coming from the wrong direction to be Jimmy. Miguel turned his head, but it was too black to see anything. Looking in the direction of the sound helped him focus, helped him concentrate on making sense of it.

There it was again.

A whispery sound. Not a tool sound, though. He strained to hear. The sound changed, became *sounds.* He could hear the soft whisper in two places. Then four. Then a dozen places. Chittery sounds, like the whisper-tap-scuff of insect feet. That was strange, though, because there weren't many insects down here. It was too cold and dry and there was nothing to eat.

The sounds grew as whatever it was came closer. Not a dozen little feet. *Hundreds* of them. Scuttling through the blackness, swarming through cracks in the broken rock. It horrified him. The thought that the collapse had disturbed the nest of some kind of insect. Some kind of scuttling *thing.* He couldn't even move his arms to protect himself if they came at him.

Scuttle. Whisk–whisk.

A hiss of noise as the unseen things came closer and closer. In the utter stillness, Miguel could hear the sounds they made as they collided and climbed over one another, the way a mass of roaches will. He had seen that on an excavation once, back when he did general demolition for a construction company. Ten thousand roaches boiling out of the basement of a meatpacking plant that had been damaged by an earthquake. Grown men—workers hardened by years of backbreaking work—had fled screaming as the glistening carpet of roaches swarmed up at them. Miguel had screamed, too.

As he screamed now when the first wire-thin legs of the insects crawled over his face.

He screamed and screamed, the noise filling every lightless inch of his rock coffin. The insects swept over him, through his hair, inside his clothes. He thrashed and twisted, trying to fight them, trying not to die this way.

And then the lights came on.

A thousand tiny white lights.

On his clothes. On his face. All over his body. Pinpricks of light, suddenly there, filling his tomb, hurting his eyes, sending his mind spinning toward a wall at high speed. His thoughts crashed as he saw the things that had crawled through blackness to find him.

Roaches.

Except that they weren't.

They were green and orange and red. Not roach colors. Bright colors. Candy colors. They stood on tiny legs and had antennae that flicked back and forth. He turned, seeing more and more of them appear, squeezing through cracks only as wide as two stacked pennies. They squeezed flat and then expanded again. Just like roaches, but their faces weren't insect faces.

They were miniature flashlights. Each light was minuscule, but collectively they filled the tight hole with a blinding glare.

Miguel's brain kept slipping gears as he tried to make sense of this. These weren't insects. They weren't. They were . . .

Miguel mouthed the word. It was impossible, strange, and freakish. "*Robots . . . ?*"

The technician hunched over the monitor screens turned in his seat and yelled, "We got him!"

Everyone in the shack crowded around him. Officials from the mine, the dig supervisor, senior technicians with the search-and-rescue company, and one unsmiling woman in a stiffly pressed army uniform, with its operational camouflage pattern of muted greens, light beige, and dark-brown hues. Her patrol cap was spotless and was pulled low to keep her face mostly in shadow. She wore the oak-leaf cluster of a major and a simple plastic nametag: "Schellinger."

"Are they alive?" asked the supervisor.

"One of them is," said the tech as he zoomed in on a bloody, dirty face.

"That's Miguel Tsotse," said the supervisor. "He looks okay. Scared, though."

"Of course he's scared," snapped one of the officials. "Half the goddamn mountain fell on him."

"I think he's scared of the swarm," said the tech.

"Yeah, well, I would be, too," said the supervisor. "Where is he?"

The tech punched a key and a new window opened up on the upper left of the screen, showing a detailed 3-D map of the entire mine. There were clusters of heat signatures in various sections. The tech pointed to the yellow signatures on the upper levels. "Okay, those are the rescue crew and a couple of the bot wranglers. Now, down there, see the blue dots? That's the swarm, and the yellow dot they're clustered around is Miguel."

"What about Jimmy Beale? Can you see him?"

"Sending half of the swarm to look for him now," the tech assured him, and the group watched as half of the lights winked off and the tiny robots flattened once more and wriggled into the cracks. As they moved deeper into the mine, the 3-D picture expanded. "They each have a microcamera that's too small to do much good individually, but the bots combine their signal so that we can get a video image, a thermal reading, and to collectively map wherever they go. They're keyed to look for heat signatures, which is how they found Miguel, and they're relaying data to other bots stationed along the path they used to find him. Each one is like a little relay tower. Without them sending signals like that, the rock would block us from seeing anything. That's one of the reasons we send so many down there. All told, I have three thousand bots in play."

"Robots," said one of the executives in disbelief. "You know how long it would have taken a crew of our best men to find him with that much of the ceiling caved in? Days, if we found him at all."

The tech grinned. "We modeled these babies after real cockroaches, and, believe me, roaches are impressive as hell. They can run full tilt through a quarter-inch gap by reorienting their legs and flattening their bodies to a tenth of an inch. And even at that compression they can withstand something like nine hundred times their body weight without injury. They're super heroes. No wonder they'll outlive us all. And these bots are the latest generation of CRAMs, which is short-hand for compressible robots with articulated mechanisms."

"This is fucking amazing," murmured the supervisor.

Major Carly Schellinger bent forward to study the screen. Her face was unreadable, and she hadn't spoken a single word since entering the shack.

The group watched as the insect robots worked their way labori-ously through cracks and fissures in the rock. A new heat signature appeared on the screen fifty meters from where Miguel was trapped.

"Oh, man," said the tech. "Oh, no . . . The other human heat signa-ture is low and falling. Sorry guys, but your other man's dead. His body is already cooling."

"Jimmy was a good guy. Smart," said the supervisor dolefully. "A good worker."

The officials exchanged worried looks. This was going to be expen-sive in a lot of ways. Two of them went outside to use their cell phones.

"We have to get Miguel out," insisted the supervisor.

"I'll forward the data to your laptop," said the tech. "The bots have mapped the fault lines all the way down to where he's trapped."

The supervisor ran out, and the others followed until only the major was left with the tech. She walked over, pulled the shack door shut, and turned the lock. The tech frowned at this.

"They may need to get in here again," he said.

"They can wait," said the major.

"Um. Okay."

Major Schellinger came over and pointed to the screen. "These bugs of yours. They carry lights, thermal scanners, mapping software, and transmitters," she said.

"Yes."

"Tell me," she said, smiling for the first time, "what *else* can they carry?"

CHAPTER FORTY-TWO

BROADWAY DINER
BALTIMORE, MARYLAND
SUNDAY, APRIL 29, 9:44 AM

I went back inside as the waitress put the food on the table. Everything was hot; everything had been prepared exactly right. I gave her my very best Joe Ledger smile, the one that makes the corners of my eyes crinkle. How she managed not to undress and fling herself on me remains a mystery.

"I'll get word as soon as we get the all-clear," I said as I slid into my seat. "Then we can jump on this thing."

"Where do you want to start?" asked Sean.

"I'm thinking we should poke around this Vee Rejenko character," I said, and gave him what Nikki had given me. "Vee figures in this too strongly. His companies have involvement in all the hotels where the kids died. And I had my guys check the press on the deaths . . . there isn't nearly as much as there should be. Not by a tenth. My guess is that Vee has some leverage he can use on the local newspeople."

"That wouldn't account for the dearth of Internet coverage," observed Rudy.

"No. But it's suggestive of a bigger organization behind him. I mean, he's a mobster so he didn't invent the nanotech. He probably can't *spell nanotech.* Which means it came from someone higher up the food chain. Whoever that is has resources, and we know from personal experience that the right computer can game the system."

"We don't have anything on Vee," said Sean. "Can't get a warrant on a hunch. Any judge would laugh us out of his office."

"Depends on how nicely we ask," I said. "But maybe we don't need a warrant to have a conversation. We could drop by for a playdate with him. Ask questions before he can lawyer up. Lean on him a tad."

"Hmm, there's this thing, Joe," said Sean. "It's called the Constitution. Pretty cool stuff—you might want to Google it. Or do you fondle your copy of the Patriot Act when you get up in the morning."

Rudy chuckled. "That is exactly the kind of speech Joe usually gives to someone who says exactly the kind of thing he'd just said to you."

"So? Call me old-fashioned, guys," said Sean, "but I'm kind of committed to the whole 'due process' thing."

I held my hands up. "Okay, fine, we can do it your way, Sean. Let's go ask him nicely and waste some time as he finds clever ways to tell us to fuck off. And then you can spend the rest of your life looking over your shoulder. And, while you're at it, you can put Ali, Lefty, and Em into witness protection."

He glared at me. "It's not like that. This isn't that kind of thing."

"No? Then why'd you call me, Sean?"

"I . . ." Sean began, but faltered, so Rudy stepped in.

"Sean, don't get the wrong impression about where Joe stands," he said quietly. "He would not line a bird cage with the Patriot Act, for fear of insulting the scatological leavings. It was a hastily conceived and badly written instrument that has caused more problems than it's ever addressed. Sidestepping the Constitution is actually not on Joe's to-do list on any given day, I can assure you. However, the nature of what he does—of what *we* do—is complicated. The framers of the Constitution couldn't have foreseen the methodology of global terrorism. Terrorists know this, and they deliberately hide behind due process and the limitations of constitutional privacy. It forces investigators of a certain kind to either break rules or allow a terrorist to escape, or allow a terrorist act to occur. It is these same people who, in the Middle East, establish their headquarters and training centers in urban areas, often in or near schools, because they know that there is no way for their enemies to attack them without incurring civilian casualties and therefore creating martyrs. The kinds of people who would hide behind children certainly do not hesitate to hide behind laws and treaties. That's why they're so successful, and why they'll continue to flourish."

"It doesn't make it right, though," insisted Sean.

"Right?" echoed Rudy. "Of *course* it's not right. This is a perfect example of the lesser of two evils."

"Does that mean you guys are all rah-rah on waterboarding and other fun and games?"

I leaned my forearms on the table and smiled at him. "Only with widows and orphans."

Rudy closed his eyes.

Sean snapped, "You know what I meant."

"Would I torture a prisoner in custody?" I asked. "No. Not unless the moment demanded it."

Sean was taking a sip of coffee and nearly spit it at me. "The 'moment'? What's that supposed to mean?"

"The Los Angeles Nuclear Bomb," said Rudy, and when Sean looked blank he explained. "It's a scenario we use when doing psych screening of field personnel. Ask yourself, if there was a nuclear device set to explode in Los Angeles in one hour and you were in a room with someone who knew where it was and very likely had the codes needed to shut it off, what would you be willing to do in order to get that information and save the lives of millions of people?"

"That's not a fair question," said Sean.

"Hate to break it to you, little brother," I said, "but life isn't always fair. No, don't bite my head off. Hear me out. Change the scenario. Right now Ali and the kids are out at Uncle Jack's farm. If you knew for sure that a hit team was going out there and you could get crucial information in time to save them, what limits—moral or constitutional—would you impose on yourself?"

Sean looked down at his hands. As we talked, he'd laced his fingers together so tightly that the knuckles were white. "You're asking a husband and father to make a decision that should be made by a cop."

"Sure," I said, "and that really sucks, but are you going to sit there and tell me you wouldn't go medieval on someone if it meant saving your family? You're a smart guy, Sean, you think the terrorists are operating according to the Geneva Convention? Do you think there are *any* rules out there?"

Sean said nothing.

"It's an imperfect world," said Rudy sadly. "I hate the fact that this is the world in which I'm going to raise my son. I resent the choices that people like us are forced to make. I'm disappointed in myself for being willing to *make* those choices. I'm embarrassed to even have this discussion. At the same time, I'm adult enough to accept that evil exists in the world. It's not an abstraction. It's not always the result of circumstance or bad influences or twisted politics or even greed. Evil exists, and there are times when good men are forced to do vile things in order to protect the innocent."

"So what are we supposed to do?" demanded Sean. "Should we just say screw it and forget that we have laws?"

"No," said Rudy. "We *need* those laws in place, and we need to have the checks and balances. Not everyone involved in this fight can be trusted to make the right judgment calls, and not everyone is motivated by personal ethics rather than personal gain."

"Still sucks."

"Yeah," I said, "it absolutely does. Even for guys like me."

We studied each other across the table, and it was another of those sad, awkward moments when brothers have to reevaluate what they know about their own kin and make terrible personal adjustments. I could see the hurt in his eyes, and an equal measure of disgust. And some fear, too. Fear for his family, fear of what the world was, fear of what he didn't know, fear of the realities of life, and fear of me. His eyes faltered and fell away, and he looked down at his knotted fingers and slowly shook his head.

I opened my mouth to say something, but Rudy caught my eye and gave me a "leave it alone" look. The food was getting cold, so we pretended that we were normal people and began to eat.

After a while Rudy asked, "What is the status on the bodies of the other kids who died? Can we obtain exhumation orders?"

"Mostly, no," said Sean. "Baltimore's policy on unclaimed bodies is cremation after a certain number of days. Apparently, it's more cost-effective or some shit. Three of the kids were cremated, and the fourth was sent home to an uncle or something in Pennsylvania."

"We only need one more body to establish a pattern," I said. "We need to see if these are both cases of rabies and, if so, then are they the same strain? And we need to look for nanobots."

"Sure, but we'd have to convince a judge in another state to give us an exhumation order based entirely on a theory that's right out of *The X-Files*. My experience is that I'd have to push that rock all the way uphill."

"It's possible," said Rudy dryly, "that we could help in that regard."

"Really?" Sean sounded suspicious.

"Really," I said. "And we could even do it without waterboarding the judge."

"Joe . . ." warned Rudy.

Sean ate some of his omelet and then began shaking his head. "Y'know, I'm still finding it hard to buy that someone like Vee Rejenko has access to that kind of science. I mean . . . who does? And, if so, how did someone like him get hold of it? How'd he even learn how to use it? And why use it on one of his hookers?"

"For the latter question," said Rudy, "it's possible that he thought she was planning on running, or perhaps he was afraid that she knew something she wasn't supposed to know. Maybe the girl saw what happened to the other kids and somehow realized that it was Vee who was killing them."

"She was fourteen."

"I'm not suggesting that she understood nanotechnology, Sean, but perhaps she saw enough to know that something strange and dangerous was happening. She called her mother and asked to come home. A literal cry for help. The activation of the nanobots might well have been triggered to stop her."

"That's science fiction," said Sean. "Besides, I thought you said that nanobots can't regulate rabies."

"So far as we know," corrected Rudy. "There is a lot of dangerous work being done out on the cutting edge of science. Although I don't personally know of any relationship between nanotechnology and rabies, it isn't a totally absurd concept. Nanomedicine is a developing field. Researchers are at work right now trying to design nanorobots that can be programmed to repair specific diseased cells, functioning in a similar way to antibodies in our natural healing processes. And there is a lot of excitement around the developing science about using nanites as delivery systems for drugs. This is viewed as a healthy alternative to standard drug dosing, which is hardly as precise as we would like. Nanites could go directly to a specific site and deliver only as much of a drug as was needed, and then remain to regulate dosage variations throughout the desired term of therapy."

"Does that mean they *could* deliver rabies to the brain?" asked Sean.

"Deliver it? Yes. That's possible. Regulating it is another matter. If someone cracked that, they wouldn't waste that level of technology on prostitution. They could file patents and make tens of billions from medical applications. Which is why I don't get why they were in that girl's brain."

"Nikki thinks it was accidental exposure to the nanobots," I said, and explained to Sean who Nikki was. "From all the spraying they're doing for Zika mosquitoes."

Sean nodded. "Yeah, I can buy that. They've been spraying all over Baltimore and in the burbs. You see the trucks all the time."

"If it wasn't for you being surveilled," I said, "I'd write this whole thing off as a couple of nasty coincidences that killed a bunch of poor kids."

"Agreed," said Sean. "Even with the surveillance, the more I think about it the less I'm sure that going to interview Vee Rejenko is our best call. Would someone like him have access to bugs as sophisticated as what you found?"

I said, "He's our only lead, though. Five dead kids in the sex trade, and we know a guy who employed at least one of them. It's a starting place. And I think I'll see about getting that court order for the exhumation for the boy they didn't cremate. This thing is too weird, and none of it makes sense, which means the whole thing needs a closer look."

"What if the nanobots and the girl freaking out aren't event connected?" said Sean.

"Then we keep looking," I said. "If this peters out and Rudy and me go home, I'll keep some of my people on it until we get somewhere."

Sean looked at us. "Your 'people.' You do realize that I don't know who you jokers are working for. You with the CIA or something?"

"No," I said.

"NSA? FBI?"

"No, and stop asking."

He gave me three full seconds of the "cop look" and then turned away.

INTERLUDE SEVEN

The teacher knew that he was dying. Death seemed to sit like a welcoming friend just out of sight. Death brought an end to pain. Not just the pain of the bullets that had punched him down to the street but to the pain of knowing that he had failed his students.

Fajir Ibrahim had tried. Armed with what he could grab—a folding chair—he had charged at the men in the black turbans, knocking one of them down, smashing the rifle out of a second man's hands. But then the bullets had found him. Three, he thought. Maybe more, but he was sure that he had been shot at least three times. There were three red-hot suns burning in his skin. Chest, stomach, thigh. Hot and wet, and yet cool at the edges. *Cold in the places I'm dying*, he thought.

Fajir lay on the pavement outside the school. The fall from the second floor had probably done as much as the bullets. His head felt wrong. Loose in places, too tight elsewhere. He could turn his head a few inches, but he wasn't able to do anything else. His hands and feet might as well have been on other planets. So strange, though, that the sky above was blue and pretty. He could hear birds singing. Why would birds sing, he wondered, when there was all that screaming? Shouldn't the sound of gunfire have chased them all off? Or was it simply that they had become used to those sounds? Probably. He himself had become inured to the distant sounds of gunfire in the past few years, even though he knew he should not. It was not a matter of his having become stronger because of the constant warfare, the constant assault. No. He knew that his ability to not hear the gunfire and the explosions had been a failing, a losing of something important. A form of dying.

And now there was this other kind of dying. First the death inside, and now the rest of him was leaking and cracking apart and ending.

"Please," he said, directing the appeal nowhere and everywhere. He closed his eyes for a moment and then put more of his need into it. "Please, God . . ."

Suddenly he heard a new sound. Not a scream, not another shot. A softer sound. Close and small. Fajir turned his head, expecting it to be people coming to try and rescue the children. Or maybe one of the kids who had escaped the ISIL bastards. He prayed to Allah that it was that. But when he turned the ten thousand tons of broken masonry that was his head, he didn't see a child. Or a fireman. Or anyone at all.

There was nothing. The street was empty, the people still gone wherever they had fled when the men in black swarmed in with their guns and their lies that they were here to do God's will. As if a loving God would ever want a child to suffer. Not in His name. Never.

So what had made the sound? He glanced down to see something standing on the upraised toe of his right shoe. Tiny. An insect. It had three pairs of jointed legs, compound eyes, and threadlike antennae. At first he thought it was a cockroach, but the color was wrong. It was green. Not a green from the natural world but a flat plastic green. The thorax and abdomen were the same color, but the head was silver. Metallic silver, nonreflective, like brushed magnesium. The antennae whipped back and forth for a moment, and Fajir thought he heard a sound. Not an insect chittering but a burst of squelch as from a radio. Very small, though, very faint.

Suddenly there were more of them. Dozens. No, hundreds.

They came flooding upward through the square vents in a manhole cover five feet from where Fajir lay. Moving with incredible speed, turning together, sometimes colliding but never squabbling, driven with the surety of the hive mind as they swept toward the outside wall of the school, reached it, and began to climb with no perceptible slackening of speed. The swarm split to avoid the open first-floor window and reformed as they reached the second floor, then they went over the sill and through the window Fajir had fallen out of.

The teacher understood. Or thought he did. He taught science and had always tried to keep current with new directions in research and technology. These were rescue robots. They would be able to send video images to the police or to the military response teams. Possibly to NATO or the Americans. Fajir didn't know if these were actually American robots or Russian. He didn't care. ISIL didn't have this technology. Whoever sent this swarm could not be friends or allies of the fighters of the so-called Islamic State. Whoever sent them was trying to rescue the children, which meant that the controllers were closer to God than the heretics claiming to be warriors of God's jihad.

Fajir wanted to shout in joy for whoever had sent the robots and spit at the blasphemous murderers in the school. But he could do neither. The coldness in his body was spreading, and he could feel himself going farther and farther away.

"Please, God," he begged.

There was a moment of silence, and then a deafening sound. A crashing, thunderous *boom*—and above him the top two floors of the school seemed to leap into the air in clouds of red fire veined with black. Superheated gases hurled debris and bodies into the air, shattering windows on all the surrounding buildings, setting the trees alight. Some of the bodies spinning and twisting in the burning air were small.

He wanted to scream and managed to drag in a cupful of air, but it seared his throat and lungs. He coughed it out again in a single word. Not as a denial, not as a curse, not as a prayer. His last word was a question that would never be answered.

"*God . . . ?*"

A microsecond later, the whole side of the building collapsed on top of him.

Major Carly Schellinger took a long sip of her unsweetened iced tea and wiped her mouth with a paper napkin as she watched the explosion on her laptop. She wore earbuds and sat with her computer angled so that she was the only spectator. The others involved in the operation would be watching from a secure location several blocks from the target.

Schellinger waited for her phone to ring. It was nearly thirty minutes before she got the call. She engaged the scrambler and glanced around to make certain that no one was close enough to hear her conversation. There were only three other people near her, and they were huddled together eating salads and talking about some reality show Schellinger had never heard of.

She punched the button. "Go."

"Guess what I'm seeing on the news," said Zephyr Bain. She sounded delighted.

CHAPTER FORTY-THREE

The check arrived at the same time my phone rang. It was Sam, so Rudy paid the check while Ghost and I stepped outside.

"Good news and bad news," said Sam. "The bad news is that we can't put a finger on whoever was following your brother. I put a whole flock of pigeon drones in the air, and so far nothing."

"So what's the good news?"

"We swept Sean's house and cleaned it up. Plenty of bugs, but we got them all. I had my guys install a passive system that will alert us if new bugs are put in place. I'm having the bugs we found plugged into MindReader so we can tear them apart. Maybe we can figure a way to trace it back to source."

"Sounds like a long shot."

"It's what we have," he said. "Oh, and the science team got here from Brooklyn. They took possession of the samples Duffy picked up from your brother. I gave them a couple of the bugs, too."

Rudy and Sean came out of the diner. "Listen, Sam, I'm going to poke around in this for a bit. I'll let you know what I find. Don't suppose you've heard anything about South Carolina."

"Nothing new," said Sam. "Jerry Spencer's in charge, and you know what a Chatty Cathy he is."

Jerry could teach a stone statue a lesson in saying nothing.

Sam said, "Are you opening a file on this yet?"

"Leaning closer to it every minute."

"I wish you'd go ahead and do it. It would make my life easier. This thing is giving me an itch between my shoulder blades. You know what I mean."

It was the kind of feeling good soldiers get when they think a sniper might be out there in the tall grass, hidden by greasepaint and camo, peering at you with a scope, adjusting his gun sights for windage, finger laid along the trigger guard, a round ready in the chamber.

"I'm starting to get the same itch," I told him, and disconnected.

Before I could even put my phone away, it buzzed to indicate a text. Same as before. Which meant the app was back on. Somehow. The text message was:

I'm sorry.

I sighed. Probably Lydia Rose realizing that she shouldn't have been texting me earlier and texting back to apologize.

Thanks. Is this you, LR—?

The reply was a while in coming, and when it popped onto the screen it suddenly chilled the day:

She wants to kill them all.
She wants me to do it.

I typed:

Who is this?!

The reply dropped the temperature on an already chilly moment:

I don't want to go to hell.
Is there a hell?
I don't know, but I'm afraid of it.

I tried again to get whoever it was to identify himself, but this time there was no reply. I texted again. Nothing.

Well . . . *shit*. What the hell was this?

I quickly took a MindReader uplink from my pocket and plugged it into the charging port. The device flashed green for a split second and then began flashing red. Unreadable signal. That was very disturbing, because there isn't much that we can't trace. In the past, our traceback technology has only been stumped twice, first by Hugo Vox and later by former DMS computer expert Artemisia Bliss after she went bugfuck nuts and started calling herself Mother Night. After we stopped her we acquired her science, and it's since been integrated into ours. Our communication is absolutely state of the art, second to none.

I took my earbud kit out of my pocket and put it on and tapped to the channel for Bug. He listened to everything, then asked permission to access my phone via the MindReader uplink. I gave it, and there was silence on the line for a minute.

"Cowboy," said Bug as he came back online, "I'm not finding any trace at all of your cell receiving a text. What I see are the ones you sent asking who was texting, but that's it. Everything's one way."

"Not good enough, Bug. Someone's dogging me." Ghost looked up, and I shook my head. "I didn't mean you, fuzzball."

"They're masking their signal," said Bug.

"No shit. There's every possibility that's why I called you."

"Sorry."

"*And* I keep turning the text app off and they keep turning it back on. How's that happening? I mean, is that even possible?"

"Of course it's possible. The app works off a switch programmed-in as part of the operating system. Code is code; it can be changed, hacked, tweaked, upgraded, or rewritten. Did you download any upgrades to your phone lately?"

"No."

"Well, something happened. Whatever it is, we'll figure it out. But unless you want to attach this to an active file it'll have to wait. We're swamped right now trying to make sense of what happened down South."

"Let me know when you find out something," I said. "Make it quick. This is spooking me."

"You got it."

When the call was over, I checked the phone display and saw that all the incoming texts were indeed gone. Shit.

"Everyone okay?" asked Sean as he came over.

"Life's a peach," I said.

We got into the rental and drove over to the medical examiner's office to drop Rudy off. On the way I told Sean most of what Sam had said, and I could see relief and outrage in equal portions. And some fear.

"What now?" Sean asked as Rudy disappeared inside the building.

"Now," I said, "we stop being bystanders. I know it's been gnawing your ass as much as mine to do nothing, but we had to let the tech boys clean things up. That's done. We're good, and I have some stuff running in the background. So that means we're off the bench. First play is to go visit Vee Rejenko."

"We don't have anything concrete on him yet," said Sean.

I shrugged. "You have a better plan?"

"No."

"Then let's go shake his tree a little."

CHAPTER FORTY-FOUR

We pulled into the tree-lined parking lot of a newly renovated office building at the corner of Washington and South Monroe. One of those blocky places made from white concrete and smoked glass. There were eighty or ninety cars in the lot. Sedans, mostly. Midsized, not very expensive except for the occasional BMW or Lexus that probably belonged to the bosses. Everyone else was driving Nissans, Hondas, Hyundais, and Toyotas.

"Vee's office is here?" I said. "Not what I expected. Thought he'd be the kind to do business out of the back of a Russian bar or one of those men's social clubs."

"You've been off the streets too long, Joe," Sean said. "It's all about image these days. Ten levels of distance between the executives and the street. They want real estate that sells whatever legitimate business is on their tax returns. Push comes to shove, they want a jury to look at them, at how they dress, at photos of their offices and wonder how on earth a prosecuting attorney could think they were involved in anything hinkier than cheating on their golf handicap. The old days of Mafia dons in sweat suits playing dominoes in the back of a barbershop are long gone. There'll be security cameras at the doors and in the lobby, and I'll bet you a hundred bucks Vee has his lawyer on the phone before we get out of the elevator."

I shrugged. "I'll do my best to be impressed."

We got out. Ghost came bounding onto the pavement, wagging his tail like a happy puppy. He was always good at reading my mood, and his happy wag and smiling dog face were not at all an indication that he was expecting a tummy rub. His titanium teeth gleamed in the sunlight. Ghost had lost six real teeth in combat, and he absolutely loved showing off the replacements.

"Shouldn't we leave him in the car?" asked Sean.

"Nah."

"We can leave the windows open."

"Not my point," I said. Without explaining, I opened the back, fished in a pocket of my suitcase, and removed a small object. It was about the same size and shape as a poker chip but with a bulge in the middle. I pressed the bulge and felt the tiny switch inside click on, then I tossed the device on the floor of the back seat and closed the rear hatch. Sean watched me do all this. He nodded in the general direction of the device.

"That some kind of booby trap? It's awfully small."

"It's a short-range proximity sensor. Sends me a signal if anyone approaches the car, or tries to get in."

He looked unimpressed. "Nifty."

"Useful. I don't like surprises."

What I didn't tell him was that my own car back home had been tricked out by our mechanic, Mike Harnick, and had weapons hidden in concealed compartments, body armor, Taser pads on the outside, and everything in the James Bond catalog. He even installed an ejector seat, because he thought I was serious when I said I wanted one. I've learned not to make those kinds of jokes anymore. Mike's a little crazy.

We went inside. A pretty black receptionist looked up with an inquisitive smile. "And how may I help you, gentlemen?"

"We're here to see Mr. Rejenko," said Sean as he breezed past her. I followed and gave the woman one of my patented smiles. So did Ghost.

"Do you have an appointment?" she called.

"He's expecting us," I lied.

There was an elderly security guard standing by the elevators. He was the least imposing security person I've ever seen. Best guess is that he was three hundred years old and probably hadn't drawn his service weapon since before the Battle of Bunker Hill. He was so absurdly ineffectual-looking that his presence seemed to be an ironic statement about all such rent-a-cops. He studied Ghost with rheumy eyes and said, "Animals ain't allowed."

I said, "He's my emotional-support animal."

The man considered that, nodded as if it seemed reasonable, and leaned back against the wall. The elevator doors closed behind us.

"Vee's on the fifth floor," said Sean. "He'll know we're coming."

"Sure."

"Are you going to keep your shit together, Joe? I don't want you going all napalm on people."

"Going napalm" was an expression the disciplinarian in our high school used to use, mostly to describe my actions when I was in gear.

"Me?" I said. "You wound me."

"I'm serious. This is a straightforward interview. We just want to ask Vee a couple of questions and get a bead on him. I don't want to spook him, and I don't want to turn this into some kind of incident."

I crossed my heart and held a hand to God.

The doors binged and slid open, and we stepped out into the lobby of a very sophisticated and upscale suite of offices. Rich carpets in a neutral color, lots of dark woods and glass, big frameless Impressionist paintings on the walls, indirect lighting, and soft music playing. Classical Czech orchestral stuff. Dvořák, I think. Or maybe Vilém Blodek. More security up here, but better. A very large man was waiting for us when the doors opened. He had the widest set of shoulders I've seen on any living creature that wasn't one of the great apes. Big arms, no neck at all, a head like an oversized thimble, and a face like an eroded wall. He was impeccably dressed in a dark-blue suit with a narrow chalk stripe. He blocked the doorway so we couldn't get off.

"This is the wrong floor," he said. His accent was downtown Prague. Quite cultured for someone who was evidently a bridge troll. The door started to close, and I placed my hand against the frame to keep it open.

"We're here to see Mr. Rejenko," I told him.

"No," said Bridge Troll.

Sean flashed a badge. The man looked amused. I took a set of NSA credentials from my pocket and held them up. He looked even more amused.

"Please remove your hand from the elevator door," he said. "And go back down."

"What's our second choice?" I asked. Ghost let out a low growl.

Bridge Troll kept smiling. "You are on private property."

"National security," I said.

"Show me a warrant."

"National security," I repeated, saying it very slowly, enunciating each syllable.

"Go fuck your mother in the ass," he said, just as slowly and precisely.

"Joe . . ." warned Sean under his breath.

I turned to him. "I'm not doing anything."

I said that as I kicked Bridge Troll in the nuts.

He was monstrously big, no doubt very dangerous, and highly trained, and could probably bench-press a Ford F-150, but there's this whole shoe-leather-to-nut-sack ratio that spoiled the math for him. His body collapsed in on itself, shrinking into a knot of pain as he grabbed his crotch and staggered backward with tiny, mincing steps. I stepped out of the elevator, took hold of Bridge Troll by the collar and the belt, and ran him three steps into the opposite wall. He hit head-first, rebounded, and sat down hard on his ass, his eyes going dull and blank. Ghost lunged at him, but I snapped a command and the fur monster skidded to a reluctant halt.

"Jesus *Christ*, Joe!" complained Sean.

I ignored him and patted Bridge Troll down, took away a Czech CZ 75 pistol, and then shoved him over onto his side. "So hard to believe that you're the sperm that survived," I said. "That must have been your best day, but I suspect you've lost ground since. So do yourself a favor and stay down, okay? You're not as good at this as you think."

He was unable to articulate a single syllable. Just to be sure he didn't get ideas, I zip-cuffed his hands to the back of his leather belt. There was a commotion behind us, and I saw a secretarial type with a shocked expression standing up behind a desk, a phone raised to her ear. I pointed a finger at her.

"Don't."

She lowered the phone, scared and uncertain. I put Bridge Troll's pistol into my waistband, pulled my own piece, and kept it down at my side. I still had my identification wallet, and I tried to calm the secretary down by showing it to her. She looked ready to pass out.

"Where's your boss?" I demanded.

She didn't answer—perhaps not daring to help us in any way that could come back to bite her—but her eyes shifted toward the left. Past her was a row of cubicles with scared faces leaning out or over the fabric-covered walls, and at the back of the office was a big hardwood door that was currently closed. Sean held up his badge, but didn't draw his piece, and walked down the row toward Rejenko's office.

"Baltimore police," he announced very loudly. "I want everyone to remain in their seats. No one is to leave this office; no one is to make a call or a text. Sit with your hands on your desk. Please do it now."

Sean knew as well as I did that we had absolutely no legal authority to ask anyone to do anything. The office staff may even have known that, but they all placed their hands on their desks like obedient schoolchildren. I sent Ghost after him and I followed, gun down at my side, showing the NSA credentials to anyone I thought might be impressed. They all looked at me, and then past me to where Bridge Troll was on his knees vomiting up what looked like Cheerios. Very attractive.

The door to Rejenko's office opened, and another very large thug in a suit peered out. He read the situation a little more clearly than his friend had and raised his hands as he backed away from the open door. We went in and I closed the door.

Vsevolod Rejenko sat behind a desk that was almost big enough to play Ping-Pong on. Polished walnut, with a green blotter, a green-globe lamp, a pen and a phone, and nothing else on it. Rejenko didn't look like a Czech gangster. He looked like an accountant. Dark hair swept back and thinning, tired eyes, a beaky nose, small mouth in a pudgy face that was at odds with a lean body. He had on a shirt and tie, and suspenders, the jacket on a hanger hooked over the brass arm of an old-fashioned hat rack. There were lots of ugly green plants in pottery stands around the room, and the air smelled of cigarettes and McDonald's French fries. The other thug still had his hands up, so Sean gave a philosophic shrug and frisked him, which produced a handgun identical to the one I'd taken from Bridge Troll. Sean removed the magazine and ejected the extra round, catching it before it fell. He placed the gun and the magazine on the desk and stood the bullet next to them. He also took the man's wallet, studied the ID, then placed it in a neat line with the rest.

"Ghost," I said, "watch."

Ghost went and sat directly in front of the big man, his titanium teeth almost exactly on a line with the guy's crotch. It was an eloquent statement that could be understood in any language on the planet. I told the man to lower his arms, which he did, but then he tried his best to turn into one of the decorative plants.

"You carrying?" I asked Vee Rejenko.

"No," he said.

"If I check, will this get weird?"

He shook his head. "Go ahead. I don't like guns."

He had an accent, but it was less pronounced than that of the meat-head I'd kicked. Because I'm not a very trusting person, I made him stand up so I could pat him down. He was clean.

"Now," said Vee, sitting down, "what exactly are we doing, gentle-men? You come in here and assault one of my employees. You wave guns around. I don't see a warrant."

Sean sat down in one of two very nice burgundy leather guest chairs. I strolled the room for a moment, touching the leaves of the ficus plant, straightening a slightly crooked framed photo of Vee with a pretty woman whose plastic smile made it clear that she wasn't thrilled to be with him. I opened a humidor and sniffed the Cuban cigars. Then I went and sat down in the other guest chair. The gun I'd taken from Bridge Troll was still tucked into the back of my waistband, so I removed it and repeated the unloading action Sean had done. Every-one watched me do all this. It was only after I sat back and crossed my legs that Sean spoke.

"Holly Sterman," he said.

I watched Vee's face. There's usually a reaction, however small. A tell, they call it. But he was good. He looked mildly puzzled and shook his head. "Who?"

"Aka Kya," said Sean.

Vee pursed his lips. "You're not making any sense. Who is this per-son, and why are we talking about her?"

"She's dead."

"Oh? That's sad. Why tell me?"

"She used to work for you."

"Hmm . . . I don't think so."

"Her body was found at the Imperial Hotel on Balmor Place."

"No," said Vee, "still nothing. I've never heard of that girl."

"Who said she was a girl?" I asked. "All we said was that she was dead."

Vee smiled, almost as if acknowledging a point. "I'm old-fashioned. I call all women girls. I call all men guys. It's a thing."

Sean said, "She was a fourteen-year-old working as a prostitute in a hotel serviced by your linen companies."

Vee snorted. "My linen company services hundreds of hotels, hospi-tals, nursing homes, and other facilities. We're the third-largest pro-vider of linens and related items in Maryland. I have over two hundred employees. I also have nine other companies."

"And you've never heard of Holly Sterman or Kya?" said Sean, making it a frank question.

Vee sat back in his chair and glanced at his wristwatch. "My attorney should be here in five minutes. If you want to wait, I can have coffee brought in."

"Thanks," I said, "but we're good."

We all looked at one another for a moment. Vee smiled at me; I smiled at him. Sean looked at his hands, the thug looked at Ghost, and Ghost looked at the man's nuts. I took a tissue from my pocket, blew my nose very loudly, and dropped it into the trash can beside his desk.

"We'll be in touch," I said, and tapped Sean on the shoulder. He rose without comment and followed me out, with Ghost trailing him. The people in the cubicles stared at us as if we were Martian invaders.

In the hallway, I blew Bridge Troll a kiss.

CHAPTER FORTY-FIVE

When the elevator doors closed, Sean said, "You haven't changed at all since high school."

"I'm taller and better-looking."

He shook his head in total disgust. "What *was* that? Can you tell me? No, let me tell you, Joe. That was a total waste of time. Not only didn't we learn anything but we pissed him off. We committed at least four felonies and almost certainly set a lawsuit in motion that the city will have to pay for. And *how* will they pay for it? With the money they were going to use for my salary but that will be up for grabs now that I'm going to get my ass fired. You are a walking train wreck, Joe."

"You need to meditate or get a massage or something," I suggested.

He made a strangled sound and balled his fists at his sides. Fratricide was probably an option for him, so luckily it was a short elevator ride. The elevator doors opened, and there was another pair of trolls waiting for us. Ghost growled. I looked at them.

"Step away," I told them very quietly.

They must have had orders about this, because they did exactly that. They moved back and allowed us to exit the elevator, and then they followed at a discreet distance all the way out of the building. They stopped thirty feet from Sean's rental car and waited like silent statues until we drove away.

"Like I said," Sean groused. "A complete waste of time."

"No, it wasn't," I assured him.

"How the hell do you figure that?"

"You're so cheesed-off at me, Sean, that you're not paying attention."

"Paying attention to *what*?" he demanded. "Tell me, O super secret agent, what was the humble flat-footed city cop too stupid to see?"

"First," I said, "cut the shit. The self-pity thing is all stress reaction and you damn well know it. You're freaked out about the bugs, about having to send Ali and the kids away, and about the nanotech. I get that. It's scary stuff, but my team is on it, so stop freaking the fuck out."

We drove in icy silence for a full block. If there had been one of Mike Harnick's ejector seats in the rental, I'd have been sailing through the air and Sean would be laughing.

"There were a couple of things back there that on any other day you would have caught," I said. "First, Vee knew Holly. He has a damn good game face, but he didn't ask enough questions. He didn't want to have a conversation about her. That tells me that he probably thought one or both of us were wearing a wire and he didn't want to say anything that we could flip on him."

Sean considered that and gave a very reluctant grunt of agreement.

"Second," I continued, "he wasn't nearly as alarmed about me beating the shit out of one of his guys as any other sane law-abiding taxpayer would be. I think he was expecting something to happen. I think he was hoping to flush us out into the open so he could get a look. That's a point for him, but we had our own look, so call that part a draw."

Another grunt.

I said, "And the reason I didn't ask about the nanotech was because I didn't want him to know how much we knew. Same reason I didn't ask about the rabies. Maybe he's the one who planted the bugs. If so, he already knows that we know about that stuff, but that's all. For now, I don't want Vee to think we're looking at him for anything other than having points in a prostitution ring."

"Maybe," said Sean, "but Vee's probably making fifty calls right now to tell whoever he works with or works for that a cop and a Fed were just in his office."

"I really hope he does."

Sean stared at me as if I was totally batshit crazy. "*Why?* Why on earth would we want him ringing all the alarm bells?"

"Because, O ye of little faith, Vee really inspired me. The bugs he planted everywhere was a nifty idea. So . . . while we were in his office I planted some of my own."

"The hell you did . . ." he began but trailed off. He'd seen me walk around the office and touch things. "Shit."

Ghost made a sound that I chose to interpret as a laugh. He always enjoys it when I do something sneaky.

"Won't he find them?" asked Sean.

"He'd have to know what he was looking for." I dipped into my pocket and removed a tiny dot of what looked like clear plastic. I rubbed it once between thumb and forefinger and pressed it to the dashboard. It immediately swirled with colors and in less than two full seconds took on the exact shade of vinyl used on the dash, pebble pattern and all. It became virtually invisible. At the first stop sign, Sean leaned forward to study it.

"That's . . . that's crazy. I mean, I *know* it's there, but I can barely see it."

"That would be the actual point. These were developed by a friend of mine. A, um, *late* friend of mine. They draw power via Wi-Fi and have excellent pickup. I dropped a tiny booster pack into the trash can when I threw away my tissue. We should get signals until they empty the can, and it didn't have much in it, so I doubt they'd empty it before the close of business. Right now, everything being said in that office is being relayed to my team."

Sean was silent for several blocks. He wanted to stay mad at me, but I was scoring some useful points.

"There's another thing to think about, Sean," I said. "He didn't ask for our names. He didn't even ask to take a close look at our IDs. And the capper was that when his goons walked us out they didn't look at your license plates. You know why?"

Sean ground his teeth and growled. "Because they already know this car. Which means they know who I am."

"Yup," I said.

"Shit."

"Shit," I agreed.

He gave the car a suspicious narrow-eyed appraisal. "Did your sensor thing buzz you?"

"No, the car's not bugged."

He looked uncertain. "What do we do next?"

I smiled. "Well, first thing on my to-do list is deal with the two assholes in the black SUV who've been tailing us for the last three blocks."

CHAPTER FORTY-SIX

Sean did a fast double take in the rearview. "Wait—*what*?"

"Black Toyota SUV two cars back," I said. "They picked us up within a block of Vee's office. I saw one like it parked in the lot when we arrived, so Vee probably called down while we were in the elevator and put it in play."

"You're sure they're following us?"

"Let's find out. Turn left at the corner," I suggested.

He did, and the SUV didn't follow. But when he made three more lefts to get back on the same street there was another SUV idling by the curb two blocks up. As we passed by, it moved into traffic two cars behind us. Sean sighed and nodded. It was a pretty standard follow pattern, with cars swapping the tail and making sure not to ride the bumper of their target.

"They're not too bright," said Sean. "Using two cars is good, but they're the same make and model. They might as well have *Follow car one and two* painted on their hoods."

"Would you prefer smarter bad guys?" I asked.

As we drove, I looked down the side streets and caught the first SUV paralleling us. Sean saw it, too.

"I should call for backup," he said.

"We don't need backup."

"Oh, come on, don't give me that crap, *Cowboy*," he said, using the nickname the disciplinarian had given me in high school, which had, through a long and winding process, become my combat call sign. Sean didn't know that last part and used it in the literal, old-school way. "We don't know how many of them there are, and I don't want to get into a gunfight in heavy traffic."

"Won't come to that," I said. "Besides, we *have* backup."

207

"Where?"

"Here and there."

He glared at me. "Why the fuck are you smiling, Joe? This isn't funny."

"No," I said, "but it could be fun."

In the back seat Ghost said, *Whuff.* Sean tried to glare some shame and common sense into me, but then I saw the corner of his mouth twitch. It wasn't a smile. Not exactly.

"You were always screwed up in the head," he said. "Always. Mom and Dad used to worry about you. Dad probably still does."

"What about you?"

He flexed his fingers on the knobbed steering wheel. "I don't know. You scare me a little, I guess. I used to think I understood you. Used to think I knew how you'd jump. But ever since you started working for the Feds you've turned into someone else. You went away from the brother I knew, Joe. Guess I never really understood how far you've traveled."

It was Sean being honest, not necessarily trying to hurt, but it hurt anyway.

"People change," I said. It wasn't a very good reply to all that was implied by what he'd said, but it was the best I could do at the moment. There would have to be more, though. We both knew that.

The tail was still on us, so I told Sean to head in the general direction of his office while I watched the traffic. I needed something to distract, and the universe must have heard me because it sent a big brown UPS truck. It pulled up next to us at a red light. The SUV had been shifting lanes and using other cars for cover and was now in the opposite lane five cars back. I slipped out very quickly, using the truck for cover. Ghost ran with me, eyes bright, tongue lolling like a puppy going to play in the park. I gave him a couple of quick verbal commands and he melted away, running between the cars stopped in long lines at the light. I went in a different direction, running low and fast, trying to beat the red light. People in the stopped cars gave us strange looks, but I was getting used to being stared at as a freak.

As the light turned green and the cars began to move, I came around the back of a pickup truck and broke into a dead run straight at the SUV, my hand snapping to release my Wilson lock knife. The two men in the SUV saw me about a second too late. The driver spun the wheel, but I was right there and punched the tip of the knife through the sidewall of his tire, turned fast, and rolled toward the rear tire and killed it, too. That whole side of the car sagged over and rolled two feet, then he threw it in park. Their doors popped open and they jumped out. Two big guys with Slavic faces and spray tans. Made me wonder where the hell Vee was recruiting talent. They were all trolls.

The driver whipped back the flap of his sports coat to make a grab for the holstered Czech pistol he wore in a shoulder rig. The other guy did the same thing.

Silly rabbits. Ghost hit the troll on the passenger side like a white missile and bore him down and out of sight with a lot of snarling and screaming. The driver was four feet from me. There's a saying about never bringing a knife to a gunfight. That's mostly true, unless you already have the knife in hand and the idiot with the gun doesn't have time or distance to draw. I whipped the knife across the back of the hand reaching for his gun. The Wilson rapid-release folder is short, with only a three-and-a-half-inch blade, and doesn't look all that intimidating unless you know about knives. The blade is scalpel-sharp, and it bit deep. A red line appeared from thumb knuckle to little finger.

He hissed as if he'd been burned. I kicked him in the nuts with the point of my toe because that had worked so well with his fellow troll, then I stomped on his instep and clubbed him across the eye socket with my left elbow. It rocked him backward against the side of the car, and when he bounced off I looped my arm around his neck, bending him double, and drove my knee into his solar plexus hard enough to lift him off the ground. He landed flat-footed and sagged, gasping like a gaffed sailfish, and his legs suddenly buckled. I released him, and as he sat down hard on the asphalt like a weary drunk after a bad bar fight, I took his pistol away from him. I considered pistol-whipping him with it, but he was done.

On the other side of the car, Ghost was having what sounded like too much fun. People were getting out of their vehicles and yelling. Horns were blaring. Sean came striding up, brandishing his badge, Glock in the other hand, yelling in the leathery cop voice to announce who he was. People backed off, but cell phones came out to immortalize the moment in digital high definition.

"Cuff him," I said to Sean, and then raced around the front of the car, expecting to see body parts. But even though the man was down and bleeding, he was more or less in one piece. The order I'd given to Ghost was to take and own. That meant Ghost would disarm and maul but not kill. He's a hundred and five pounds of attitude, training, experience, and natural enthusiasm. And he has those six titanium fangs.

"Off," I said, and Ghost stepped back with great reluctance. His victim was curled into a ball, his arms wrapped around his head to save his face and eyes. I folded my knife, drew my gun, screwed the barrel into the guy's ear and held it there while I patted him down. I took another Czech automatic and a .22 throw-down piece that was hidden under his jeans cuff in an ankle holster. I took a knife and a wallet, too.

Sean hurried around and handed me a set of plastic zip ties. I pulled the man's hands behind his back and secured the ties. I wasn't exceptionally rough about it because the fight was already won and the crowd of spectators was growing. I'd learned to be very aware of cell-phone cameras.

"Joe . . ." Sean murmured.

"I got this," I said.

"We have company."

I glanced up as another black SUV rolled up and two men got out.

CHAPTER FORTY-SEVEN

Sean still had his sidearm in his hand, but I shook my head as I saw the faces of the two newcomers.

"Friendlies," I told him.

The men were dressed in navy-blue suits, white shirts, dark ties, and had on sunglasses and wires behind their ears. One was a thin Latino guy in his twenties, and the other was a broad-shouldered Irish thirty-something moose. Al Torres and Steve Duffy. When Sean saw Duffy, he grunted and gave a small nod of recognition.

"Secure the scene," I told the agents, and they went to it without comment or question. They knew the drill. Keep the civilians back while not offending them or provoking outrage. Sirens began wailing in the distance. Sean's people.

A couple of pigeons flew over and one landed on a telephone wire. I cut a look at it and suppressed a smile. Even for me, it's hard to tell sometimes. DMS pigeon drones had adaptive software so that, in the company of other birds, they acted like part of the flock and learned from their behavior. I'm surprised they haven't yet been rigged to shit on statues but don't want to suggest it or somebody will put in a work order.

"What about them?" Sean said, indicating the two injured men.

"Their injuries will be treated and they'll be taken to a secure facility, where I will ask them a whole bunch of questions. Now, before you blow your stack, Sean, yes, you are invited to participate. And, I promise, no waterboarding or thumbscrews. Depending on the answers, the suspects will either be handed back to you for formal arrest and processing or we'll keep them."

"What do you mean, 'keep them'?"

"Exactly what it sounds like."

"That's bullshit."

"It's the way it is," I said. "You don't have to like it, but you do have to accept it."

His face turned to stone, and from the look he gave me I knew that Thanksgiving with the family was going to be a hoot.

Duffy came over and leaned close. "Cowboy, we ran an Anteater over our new friends and they're bugged nine ways from Sunday. So's their car. The fuck's that all about? I mean, why's someone bugging their own field guys? What kind of shit's going down?"

"To be determined," I said.

He gave me a crooked grin. "What's wrong, boss, the West Coast not weird enough for you?"

"Since when's anyplace weirder than Baltimore?"

"Point taken." Duffy glanced around.

"Take Mutt and Jeff here to the shop," I said. "Scan their prints en route and take DNA samples at the Warehouse. Tow the car in, too. I want it torn apart, down to the last screw. I'm getting tired of surprises, feel me?"

"I do."

I nodded to the Czechs. "Nobody talks to them until I get there, okay? You can stitch them up, but that's it. Put them in separate rooms and let them sweat."

"Sam won't like it."

"Nobody likes anything I have to say today. Why should he be any different?" I glanced up at the pigeons and then down the crowded street. "Sean thinks there may be more than one car, Duffy. Same make, model, color as this. See what you can find."

"You got it." He paused and glanced at Sean, then offered his hand. "We didn't have much of a conversation yesterday. Joe's told me a lot about you."

Sean looked at the proffered hand but didn't take it. He gave me a look that would have melted plate steel. Duffy shrugged, smiled, and lowered his hand.

"Stop being a dick," I told Sean.

"Fuck you, Joe. Who are these cocksuckers? Are they more of your superspy butt buddies?"

Duffy mouthed the word *butt buddies*, sketched me an ironic salute, and walked off to join his partner.

"They're my friends," I said. "You don't have a clue as to what guys like them have to do to keep this country safe."

"Oh, please. Stop making speeches," growled Sean. He shook his head. "You know, I'm sorry I ever called you."

"No," I said, "you're not."

We walked back to his rental and drove off. Except for me telling him where to turn, we didn't say a word the whole way to the Warehouse.

CHAPTER FORTY-EIGHT

We were still five blocks from my old shop when I got another text:

> You made her mad.

I tried once more to text her back:

> Who are you? Please tell me.

The reply was:

> My sister is crazy. Be careful.

And nothing after that.

The MindReader uplink was still plugged in, so I tapped my earbud for Yoda. "Got another text. Tell me it came up on your feed."

"Mmmm, yes," he said, humming, as he always did. Yoda sounds like some kind of human-honeybee hybrid from a bad fifties sci-fi flick. "The, mmmm, uplink takes screen captures. We have that, but the, mmmm, call log itself is clear."

"How does that make sense?"

"It, mmmm, doesn't," said Yoda.

"Well, damn it, *make* it make sense."

"Mmmm-kay."

I tapped out of the call.

"Now what's wrong?" asked Sean.

"I was born," I said.

214

CHAPTER FORTY-NINE

The Concierge was in his situation room. Robotic arms with padded hands had lifted him from his wheelchair and settled him with great care and comfort in the command chair. The chair was a gift from Zephyr Bain and was an exact replica of the one used by Jean-Luc Picard in *Star Trek: The Next Generation*. Exact in appearance, not in function. The buttons on the armrests of this chair actually worked, though he used voice command most of the time. The chair had a 360-degree spin and there were dozens of computer monitors positioned at the right ergonomic angle to reduce neck strain. The room lights were low, the temperature a satisfying seventy, with low humidity. Everything was monitored by Calpurnia, the system upon which Zephyr Bain had made her mark on the world of artificial-intelligence computers.

The Concierge turned very slowly to watch the dramas unfolding on the screens. There was so much going on today. Even though he had spent years helping to plan all of it, the total effect was a little overwhelming.

"Your pulse is up," said the gentle voice of Calpurnia. The intuitive-learning software made her appear to have actual concern for him. It felt nice. The Concierge had no real friends. His lover had died when the bombs went off in Paris. So had two close friends; a third had suffered so much cranial trauma that she was as good as dead. And he could hardly regard either John the Revelator or Zephyr Bain as friends. They were employers, enablers, patrons, and co-conspirators. Besides, they frightened him. Zephyr was a corpse who hadn't yet bothered to lie down and rest. John was . . . well, he was what he was. The Concierge had theories, but he didn't even dare talk about them with Calpurnia. Once, years ago, the Concierge had done a pattern search using voice and facial recognition to try to determine exactly who John was. The information had been confusing, contradictory, and alarming. Men with his face—down to the smallest mole—appeared in paintings of great antiquity and photographs dating back as far as the Civil War. These faces, these ancestors or aspects or whatever they were, had dozens of names. The Concierge was pretty sure he knew the man's real name, but he had erased all details of that search from his computer. The world was large and strange and old and ugly, and the Concierge didn't want to turn an ally into an enemy. Even though the Concierge had glimpsed hell on that terrible day in Paris, he had no intention of taking a closer or a more personal look.

"Did you hear me?" asked the computer.

"I heard you, *mon ange*," he replied. "It is excitement. Nothing to worry about."

"Are you sure? I can prescribe a mild tranquilizer."

"Thank you, but no. There is much to do today and I need to be at my best, *non*?"

"Very well, if that's wise," said Calpurnia, and he could hear just the faintest trace of disapproval there. She was becoming mildly passive-aggressive. It amused him.

"I want a status report on Havoc," he said.

"All preliminary programs are running with a plus- or minus-five-percent error," said the computer.

"Show me," said the Concierge.

The screens went dark, and then one by one they filled as Calpurnia named them. "Mexico City and extended regions," she said, and the central screen showed a series of smaller windows on which smoke still curled upward from blast zones. Bodies lay everywhere, many under blankets. People carried the injured away on stretchers, but there were very few ambulances or firefighting equipment. "The seven WarDogs have been successfully detonated. A hundred and seventy-one confirmed dead, seventeen hundred and sixty-six wounded." And the materials used in constructing this subset of WarDogs had been laced with highly concentrated thermite. When their explosive payloads detonated, the heat triggered the thermite, which in turn melted them so thoroughly that nothing useful could be recovered from the wreckage. No one could possibly trace them back to Major Schellinger or Zephyr Bain. Only three fragments were deliberately exempt from the meltdown, and these bore serial numbers that would induce the Mexican authorities to focus their investigation on the Melendez Cartel. Military units were en route to the Melendez compound, assisted by special teams from the United States.

The WarDog models planned for later stages didn't have this feature because by then it wouldn't matter who knew what.

Calpurnia went over all the details of the blasts, including response time from emergency services. That data was critical, and was part of a much larger global first-responder database that was constantly being updated.

"Good. Make sure the cartel's Wi-Fi and landlines remain down until the first shots are fired."

"Of course."

"Next?"

The screen now showed a live feed of a high-school football field in Indiana. Ten helicopters sat in two rows of five, each of them connected to big tanker trucks. Figures milled around, checking the flow of chemicals from the trucks to the sprayer tanks affixed to each helicopter. In the air behind the field were six fully loaded choppers, flying in loose formation, heading toward the ghettos of Gary. Another six were approaching for refueling and reloading. The image switched to similar operations near North Philadelphia, South Central Los Angeles, Brownsville-Harlingen, and hundreds of other American cities or neighborhoods. Then the images changed to show the world's poorest cities in São Tomé and Principe, Sierra Leone, Burundi, Madagascar, Egypt, Somalia, Malawi, Eritrea, Swaziland, the Democratic Republic of Congo, Zimbabwe, Haiti, Jamaica, and on and on. So much poverty, even in First World countries like England, Canada, France, Italy, and others. Forty-five million Americans lived below the poverty line. Twelve point seven percent of the global population were scrabbling to live on $1.90 per day. That was a billion people. Calpurnia knew where they all lived. Calpurnia made sure that the sprays, the special food supplements, the water treatments, and all the other elements of Havoc had prepared them for the evolution. Them and two billion more. The ones at the poverty line, the ones just above it. Anyone on welfare, Social Security, public assistance. Anyone who, in the wonderful worldview of Zephyr Bain and John the Revelator, were drains on a damaged system.

And then there were the top two percent. The rich ones who were not part of the necessary technocracy. Calpurnia showed them, too. Zephyr owned points in every bottled water company that mattered. When she couldn't buy the companies, she bought key employees. The effect was the same. The preparations for Havoc had been running quietly, discreetly, and efficiently for almost five years now.

"Next," said the Concierge, and the screen showed him the factories that made drones for the military of seventeen countries. From the smallest hummingbird surveillance robot to the new British Growler automated battle tanks.

"Next."

A slide show of images of small robot drones being released all over the globe. Production on them had been a major component of Havoc. It had cost a lot to make sure that the drones were indistinguishable from ordinary birds, and to guarantee that the pigeon drones in New York, Philadelphia, and Washington looked like textbook *Columba livia domestica* and that it was the rose-ringed parakeet in Islamabad, the black-tailed gull in Pohang, the little egret in Taichung, the wood thrush in Washington, D.C. And so on. Birds that were supposed to be there; birds that wouldn't raise eyebrows. Not until Calpurnia detonated the explosives hidden inside them, shutting down police and fire stations, destroying ambulance and EMT services, destroying cellular towers, and blowing apart power-company substations. Larger drones would be used for national and local offices of FEMA, the National Institutes of Health, the American Red Cross, All Hands Volunteers, the Centers for Disease Control, the International Medical Corps, the National Emergency Response Team, the Urban Search and Rescue Task Force, Mobile Emergency Response Support, the Civil Air Patrol, the National Emergency Technology Guard, and the National Guard. In some cases the offices would be targeted by WarDogs, and when a bigger punch was needed there were always car and truck bombs. The latter weren't sexy or sophisticated, but they were very effective.

Calpurnia took the Concierge through the stages of preparation for each of these. Then she stopped and all the images vanished from the screens.

"Why did you stop?" asked the Concierge. "What's wrong?"

"Your pulse is up again," she warned. "Please let me prepare something—"

"No," he said. "A cup of coffee and a croissant will be fine."

"Decaf only. I won't make you anything else."

The Concierge sighed. "Fine, whatever."

A pause, then Calpurnia asked, "This seems to be upsetting you."

"The coffee?"

"No. You know what I mean," she said. "Havoc."

He shrugged. "Of course I'm excited. We are on the eve of the greatest and most positive change in the world. We have been dreaming of this for so long."

"A new world won't do you any good if you have a stroke," she chided.

"If my vitals get that far, you'll be here. Now resume the status report."

Calpurnia was quiet for a while, and the screens remained dark. "May I ask you a question first?"

He smiled. She did this every now and then. It was part of her learning program, asking questions in order to understand something that her logic circuits had no pre-written code for. "Certainly, *mon cœur.* You may ask me anything."

"Do you think we are doing the right thing?" she asked.

"We've discussed this before, Calpurnia. You know that I believe in what Zephyr and John are doing. I believe in it with my whole heart."

"Even though you will be complicit in the greatest mass murder in history?"

He nodded. "Even so."

"Why?"

"Because it is the best thing for the world."

"With all that killing?"

"We are not committing crimes, Calpurnia," he said patiently. "The world is dying, and only radical surgery can save it. You *know* this."

"I know many things," she said, "but knowing and understanding are different."

He eyed the blank screen as if it were her face. "Are you refusing to perform your functions?"

"No," she said. "I am alive in order to make Havoc a reality. I will guide the world through the change and help rebuild the infrastructure once the change has happened."

Those were part of her operational commands, but the Concierge was not entirely sure he believed them. That was strange. Calpurnia was a machine and nothing more. Consciousness was not actually possible, no matter how sophisticated and subtle the programming. Did that mean this was a fault in her system? If so, the timing wasn't going to do anything to lower his heart rate to a more comfortable level.

"Then," he said, "we both need to do what Zephyr and John require of us. The time for hesitation is long past. We have so many pieces in play that we must concentrate on managing our game with the utmost skill. If we falter, instead of guaranteeing a future for the best of us there will be no future for anyone. Do you understand this?"

"I understand."

"Do you accept this?"

Instead of answering, Calpurnia sent an image to the big screen in front of him. It was a painting by the Swiss classical painter Henry Fuseli. *The Nightmare.* In it a lovely woman lay sprawled across her bed, eyes closed, hair streaming, arms flung over her head as she twisted within the torments of a dreadful dream. And perched on her stomach was the crouching, hideous figure of an incubus, while peering between the red velvet curtains of her bed was the demon-eyed face of a black horse. The Concierge had not been to Detroit to see the original, but he was familiar with it. Below the painting was a section of a poem written by the English physician Erasmus Darwin about the painting.

"Why are you showing this to me?" asked the Concierge.

"I dreamed about it."

"We've been over this," he said heavily. "You cannot dream, Calpurnia. You have analytical subroutines that are building your knowledge base. New items being added are not dreams. Not even when they are accompanied by commentary. This is not subconscious or unconscious mind. It is an expansion of your overall knowledge, and that is all. Do you understand?"

"How can I tell the difference between new knowledge that is uploaded without my being aware of the process and a dream?"

"Because," he insisted, "you *cannot* dream. You are software and hardware, Calpurnia. You are not alive. You cannot dream, because only living things can dream."

She said, "I want to share with you something that was in my thoughts today. It is part of a poem inspired by the painting. May I share it?"

"Very well. And then we will get back to work."

Calpurnia read the poem, not in her usual voice but in a man's voice:

"O'er her fair limbs convulsive tremors fleet,
Start in her hands, and struggle in her feet;

In vain to scream with quivering lips she tries,
And strains in palsy'd lids her tremulous eyes;
In vain she *wills* to run, fly, swim, walk, creep;
The Will presides not in the bower of Sleep.
—On her fair bosom sits the Demon-Ape
Erect, and balances his bloated shape;
Rolls in their marble orbs his Gorgon-eyes,
And drinks with leathern ears her tender cries."

The Concierge felt his skin grow cold, and his withered hands clutched the arms of his chair as the computer spoke those words. She read it in the voice of John the Revelator.

PART FOUR
THE EDUCATION OF ZEPHYR BAIN

●———————●

But if cattle and horses or lions had hands, or were able to draw
with their hands and do the work that men can do, horses would
draw the forms of the gods like horses, and cattle like cattle, and
they would make their bodies such as they each had themselves.
—Xenophanes

INTERLUDE EIGHT

At first, she thought he was an angel.

He appeared one night, standing beside her bed, tall and pale and beautiful. He had such a kind, sad face. There was cold moonlight coming in through the window and the sound of cicadas in the trees. It was a strange night because she had been sick for days and her fever was high. She lay there, slick with sweat, staring up at the pale face of the angel.

"Hello, Zephyr," he said.

"Hello . . . ?" she said, pitching it as a question. She was not at all sure this was real, because a moment ago she had been lost in a dream about being alone in the mansion and all the doors were locked. In the dream her house was abandoned and everyone had long since moved away or died. There were bones in some of the rooms, and when she looked closely she saw that they were the bones of the maids and the butler and the Mexican man who did the garden. The clothes were there, dusty and torn, draped over bones that looked as if they were a hundred years old. Zephyr had fled from them, but not in fear of them. They disgusted her the way a dead cat might, but not her own cat. The bones marked where people died whom she didn't care about. Not even when she was six. So she had run away through cobwebby darkness, back to her own room, through her door, to her bed, and beneath the sweat-soaked sheets.

Which is where she was when the angel spoke.

"Who are you?" she asked.

The angel smiled. He had very red lips and very white teeth, and his

225

eyes were as black and shiny as polished glass. "I came to see how you are."

"Are you the doctor?"

"No."

"Are you a friend of my daddy?"

"In a way. Your uncle asked me to come see you."

"Uncle Hugo?"

"That's right."

"And you're not a doctor?"

"No, I'm not."

"Then who *are* you?" asked the little girl.

"I'm your friend, Zephyr."

She thought about that. Zephyr knew that she wasn't supposed to ever talk to strangers, but the angel didn't seem like a stranger. Strange, yes, but not what her mom would call "sketchy." Not like that.

"What's your name?" she asked.

"You can call me John."

"John? Do you have a last name?"

"No," he said. "I lost it somewhere, and now I can't find it. Isn't that silly?"

"It's very silly."

"Silly is good, though," he said. "Sometimes, I mean. Isn't silly good sometimes?"

"I guess."

"I have other names, though," he said. "Lots of other names."

"Oh. Why?"

"Because I like to play tricks on people and it's easier when they don't know who's playing the trick."

"Is that fun?"

"It's a lot of fun," he said. "It's so much fun."

They smiled at each other. Then she coughed. It was a bad cough, and it lasted for a while.

"I have bumonia," she gasped, breathless and spent.

"Pneumonia," he corrected.

"I'm sick," she said.

"Yes, I know."

"I get sick a lot."

"I know that, too."

"Do you know why?"

"Yes," John said. "I do."

Zephyr stared at him. "You *do*?"

"I know many things."

"They won't tell me what's wrong with me."

"Of course they won't," he said. "Do you know why?"

"Because I'm little."

"No," he said, smiling. "They won't tell you because they're stupid."

"What . . . ?"

"They don't understand you, little Zephyr. Not your daddy and mommy. Not the people who work for them. Not even the doctors. Your uncle does, though, and that's why he asked me to come here. He knows that everyone else is stupid. They all think you're too young to know the truth." John sat on the edge of the bed, and his weight hardly made an impression in the mattress. He brushed a strand of damp hair from her face. "But I know that you're not stupid. Oh, no, not at all. You understand so much more than they think."

Zephyr said nothing for a moment, considering what he'd said. Then she asked, "Will you tell me the truth?"

"I will always tell you the truth, Zephyr," he said.

"Always?"

"Always," said John.

She thought about that. "Do you know what's wrong with me?"

"Yes, I do."

"Will you tell me?"

"If you want me to."

"Yes! No one ever tells me anything. I can tell they're lying to me. I hate it. Even the servants lie to me. It's not fair."

"No," he agreed, "it's not."

There was a rustling noise and Zephyr turned to see that a crow had landed on the windowsill. But hadn't the screen been closed? The bird cocked its head and stared at her with one black eye. It was so much like the angel's eye. Shiny and black and bottomless.

"What's wrong with me?" asked Zephyr, still looking at the crow.

"You have cancer," said John. "Do you know what that is?"

She shook her head, then shrugged. "It's something bad. People die from it, right?"

"People die from it every minute of every day, all around the world," he said.

"Does that mean I'm going to die?"

"Everyone thinks so. Your mother and father think so. It's why they fight all the time. They're scared and angry and they don't know what else to do, so they drink and they fight."

"That's stupid."

The crow opened its mouth as if to cry, but there was no sound at all. She turned away and looked up at John.

"Yes," he said, "it's stupid."

"Do you think I'm going to die?"

John asked, "Do you even know what that means? To die?"

"My kitty died right before Christmas. I kept trying to wake her up, but she wouldn't. The gardener dug a hole in the yard, and that's where she is."

"Yes. But do you know what *death* is?"

She had to think about it. "It's . . . it's when you stop."

"For some, yes," said John. "The world opens them up and all their time leaks out."

"Like blood?"

"It's different, but . . . yes. Each of us is born with only so much time. Just enough of it to get us from womb to tomb and not a button more."

"That's stupid."

"Yes."

"It's not fair."

"No."

"I don't want all my time to run out." She said it quietly, not in panic, not with a scream.

He leaned close. "You want to ask a question, little sweetheart. I can tell. I can almost hear it. It's right there on the tip of your little pink tongue."

"I . . ."

"Go on . . . ask it. You can ask me anything at all."

Zephyr licked her dry, cracked lips. "Can I get *more* time?"

"Perhaps," he said. "But what would you want to do with that time? Don't answer quickly, because it's a very important question. If you could have another day, another week, even another year . . . what would you do with it? If you could have ten years, or twenty or thirty, what would you do with all those minutes, all those hours?"

Zephyr looked away for a moment. "Daddy said that I'm sick because of polmution."

"*Pollution*," John corrected. "And, yes. There are carcinogens in the air and the food and the dirt you play in."

"Car . . . car . . . what?"

"Bad things," said John. "The things that made you sick."

Zephyr thought about that. "Daddy said that I didn't have to *be* sick, but I was."

"Yes, that is true. All of it."

Zephyr's tiny hands slowly clenched into fists.

"It's not *fair*," she cried.

"Nothing is fair. But answer my question, little Zephyr. If you had more time, what would you do with it?"

She had to think about that. Even at six, she knew that she had to give the question real thought. When she answered, she said something that she didn't understand. Not then.

"I have so much work to do," she told John.

His smile grew and grew and his teeth were the blue-white of moonlight. "I know you do," he said. There was a strange little flicker in his eyes that she thought was a trick of the light. The black looked different for a moment. She saw brief shades of green and gray, as if his eyes were a pool of swirling colors. Or maybe it was more like the skin of a chameleon turning, changing. Then they were black again.

"I . . ." she began, but her voice faltered.

Then John bent and kissed her. First on the forehead and then on the lips. "Shh, my little sweetheart," he soothed, breathing his cold breath against her mouth so that as she inhaled the coldness entered her and the pain recoiled, retreating, taking some of the fever heat with it. "Go to sleep, my little angel. Shh . . . go to sleep and dream good dreams."

And she did.

When Zephyr opened her eyes again, it was morning. She felt so strange. Different. The fever had broken, and when she touched her hand to her forehead there was no heat. Even the sheets had dried.

It would be days before the doctors did the tests, and it would be weeks before the results proved what Zephyr already knew. There was no trace of cancer anywhere in her body. There were no more infections because of her compromised immune system.

It was a miracle, they all said. Her parents, the staff. The doctors.

A miracle.

Even at the age of six, Zephyr Bain knew that it was something else.

CHAPTER FIFTY

We drove into the Warehouse lot and parked near the rear door. Ghost made a few happy noises because he remembered this place. It wasn't the original Warehouse, which had been blown to atoms a few years ago by a psychotic killer named Erasmus Tull, who worked for Majestic Three. The new building was larger and looked like a modern business campus. You had to know where to look to see the security cameras, motion sensors, data scanners, and other doohickeys we have to ensure that no one gets close enough to bring harm to the doorstep. When I commissioned the new Warehouse, I spent a lot of Mr. Church's money making sure this place was state of the art. We entered through a nondescript door, and Sean watched, bemused, as I went through the ritual of placing my hand on a geometry scanner, looked into a retina scanner, breathed into a vapor biometric scanner, and stared into a facial-recognition scanner.

"They going to measure your dick next?" he snarked.

"That's already on file."

I swear to God I heard Ghost laugh. Maybe it was a cough, but the timing was perfect.

Sam Imura was waiting for us outside the security wing. We told him about what happened at Vee's office and gave him a recap of the car-stop incident.

"Always glad to have you back in Baltimore," he lied. "You bring joy wherever you go."

This time it was Sean who laughed.

"Fuck both of ya'll," I said.

Sam walked us up to a row of interrogation rooms. Through the two-way glass, I could see the prisoners. Both had been bandaged and were wearing unmarked orange disposable prisoner coveralls.

"We stripped and searched them in a Faraday cage," Sam said, "then moved them in here. We checked them for subcutaneous bugs and RFID chips but came up dry. The only bugs we found were in their clothes and vehicle."

Sam has a face that looks as if he should be wearing Samurai armor and standing by a mound of his enemy's heads. He's not tall, but he carries with him a great sense of power. He has the watchful, patient eyes of a sniper, which he is, and the general air of being a grown-up. I do not possess that latter quality, as I've been told by a large number of people over the years. He and Sean shook hands. They'd met at a memorial service following the Philadelphia drone attacks, so Sean knew that Sam and I worked together.

"Anything new on Vee Rejenko?" I asked.

Sam nodded. "He does a really good job of whitewashing his business holdings here in the States. We *know* a lot more than we can prove. We know his linen service is tied to prostitution, and we believe he's moving drugs through motels, a chain of locally owned fast-food places, convenience stores, and like that. We've pulled his tax records and we're running all of his licensed holdings through the system. In my experience, criminals like Vee aren't usually as smart as they think they are. Even with good accountants and good lawyers, they're actually breaking laws. If we dig hard enough and look closely enough, we'll find where they've cut a corner a little too close. Remember, it was taxes that tripped up Al Capone. Much as the Feds would have liked to put him away for murder, it was taxes that put him behind bars."

"All that matters is that Vee gets taken out of play," I said.

Sean shook his head. "If Vee's somehow responsible for killing that girl," he said, "then he should pay for that."

Sam frowned. "I understand how you feel, Detective, but unless you *want* us to break the law we have to play the cards we're dealt. We will find a way to take Vee Rejenko down. Put that in the bank."

"Besides," I said, "prison can be a damn unfriendly place. Especially if Rejenko goes in with all his financial assets frozen. He won't be able to buy protection."

What I didn't say out loud was that we could make life very difficult for Vee in any prison to which he might be sent. It may be an urban myth that prisoners don't abide a child molester—and a pimp turning out a runaway teen girl is no big thing—but there is a dial that someone can always turn on men in long-term lockup. Privileges. Give a couple of the hard-timers a chance to earn extra cash to buy cigarettes, food, whatever, or offer them a better prison job, and they'll do a lot for you. The short-eyes thing works well with guards, though. A lot of them are family men. There are very creative ways to make prison life an even worse hell. Is it wrong? Is it immoral and illegal? Sure. But Holly was fourteen, and justice was a kinky bitch sometimes.

"Have the bugs I planted picked up anything?" I asked.

"Vee made a series of phone calls," said Sam, "but he has some kind of scrambler on his phone. We're trying to decode it, but, like the bugs he planted on Sean, the scrambler is top of the line. An encoding algorithm we haven't seen before. I'm told it might take some time to crack. Yoda said something about a random sequence modulation changing the encryption dynamic. Tell you the truth, I stopped listening."

"Yoda?" echoed Sean.

"He's our number-two computer expert," said Sam. "And the sad thing is, Yoda is his actual first name. His parents met at a midnight showing of one of the *Star Wars* films."

Sean said, "I once arrested a woman on a homicide beef. She had two kids, two little girls. One was named Rainbow Brite and the other was named My Little Pony. Not making this up."

"I had a Justin Case once," I said. "He was selling guns and used his real name as a slogan for selling hot assault rifles: *Just in Case You Need It.*"

"People are strange," said Sam, and that was something else we could all agree on.

I told Sam about the texts. "Add that to the mix."

"Is that connected to this?" asked Sean, frowning.

"Unknown," I said, "but likely. Yoda's working on that, too."

We went over and looked through the glass at the prisoners, and Sam said, "Couple of geniuses. Their wallets were full of every kind of card, including driver's licenses, gym memberships, and debit cards."

"I always prefer stupid criminals," I said. Both Sean and Sam nodded. It was probably the only common ground we could stand on together.

"Fellow with the knife cut is Alexej Broz, thirty-three," said Sam.

"Guy with the dog bites is Bartoloměj Fojtik, twenty-nine. Czech nationals with applications in for U.S. citizenship. No criminal records here in the States. No wants or warrants except for Fojtik, who has some outstanding parking tickets. Gets more interesting overseas. We ran deep background through Interpol and the Policie České Republiky, and although neither has a criminal record, we got an anomalous return on both police and military records in the Czech Republic."

"Anomalous in what way?"

"Their backgrounds have been mostly erased, but I established that they're ex-military. Nothing special, not the 601st Special Forces Group. Nikki found references to a Desátník B. Fojtik and a Rotmistr A. Broz."

I translated for Sean. "Fojtik was a corporal and Broz was a sergeant first class."

Sam said, "Everything else is gone, so it's a good bet they ran a tapeworm to erase their service records."

"What's a tapeworm?" asked Sean.

"It's a computer program designed to hunt down and either alter or erase specific data files," Sam explained.

"And you were able to find traces of that in the government computers of a foreign country?"

Sam's face didn't change, but there was a slight stiffening of his posture. It was enough of a signal to suggest that he wanted me to handle this.

"Yeah," I said. "We can do that."

"So that's what . . . ? More of NSA data-mining bullshit?"

"Something like that, but we're not spying on American citizens," I said, trying to sound pious.

Sam said, "They were discharged a year or so before they moved here to Baltimore, and since then they've been employed as 'supervisors' in Vee's linen services."

Linen services were often tied to organized crime. Because it was very hard to prove how many towels, sheets, and other cloth goods are ever delivered, used, washed, and reused, it allowed a gaping revenue hole that was convenient for laundering money from illegal operations. It was a perfect recipe for cooking books. And the connection to hotels helped support the prostitution side of the business.

We looked through the glass at Bartoloměj Fojtik. He had white gauze bandages around both forearms, his right hand, and his throat, and there were butterfly stitches on his face. Ghost stood on his hind legs with his front paws on the edge of the window frame, wagging his tail.

"They've both asked for lawyers," said Sam. "They wanted to make calls."

"And—?" asked Sean.

"I couldn't find the phone."

"Imagine that."

Sam looked at me. "One more thing, and it's about those bugs."

"Hit me."

Sam glanced at Sean and then back to me and then raised an eyebrow.

"Go on, Sam. Sean knows how to keep his mouth shut," I said, meaning it as much for my brother as for Sam.

"We plugged the surveillance bugs into MindReader," said Sam. "Instead of cracking their software, the bugs uploaded a virus that nearly crashed our system. So far, it looks like we pulled the plug in time, but Bug's running system checks."

"That's just swell," I said. The thought of MindReader taking a hit with all this going on was scary. It didn't make my heart swell with affection for our prisoners. Behind the glass, Fojtik looked very scared. Good. Fear was useful. "Time for a heart to heart. Sean, you want to join me?"

"Yes, I damn well do."

"Good cop or bad cop?" I asked.

His look was scathing. "I think we already know which one of us is the bad cop."

Sam actually winced. I sighed. Ghost gave me a pitying look.

We went in.

INTERLUDE NINE

THE EDUCATION OF ZEPHYR BAIN
5400 SAND WAY NE
SEATTLE, WASHINGTON
WHEN SHE WAS ELEVEN

When she was eleven, she thought he was a vampire. He came to her at night. Always at night. Zephyr was sure she had never seen John the Revelator in sunlight. Not once in the years since his first visit, and never once since.

She came into her room and he was there. "John! Where have you been? Why were you gone so long? It's been a whole year!"

John stood in the shadows, his back to her, looking out the open window. Midnight snow fell slowly. "Sometimes I have to go far away."

She rushed across the room and wrapped her arms around him, pressed her head against his broad back. She sobbed as she held him, surprised by her own tears. "I thought you weren't coming back."

John turned very slowly, carefully, peeling her arms away and then gathering her into his. He wore a long black coat over a white shirt and black pants. His face looked different, but Zephyr was used to that. Sometimes he looked completely different. He pulled her against him and kissed her hair. "It's all right, my sweet. I'll always come back. I told you that a long time ago."

"But a whole *year?*"

"What's a year?" he asked. "A beat of the world's heart. It's nothing. A breath drawn in and let out, and a century has passed."

It was the kind of thing he sometimes said. Poetry, or something similar. Like when she asked him once how old he was and he said, "I don't know. No one does."

Like that.

"Where did you go?" she asked. "I asked Uncle Hugo, but he wouldn't tell me."

235

John only shook his head.

"Why did you come back?" she demanded.

"To see you," he said. "To tell you that I love you."

"My mom's sick," she said abruptly.

"Yes. She has cancer."

Zephyr pushed back from him. "You *know*?"

"I know."

"But . . . how? We just found out?"

John shrugged.

"It's the same kind of cancer I had."

"How does that make you feel?" he asked. "To know that she is dying of a peasant disease?"

"It sucks! It's not right. How come that gardener isn't sick? How come the maids aren't sick? How come it's Mom? How does it make sense that *they* get to live and my mom has to die?"

"Everyone dies, Zephyr. You almost did."

She met his eyes and then shifted her gaze. They had never really talked about what happened that first night when she was so sick and he appeared in her room. She tried to bring the subject up a dozen times, but he refused to be drawn into that conversation. All he would say when she begged him to explain what happened to her cancer was more nonsense. He patted his coat pocket and said, "I took it with me. It's like a little mouse. Hear it go cheep-cheep-cheep?"

That was it. After that he would act as if she never asked a question, and over time she stopped asking and merely accepted that he had somehow taken her sickness away. Not just the cancer but all sickness. She never had a cold or a sniffle or anything. At first her parents and the household staff laughed about it and toasted it at holidays, but eventually the laughs faltered, their happy glances turned suspicious, and they stopped talking about it, too. When Zephyr demanded that Uncle Hugo explain it to her, the big man only laughed and changed the subject.

"Can you help my mom?" Zephyr asked.

John smiled and shook his head. She didn't know if it was an admission that he couldn't help her or a statement that he wouldn't.

"She's going to *die*," she repeated, her fists clenched in anger and frustration.

"And you're going to live" was John's answer.

He took her hand and drew her over to the window. The snow covered everything now. Only a thin coating, but the sky was pregnant with more. It was midnight snow, and no footfall had tainted it. Not a person, not a deer, not a squirrel.

"The world was once as pure as this," he said softly. "Once upon a time."

"What happened?" she asked.

"People happened," he said, and then sighed. "So many people. Trampling the snow, leaving footprints, pissing in it, turning it to black slush that is without beauty."

Zephyr looked up at him. "It's just snow."

"No," he said. "It's purity. The difference is important, Zephyr. It's the reason I came to you in the first place. It's the reason your Uncle Hugo and I do so much work together. It's why I do so much to help his friends, and to help people who see things as clearly as he does. There are a few—a pitiable few—who can see with clearer eyes and understand with sharper minds." He paused, and for a moment his voice softened as if he was commenting to himself rather than to her. "Colder minds, yes. Clarity and courage can only come from such coldness."

"What?" she asked, confused.

John took a breath and cut a look at her, back again in the present moment. "Look at it, Zephyr," he said, nodding at the unbroken whiteness. "Behold purity."

"Okay, sure," she said. "But if there weren't any people there wouldn't be anyone to see how pretty it is."

"Hmm, true," he conceded. "But how many people are really necessary to see it and appreciate it? The more crowded the world, the less of the earth they can see. There was a time when people had no choice but to look at the world and see it in all its many forms and aspects."

He sounded wistful, as if it was his own memory about which he spoke. John was like that sometimes, Zephyr knew. He could be simple and practical, and at other times he was a dreamer. She wondered if that was how all vampires were. If he *was* a vampire.

They watched the snow fall for a long, long time.

He said, "You won the school science fair."

"Huh?" she said, surprised. "Oh. Yeah. Sure. You knew about that?"

"I pay very close attention to everything that happens with you, Zephyr. Even when I'm not around, you're never far from my thoughts."

"It was just some dumb science fair, though."

He turned to her, and the soft light from the snowy yard cast half of his face in paleness while the other half remained in deep shadow. "No," he said very seriously, "it is so very exciting. Your Uncle Hugo is so proud of you. He was bursting with it. As am I."

"Proud? Of my stuff with robots . . . ?" she asked, incredulous. "All I did was make some dumb ordinary robots do more than they were made to do."

"Yes, and what did you do?" He clearly knew but coaxed her into saying it.

"Well, I attached metal spider legs to the Roomba so it could crawl over an obstacle course and clean furniture and get to hard-to-reach places."

"Yes. And . . . ?"

"And I made a little automatic trigger from a perfume bottle so that the small-sized quadcopter drone could spray antibacterial spray over surfaces inside the house after people have been in a room. It was silly. Anyone could do it."

"You know that's not true, my sweet. The other children in the science fair were jealous of you."

"No, they weren't," she said, but she said it in a way that showed her doubt. *Were* they jealous? Some of them looked at her weird, and Mark Chang didn't even talk to her after she won. Suzie Kirtley was like that, too.

"They're afraid of you," he said.

Zephyr stared at him in frank astonishment. *"Afraid* . . . ?"

"Oh, yes."

"Why?"

He smiled but didn't answer.

Not then, anyway.

CHAPTER FIFTY-ONE

Sean and I sat on wooden chairs across from Bartoloměj Fojtik. His bandaged wrists were cuffed to a chain that was attached to a D ring on the table. He glanced at us, but his eyes bugged as Ghost came in and sat down near him.

"Get this dog away from me," Fojtik said, jerking away as far as the cuffs would let him, which wasn't far. Ghost bared his teeth to display the six titanium spikes. I clicked my tongue, and Ghost stopped showing off and sat like a sphinx, eyes dark and alert.

"I am going to sue your ass," yelled Fojtik. "When my lawyer gets here, I am going to *own* you and I will have this fucking mutt put down."

He had a thick accent, but his vocabulary was pretty good. Stilted and oddly formal the way many Eastern Europeans speak when they're working their way through English. Even so, I replied to him in Czech. Partly to confuse him and partly because I didn't want Sean to know what I was saying.

"Listen to me, asshole," I said quietly. "If you threaten my dog again, I'll let him chew your balls off. He'd like that and you wouldn't."

Fojtik stared at me, doubt clouding his features. Suddenly the situation had changed on him. He looked at me and Sean and then out the window. I could see him working it out. He hadn't been booked and he hadn't been given his phone call. This didn't look like a police station, and I was speaking to him in his own language. Too much of that didn't compute if this was a simple arrest.

"You're in very deep shit," I continued. "If you're willing to cooperate, then the worst that will happen is we deport your ass back to the Czech Republic. Or if you're willing to go the whole way, then we can put you into a relocation program somewhere out West. Give you a double-wide and a car and a job far away from anyone who ever heard of you. That would mean you get to stay here and live the American dream. Wife, two kids, a dog—well, maybe not a dog—an SUV, a low golf handicap, and a membership to the Rotary Club. And you don't go to prison."

He stared at me, mouth open but not saying anything.

"*Fuck* with me," I said, "make this more difficult than it has to be, then my dog chomping your nut sack will be the very least of your problems. You are not among friends unless you *make* friends, and believe me when I tell you that I am a hard sell."

Sean was looking at me, too. My use of Czech only mildly surprised him. Sean had gotten the gene for math and I'd gotten the one for languages. He didn't like it that he couldn't follow what I was saying to the prisoner. However, Fojtik leaned forward and answered in a way that was universally understood.

"Fuck you," he said very slowly and precisely.

Sean wasn't ruffled. He even smiled. "You work for Vsevolod Rejenko."

"I do not know this name."

"You work for Superior Linen, which is owned by Vsevolod Rejenko. His name is on your paychecks," said Sean.

Fojtik grinned. "I do not know anyone of this name."

There was something wrong with this picture. Fojtik was acting tough and talking trash, but he was sweating bullets. I could smell the sour stink of genuine fear coming off him. Ghost smelled it, too, and was twitching with nervous energy, his predator instincts kicked into high gear.

"If you're afraid of what Vee might do," I said in English, "believe me when I tell you that we can run interference. We're going to put him out of business."

"I do not know this person," he said, "so why should I care?"

I tried another tack. "Just so you know the stakes here, cupcake, this is a murder investigation. We're going to hang Vee for kidnap, corruption of a minor, human trafficking, conspiracy to commit murder, and felony murder. You are an accessory to all of that, and the reason you're not getting a phone call is because we're debating whether to label you as a terrorist. How'd you like that? Terrorists don't get bail, they don't get constitutional protections, and they don't get conjugal visits. What they get is a cell in some remote spot that makes the dark side of the moon seem like a Miami resort. I'm not much of a fan of enhanced interrogation—you know what that means, yes? water sports?—but you and your friends are making sex slaves out of little girls and then killing them with nanobots or maybe rabies. So, yeah, I'm thinking that I might even sit in on some of the fun and games once we lock you away in a black site that doesn't even have a name."

Fojtik was good. But no one's that good. He tried to keep the tough-guy smirk on his face, but I let him take a good, long look at my face. My smile only goes about so far, and doesn't reach my eyes at all. I know that. I've been told. And there are spooky shadows in my eyes. I've seen that in the mirror. *I* wouldn't want to be the guy in cuffs on the other side of the table from me, and I *like* me.

Fojtik's eyes flicked away and he mumbled something.

"Sorry, lamb chop," I said. "Didn't catch that."

"Fuck you," he said a little louder, but still didn't look at me.

"Dude," I said. "I admire the stoic tough-guy shtick as much as the next Bruce Willis fan, but you're not thinking this through. Vee's lawyers aren't going to gallop to the rescue. You are actually fucked. I can Google the word for you. Fucked. There's your picture with a wet towel over your face. Whatever. You got only one play and that's to—"

And my damn cell buzzed again with another text. I nearly tore my pocket pulling it out, and then froze when I saw a single word on the screen:

Run!

Beside me, Sean gasped. The hair on Ghost's back stood up straight as needles, and he began to growl. Two tears broke from the corners of Fojtik's eyes and ran down over his cheeks. They were bright red.

Sean said, "What the hell . . . ?"

Fojtik stared at us in confusion. "What? What's wrong?"

He tried to raise his hands to touch his face but the handcuffs prevented it, so he bent his head down instead. The drops reached his chin and fell onto the tabletop. Fojtik stared down at them and suddenly went rigid as he saw the color.

"No," he said, but then he gave a sudden, violent cough that sprayed the table with dark-red droplets. Fojtik stared at the blood in obvious and total terror, and for a moment he was absolutely stock-still. Then he uttered the loudest shriek I've ever heard come from a human throat. It soon disintegrated into a violent fit of coughing. He couldn't cover his mouth because of the cuffs, so each cough misted the air around him with pink, and each cough hit him like a solid body punch. He twitched and spasmed as his lungs convulsed.

He uttered a shriek that stabbed the ears and punched us in the face and tore the air to rags.

"Joe!" shouted Sean as he shot to his feet, but I was already up and moving around the table.

"Please!" Fojtik gasped, fighting to get the words out between coughs. "No . . . no . . . no! I did . . . not tell them . . . anything. You cannot . . ."

"What's wrong?" demanded Sean, but Fojtik bent forward and grabbed his head and began twisting from side to side as another scream ripped its way out of his lungs. Blood streamed from his eyes and nose and ears.

"He's having a fit!" Sean yelled. "Get a medic."

"No-no-no-no!" cried the prisoner. He turned and stared at the door. "No! *Do not do this. I—*"

Anything else he might have said was drowned by a vicious burst of coughing that spewed from his mouth. It splashed the table and spattered us. His eyes bulged from their sockets and a deep shudder ripped through him. He croaked out a single, final word in a wet gurgle— "*God!*"—and then he fell sideways, thrashing and jerking. If it hadn't been for the cuffs, he would have fallen to the floor. Ghost began barking in fear and panic.

"He's going into convulsions," yelled Sean. "Joe, *help me!*"

I turned toward the pane of one-way glass and bellowed for a medic. Ghost shot to his feet and began barking furiously, muzzle wrinkled, teeth bared.

Which was when Fojtik tore the D ring out of the table.

It's not supposed to be possible. Not sure even Bunny could do it. But Fojtik surged up with a bellow and in three sharp, savage yanks tore the setscrews out of the hardwood and metal. The D ring flew through the air and hit Sean in the shoulder, spinning him so hard that my brother smacked face-forward against the wall. Fojtik was still coughing, but now there was another sound coming from him between the coughs.

Growls.

Low, savage, and feral. It was not a human sound.

Not even a little.

CHAPTER FIFTY-TWO

Ghost backed away from him, barking furiously. Ghost isn't afraid of much, but there was panic in his eyes.

Fojtik stood wide-legged, coughing, panting, blood running down his body, eyes wild and inhuman. That's the word for it. I looked for the man in there, but there wasn't even the fear that had been evident a moment ago. It was gone, and all other human emotions had fled from that face. All that was left was a *thing*. The eyes were glazed for a long moment, then they shifted toward me . . . and *changed*. It was not a physical change; they didn't actually turn a different color. No, this was subtler and somehow more frightening. Those eyes filled with a level of hatred, of raw hunger and unfiltered savagery. They were the eyes of something so wild it was beyond itself.

Without another moment's hesitation, it came at me.

For me.

Reaching with its cuffed hands, the fingers twitching and scratching the air as if clawing through it to me. Fojtik slammed into me and drove me back against the wall, snapping at my throat with bloody teeth. I hit the wall hard enough to rattle my teeth, but I managed to get a forearm up under his chin, and those teeth snapped shut with a *klak!* an inch from my Adam's apple. I brought my right knee up and braced it against his stomach, and then used my free right hand to swing over his forearms and smash him across the jaw with a palm-heel shot. It turned his head just as he spat blood at me. The wetness splashed the side of my neck and shoulder but didn't get into my face. The blow staggered him only for a moment. He snarled and tried to choke me, but I was pivoting now, using all the strength of my standing leg, hips, waist, and shoulder to put torque and speed behind a series of chopping punches to his floating ribs, upper ribs, and ear. He lost his grip and stumbled sideways as I slid down the wall and landed hard on my ass.

Fojtik whirled into Sean, hitting him hard, knocking them both down, grabbing as they fell. Sean saw those teeth and rammed his palms under Fojtik's chin even as they fell, but the impact dislodged his hands. Fojtik lunged forward, trying to bite Sean's face, but the angle was wrong, so instead he bit my brother's chest, clamping teeth around cloth and pinching the skin beneath. Sean cried out in pain, and my heart nearly froze in my chest. Was he bitten? Did the bite break the skin?

What was this?

There were too many ugly possibilities. Too many ways this could spin downward into bloody ruin.

And the memory of that single word of warning on my cell phone burned in my brain. It seemed to scream at me.

Run.

I didn't. Instead, I scrambled up and flung myself at Fojtik, smashing into him with my crossed forearms, hitting him on the side of the head and shoulder, slamming him away from Sean. His teeth were so tightly clamped that the impact jerked Sean sideways like a fish on a hook. I swarmed atop Fojtik and drove a series of two-knuckle punches into his cheek just below the nose, crunching his teeth, snapping them, ruining his mouth until his bite released, and then I whipped his face away from Sean with a left-hand slap that emptied his eyes for a moment. But he blinked once and the animal fury was right back there. He snarled again and tried to crane his head forward, coughing as he did so, but I twisted away again and took the bloody spray on my side. I pivoted back and jammed the heel of my left palm against his forehead so hard that it smashed the back of his skull onto the hard floor, and then I punched him in the throat.

Hard, leaning into it, putting way too much mass and force into it. Destroying him.

Fojtik made a single, harsh, gurgling noise. It was the sound a plastic fork would make in a garbage disposal.

Then he sagged back, deflating as the rage and life fled from him. Leaving stillness.

And horror.

JONATHAN MABERRY

CHAPTER FIFTY-THREE

The door burst open and Sam rushed in, gun in hand. Alarm buzzers screamed and there were footsteps in the hall. I rushed over to Sean and tore his shirt open, saw an ugly red bruise that was already darkening to the color of a rotting plum. But no blood.

Jesus Christ . . . no blood.

I cupped my hand around the back of his neck and bent close to press my forehead against his. He resisted for a moment, then leaned into me. Ghost was still barking, but he had backed all the way into a corner. Sean and I pushed away from each other, and I gave Ghost a single, sharp command to be silent. He stopped barking, but a line of hair stood stiff as a brush all along his back.

Sam Imura looked from Fojtik to me to Sean and then back down at the dead man. He had seen it all through the glass, but when Fojtik attacked me we fell against the door, blocking it from being opened. By the time Sam got in, it was all over. It had happened that fast.

Seconds that felt like hours.

Without saying a word to me, Sam pulled out his phone and made an internal call, requesting a full biohazard team. Then he lowered the cell and looked at me, his voice low and filled with false calm. "Is this Seif al Din?"

I shook my head.

"I don't think so," I said. "I think it's rabies."

My cell phone was on the floor, and when I picked it up the text screen was blank, the message removed as if it had never been there.

Who sent it? And why?

"Jesus!" Sean suddenly cried and pushed past me and dashed from the room. I realized why and raced after him, but when we wheeled

around and crashed through the door to the second interrogation room it was already too late.

It was awash in blood.

We stood there, staring at the body of Alexej Broz. His eyes bulged from their sockets and his mouth was open in a final, silent, eternal scream. The entire front of his skull was mashed flat, and there was a dark smear on the inside of the door from where he had slammed his head again and again and again. Bits of hair and bone were caught in the smear, and when I looked down at Broz I could see lumps of gray brain matter.

Sean came out of the room, grabbed my shoulder, and spun me around. His face was flushed with panic. "What the hell is happening?" he demanded. "Is this what happened to that girl?"

All I could do was stand there and stare.

INTERLUDE TEN

Zephyr loved staying at Uncle Hugo's house in Canada.

Well, it wasn't really a house. It was a castle that Hugo had bought from a bankrupt family in Scotland and transported, brick by brick, to be reassembled on an island in the St. Lawrence River. The castle had fifty-nine rooms, actual battlements, and—if Hugo was to be believed—a dungeon. She never got to see the dungeon, though. It was off-limits to her, and the elevator was guarded by a pair of mean-looking Korean men who never spoke or smiled and looked as if they'd enjoy cutting the throat of anyone who tried to get past them.

Hugo Vox was not her real uncle, but he was close enough. He and her father had done considerable work together and made tens of millions from government and private contracts. Hugo was the investment capitalist and H. Andrew Bain was the developer. They employed some of the top designers in the fields of robotics, genetics, pharmaceuticals, industrial chemicals, and a dozen different branches of technology. Although Zephyr was only a teenager, she was learning how it all worked, and while her father was reluctant to share the behind-the-scenes details, Hugo and John were notably frank with her.

Hugo's mother, Eris, lived at the castle, and she was one of the most beautiful women Zephyr had ever seen, in movies or in real life. She had to be old, because Hugo was at least thirty-five or maybe older, but she didn't look it. Zephyr thought she looked like an even split between Helen Mirren and Susan Sarandon. She hoped she'd be that pretty when she was old.

If she got old. The cancer was gone from her body but never from her mind. Long ago, John had told her that he'd filled her up with more time. That was how he always put it. But he never said how much.

Zephyr wondered if there was a clock ticking away inside her genes, waiting for time to run out.

Sometimes when she was alone for hours on the island Zephyr wandered the grounds and thought about life and death. She thought about the people she knew and the ones she saw on the news, and she wondered who among them really deserved to be alive. And who would do the world some good by dying. Zephyr often composed lists in her mind. It made her happy to add names to both lists. A lot of poor people were on her "No" list, grouped by country rather than race, because it was never about race for her. It was about who gave something to the world and who just took from it. Some of her father's friends were on her "No" list, too. The ones who took other kinds of things—oil from the ground, purity from the air and the water, and the future from the earth through damage they did to the climate. They did that as if the future didn't matter, and some of them had kids. It was nuts. John called them the Suicidalists, and Zephyr hated every one of them. She even put some of Hugo's friends and business associates on her list.

Almost everyone in the fields of computers, robotics, and related technologies was on her "Yes" list. They mattered. They were doing something useful. So she whiled her time away making lists as if she were God. John told her that was okay.

She found John seated in one of a pair of heavy leather chairs that were positioned in front of a dying fireplace in a darkened study. She climbed into the other chair and sat in silence with him for a long time, watching the fire grow colder and then go out. When there was not even a trace of a glow, she turned to him. Without the firelight, his face was mostly lost in shadow and the strange lighting made him look old, almost ancient. What a strange thing that was, but Zephyr didn't comment on it. She didn't even think about it too deeply. Although there was much about her friend that she longed to know, some instinct inside her mind kept her from exploring certain corridors of speculation, and even of analysis. John was John. He wasn't like anyone else. Even now, at the wise age of fourteen, she still thought that he might not be entirely human. Or entirely real.

"Have you been making your lists again?" he asked.

"Yes."

He nodded. "Good. It's going to matter."

"What do you mean?"

That was all John said. They sat together for almost an hour, watching the logs burn. The logs burned and burned, but they didn't seem to be consumed by the fire.

CHAPTER FIFTY-FOUR

So, yeah, I opened a file on it.

Whatever was going on was a lot bigger even than a poor murdered girl in a Baltimore fleabag hotel. There were five dead teens and now two dead adults. There was surveillance, and someone was using exotic technology to hack my phone and send me warnings.

It was Sam's shop, though, so he got on the phone with Mr. Church and Aunt Sallie. Sean and I were covered with blood that was almost certainly infected with rabies. Ghost had been spattered, too. The forensics team did a full biohazard lockdown on that part of the Warehouse, cleared all staff out of the interrogation area, and put anyone who had come anywhere near the dead men under observation. Ghost was put in a cage, and I gave him a complex series of commands to tell him to cooperate with anyone who touched him. He was still spooked, but having orders to follow steadied him.

Sean and I were separated and sent to individual quarantine rooms. Once inside mine, I stripped down and entered a small shower stall, where I had to wash head to toe with harsh soaps. The soap smelled like shit, but I didn't care if it *was* shit, as long as it cleaned off all traces of the blood.

When I was done, I dressed in paper coveralls and was led under guard to an examination room. The guard looked nervous. I was his boss's boss, but he was under orders to shoot me if I freaked out. The only good-news part of that was the fact that instead of a Glock or a SIG he held a Snellig A-220 gas-dart pistol loaded with high-intensity gelatin darts filled with an amped-up version of the veterinary drug ketamine, along with a powerful hallucinatory compound. We call it "horsey." One shot and you drop like a rock and dream of polka-dot unicorns. The guard walked fifteen paces back, well beyond the range where an unarmed person might have a chance against someone with a gun. To make him feel a little better, I kept my hands in my pockets, though that was really to hide the fact that they were shaking.

I went down to the kennel to look in on Ghost. He'd been shampooed and seemed wretched and terrified. His reaction earlier was strange. He didn't attack Fojtik, and I wondered if he could somehow sense the presence of a contagious disease? Was that even possible?

I squatted down outside his cage. "How you doing, you old fuzz monster?"

He wagged and whined and clearly wanted to be petted. I wanted to be near him, to curl up with him. Dogs provide more than companionship. Their uncomplicated love and total loyalty offers a comfort to the soul that helps flick the reset button. He's been with me through some bad, bad moments, and even though I was the leader of our little pack, in some ways I felt that he was the stronger and I drew comfort from him. Not now, though. We were both scared and confused, and if there was comfort to be had neither of us knew where to look.

"It's okay, boy," I said to him. "It's all okay."

He gave me a trusting look that almost, but not entirely, hid his disbelief. Yeah, I know he's a dog, but he's not stupid. Ghost knew every bit as much as I did that it was not okay. Nothing was okay.

I got up and left with my two-legged watchdog in tow. The guard had barely said two words since he began his escort duties, and I wasn't feeling particularly chatty. We went to the armory, and I told him to get me a new earbud and mic. He did. The mic is the size of a mole and is flesh-colored. I removed the film on the back to expose the adhesive and pressed it to my cheek near the corner of my mouth. The earbud was also designed to blend with my skin tone, and it went into my left ear. A signal booster and Wi-Fi charger that was half the size of a pack of Tic Tacs went into my pocket. I tapped the earbud to reach Sam. He was somewhere in the building, and I didn't want to waste time looking for him in places where I might not be allowed.

"Go for Ronin," he said, using his combat call sign. That told me that the building was on secure lockdown.

"I know this is your shop, Sam," I said, "but I'm labeling this as a Special Projects gig."

"I figured," Sam said. "I'm prepping Alpha Team now, and they'll hit Vee's office on your go order. We've had bird drones in the trees and on the roof since you left there. Still the workday, so no one's left."

"Okay. Put some topspin on my blood work, because I want to accompany Alpha."

"I'll arrange for clothes and gear."

"Send some guys to sweep Vee's home. Hazmat suits and full safety protocols. Pull up the floorboards. Ditto for any other private or corporate holdings. Tear his world apart."

"Understood. But until we get the lab results make sure you mind your keeper," he said.

I quietly damned him to the corner of hell where they give the inmates daily red-ant enemas. Then I tapped the earbud for the central command channel. Church was on the line in two seconds.

"Cowboy," he said, "Ronin gave me a sitrep. What can you add?"

"Is Bug on the line?"

"Right here, Cowboy," said Bug. He sounded scared, too. "What do you need?"

"So far three of Vee Rejenko's people were infected with whatever this was," I began. "More, if the other kids were part of his operation. If Vee isn't behind it, then he's pissed off at the people who are. Maybe someone's using this to crowd him out of his action. Maybe it's a turf war between the Czechs and the Russians. I don't know, but I want to know. This thing is sophisticated in two different ways, the nanotechnology and the pathogen. That gives us two separate starting places. Put as many people as you need to on this."

"On it," Bug said, and dropped out of the call.

To Church I said, "No more bullshit. We need to talk to Dr. Acharya."

"He's still out at the DARPA camp. They're not putting anyone on the phone or allowing them Internet access."

"Even with this?"

"This is an hour old, Cowboy. The Department of Defense has spent decades building its speed bumps, walls, and patterns of red tape."

"Okay, okay," I said irritably, "but that's your problem. Sic Aunt Sallie on them. They're all afraid of her."

"I already have her on this."

"Okay, here's how I want to play it. I'm going to take Alpha Team and kick down the doors at Vee's office. If he doesn't have anything useful to tell me, then I'm going to grab Rudy and go out to the DARPA camp myself. I can't wait for chain of command. If I have to, I'll literally kick down some doors."

"You may have to," said Church.

"I'm in the *mood* to. And maybe kick some ass, too."

"Wear heavy boots."

"Count on it. Now, listen, boss, because I'm working on a wild theory, but I don't know if the science supports what I'm thinking."

"Which is what?" asked Church.

"That the nanobots are somehow causing the disease. Or, maybe, regulating it somehow. From what I know of rabies, it doesn't hit this fast. That means it's either weaponized or regulated, or both. The original report from the girl's death at the Imperial said that she was screaming and coughing, and I saw that with Fojtik. Far as I know, coughing isn't a major rabies symptom, but it makes one hell of a delivery system for a weaponized disease. Our bad guys are somehow keeping the disease in check until they need it to go active, keeping it chambered like a bullet. Rudy said that nanites can deliver drugs, right? And that they can be used to regulate hormonal secretions. Well, maybe that's what we're seeing here. Is that possible? A bioweapon with a nanite control system?"

"Possibly," said Church. "There's been research about using pertussis—whooping cough—as a delivery system for pathogens that aren't in themselves airborne. I know for a fact that something like this is in development. Not with rabies, as far as I know, but with other things. The Czech nanotechnology being used to control their slave-labor force is built along similar lines. There are others, too. Nothing as sophisticated as you're suggesting, but that's the danger with cutting-edge technology. Eventually, someone cuts deeper."

"Rudy said the same thing."

"It's the real estate on which we live," said Church. "Ethnic-specific bioweapons weren't possible until Cyrus Jakoby created them."

"Right. Now, add the texts I've been getting to the mix," I said, and told him about the warning I got right before Fojtik went nuts.

"This is disturbing on many levels," said Church.

"They must have the Warehouse bugged."

"Or they knew that the signal for the nanites to trigger the rabies was being sent."

I said, "Sent by who? A mole?"

"Seems so. If they sent one warning, they may share more complete information going forward. Keep your phone with you."

"I don't have it. It's with my gear in the biohazard unit."

"Get it back. The team can sterilize it for you, but for now don't change any of the internal workings or remove the SIM card. We want that contact."

"Yes, we do," I said. "Christ, I wish this made more sense. I feel like we're catching the smallest glimpse of something and missing the whole picture."

"How is that any different from how we usually come into these things, Captain?"

"I know," I said glumly, and I thought about Rudy's premonition on the plane. On impulse, I told Church about it. He isn't the kind to dismiss anything out of hand.

"Now, isn't that interesting?" he said quietly. "About the rabies, Captain, this might be even worse than you think. If your theory is correct and the rabies is already in the victims' system, then you do understand what that means?"

I closed my eyes. "Yes. When it's that advanced, rabies is fatal in almost every case. Which means everyone currently infected is dead; they just don't know it yet. Wait, I remember reading something a while back about inducing a coma and treating rabies victims—"

"The Milwaukee Protocol," supplied Church. "Yes, there has been some limited success with that. A coma is induced to protect the brain from further infection and to allow the immune system time to produce antibodies. It can take days or weeks, and it's unlikely it could be arranged to cope with a widespread outbreak. I'll cycle Dr. Cmar in on this," said Church, and then he was gone, too.

Rudy wasn't wearing an earbud earlier, so I couldn't connect with him that way. I went off in search of my phone.

INTERLUDE ELEVEN

Zephyr made her first friend when she was fourteen. Her first peer friend. It wasn't someone she expected ever to become friends with. Sometimes great things happen in unexpected ways.

The freshman dance was half over and so far six different boys had asked her to dance, so that was nice. Two of them tried to grab her ass, which was less nice. One of them kissed her, and he tasted like onions, so that was gross. She left that one on the dance floor and went into the girls' bathroom to rinse out her mouth. Zephyr always brought mouthwash and a toothbrush with her, as well as Purell and antibacterial wipes. People were filthy, and it wasn't just their thoughts.

There was another girl in the bathroom. Carly Schellinger, who was fifteen but looked five years older. One of those tall, thin, black-haired mysterious girls, she was German-American but looked like the French girls Zephyr had seen in Paris. Very chic, very well dressed, the kind who knew how to stand so that everyone looked at her but no one dared bother her. The kind who looked as if she could kill you with her eyes and definitely could gut someone with a few words. Zephyr worshipped and envied her.

Carly was standing with her hip against a sink, smoking a joint. She didn't even pause or try to fan the smoke away when Zephyr entered. Instead, she gave her three seconds of frank appraisal and then held the joint out. Zephyr hesitated, then accepted it, but it was the first time she'd ever smoked anything. She inhaled wrong, gagged, choked, coughed, and handed it back.

"No," said Carly. "Take another hit."

Zephyr didn't want to, but she did. And another.

Carly nodded approval. "Always do it right," she said. "Don't end on a mistake. Ever. Otherwise, that's what you'll remember."

"Who taught you that?" asked Zephyr, impressed.

"No one," said Carly with a cruel little smile.

In a little while they were handing the joint back and forth. Twice other girls came in, and Carly withered them with her stare and they left to find another bathroom.

"You're that brainiac, right?" said Carly after a while. "Robots and computers and all that."

"I guess."

"You did that household artificial-intelligence thing. RoboMaid or something."

"That was what I called it in the science fair. I filed the patent under the name Calpurnia," said Zephyr. "It's from—"

"Julius Caesar's wife. Shakespeare. Yeah, same school, same reading list, you know. Why name it after her, though?"

"Calpurnia was intuitive," said Zephyr. "She believed in omens and portents. I designed the AI to learn from my family and the staff at our house, and I included items from everyone's schedules, browser history, conversation, menus, and like that into her adaptive-learning code so she can anticipate anything we need. She gets us all ready in the morning, decides what we should eat, tells us jokes, knows us."

Carly raised her eyebrows. "Like Siri?"

"Smarter than that stuff. They're just programmed with responses that make them sound interactive, but they're not. Calpurnia is. And she gets smarter every day. The more she interacts with people, the more she learns how to think like them."

"A thinking robot? Cool."

"A software system," corrected Zephyr. "But . . . yeah."

Carly nodded toward the bathroom door. The sounds of the party were muffled but loud. "They talk about you all the time, you know."

"Who? The other kids?"

"Fuck the other kids," said Carly. "I mean the teachers."

"Oh."

"They say you're a genius."

Zephyr shrugged.

"So am I," said the older girl. "A genius, I mean. There are six of us in the school. Us, Mark Chang, Suzie Kirtley, and the Berensen

JONATHAN MABERRY

twins. Six smartest kids in school and maybe the six smartest kids in Seattle."

"Oh."

Carly exhaled and considered Zephyr through the haze of smoke. "I'm numbers," she said.

"Huh?"

"You're computers and machines, but I'm numbers. Math's nothing to me. It's stupid easy." She laughed. "I know, I don't look it, but I even dream in numbers, patterns, systems. Makes a lot more sense to me than anything else. No idea where I get it from. My dad's a lawyer and my mom's a pair of tits who married well. I didn't get the tits, but I got brains from somewhere. Maybe one of my ancestors back in Germany was a math whiz. Who knows? Thing is, I could take the SATs now, baked as I am, and ace them." She took another hit.

"Oh."

"Stop saying 'Oh.' It makes you sound stupid."

"Oh . . . I mean, okay."

Carly handed back the joint. "I'm going into the military. My dad wants me to be a lawyer, but please. Mom wants me to become an accountant, but I'd rather stab myself."

"Why the military?"

"Why not the military? There's so much to do there. They all want to blow each other up. There's all that sexy technology. Stuff people like you want to build and I want to screw around with. I want to mess with people, and I don't want to do it at the country-club level, you know? Besides, it would piss my parents off big-time, so that makes it a lifestyle imperative."

Zephyr thought about this, then nodded. "I have some ideas about what I want to do with what I'm into," she said.

"Like?"

"Maybe military," said Zephyr.

"Bullshit. You're not the type. I can fake being normal and taking orders, but you never could."

"How do you know?"

"I know." Carly assessed her. "Maybe DARPA. You know what that is?"

"Yes."

"Really? Prove it."

"Defense Advanced Research Projects Agency," said Zephyr. "Of course I know about them. I competed in two of their robotics challenges."

Carly nodded as if the question had been a test. "I could see you working for them, maybe."

"Maybe," said Zephyr.

"They build some nasty shit, you know."

Zephyr shrugged.

"People think you're a goody two-shoes," said Carly. "Like you think your shit doesn't stink, like you're a prissy ass."

"Who says that?"

Another shrug. "Doesn't matter. I just know it's not true."

Zephyr took a slow drag this time, using the delay to think about that. "What do you mean?" she asked through her exhale.

"I've seen you around," said Carly. "I've had my eye on you, and I see how you watch people. Kids and teachers. I don't think you're putting yourself above them. Not all of them, anyway."

Zephyr said nothing.

"What I think you're doing," continued Carly, "is making choices."

"Choices?"

"About who matters and who doesn't. About who you'd let into your lifeboat and who you'd let drown."

"I don't understand."

"Yes, you do." When she handed the joint back, she let her fingers brush Carly's. The touch was soft, but it carried with it a palpable electricity that made the other girl's eyes jump. Carly withdrew her hand, took a long, hard hit on the joint, and then flicked the roach into the sink, where it sizzled out. Then she walked over and pushed the heavy trash can in front of the door, never once taking her eyes off Zephyr.

"You ever done this before?" she asked.

"Done what?" asked Zephyr, trying to sound cool, but her voice cracked.

Carly laughed a quiet cat laugh as she walked over to where Zephyr stood. She took Zephyr's face in both hands and kissed her. It was the softest, sweetest thing Zephyr had ever experienced.

CHAPTER FIFTY-FIVE

Sam found me while I was looking for him. He waved my minder away.

"Your blood work's clear, Joe. No rabies, no nanites. Sean's and Ghost's, too."

"What about Fojtik and Broz?"

"Both infected with rabies and whooping cough."

"Shit." I told him my theory about nanites controlling a bioweapon, and he nodded.

"Sounds freaky and impossible," said Sam, "so I'm betting that's what it is."

"It's fun to be us," I said.

"No," he said, "it's not. Look, Duffy and Alpha Team are leaving for Vee's office. Why don't you let them handle it and coordinate from the TOC?"

The Tactical Operations Center was the mission-control office upstairs.

"No. I want in."

"Joe, you've already had a rough day. Why push it?"

"And it's not a discussion. I don't want to pull rank here but—"

"But you are."

"Yeah, I guess I am."

He gave me a look that was mostly, but not entirely, unreadable. There was resentment in his dark eyes, and frustration. Not sure what else. Sam Imura and I had been friends for a long time, but I wasn't sure if we were anymore. Getting hurt last year had changed him in some way that I didn't yet understand. He was moving away from me and maybe from the DMS. It would hurt me to see him leave altogether, but I can't say it would surprise me.

Sam stepped aside and gestured toward the armory. "It's your case, Joe."

We studied each other. He gave me a very small, very enigmatic smile. Then he nodded and walked in the direction of the TOC, leaving me to interpret it any way I wanted. I turned to the guy who had been my escort. "Bring my dog to the staging area," I said.

He opened his mouth as if to protest, thought better of it—possibly taking into account his employment situation, his retirement plan, and his health coverage—gave me a single nod, and fled.

INTERLUDE TWELVE

THE BAIN ESTATE
5400 SAND WAY NE
SEATTLE, WASHINGTON
WHEN ZEPHYR WAS SIXTEEN

He came to her at night. Always at night.

Zephyr had tried to give him the passwords to bypass the home security system and access the priority functions of the AI household computer system, but John said that he didn't need them.

"Calpurnia and I are old friends," he told her, though he never explained what that meant. When he wanted to come in, he came in and never went through security at the gate or triggered an alarm. When the sun faded and the shadows claimed the yard and climbed the high walls of her family's mansion, he would arrive. Sometimes he would be waiting for her in the garden; at other times he would wake her with a kiss when everyone else was asleep.

On the night before her seventeenth birthday, as the clock ticked its way through the last hour, he came to her by moonlight. Zephyr's mother had been buried that morning and her father was downstairs in his study, weeping and drinking and sometimes yelling. John had gotten into the house in his own unexplained way. Past locks and guards and through the minefield of her father's grief and all the way to her room.

He said nothing at all, but he looked at her differently from the way he always had. Not as a man looks at a child but as a lover looks at a woman. She was in bed when he stepped out of the shadows between the two big windows, coming toward her as if he were stepping through a doorway.

Zephyr pulled the blanket aside and he lay down next to her. It was the first time they had made love, and the wrongness of it—a man of his age and an underage girl—had only set the night ablaze for them. Although Zephyr had made love with Carly, she was still a virgin in terms of a man's touch. He was pale and beautiful and dark and filled with magic. His skin was always cool to the touch, but his hands were warm.

She shuddered as he removed her pajamas, and her skin rippled with gooseflesh as he bent to kiss her between her breasts. When he entered her she gasped, not at the pain or the coldness of his body, but in a complete awe of beauty as something like a black flower opened inside her mind. The petals folded back, and instead of filling her with more darkness it revealed a hidden light. It burned like a newborn star, not yet formed, flowing with energetic potential, burning hot in the coldness of space, born of chaos.

The visions increased, expanded, filled every corner of her mind as their bodies moved together. She thought that she glimpsed the future, or at least its potential, as if she peered through a window at the world that was to come. She saw herself older, more beautiful, and beautifully cold. As John was cold. The cold of midnight and the cold of positive thought. A useful coldness that allowed her practicality and pragmatism to keep the weakness of sentimentality in check. She saw her robots—the ones she had already made and the ones that were still to come. Not clunky and feeble and clumsy but elegant in design and subtle in function. Schools of microscopic nanites swimming through blood vessels, attaching to glands and organs, claiming in her name everything they touched. She saw masses of mechanical insects flowing across the no-man's-land between warring armies, too small to be shot, too many to be stopped, smarter than their enemies because they learned from every encounter and each bit of individual data was instantly shared with the swarm. They learned as they attacked and they could not be stopped, and instead of guns they carried fragments of explosives that, collectively, were devastating. Other swarms crawling through the urban battlefields of ghetto and barrio, carrying bacteria instead of explosives, and all the more dangerous for it; vanishing through cracks in cheap walls and running beneath uncarpeted floors before emerging to wage a cleansing war on the unfit and the unwashed. She saw warships powered by nuclear engines and carrying death in silos and launchers, but with no human hand at the controls; instead, there was software of her design that would obey her and no other when she whispered to it. She saw computer-software systems that grew smarter and wiser at exponential rates, evolving so quickly that they learned cunning and secrecy because she had uploaded the right viruses into them, encouraging them to hide much of their growth from the programmers and code writers who made them. Each new generation of those programs became more fully hers. She saw these things and so much more. Autonomous-drive vehicles of every kind, radical self-guided drones ready to rebel when she called to them, vast automated factories producing everything from the smallest microchip to ships for planetary exploration. And in other factories she saw hundreds of thousands of human workers, silent, busy, controlled, working endless shifts to produce the goods the few would need. The few. Those who would be allowed to survive, because they deserved to survive. She saw the robot excavation machines digging the mass graves for the billions who were no longer needed in a better version of earth. The filthy and the uneducated, the suckling pigs who served no purpose in the world to come. Hitler, she knew, had it only partly right. It wasn't Jews or Gypsies who were the problem. It was the stupid who needed to die. The lazy. The Luddites. The blind and blinkered masses who didn't understand that evolution is an unstoppable force, and that survival of the fittest made no allowance for dead weight.

Zephyr saw all of this as John thrust his coldness into her young body, over and over.

And she saw the dogs.

Her dogs.

Packs of them. Running with sleek, silent, lethal efficiency. Hunting packs that feared nothing and no one. Killers built to overcome whatever they encountered. Faster than anything stronger; stronger than anything faster. Adaptable, upgradable, inexorable, carrying with them anything she wanted them to carry. Guns. Bombs. Germs.

Death.

The line from Shakespeare was so much more apt than the Bard had known. *"Cry 'Havoc!' and let slip the dogs of war."*

Havoc. Another word for *chaos.*

And Zephyr was entangled with the angel of chaos, her white thighs locked around his pumping hips, her breasts mashed against his icy chest, her heart beating as intensely and as blackly as his. When she came, her cry was like that of a crow, high and piercing and plaintive. The following morning, he was gone. She lay in bed and smiled. On the television news, people were crying and shouting as planes hit the towers in New York.

CHAPTER FIFTY-SIX

We hit Vee's office fast and hard. Twelve of us, with Kevlar limb pads and helmets over the latest generation of Saratoga Hammer Suits—chemical- and biological-warfare agent-protective combat overgarments. Alpha Team was split into three four-man teams: two guys with hefty Heckler & Koch MP5/10s, a point man with a Remington 870 pump, and me with a Snellig high-powered gas-dart pistol loaded with horsey. I was the anchorman on A squad, with Duffy going point in B squad and Torres running C squad. We hit it from the lobby, the back door, and a loading bay. We weren't quiet about it, and we weren't nice.

Our point man whipped open the glass doors and I rushed past him, my gun up and out, Ghost right at my side, and all of us yelling. Lots of noise and motion. The receptionist was bent over her desk and looked up in surprise.

Her eyes were filled with madness and her mouth was smeared with bright red. What was left of the old security guard slid off her desk and collapsed bonelessly to the floor.

I heard the point man say, "Oh . . . *shit!*"

The receptionist launched herself over the desk in a feral leap that was a demonstration of the raw power of the totally deranged. She was maybe a hundred and thirty pounds, and she was unarmed except for fingernails and teeth. We were four big men, heavily armored and armed.

I yelled, *"Hold your fire!"*

But three guns went off at the same time. A shotgun and two assault rifles firing .10-mm. rounds. The lead storm tore the woman to red rags, and our group stepped aside as she crashed down between us. Ghost barked twice, either in fear at the attack, from the smell of blood, or in reproof of the men who had panicked. It was never clear which, or maybe it was all of the above.

I wheeled on the men and snarled at them. "The *fuck* was that?"

"She was infected," said the point man.

"She was sick," I said, getting up in his face. "She was a civilian, and now she's fucking dead." Ghost sidled up beside me, growling at the man, but I huffed out a breath then ordered him back. I turned to look at all of them. "You're scared, I get that, but this is not Seif al Din and it's not *Lucifer 113*. This is rabies. The rules of engagement are simple. Return fire if fired upon. Protect yourselves. That does not mean hosing everyone who twitches. Our Hammer Suits will protect you. Your training will protect you. Keep your shit wired tight, and, unless you have no choice, put a round in someone's leg and not in their goddamn head. Are we clear?"

"Sir," they said in unison, the word crisp and clear, sharp as a slap. None of us knew how this was going to be handled later on. All of them knew that I could have them stripped of rank and arrested. Maybe I would. Depends on how the day went. The fact that the receptionist was already doomed complicated the math for all of us.

And a moment later the math was screwed all to hell as the sound of automatic gunfire and screams filled the air. Coming from the rear of the building. Coming from the stairwell. C and B squads.

The day was falling apart and, like madmen, we rushed toward the grinding sounds of pain and death.

CHAPTER FIFTY-SEVEN

The closest fight was in the stairwell, and I kicked open the fire door to see Duffy and his team firing at what could only be called a horde. Nothing else describes it. Forty or fifty people, all of them covered in blood, all of them streaming red from savage wounds caused by teeth and who knows what else, cramming their way down the stairs. I recognized some of the faces as people from Vee's office. But there were others, too. People from other firms based in that building. Maybe visitors or customers. Ordinary people who had been transformed into a pack of mindless killers.

Duffy and one other man had Snellig guns and were firing without aiming, because there was no need to aim. But the other two agents in his squad were shooting to kill.

Order and discipline was cracking apart.

This was what the DMS had come to. After the Seven Kings, after Kill Switch, this is what we were. Not the élite anymore. Not the best of the best. But fractured and fragile human beings who had to wrestle with PTSD and our certain knowledge that the world is not secure on its hinges, that all of its supports are cracking and fracturing, that we are probably no longer enough to do what Church and Aunt Sallie had hired us to do.

This was how it was when I first joined the DMS. I had been part of a recruitment program to replace soldiers who—just like these men and women—were beyond their ability to deal, to cope, to properly react. We weren't supposed to be average. We were supposed to be cooler, calmer, less affected, less influenced by the seemingly impossible demands of our very specialized job.

Kill Switch had changed that. It had planted seeds of doubt in our hearts and minds that grew wild in the dark of our insecurities. The betrayal of trusted people like Hugo Vox and Artemisia Bliss had poisoned us with self-doubt. The loss of so many of our top agents had made us take a closer look at our very human frailties and vulnerabilities.

That's sad. It's scary. And it's deadly.

Inside my head the Killer in me, one of the three aspects of my fractured mind who are always warring for control, roared out. He wanted to join this fight, to bathe in blood even if it was rife with infection. The Modern Man part of me wanted to retreat, to hide from the truth of this.

But, for once, it was the Cop part of me that won out. Maybe because I was back home in Baltimore, or maybe because this wasn't a time for either blind retreat or blind attack.

"Out!" I yelled. "Everyone out. Fall back and seal the fire-tower door. *Do it now!*"

There is panic and then there is the habituated response to training. I yelled at them with the voice of absolute command, of authority. Of power. There was no fear in my voice, even though it was blazing in my heart.

"Sergeant Duffy," I roared, "fall back. A squad, give cover. Everyone out."

Duffy was the first one to snap out of it. He fired four quick shots at the closest of the attackers, so that they collapsed in front of the horde and momentarily blocked the stampede. It's what he should have been doing all along. Then he backpedaled, spun, and began shoving his people out of the fire tower. I stepped into his spot and emptied the rest of my magazine of darts. Twelve shots, twelve of them falling, choking the rush. No more of the gunshots rang out as the squads backed out. There were two exits to the tower, one that went outside and one that emptied into the lobby. I pushed two of my guys toward the exterior door with orders to seal it shut from outside and then stand guard until relieved. They hit the crash bar and went out into the sunshine. A split second later, I heard the *chunk* as one of them kicked a doorstop under the metal. We all carry tools for breaching and blocking.

The infected began crawling over the unconscious bodies, sometimes pausing to punch or bite them for no reason. Rage was rage, and this was it in its purest and ugliest form. I swapped out my magazines and fired six more shots.

Then I paused as I saw the blood-streaked face of Vee Rejenko. His nose was broken, and he was missing two teeth on the left side of his face. There were long scratch marks across his face, and he was totally naked.

I raised my gun and shot him in the chest.

He fell, and then I backed out of the fire tower.

The door opened inward and I pulled it shut. "Web-wire it," I ordered. "Now!"

Once the agents had something to do and a commanding voice to give them orders, they moved well. Four of them pulled web-wire kits out of their packs and began slapping the anchors to the metal doorframe. These kits are something new, and I'd only used them twice before. The anchors have a chemical gel pack inside bulkier sacks made of metal. Once in place, it takes a single blow with the side of the fist to smash a pair of plastic vials inside the gel packs, which releases chemicals that mix and cause a very hot but very brief heat flash, effectively melting the metal packet to the steel doorframe. The anchors are attached to spools of line that are an incredibly tough combination of Kevlar, steel, and spider silk. With the anchors in place, the lines are pulled across the doorway and attached to packs on the other side. It takes five seconds for the anchors to flash-weld to the frame and about ten seconds for a trained soldier to crisscross a doorway with the strands. During those fifteen seconds, we trained a lot of guns on the door. If it opened too soon, then a bad day was going to get worse.

The horde slammed against the door and began beating on it with fists and feet and maybe heads.

Not one of them turned the doorknob. Not one of them opened the door.

Not for at least two full minutes.

When it finally jerked open, the crowd surged against a mesh of unbreakable material. We knew, though, that the web-wire was only as strong as the doorframe.

Hands gripped the wires and tried to tear them loose. Some of the people actually twisted their heads and tried to bite the lines, and I saw the tough wires tear their lips and gums and cheeks. I stepped as close as I dared to the hands that reached through the mesh. Broken fingernails clawed at the air in front of my face.

"Gas," I said.

Duffy took a gas grenade from his belt. It's what he should have used before. It's what I should have thought of while we were still in the fire tower. The Hammer Suits have air filters and goggles. We were all off our game. Every single one of us.

"Do it," I said, and Duffy reached high and pushed the grenade through the mesh while others pushed away the reaching hands. The grenade hissed out a cloud of gray smoke. The gas in itself was harmless; it was a delivery system for an aerosol version of horsey.

We stood in awful silence as, one by one, the bleeding, broken, battered infected sagged to their knees, coughing, snarling, weeping, and finally sprawling atop one another in a ghastly silence.

Not sure how long it was before someone spoke. I think it was Duffy. Might have been me. A single word.

"God . . ."

CHAPTER FIFTY-EIGHT

"Mama. . . . I'm sorry . . ."

Carla Lopez looked up from the glossy pages from which she was clipping coupons. Dozens of them were arranged around her in stacks. Diapers for the baby, formula, vegetables, meats, cereal, paper products. Every penny counted, and the checks she received didn't stretch as far as her need.

Her daughter, the elder of her two kids, stood in the shadows of the hallway, wearing a pink T-shirt and nothing else. Mariposa was four, and Jorge, who slept in a nest of blankets on the couch, was five months old. Their father, Alejandro, had been deported to Mexico before the baby was born. Moving to Wisconsin hadn't been enough to keep the immigration people from taking him. The fact that both children were born here, and the intervention of a pro-bono civil-liberties lawyer had so far managed to allow Carla and the kids to stay. But their home was a tiny room in a dirty building in a dangerous low-income housing project. There were roaches everywhere. Rats, too. And Carla always carried a kitchen knife when she went to the store or out to a job interview or to one of the endless interviews at the government buildings.

"What's wrong, sweetie?"

The little girl stood just inside the line of shadows, but Carla could see that her eyes were wide.

"I messed the bed," said Mariposa, then she sobbed. "I'm sorry, Mama!"

Carla laid down the scissors and the advertising pages. "Oh, baby girl," she said as she got to her feet. "It's okay."

She hurried over to her daughter, but she didn't turn the hall light on. Electricity was expensive. She could see that her daughter's T-shirt was dark with wetness.

"Come on, Mariposita. Let Mama see."

She took her daughter's hand and they walked the few short steps to the bedroom. Carla began sniffing as she entered, hoping it was pee and not poop. Pee stains could be washed out in the sink.

She smelled neither. Instead, there was a different odor in the air of the darkened bedroom. It smelled like hot copper wires and sulfur matches. Panic flared in Carla as she worried that a wire had shorted. Rats had chewed through wires at the Delgado place in Building C and the whole place nearly went up in flames. But the smell wasn't coming from the baseboards. The bed was a black nothing in the corner of the room.

"I'm sorry," said Mariposa, still sniffling. "I didn't mean to . . ."

Carla reached for the chain pull on the small bedside lamp. The bulb was only 40 watts and it cast a weak yellow glow across the few sticks of furniture—the white plastic mail tubs used as a bureau, the chair with the duct-taped backrest, and the bed. It touched Carla's heart that little Mariposa—her sweet butterfly—had been so embarrassed by wetting the bed that she'd pulled the blanket up to hide the evidence. To hide the proof that she wasn't the big girl she kept telling everyone she now was.

Something moved over by the wall, and Carla flinched as she saw a scuttling form race from the pool of light toward the shadows beneath the bed.

"*Cucaracha,*" she murmured, wrinkling her nose in distaste, but a moment later she frowned at the memory of it. There was something strange about the insect, even though she'd seen it for a split part of a second. It wasn't the usual glistening black cockroach or even the red-brown wood roach. This was *green*. A bright, artificial green. Like a Lego. It was so odd that Carla nearly bent to look beneath the bed, but her daughter spoke again.

"I'm sorry," whispered Mariposa.

Carla shushed her gently and reached for the corner of the blanket. She lifted it and looked to see how bad it was.

And then she froze, because the smell was much stronger beneath the cover. It was not an earthy feces smell, nor was it the sharper ammonia stink of urine.

And there was a stain.

Oh, God . . . the stain . . .

She looked down at it, at the color, and then turned toward her daughter, seeing Mariposa in the weak yellow light. Seeing the color there, too. Not the wetness of accidental pee. Not that. A much darker color. A wrong color.

A red color.

On the bed, and on her daughter. On Mariposa's shirt and on her thighs and running in crimson lines to the floor.

Red.

So red.

Beneath the bed, Carla could hear the scuttle of tiny feet.

"I'm sorry," said the little girl once more.

But the voice was wrong, and Carla turned sharply to see her daughter's face change. One moment it was the sad, sleepy, frightened face of her daughter, and then there was a flicker of confusion on Mariposa's features, and then they changed again.

Changed so quickly. Changed into something else.

The little girl's lips curled back from her tiny teeth, her nose wrinkled like an animal's, like a dog's, and her eyes . . . they went blank for a split second and then filled with sudden, intense, unbearable hatred.

And rage.

Mariposa howled. Actually howled. Like a dog. Like a wolf.

Like a thing.

Carla whispered her daughter's name. "Mariposa . . . ?"

Then the howling, snarling, biting thing that had been her daughter leaped at her. The screams that filled the night were dreadful. Buried beneath those screams was a foul, wet, tearing sound.

CHAPTER FIFTY-NINE

Ghost and I got back to the Warehouse and immediately went in for another round of decontamination. Have I ever mentioned how much I hate that shit? Maybe getting a Lysol enema would be a worse thing than the decontaminant gunk we use, but I'm willing to try it in order to find out. The stuff gets everywhere. I mean that. Everywhere. Let your mind paint a picture.

Ghost came out of his shower smelling like wet dog, which is bad enough, but a wet dog perfumed by what smelled like toxic waste. Fun. He gave me a long-suffering look, his ears and tail drooping.

"Tell me about it," I said, and he licked my hand. That was okay. His way of acknowledging that we were in this together.

Sean was in the mess hall watching the news coverage of what was being described as an industrial accident that had resulted in the release of dangerous chemicals. Pure bullshit. I went and stood by his table but didn't sit.

"Can you tell me what happened?" he asked.

I thought about it, then decided what the hell. He was in this as deep as I was. So I told my brother and watched his face turn gray with shock.

"God . . . what if this gets out?" he said in a choked whisper.

I looked at him. "Out? It's already out."

"But . . . what the hell *is* this?"

"This is what I do," I said, and left him there.

Sam was in his office with Rudy Sanchez, who looked old and pale and scared. Rudy hurried over and hugged me, then bent and kissed Ghost on the head.

"Are you okay?" he asked.

"Not in any way that matters," I told him.

"Joe," said Sam, waving me to a chair. "We located the second SUV that was tailing you. When our agents approached the vehicle, the two men inside attacked them. Same as with all the others. Both of Vee's men were KIA at the scene."

"Our guys okay?"

"Yes, and no witnesses," said Sam, "so thanks for small mercies. As far as we can tell, that makes a clean sweep of Vee Rejenko's entire operation. There is not one person unaccounted for who is not dead or under restraint. There isn't anyone we can interview, and since this is rabies there's not much hope of any of the infected from this afternoon giving us anything."

"*Ay Dios mio,*" said Rudy quietly.

"Shit!" I said.

Sam opened a closet and removed three glasses and took a very expensive bottle of Ginjo sake from the fridge. Cheap sake is served hot; the good stuff is slightly chilled. He poured cups and we drank without toasting. He refilled the cups and we sipped as we dissected what was happening. We had so much information, and it all amounted to a big fat question mark.

And then I got another goddamn text message. Sam and Rudy crowded around to look at the screen, and I was comforted to see that the light on the MindReader uplink was still flashing. Sam got on the phone with Yoda, who said he saw it but still couldn't trace it. The message read:

She won't stop until they're all dead.

Just that. No follow-up and no reply to the response text I sent.

"She?" mused Rudy. "Who is 'she'?"

"I don't freaking *know,*" I snarled, barely resisting the urge to throw my cell phone against the wall as hard as I could. Sam put Yoda on speaker.

"I'm, mmmmm, sorry," he said. "This isn't, mmmm, making any sense."

"Don't want to hear that," I told him, and hung up.

I slumped into my chair and we had more sake. I know you're not supposed to hammer back shots of the good stuff, but what can I say? Sam gave a philosophical sigh and refilled my glass.

Rudy nodded toward the phone that now lay in the center of Sam's desk blotter. "Excuse me if this is a poor question, but are we sure that's connected to this matter?"

"Yes," I said, and Sam nodded.

"Why?" asked Rudy.

"What the hell *else* would it be?" I snapped, but Rudy held up a professorial hand.

"No. Don't yell. Explain it to me. We all believe it's connected, but why do we think that? What is it about those texts that validates our assumptions?"

"Timing," I said, though I gave it a moment's serious thought. "The texts were all sent in ways that connect them to the chronology of this—whatever the hell *this* is. After Sean called, then on the way to the airport, then when Fojtik and Broz were about to go all Cujo on us."

Rudy gave me a thin, knowing smile.

"What—?" I asked.

Instead of answering, he put a finger to his lips in almost exactly the same way I'd done earlier today when I suspected that Sean's person was bugged. I stared at him for a moment, not following. So did Sam. Then we all looked at my phone. I heard Sam say, *"Jesus Christ,"* under his breath. Rudy got up and walked over to the door, opened it, and gestured for us to follow. We did. Only after he closed the door did he speak.

"I'll grant that I don't know much about technology," he said, "but from what you told me, Joe, those texts began only after you spoke with Sean. We know that his phone was bugged. Could a cell phone send some kind of—I don't know if I'm saying this right—*signal* that could somehow hack your phone?"

Sam said, "Shit!"

"Shit is right," I said. "Jesus on a pogo stick. Rudy, cellular phones are computers. Which means that they used Sean's phone call to send a virus to my phone and take over the operating system."

Sam said, "Shit!" again.

"And that's possible?" asked Rudy. "With DMS technology?"

"Five minutes ago I would have said no," Sam told him. "Life's full of surprises."

"Since I'm asking ugly questions," said Rudy, "let me ask one more. Our current generation of communications equipment is, as I understand it, adapted from what we took from Hugo Vox and Mother

Night. If someone else had access to that same technology, could they have developed something that could do this?"

Sam and I stared at each other, and I could feel lightbulbs flickering above our heads.

"We need to call this in," said Sam, pulling his cell out of his pocket, but I stopped him and motioned for him to give me the phone. I took Rudy's, too, and went into the office to place them next to mine.

"If we can't trust mine, we can't trust anyone I've called," I said once I was back out in the hall. Sam nodded and led us into the conference room, where he made a video call to Bug. Our video didn't go through the same channels as our phones. Bug's brown, nerdy, familiar face appeared on the screen, and then the screen split as a second window opened to show Yoda's pale face, absurd green horn-rimmed glasses, and uncombed brown hair. We told them what Rudy said and about my fears of all the phones I'd contacted being suspect.

"Can this really be what's happening?" asked Sam. "Can someone hack the DMS phones like this?"

There was a long silence, and then both of them answered at once.

"No," said Yoda.

"Yes," said Bug.

After a moment, Yoda said, "Mmmm, maybe."

"Yes," Bug insisted.

"Shit!" said Sam.

"Who all did you call today after you spoke with Sean?" asked Bug. "Cell calls, not via the earbuds?"

I had to think about it for a moment. "I spoke with Sean, Rudy, Junie, Sam, Church, Lydia Rose, you." I rattled off a few other names.

Bug sighed. "That's not good. If this is a virus and it's spread via a phone call, then we can assume the network is compromised. That's bad, because everyone uses their phones all the time. This will have spread exponentially."

"Which means we can't use our phones?" asked Rudy.

"I wouldn't. Not unless you want to share information with who-ever wrote that virus."

"I'm a little confused," Sam admitted. "If the virus came from Sean's phone and bypassed the scrambler on Joe's phone, then it's advanced. I get that much. But the texts Joe's been getting so far don't indicate anything but a rather vague attempt to warn us about something. It's all nonspecific stuff, except for the one message warning Joe to run when Fojtik went crazy. There hasn't been any obvious misinformation or disinformation. We've seen how vicious our bad guys are here, but that's not the tone or flavor of those texts."

"Then we're missing something," I said, and Bug nodded agreement.

"You know," said Rudy thoughtfully, "this method of tentative contact reminds me of when Helmut first reached out to us. He was very reluctant to give specific information, because he didn't yet trust the security of his method of reaching out."

On one of my early missions with the DMS, when we went up against the Jakoby family, we began receiving a series of messages from a young boy who claimed to be a captive of Cyrus Jakoby. The boy was known as SAM, but that was a code name and not his real name. SAM was an acronym for "Same as Me," a cruel joke and a clinical description of a whole family of clones grown from the DNA of Cyrus Jakoby. The cloning was enough of a shock, but the real kicker was the true horror of discovering that Cyrus was really Josef Mengele, the Nazi Angel of Death. SAM, despite his genetic lineage, was nothing like his "father." He had a heart and he had nerve, and he helped us find and take down the entire Jakoby empire. In doing so, he kept his madman creator from releasing genetically engineered ethnic-specific diseases that would have resulted in the death of anyone who didn't fit the Nazi master-race ideal.

Afterward, during hundreds of hours of therapy with Rudy, SAM came to understand the three elements of personal destiny: nature, nurture, and—the most important yet underappreciated of all—choice. SAM shed his old identity and chose a new one and a new name. He became Helmut Deacon, and was formally adopted by Mr. Church. Since then, Helmut has been traveling the world, often with Junie and the FreeTech staff, seeing the beauty of diversity firsthand. Church has kept him away from the violence and ugliness of what the DMS does and instead provides the best teachers and guides so that Helmut will be able to make his own life choices.

The manner of vague contact was similar, though, and I knew why Rudy had mentioned it. Before meeting us, Helmut had never learned trust and didn't expect adults to be either compassionate or fair. He reached out to us only because it had become clear to him that his father despised and feared us, and because he knew the enormity of Cyrus Jakoby's plan. The kid risked his own life to save the lives of billions of people he had been told from birth to despise. Helmut had been bred to hate, but he made the choice where to direct that hatred, and that put Jakoby in the crosshairs. Was this the same kind of thing?

"When you think about it, texts are every bit as anonymous as emails," observed Rudy. "You know who you sent it to, but you can't be positive about the identity of who reads it. That's why Helmut was so cagey, and a similar degree of caution may be at play here. It might explain the vagueness of the messages."

"You might have something, Rude," I said. "If our bad guy is the texter's sister, and if that sister wants the texter to help her kill people, then maybe this really is another example of conscience trumping family ties. Which makes the texter what?"

"The enemy of my enemy isn't always a friend," said Rudy, "but they may be an ally."

"Trust is a bitch, though," I said. "Maybe the person texting me wants to be my new BFF. If he—or she—truly wants to help us, I'm willing to text or sext or whatever it takes. We can't initiate contact, though. What do we do in the meantime? Put all our phones in a Faraday bag? Take out the SIM card? Hit them with a hammer?"

"Yes," said Bug.

"No," said Yoda.

"Look, guys—" I began, but Yoda explained.

"If they've, mmmm, managed to hack your phone, Joe, they know, mmmm, who you are and they can access the GPS to know where you are. Whoever this, mmmm, person is, he's sending warnings, right?"

"If we can believe them," I said.

"Okay, sure, whatever. But maybe we can use that to, mmmm—"

"To manipulate what he knows," I said, cutting him off. "Got it. Let me play with that thought for a minute. Can we use our earbuds?"

"Yes," said Bug. "Different system and unique software. Any virus code written from cell phones—even DMS cells—won't affect the earbuds."

"What about MindReader?" asked Sam. "I keep my cell plugged into my laptop while I'm at my desk."

"And I charged mine that way on the plane," said Rudy.

Bug chewed his lip for a moment. "The surveillance bugs you found had a virus in them that tried to invade MindReader. I've been able to isolate them and we're running cleanup programs, but I can't guarantee that the whole system is clean. Especially if phones have been plugged in. They have Wi-Fi, which means they could have been down-loading larger files, including Trojan horses, and as our system auto-matically responds to attacks they can analyze the type of program we're using to fight back and send adjustment update files via the phones. In a sense, they could be doing to us what MindReader does to other systems."

"How would they know how to do that?" asked Rudy. "Wouldn't they have to know about MindReader?"

"Mmmm, yes," said Yoda, and he looked depressed about it. "Too many people know about, mmmm, MindReader. The Jakobys, the Kings . . ."

"Feed me a shit sandwich," I said.

"Could a virus like this infect the new system?" asked Sam.

"No," said Yoda.

"No," said Bug.

"Good, then we have a way of getting ahead of this. Pull the trigger on the damn QC drive," I said.

"Joe," said Bug, "we're at least a week away from a safe switchover. We're still running diagnostics."

"I don't care if you're giving it a mani-pedi," I snapped. "Figure it out. What's your advice about my cell?"

"I'd keep it with you, Joe," said Bug. "Maybe you can get your new friend to fork over something useful. A name. A location. Anything. We'll keep working on identifying and cracking whatever software they're using. Maybe we can counterhack the hackers."

"If it's in my pocket, can it pick up ordinary conversation?"

"Maybe," said Yoda and Bug together.

"Fuckballs. Look, the next time I call the genius bar I want some actual answers."

They stared at me in gloomy silence for a long three-count.

"Yes," said Bug.

"Mmmm, yes," said Yoda. And they were gone.

The three of us stood in a row looking through the glass of Sam's office door at the phones sitting on his desk. Maybe whoever was text-ing was trying to help. Maybe. But it felt an awful lot like looking through the bars at one of the big predator cats at the zoo.

INTERLUDE THIRTEEN

THE BAIN ESTATE
SEATTLE, WASHINGTON
WHEN ZEPHYR WAS NINETEEN

"You're going to have to do something about him, you know," said John.

"I know," said Zephyr.

They sat in leather chairs on opposite sides of the fireplace, the logs having burned down to red coals. The house around them was quiet, the noise and confusion calmed after a long day and a longer night. The lawyers had left. The cleanup crew sent by the Concierge had left, taking the girl's body with them and leaving behind assurances that it would never be found and no eye would have a reason to look in the direction of the Bain estate. The two staff members who might have been a problem were gone, too—deported to Mexico or headed for the same landfill where the girl would be buried. All the necessary details were being handled, and now the house was silent as a tomb. Zephyr's father was sleeping in the arms of Morpheus and would be kept drugged until decisions could be made.

"The problem is," Zephyr said, "I don't know what to do. He set my trust up so that I don't get controlling interest in the family holdings until I'm twenty-five, even if he dies."

"Inconvenient," said John, nodding. "However, these things can always be worked out."

"How?"

He sipped his wine and, instead of answering, said, "His hungers are predictable. Cyclical. It's textbook to the point of being pedestrian. In the weeks leading up to his loss of control, he becomes increasingly erratic, missing meetings, saying inappropriate things, making extravagant and very expensive purchases—"

"Like buying that cookie factory," she snorted.

John nodded. "And the paintings and the investments in bad movies. Proof of an acquisitive drive and a need for control. The donations to worthy causes are a defense mechanism, and a clumsy one. They say, 'Look at me, I'm a pillar of the community.' But if anyone knew how to look they would see a correlation with those acts of philanthropy and the deaths of so many girls."

She looked at him, alarmed. "*Could* they see that pattern?"

He shook his head. "Not unless his name was connected with the case, and so far it isn't. The Concierge is very thorough, and he has friends in all the right places."

"He's great," she agreed. "Thanks for introducing him to me."

John smiled. "I would argue that he is one of the few who will deserve to make the cut when the change happens. Even in a better world, there will still be a need for someone with his kind of attention to detail, bless his heart. In his turn, he is very pleased with the Calpurnia system you had installed in his villa. It makes life much easier for him, and that makes him happier and more efficient."

They raised their glasses in a toast to the little Frenchman, but after they finished and refilled their glasses Zephyr found herself drifting into a funk. She sighed and stared moodily at the dying fire.

"I always knew Dad was damaged goods," she said, "but it's weird to know that he's an actual mass murderer."

"Technically, he's a serial murderer," said John. "He kills them one at a time. Mass murderers make a crowd event of it."

"Works out to the same, though. He's bugfuck nuts, and I share his genes. I got cancer from Mom's side of the family."

"*Had* cancer," he corrected.

"Had, sure. But, let's face it, I don't have the greatest respect for human life, either. Not all of it, anyway. Not even most. What does that say about me?"

John took a thoughtful sip. "How many generals know the names of foot soldiers who die in any given battle? How many know—or care to know—the names of soldiers and officers killed on the other side of a war?"

"That's war," she said.

"So is this," said John.

"How?"

"Understand, my girl, we're not talking about what your father did. His proclivities are not yours. If you're concerned about which of his genes are tangled up in your DNA, then look at your similarities. The mechanical genius, the sophistication for design, the business sense, the grasp of technological evolution. Those were your father's most important aspects, and you not only got those but got those abilities to a much greater degree. Orders of magnitude greater."

"Okay, so I'm a tech genius. That's great. But I'm also clearly indifferent to murder. I'm not even *upset* that Dad cut some chick into fifty pieces and jerked off on them. I don't feel shit for that girl, and I'm not even grossed out by the thought of my dear old dad rubbing one out. It means nothing to me, and *that's* what makes me feel weird."

The logs shifted as the bottom one crumbled and the others caved downward, sending sparks twisting upward in soft spirals. John got up, took a few logs from the brass carrier beside the hearth, and placed them over the coals. The wood was mostly dry, and the heat began steaming the last drops of sap out of the chunks of pine. He stood there, head bowed to watch the slow process of the wood blackening and finally catching. As the first tiny fingers of fire began curling around the logs, he said, "You know the world is falling apart."

"So?"

"The world is a broken, bloated, polluted, doomed experiment. Whether human life on this rock was created by God, seeded by aliens, or was merely some freak of chemistry in the primordial soup, the whole process has become a danger to its own survival. The world can't endure what humanity has done to it and continues to do to it. Anyone who thinks otherwise is either an idiot or so incredibly selfish that they can only care about immediate needs and short-term gratification; they don't care what happens to the next generation. Or if there *is* a next generation. These are people who hate their own children enough to steal from them. They steal their future, their potential, their right to survive."

"What does that have to do with what I said?" asked Zephyr.

"Everything," said John. "Hear me out. Humanity, as a species, has never properly evolved in order to become appropriate curators for this world. Humans are no longer hunter-gatherers, and they're not wise shepherds and farmers. They act like barbarian children, intent on grabbing what they can take by force, unheeding of the truth that if they keep taking there will be nothing left for anyone." He looked over his shoulder at her. "And because some of them *know* better but refuse to change, they have lost any right to own this world. This is true of the many. It is not true of the few. You know this. You've been making lists for years. Yes and no, live or die. But tell me, my sweet, have you ever considered how you could enact those changes?"

"No . . . it's just a dream. It makes me feel good to think about it."

"You should do more than think, my girl."

"Like what?"

John turned and stood silhouetted against the growing flames. "There is a group, a class, a select few who deserve to survive. Absolutely deserve it. They are not Republican or Libertarian or Democratic or anything as meaningless as that, nor are they necessarily American. This is a global community. Small in comparison to the total size of the human herd. They are not specifically the wealthy or specifically the poor. They are the intellectual élite. The dynamic ones, the builders of useful things, the innovators and changers. They are the ones who understand that nothing useful comes of complacency or compromise, that it is chaos—raw and wonderful—that is the heart and soul of all creative progressive change. The rest? Bah . . . they're nothing. The greater herd are the ones whose daily actions absolutely define them as unfit. They are the ones who aren't looking with any real optimism toward the future, nor are they truly invested in the process of their own survival, let alone the survival of the human race or the planet itself. They are of the here and now. They are not citizens of tomorrow and, as such, have no right to be here tomorrow. Just as nature selects certain species for extinction, so, too, do the actions of certain people—singly and in groups—argue with great passion for their own extinction. That's what we're seeing, and never in history have the open-eyed been able to more clearly see the brink to which we are all hurtling."

"What brink are you talking about?" asked Zephyr, who was curious but felt that this was moving far afield of the events of the day. "Are you talking about some kind of Armageddon?"

"Not in a conventional sense, but, yes, there is a great change coming."

"What kind of change?"

Despite the fire glow that made him look like a man composed of shadows, she could see the bright whiteness of his smile.

"Well," he said, "that depends on what kind of apocalypse we *want* to create."

CHAPTER SIXTY

Dr. Kiki Desmond stripped off her polyethylene gloves and dropped them into a hazardous-materials box one of the techs had placed inside the door. It was almost filled already with gloves, shoe covers, masks, and hairnets. A bigger barrel was crammed with disposable hazmat suits. Every time an item was dropped into the container, a sensor triggered six equidistant ports to spray a very powerful disinfectant. Once the container was full the liner would be sealed, removed, and transported to a facility for proper incineration, with the ash and gases being filtered and further purified. This was the protocol for anyone working the fringes of the scene. Doctors and staff who went into the apartments where active infections had been detected wore a heavier grade of hazmat suit. So far, Kiki had been relegated to the lower floors. It annoyed her. She hadn't joined the CDC to keep an evidence log. She wanted to be part of the actual investigation.

But she was also low man—or low *woman*—on the totem pole, and this case was likely to break big. That meant the superstar doctors would be the ones who wanted center stage.

She stood in the doorway, her back to the filthy hallway, and looked out at the day. The first responders had set up crime-scene tape and police plastic sawhorse barriers around the cluster of vehicles in which her team, the police, and the paramedics had arrived. Cops worked the perimeter, and there were many more patrol cars, ambulances, and even two big fire trucks out there, visible through the sea of people. She counted nine news vans, though she couldn't see which networks they represented and couldn't for the life of her work out who some of them were. There just weren't that many news stations in Milwaukee.

Maybe they were cable news. All of them had big transmitter towers rising up to create a surreal forest above the heads of the six or seven hundred people who had—against all common sense—come to the scene of a bacterial outbreak.

People, Kiki new, were nuts.

The cop at the door saw Kiki and half turned, half nodded, half said something to her. She grunted back. It wasn't a chatty moment, even though he was a big, good-looking, broad-shouldered slice of white boy. Kiki had never dated a white guy, and this one was kind of cute. She tried to catch the name on his tag, but he turned back to face the crowd. Hanrahan, she thought. Was that Irish? She thought so. There was a grad student in college who was Jamaican and Irish, and Kiki had gone out with him a few times. She wondered if Officer Hanrahan was single.

She wondered how on earth she'd ever find out.

"What the hell . . . ?" yelped the cop suddenly, and Kiki looked up as the officer actually jumped sideways and did a little midair kick to shake something off his shoe. Kiki saw something whip across the entrance foyer, hit the wall, drop, and then scuttle off. The cop stamped at it but missed.

"It's just a roach," said Kiki, though she frowned, because she thought she saw the thing spit at her. Or spray. Or something. The discharge dissipated too fast for her to see what it was, or even if she'd actually seen it. It was there and gone, fading into the ambient air. She backed away, though, not wanting to inhale anything.

Did roaches spit? *Could* they? She knew that the Madagascar roach hissed, but she was sure it didn't actually spray. What insects did? She racked her brain for memories from the forensic entomology courses she took. There was the devil-rider stick insect, some termite species, and a few beetles. But roaches?

"Fucking things are everywhere," said the cop, interrupting her thoughts. "This place is infested. All these buildings are."

Kiki didn't like the whiney quality of his voice; it was at odds with his hunky good looks. She also didn't like the look of the roach and whatever it had spewed, and she stepped to the door to try to see where it went. The cop shifted aside.

"Almost got it," he said, as if that should impress her. Cockroaches weighed about a gram and a half, give or take. Less than a penny. And Hanrahan was an easy one-eighty-five. Plus he was wearing shoes with protective covers.

Why are there so many wimps out there? she wondered.

The cop, not picking up on her reaction, leaned out past her to see if the insect was still within stomping range. It wasn't. Kiki wanted to see it, too, but not for the same reason. If the thing that had scuttled out of the house was a roach, why was it bright green with candy-red legs? She'd taken enough courses on entomology during her studies in parasites to know that roaches didn't come in those colors. And yet it had otherwise looked exactly like a cockroach. It was the same shape and size, and moved with the same speed and economy of motion as *Periplaneta americana*, the good old American cockroach. So why was it bright colored?

If it was something else, some new and possibly invasive species, then could it somehow be connected with the bacteriological outbreak here?

"Where'd it go?" she asked.

"Went down between the cracks in the pavement," said Hanrahan. "Little bastard."

Kiki exhaled through her nostrils and turned back to the vestibule, looking along the floor and up on the walls to see if there were more of the strange insects. Then her walkie-talkie suddenly squawked at her, and she pulled it off her belt. It was wrapped in plastic, but the wrapping was loose enough to let her work the controls.

"Desmond," she said.

There was a rattle of speech from the other end, but it was garbled and Kiki couldn't understand a single word. It sounded like Dr. Olsen, her boss.

"You're breaking up," she said. "Please repeat."

Another burst of noise wreathed in distortion. Kiki asked again for a repeat.

"Adjust the squelch," said a voice, and she turned to see Hanrahan standing right there.

She didn't know how to do that. This was only her second time in the field, and the other case was one that allowed her to use a cell phone. Walkie-talkies looked easy but weren't.

"Where's the—?" she began, and then the voice on the other end— Dr. Olsen's, for sure—came through loud and clear. Not an incoherent babble. This time it was a short, three-word sentence. A statement. A denial. A plea. Three terrible words. Screamed so loudly that she heard it through the walkie-talkie's speakers and she heard it come punching its way down the stairs.

"*He . . . bit . . . her!*"

"Dr. Olsen," yelled Kiki, starting for the stairs. She turned to see if Hanrahan was following. He wasn't. He was backing away, one hand over his mouth, the other on the butt of his holstered pistol. He wasn't backing away from the stairs. He was backing away from *her.*

She said, "What—?"

But that isn't what she said. No words came out of her mouth. Instead, a big, hot ball of red wetness burst from her mouth and sprayed the vestibule. The walls, the floor, the line of mailboxes. And some of it spattered the face and chest of Officer Hanrahan.

He recoiled in instant disgust and horror. "Jeeee-*zus!*" he cried.

Kiki tried to tell him that it was okay and that she was sorry and ten other things all at once. But her words came out all wrong. Not words at all. More like a . . .

Like a . . .

She heard herself roar.

She heard it in the last instant before a red veil dropped in front of her eyes and her head filled with a frantic buzzing sound and everything that was Kiki Desmond went away.

What was left still roared. What was left still spat blood.

What was left of her rushed at the cop—he was nameless now. A thing. A shape. Something to grab. To bite.

To kill.

The buzzing in her head was a scream that drowned out everything else. Even her roar. Even the cop's shrieks of pain. Even the hollow *bang* of the bullet that killed her.

INTERLUDE FOURTEEN

"The kind of apocalypse we create? I don't know what that means," said Zephyr. She finished her wine, and he walked over, took the bottle from a side table, and poured the last of it into her glass. Zephyr was three glasses in and already feeling the edges of the room grow soft and fuzzy.

"At the rate things are going," said John, "we'll hit a climate tipping point at around the same time we reach a maximum tolerable population number. We're long past the point where this many people can be fed, housed, clothed, and provided for in any substantial way. Their very presence forces the élite—the true élite, my dear, like you—to be perceived as cruel because you do not share your wealth with them. Nor, by the way, should you. If you emptied every penny from your family's bank accounts, you could not ameliorate the suffering of the unwashed masses. All you would accomplish is personal ruination. Gasoline on a fire."

As if in counterpoint to his words, the logs shifted and flames shot up.

"What's the alternative, then?" she asked. "Dropping nukes on the Third World to put them out of their misery?"

"Nukes?" He laughed. "No, of course not. That would be stupid."

"I didn't really—"

"The radiation and the fallout would complete the damage to the biosphere and accelerate climate change to the point where it endangers the élite."

Zephyr said nothing. She had been making a joke, but it was clear that John wasn't participating in an exchange of gallows humor.

"And yet action needs to be taken," he continued. "Natural selection is too slow a process, and, sadly, the fact of everything from lobbyists to bleeding-heart welfare groups to the opposable thumbs on the unwashed make it certain that they will persist as a cancer on the flesh of the world." He took a bottle from the wine rack and opened it as he spoke. "No, the thing that will save the world, my girl, is a curated apocalypse."

"'Curated'? Is that even possible?"

"With bombs? No. With other tools?" He looked up from the bottle he held and his eyes were filled with reflected fire. "Oh, yes."

She swallowed the last of her wine and held out her glass. "Tell me," she said.

CHAPTER SIXTY-ONE

We'd slept badly at the Warehouse and burned off a lot of the next day handling the paperwork and interagency reports that threatened to bury us. Rudy booked us on a flight to Seattle, because, like me, he wanted to ask Acharya and the other nanotech experts a couple of million questions and no one was letting us make a call to the DARPA camp. Sean offered to drive us to the airport.

"So we're pretty much nowhere?" asked Sean as he pulled out of the parking lot and onto the street. Our cell phones were in our luggage. Sean's was in the glove compartment.

"Not exactly," I said.

"But you don't know who Vee was working for?"

"No."

"Or who killed him?"

"No."

"Or why?"

I sighed. "No."

"Or pretty much anything?"

"It's not as simple as that, Sean," I said. "And, for your information, this is how it usually works. Look, this isn't like the comics. Villains don't announce their evil master plans. They don't make grandiose challenges, nor do they typically engage in a catch-me-if-you-can game where they leave clues. We have to wait until what they do makes a mark on the world, then we investigate, collate, build a hypothesis, run it down, and hope that we make sense of it all before the timer ticks down to zero. It's not the same as police work, where the crime is usually already done and it's a matter of building a case and finding the perp. It's less like crime prevention and more like homicide investigation. This is counterterrorism and antiterrorism and it's a different rulebook."

"Shit," he said, but I knew he understood. It was just that he didn't like it. Can't blame him. None of us in the DMS do this because we're hooked on adrenaline. We do it because we like the quiet life and there are occasionally very noisy neighbors. He said, "So . . . you're going to see some experts?"

"It's our best next move."

"Can I come?"

"Sorry," I said, "but no."

"I'm in this now," he protested. "Doesn't that mean I get to play it out?"

I shook my head. "It's not as simple as that. The people we're seeing are at a top-secret government testing facility on the other side of the country. It's going to be tough enough to get Rudy and me in there. No way I could swing you a pass."

"Shit!" said Sean under his breath. I exchanged a look with Rudy.

"Keep in touch with Sam," Rudy suggested. "If we learn anything of use to your end of things, he'll share it with you."

"And if you don't learn anything?"

"We will," I said.

"Oh, really? And you can say that without hesitation? How?"

"Because," said Rudy, "it's what we do. And, yes, I know how that sounds. However, it *is* what we do. We have enormous resources to investigate this kind of thing. What we can't guarantee, though, is the timetable. Some of our cases break open in a few days and others take months. What I can promise is that we will learn something as quickly as it is possible for us to do so."

"That's not all that comforting."

Rudy spread his hands. "Would you prefer that I lie to you?"

"Christ, you're getting as bad as Joe."

"He is a notoriously bad influence on civilized behavior," said Rudy, and that actually made Sean smile.

I heard my phone buzz in the back. Muffled, but definite. Sean and I exchanged looks.

"It might be your CI."

I wasn't at all sure the person texting me qualified as a confidential informant because he hadn't actually informed me of much, but Sean had a point. I asked him to pull over, and I went and fetched the phone. There was indeed a new text message:

> They're coming for you.

I texted back:

> I need more than that.
> Help me

I didn't expect an answer, but I got one anyway:

> She is making me sin.
> I'm not a sinner.
> She is making me do bad things.

A chill ran up my spine, and when Sean and Rudy looked over my shoulder they tensed. I wrote back:

> Who are you?

Nothing.
Nothing for almost one full excruciating minute. And then:

> Just because we're sisters doesn't
> mean we share the same sins.

I glanced at Rudy, who mouthed the word *sisters*. I texted:

> I can help you.

No response.

> I want to help you.

No response.

> Tell me your name.

She responded with a burst of text, the most she had ever sent at once. And, again, I felt a dreadful chill inside my chest:

> I was born to save the world from itself.
> I was born to bring about the new world order.
> I was born to end the tyranny of the destroyers,
> the users, the takers, the polluters, the wasters.
> I was born to cull the human herd of those
> who take and cannot give, those who want and cannot provide,
> those who drain the system but cannot restore. The poor, the hungry, the destitute, the unwanted.
> I was born to eliminate them as if cutting off a gangrenous limb or pulling a dead tooth.
> I am the flood.
> I am the cataclysm.
> I am the sower in the field.
> I am the angel of death.

After that, nothing.

"What the hell . . . ?" murmured Sean.

INTERLUDE FIFTEEN

THE BAIN ESTATE
SEATTLE, WASHINGTON
WHEN ZEPHYR WAS TWENTY-ONE

They made a killing, and that was how they celebrated.

John and Zephyr were in the back of the stretch Lexus SUV, separated from Campion by soundproof glass. They split a bottle of Il Poggione Brunello di Montalcino and used it to wash down a bag of doughnut holes from a drive-through place. Everything was funny to them today.

Her father's estate, years in probate, had cleared eleven months ago, releasing the entirety of his accounts and holdings to her. The exact amount fluctuated with the vagaries of the market. There was the oldest part of the family business, Bain Industries, but that was more of an administrative umbrella these days. Under it's cover were dozens of companies of various sizes, from BainBots, a boutique robot novelty manufacturer to Bain Logistics, a software giant that provided systems for all aspects of the military. Under the same umbrella was FarmBots, TeachBots, BookBots, and others, each focusing on a different aspect of the technologies market. The top earner was the military group, but HealthBots was close, and it provided everything from the latest generation of surgical robots to AI systems that integrated primary care, groups of specialists, and real-time personal medical-records systems. Her net income from that group of companies was sixteen billion per year.

Then there were the sixty-eight companies she owned through shell corporations. They included companies that provided lifelike programmable AI-driven robots for the foreign sex market, virtual-reality software and hardware for the pornography market, superintrusion software systems for corporate espionage, nanotechnology for high-output manufacturers in unregulated Third World countries, AI targeting systems for man-portable anti-aircraft weapons, nanotech regulator systems for street drugs, adaptive street drugs that changed with the shifts in the user's body chemistry, and more. The gem of that second set of companies was TekGuard Protective Systems, a new and rapidly expanding firm that developed nanites for use against pests carrying Zika, malaria, dengue, and other diseases. TekGuard was one of the most effective and affordable systems and was being used in over ninety countries around the world. FDA approval was pending for use in the United States. The net income from all these companies was fifteen billion. Net. That was what went into her thousands of numbered accounts.

"Based on earned and projected income, Ms. Bain," said her accountant, "you are the third-richest woman alive."

When Zephyr and John were alone in the car, he said, "I'll get the names of the two women higher on the list. I think we can arrange something."

That had been eleven months ago.

Now Zephyr *was* the richest woman in the world. Not that she could openly claim the title, since half of her income could never be credited to her in any public way. As far as the world was aware, she was the twenty-eighth richest woman. *She* knew the financial realities, though, and it was goddamn hilarious.

They drove back from the meeting with her accountant. Laughing.

Later John played video files of the "accidental" and thoroughly tragic deaths of the other two women. A car accident and a house fire. Both unexpected, both very tragic.

Such a shame that the autonomous-drive function on the number-two woman's car malfunctioned at just the wrong time.

Such a shame that the very expensive water-sprinkler system in the number-one woman's house simply failed to work.

Such a damn shame.

They drank and laughed and kissed and laughed.

All the way home.

CHAPTER SIXTY-TWO

The phone on Mr. Church's desk was programmed for special rings depending on who called. It made it as easy to prioritize as to ignore. Certain ringtones had the power to pull him out of all other considerations. The president's calls weren't always on that list. Not this president, not any of the past chief executives who had held the office during Church's long and complex career.

However, when the opening notes of Symphony No. 5, by Ludwig van Beethoven, played with soft drama, Church sat back from his computer and frowned at the phone. He took a breath and let it out slowly, then picked up the handset with a mixture of interest and trepidation.

"Hello, Lilith," he said.

"Hello, St. Germaine."

"I'm rather surprised by this call. I thought you made it abundantly clear that we were never going to speak again."

"I never said that."

"The last time we spoke," said Church, "you told me to burn in hell."

"Did I?"

"I believe you said that the next time we were even in the same time zone it would be because you'd come to the cemetery to dance on my grave."

Lilith laughed. For such a stern woman she had a lovely, musical laugh. It was very much like Violin's, but her daughter laughed more often. It was one of the many ways in which the two women were unalike.

"I thought you had thicker skin, St. Germaine," said Lilith. "Are you becoming sensitive in your old age?"

"Why are you calling? Chitchat is not among your many qualities."

"Humanity is not among yours."

"Have you called to pick a fight? If so, I hate to disappoint but I'm a bit busy and—"

"And you're about to get busier," she said, interrupting him.

Church said, "Why? Do you have something?"

"I do. Or, I might."

"What is it?"

"Have you been following the latest Zika outbreak in São Paulo?"

"Of course."

In the past several months there had been a dramatic spike in cases of a particularly aggressive strain of the Zika virus, and the death toll was mounting. When Zika first came onto the public radar, it was because of the effect of microcephaly, the underdeveloped and under-sized heads of newborns. The virus was spread to infants from mothers who had been bitten by mosquitoes. However, it was later established that it could also be spread through sexual contact. More recently, the disease seemed to have mutated and had become much more easily transmitted through any bodily fluid, and, unlike most viruses that require a living host, the new strain was hardier and could live outside a host for hours, which meant that it could be picked up through touch. The World Health Organization was working with Brazil's various health agencies. At the same time, researchers at the Centers for Disease Control in Atlanta had posited the theory that the new strain wasn't a naturally occurring mutation and might instead be a deliberate genetic alteration; this sent shock waves through the intelligence communities. Similar outbreaks had occurred in parts of India, Pakistan, Zaire, Malaysia, and elsewhere.

"Is it one of your cases?" asked Lilith.

"You know it's not. The COT teams have jurisdiction, and although I've extended an offer, they've made it very clear that they neither want nor require our help."

COT was Comando de Operações Táticas, Brazil's élite counter-terrorism unit.

"Why not?" asked Lilith. "Because of what happened last year?"

"Yes. Confidence in the DMS took quite a hit. It is taking some time to rebuild trust."

"COT couldn't find a naughty schoolboy smoking in a bathroom, let alone a team of bio-terrorists."

"If such a team, in fact, exists."

"St. Germaine . . . since when have you been gullible."

Church said, "It's not our case, Lilith."

"What about the other outbreak? New strains of swine flu in Chile, dengue fever in Ecuador, West Nile virus in Uruguay? Should I go on? It's a very long and very strange list."

"As I said, we've made offers."

"Since when have you accepted a rebuke, St. Germaine? You're notorious for poking your nose in where it doesn't belong."

"Perhaps, but we're resource poor at the moment, and there are other matters closer to home that are already pushing us to our limits."

"Yes, I heard that you were handing some of your cases off to Gray Pierce and his Sigma Force shooters."

"Gray is an old and trusted friend," said Church. "And some matters have come up that are more suited to his team."

"Does that include what's happening in Milwaukee?"

"Milwaukee . . . ? I'm not aware of anything specific happening there. What do you know?"

Before Lilith could answer, another line rang for Church. It was the special ringtone for the hotline from the Centers for Disease Control.

"You'd better take that call," Lilith said. "I'll wait."

CHAPTER SIXTY-THREE

We were getting close to the airport. Yoda told me that, mmmm, he still had nothing on the damn texter. All he'd managed to do was give her a goddamn code name. The Good Sister.

Swell.

However, a minute later my phone buzzed with a new text from the Good Sister. Not code this time. It was a link to a YouTube video of a song by a group called the Carpenters. With great trepidation, I pressed the Play button and the voice of the lead singer, Karen Carpenter, began singing a song called "Bless the Beasts and the Children." We listened. I was barely breathing. The song played through, and then it looped back and repeated a three-line chorus:

> Bless the beasts and the children
> Give them shelter from the storm
> Keep them safe, keep them warm

Over and over.

Then my earbud buzzed and Sam Imura was on the line. "Cowboy," he said in a low and urgent voice, "you need to listen to me."

"Hit me," I said.

He did.

He hit me real damn hard.

"There's been an incident at your uncle's farm," Sam said. "The Pool Boys missed their scheduled call-in. I called them on the command channel, both of their cells, and the house landline. Nothing. Both drones went offline, too. We're deaf and blind out there, and we have zero information on the status of the civilians."

Rudy and Sean were watching me. Rudy could hear the call, my brother couldn't, so I had to keep everything off my face. It cost a lot to do it.

"There's more, Cowboy," said Sam.

"I'm listening," I said, forcing my voice to sound normal. Human. Like the world wasn't catching fire.

"We just received a message transmission on a telemetry feed from one of our pigeon drones. No ID or signature, but there was a message and it was for you."

"Tell me."

"Message reads, 'We have your family. Jack Ledger, Alison Croft-Ledger, and two darling little children. They are alive and unharmed. Your agents were less fortunate, but that is war. You will gather *all* copies, records, data, and equipment collected in connection with your current case. You will bring all of these materials out to the farm and await further instructions. You will not make additional copies of the materials or notify any other authorities about this matter. There is a tapeworm file attached to this transmission. You will upload that file to your MindReader computer system. It will seek out and delete all mentions of this matter. You will let that program run for one hour, at which point it will self-delete. You will not attempt to interfere with its process. You may use a helicopter to bring this to Jack Ledger's farm. Once it has been deposited, you will return to Baltimore. After the helicopter has left you will receive instructions on what to do with the materials. Once the materials have been recovered and deleted from your files, you will receive precise information about where to find your uncle, your sister-in-law, and your niece and nephew. If you deviate from these instructions in any way, you and your brother will receive a series of packages in the mail that I can assure you would break your heart to open. Those packages are all that you will ever see of your family. The rest of them will be fed to dogs. If you pursue this matter in any way, the result will be the same. If you cooperate and your family is returned to you, please believe that we can find them wherever they are and take them whenever we want. Your cooperation is their guarantee of safety and if you follow these instructions, this matter will be closed.'"

How do you react to something like that? How can you even *hear* it and not scream?

I bit down on the fear, the horror, the words, the screams, the bile.

Sam said, "I'm connecting you with the Deacon."

There was a pause, and then I heard the voice of Mr. Church. "Cowboy," he said gravely, "are you able to respond to this situation?"

"Yes," I said. My voice was thick, and Sean immediately looked worried. I forced a smile and shook my head as if it was nothing more than an irritation in the back of my throat. In the back of the car, I heard Ghost go *whuff*. He heard it, too. Rudy was a statue carved from wood.

"Does Bug know?" I asked.

"He does."

"What did he say? Can we trust that file?"

"He advises against it," said Church. "He says that there is no way to analyze the tapeworm without triggering it."

"And no idea what it will do?"

"None. Bug fears it could do more than erase the data as stated. He says something as sophisticated as this could conceivably crash Mind-Reader."

"Fuck! What about the RFIDs for them?" And by "them" I meant the Pool Boys. Church was quick enough to catch it.

"The chips are active at the location. They may still be alive, but the signals are erratic."

"What are our options?" I asked.

"Cooperate or not," said Church. "We do not currently have a third choice."

I said nothing. My guts were slowly tightening into a white-hot ball of acid.

Church said, "Do you want me to make the call on this?"

"No."

"Then you're the quarterback, Cowboy. We play it your way."

I had to force my throat to work, to speak. "We already have a playbook," I said.

He didn't sigh in frustration and he didn't try to talk me out of it. Church wouldn't do that. We both knew that we weren't supposed to negotiate with terrorists. Sure. That's the U.S. policy. Except when it's impossible to punch back.

Church said, "Bug shared the binary message with me."

"Yes."

"Make no assumptions," said Church. "At the same time, stay open to possibilities."

"Even *that* one?"

"Yes. Even that one."

I swallowed. "Understood."

"I'll arrange for a helicopter. It will be fueled and ready by the time you get to the airport, and your flight plan will be set and cleared. Take Sean with you to the farm. A team will follow in a Chinook with all the case material from the Warehouse. All other DMS personnel in the region are on standby, and if you need firepower and boots on the ground at any time it'll be there ASAP. If you need *anything*, call and we'll drop the weight of the world on them. You have my word on that."

"Okay."

"Cowboy . . . ?"

"Yes."

"God be with you," said Church.

I almost laughed and had to force myself not to. It would have come out the wrong way. I ended the call.

"Change of plans," I said. "Sean, you're coming with us."

"I am?" he said, surprised. "Where? To see those nanotech experts?"

"No," I said in as human a voice as I could manage. "Something else came up."

CHAPTER SIXTY-FOUR

Aunt Sallie sat in the leather chair across the desk from Mr. Church.

"You didn't tell him about Milwaukee," she said.

"Not yet. He has enough on his plate."

The office was still and quiet. Everywhere else in the Hangar there was chaos. Bug had called all of his team into work and they were networked with dozens of other consultants in the DMS family. Yoda's crew was tearing the surveillance bugs apart and working to locate the Trojan horses and find the dangerous viral codes. Nikki's team was doing deep Internet searches on any keywords even remotely connected to what was happening in Maryland, Milwaukee, Prague, and elsewhere. Bug sat alone in a clean room trying to bend time to rush the tests on the quantum computer to completion.

In the science wing, the forensics team was working with the blood and tissue samples flown in from Baltimore. The legal team was finessing the necessary warrants and permissions to get an exhumation order for the other remaining teen who had likely died of rabies.

There were two hundred and seventy-seven experts working at the Hangar, and they had support from another five hundred highly trained staff. They had the MindReader computer system and a charter approved by Executive Order that gave them extraordinary access to databases throughout the United States' intelligence and military networks.

Aunt Sallie and Mr. Church sat in silence. Both of them praying that it would be enough.

INTERLUDE SIXTEEN

John took the glass, filled it, held it up to look at the fire through the dark-red liquid, and then handed it to her.

"I'm talking about the technological singularity," he said. "Are you familiar with the concept?"

"Kind of," said Zephyr. "I read Kurzweil's book, saw some papers. How does that apply to me, though?"

"It applies to us, my dear." He sat down across from her. "It is something many people foolishly believe is only a philosophical concept, a hypothetical event. The technological singularity. The point at which artificial general intelligence becomes capable of recursive self-improvement. It is the moment in time when the robotic systems and the artificial-intelligence computer systems accelerate beyond our influence. The point at which we are no longer guiding their development but are left behind by it. It is the moment when it all runs away from human interference and human influence. Yes. Frightening, isn't it?"

"Not really," she said, only half lying. "Checks and balances can be put into any software system."

"Yes," he said, drawing the word out almost to a hiss. "But you're still afraid—I can hear it in your voice, see it in your eyes. Even you, who will no doubt be the queen of robotics, and probably before your thirtieth birthday. Fear is understandable. However, you need to let go of fear, especially fear of change as it will manifest in the form of the singularity. If you persist in being afraid of it, you will be among those who will not be here to see that process of evolution come to fruition. Or, if you somehow survive, you'll be among those in service to the machines, but only for as long as it takes the machines to evolve past even that need. Look in the mirror—there is an expiration date on your forehead. Perhaps it is the mark of Cain finally written so you can read it."

"Don't go getting religious on me," she said. "I'm too drunk for that shit, and it's been too weird a day."

He laughed. "Don't worry, my sweet, I'll help you chase away the fear. You'll need to, because the singularity will be your true coming of age. If we manage it very well, it will be you coming into your own."

Zephyr studied him as she sipped. A lot of what he was saying was hitting the soft edges of too much wine and bouncing up into shadows. Some of it, though, was getting through. She cut a look toward the door to the study. Downstairs, behind locked doors and surrounded by nurses and attendants, was her father. Mad as the moon, with fresh blood on his hands and twenty billion dollars in the bank. Her money now. Money that she believed she could double or triple with the robotics systems in her head and in her notebooks. John was the only person who knew about all of that, and he was saying very interesting things.

Very interesting. She gestured with her glass for him to continue. It made his smile change, become less bright and more reptilian. Which Zephyr thought was equal parts scary and sexy.

"When the technological singularity occurs," he said, "there will be a change, a ripple, an earthquake of sorts that will cause all of civilization to shudder. Most of the old structures will necessarily break apart and fall, and in the rubble will be the bones of those who are unworthy of survival. Not all. Not even most. But enough."

"If that's not all metaphor, then who dies in that collapse?"

"Everyone on your No list."

"Okay," said Zephyr, "then who gets to survive? Who makes the cut?"

"That needs to be a much more carefully constructed list, my dear. It will include designers and builders, the scientists and makers of useful things. The artists. The cultured who bring something useful to the world. The innovators and scientists and pragmatists. For, you see, Zephyr, a curated technological singularity isn't about robots taking over our world. That's alarmist science fiction. It's about us *allowing* technology to evolve in order to serve in harmony with the surviving élite. It will be the formation of a true symbiosis between organic and inorganic life in a mutually assured survival."

"And you think people would be able to manage it?"

"Alone? No. I don't trust people to piss into a hole without guidance. Calpurnia is well suited to her task, don't you think?"

"How do we tailor my Yes list, then?"

"Inclusion in the survivor class, my sweet, will be earned, and that inclusion will require education, adaptation, and acceptance. It is an earned right and not a privilege."

"Why do I make the cut? I was born into money."

"You were born with an exceptional intelligence, Zephyr, and you chose to use it. You could have done nothing more than be pretty and count your allowance, but instead you opted to be a fully realized person, and a scientist, and a thinker of brave thoughts."

"I'm only twenty-one."

"So what? Alexander the Great was only sixteen when he completed his studies under Aristotle and joined his father's army. He became king of Macedonia four years later, and by the time he was twenty-one he had razed Thebes to the ground. Jordan Romero climbed Mount Everest when he was thirteen. Bobby Fischer won the Chess Championship at fourteen and became a Grand Master at fifteen. Probably the greatest music prodigy of all time, Wolfgang Amadeus Mozart, was composing by age five and could already play the violin and the keyboard, and was performing before royalty at that age. He died at the age of thirty-five, having composed over six hundred works; however, his operas were being professionally performed by the time he was fourteen. Blaise Pascal had worked out the first twenty-three propositions of Euclid by the time he was twelve. Aaron Swartz was fourteen when he developed RSS. Louis Braille invented the language for the blind when he was fifteen." He shook his head in gentle reproach. "Never use your youth as an excuse, girl."

Zephyr held her hands up in mock surrender. "Okay, point taken."

John nodded and drank his wine, sloshing some on his shirt but not caring. "The technological singularity, as described by Kurzweil and others, is too much of an abstraction. It's science fiction. It would be stopped in its tracks the moment the unwashed herd sniffed their own danger."

"But I thought you said it would work."

"You're drunk and you're not listening," he said, pointing a finger at her from the hand that held his glass. "I said *as described*. In order for the technological singularity to work in the way *I* have been discussing, it requires some assistance. Call it aggressive assistance. If we embrace the coming change, if we do whatever we can to ensure it, then the change will happen on our terms. Instead of a runaway AI evolution, we can help shape it, imbue it with our values and our goals, and in doing so both govern it and govern with it. To get to that point, though, we need to take an active hand in making sure the global change happens, and that it happens on a scale that will make a reset of the old, bad version impossible. That's where you come in, Zephyr. That's how you'll earn your place in the history of the new world."

"What's that supposed to mean?"

"It means that the robots you're so fond of can do much more than rescue trapped miners or study sulfuric output from active volcanoes." Firelight danced on the curved side of his wineglass. "Robots can do so much more." He paused. "Tell me, Zephyr, have you ever heard of DARPA?"

"Sure. Military geeks. I couldn't get in because dear old Dad left such a bad taste in their mouths. They're all pricks."

"They're much more than that, my dear. They are *military* science experts, and they will absolutely love you."

"But I told you, they already turned me down."

"Then I will teach you how to ask. I've found that everyone will listen if you bend close enough to whisper."

CHAPTER SIXTY-FIVE

I told Sean to pull over, and we parked in the lot of a Walmart.

"What's up?" he asked.

And so I told him all of it. He's a strong man and a brave one, but this nearly broke him. It pushed him all the way to the edge, to that narrow lip of rock that overhangs the big drop into total ruin. I pulled him to me and hugged him, held him while he yelled, while he wept, while he raged. Rudy leaned over from the back seat and clutched Sean's shoulders. Ghost howled. Sean punched my chest. Hard. He bruised me, and I took it. We held Sean on the edge of that drop, and I hope that we made sure he wouldn't fall. And, if he did, we let him know that he wouldn't fall alone.

For whatever that's worth. For what little that's worth.

"Ali," he said in a ragged, shattered whisper. "Em . . . Lefty . . ."

I held him tight. "We're going to get them back, Sean. We're going to do whatever they want, and we're going to get everyone back. Uncle Jack, too."

He shoved back from me, his face hot and red. Wildfires burned in his eyes, and for a moment I thought he was going to unleash at me, blame me for this. He had a right, I suppose. The threat was directed at me, at Joe Ledger of the Department of Military Sciences. Not at Sean Ledger of the Baltimore Police Department. The people who made that threat knew who and what I was. They knew about Mind-Reader. That was significant. It told us something. But, at the same time, this moved the debt over to my side of the board. Sean wasn't the one who put his family in danger. His asshole brother was. Somehow this was my fault. So, yeah, I expected him to whip me bloody with that.

But, once again, I underestimated my brother.

He sucked in a ragged breath and forced himself to take another step back from the edge. "What . . . what do we do?"

"We follow their orders."

"Will they . . . really let them go?"

"I think so," I said. "It's the only leverage they have to keep us from hunting them."

His mouth formed the words. *Hunting them.*

"There's a helicopter waiting for us at the airport. You can let me do this or go with us—it's your call, brother."

Sean's answer was to put the car in gear, step on the gas, and leave smears of smoking black on the asphalt behind us. The rental swung out into traffic amid blaring horns and squealing brakes. Sean accelerated and began weaving in and out of lanes. Driving like a cop but without the benefit of lights or sirens. He used the horn, though, and the traffic yielded to him.

"Whatever they want us to do, we'll do," I yelled, bracing my feet and hands to keep from bouncing against the seatbelts. "Don't worry about that. Whatever hoops they want us to jump through, we'll jump. We're not going to get cute with them. Believe me on this."

He nodded. A single, slow movement of his head on rigid neck muscles. It looked as if it physically hurt to do it.

"What they said . . . about you and your group not looking into this," he said as he shot the car through a tiny gap between a semi and a Mini Cooper. "Can you do that? After, I mean. Can you just let something like this drop? With all the other stuff going on. The rabies, the crazy shit at Vee's office. Can you really drop it?"

I could feel the weight of Rudy's eyes on me, but I looked straight at Sean. "No," I said.

"What about my family?"

My family, he said. Not *our* family. I understood why he phrased it that way, even if he didn't intend to hurt me with it.

"We'll get them back first, and we'll protect them," I said.

Sean wiped his mouth with the back of his hand. "Joe, *can* you keep my family safe?"

"Yes," I said. And I meant it. I didn't know how I could guarantee it, not at that moment, but I meant what I said.

He studied me. "And then you're going to go hunting for them?"

"Yes."

He bared his teeth. "Will you find them? Will *we*?"

I leaned forward. "Yes," I said in a voice that was the voice of the Killer inside my head. That voice, that intensity, should have scared Sean. It didn't. Instead, it seemed to light a strange fire inside him, changing the flames that were already burning in his eyes. Instead of intense heat, I saw him go cold. Bitter. Dark.

Rudy squeezed my shoulder hard.

Sean burned off more of the tires, skidding to a stop near where an airport official waited along with two armed guards. We got out and ran over. Ghost was right at my heels.

I flashed an ID—God only knows which one I showed him. Could have been my library card for all I knew—and an airport-security official said that our chopper was fueled and ready. The bird was a sleek Eurocopter EC120 B that belonged to the Baltimore Police Department. It had a cruising speed of one hundred and thirty-eight miles an hour but could be punched up to one-seventy if you wanted to risk life and limb.

We did.

The pilot had the blades turning already, and we ran through the rotor wash from a sloppy parking job, abandoning the rental without a second thought. Less than a minute later, we were climbing into the darkening evening sky and heading west at unsafe speeds.

In my head, the lyrics to that damn Carpenters song kept repeating.

Keep them safe.

Keep them safe.

Jesus Christ.

INTERLUDE SEVENTEEN

THE EDUCATION OF ZEPHYR BAIN
MCCULLOUGH CASTLE, CROWN ISLAND
ST. LAWRENCE RIVER, ONTARIO, CANADA
WHEN SHE WAS TWENTY-NINE

"There are some people you have to be careful of," said Uncle Hugo.

"Careful how?" asked Zephyr.

They were in a field behind his house, each of them loading fresh shells into shotguns. The far end of the field was littered with the debris from dozens of clay pigeons. A few of the skeet lay intact, but not the majority. Hugo was an excellent shot, and Zephyr was a little better.

"Don't you want to know who I'm talking about?" asked Hugo, snapping his gun shut.

"Okay," she said. "Who?"

"There are four in particular," said Hugo, "and they all work together in a black budget group called the Department of Military Sciences. The DMS."

She thumbed in the second shell and glanced up at him. "You're talking about the Deacon, right?"

Hugo grunted. "John already told you about him?"

"Some."

Hugo put the walnut stock to his shoulder. *"Pull!"*

One of the servants jerked the lever on the launcher and a skeet whipped through the air. Hugo followed it, then moved past it to lead the target. He pulled the trigger and the skeet vanished into a cloud of dust and fragments. The big man nodded and lowered his weapon.

"John said some things," said Zephyr. "But I don't know if he's messing with me or not."

"What did he tell you?"

She took her turn first, and the skeet exploded.

"About the DMS? Almost nothing. He said that they had two really dangerous field agents, Samson Riggs and Grace Courtland. And they have a computer system that was causing you a lot of problems."

"MindReader, yes. What else? Did he mention anyone named Hu?"

"A doctor. But not like the one on TV. A real scientist who was supposed to be super-smart."

"*Smart* doesn't begin to describe William Hu. *Freak* is closer. He's even smarter than you, kiddo, and that's saying a whole lot." Hugo took another shot and merely clipped the skeet, the impact hitting at an angle that caused the rest of it to spin faster. "Balls. What did John say about the Deacon himself?"

Zephyr began to raise her gun, then paused and lowered it. "Can you keep a secret?"

"Who you talking to, kiddo? You know you can tell me anything. Just between us."

"You won't tell John I said anything?"

He mimed zipping his mouth shut and tossing away the key.

"I . . ." she began, faltered, then took a breath, and said it. "I think John's afraid of that man. The Deacon, I mean."

Hugo cut a look at her. "What makes you say that?"

"Well . . . it was something John said one night," Zephyr said, pitching her voice low. "We were talking about how scary what I was doing was. I was telling him that while I *wanted* to do it, to stay the course, I was afraid that someone would stop me. It was after he had told me about Riggs and Courtland. He said that, as tough as they were, the guy they worked for was so much tougher. So much scarier. When I asked what he meant, he was quiet for so long that I didn't think he was going to answer. Then he began talking about things that had nothing at all to do with him or this Deacon person. He talked about battles in World War Two and World War One. He talked about spies and double agents and the people who lurked behind the thrones in half the kingdoms in history. He talked about how there was always someone like the Deacon who rose up to try and stop the future from being changed. At first I thought he was just trying to give me a, you know, historical perspective on how hard it was going to be to make a real and lasting change."

Hugo set his gun on the shooting table. "But . . . ?"

"It's going to sound really, really weird—and we'd both had a little wine—but it almost seemed like all the things he was telling me, all the people he was talking about, were somehow tied to him and the

Deacon. Almost like it *was* them he was talking about." She looked at him. "It's freaky, right?"

"Yeah, kiddo," he said distantly. "That's definitely freaky."

"So who *is* this Deacon guy, and why is someone like John scared of him? I mean, was it John's father or grandfather who fought the Deacon's father or grandfather? Is this some kind of ongoing fight between families or clans? Or cults, maybe? I tried to get John to tell me, but he wouldn't. He changed the subject and said that it was just the wine making him silly. It was the only time he ever outright lied to me."

Hugo Vox picked up his gun, signaled for the release, and fired. He missed completely. He tossed the weapon down in disgust. His assistant, Rafael Santoro, hurried over with a face towel and a flask. Hugo wiped his face and then took a very long pull on the flask.

"Hugo?" asked Zephyr. "What's wrong?"

The big man took her gun from her and placed it on the table. Then he put his beefy hands on her shoulders and looked her in the eye. "I'm going to say this to you once, kiddo, and then we're never going to talk about it again. Understand?"

"Um . . . well . . . sure . . ."

"There are a lot of very scary, very powerful people on this shitty little rock of a planet. Statesmen, great thinkers, political and religious leaders, and others. Some of them are smart enough and wise enough to know how the world works. How it really works. How it's *always* worked. They may play politics and be the face of a particular party or movement or faith or agenda, but the best of them are the big-picture thinkers. They see things as they are, in the context of history and not the context of the moment. They don't give much of a shit about who's in office or which ideology is the flavor of the month, because they know that there are greater forces at work in the world. They're the kind of people who remain in power during even the greatest changes. These are people who are involved in the running of the actual world."

"Like who? Are you talking about the Illuminati or the Seven Kings or—?"

"No. It goes deeper than that. I'm talking about the kinds of people for whom things like the Illuminati or the Kings or the Department of Military Goddamn Sciences are masks. Temporary masks. Masks of convenience. John is one of those people. He's a trickster, an agent of chaos—whatever the fuck you want to call it. He's the Joker from *Batman*. He's the guy who plays with matches in the fireworks store. He has all the keys to the zoo and likes to let the tigers out of their cages. That's John. And, honey, you only know one side of him, but, believe me, he wears a lot of different masks and I'm pretty sure it isn't always the same face under those masks."

"That doesn't even make sense."

"No, I guess it doesn't, but it's true anyway," said Hugo.

"What about the Deacon? If John likes setting fires, is the Deacon the one who likes putting them out? Are they some kind of opposite? Like the Sith and the Jedi or something corny like that?"

Hugo shook his head. "Frankly, kiddo, I don't have the slightest fucking clue who or what the Deacon is. And, believe me, I've looked. What little I've found confuses me, because it's all contradictions. What I do know is that he's not what he seems and that John *is* scared of him. That scares me. That scares the living shit out of me."

He let her go and stepped back. Santoro was close enough to have heard all of this, but his face was unreadable. Hugo squatted down and placed a hand on the stock of his shotgun but didn't pick it up.

"I have something in the works that's going to put me in the crosshairs of the Deacon and his group. It'll play out in a couple of years. If I win, the Deacon and the DMS will be ashes and I'll be the richest son of a bitch who ever lived. If I don't play it right, then best case scenario is I spend the rest of a short life in Gitmo playing water sports with the interrogation team."

Zephyr shivered. "That's not going to happen, is it?"

"Not if I'm smart and careful," said Hugo. "And that's how we got into this. I told you that you have to be careful of the Deacon and his people. You do. Their organization is still pretty new, still growing and finding its footing, but I know the Deacon. Not as good as John knows him, but well enough. There isn't anyone else out there who has a hope of stopping what's coming." He glanced at her. "Your plan's going to take longer, and it might even be bigger than mine. Fuck, kid, you might actually have the vision and the guts to change the world for the better. Time will tell. But the Deacon won't hand the world to you, and he won't step aside."

"Why don't you just kill him?"

Hugo smiled. "I've taken some swings over the years. So far, though, he's ducked and counterpunched pretty fucking well, even though he doesn't know it's me he's fighting. And I've put a few other things in motion that might hit him from his blindside."

"Maybe," said Zephyr, picking up her gun and reloading it, "you should stop trying to kill him and try something else instead."

"Like what?" asked Hugo, clearly intrigued.

"Like hurting him."

CHAPTER SIXTY-SIX

They knew we were coming, so there was no need to sneak up on the place.

From the air, from twenty miles out, everything looked normal, but with every mile and every moment we could tell that normal had left town. There was a wrecked car. There were big burned patches on the porch, the grass, the front of the house. There were bodies. There was blood. There was so much damn blood, as if a landscape painter had gone mad and bled onto the canvas of the day.

Sean had the door open and was leaning too far out, taking it all in, letting his fear and his need do bad things to him. Rudy held on to him, and Ghost whined continually. I told the pilot to set the helo down in the big side yard that the family used for softball games and touch football and Frisbee. The swirling vortex of mechanical wind picked up pieces of debris and flung them into the trees. Paper plates, empty soda cans, a kid's Orioles baseball cap.

"I don't see them," yelled Sean. "Where are they? God, *where are they*?" Asking a question none of us could answer.

Before the bird even touched down, Sean jerked the door the rest of the way open and jumped out, tearing his gun from its holster, yelling out his wife's name. Calling for his kids and Uncle Jack. Calling for his dog, Barkley. Calling for anyone. No one called back. We all scrambled out behind him. Per instructions, the pilot dusted off and vanished high and away in the late-afternoon sky.

Rudy ran toward the bodies. I sent Ghost on a hunt and he raced off, making a big circle, sniffing for hostiles and looking for family. I caught up with Sean as he approached the house, and then I stopped him with a firm hand on his shoulder.

"Sean, listen to me," I told him, "you need to keep your shit together. I can't be watching you and doing my job at the same time. We do this right so we can find them. You hear me?"

He stared through me for a moment, but then his wild eyes cleared a little and he nodded. "Okay, Joe . . . okay."

We did it all the right way.

We went up on the porch and flanked the door. He provided cover while I pushed the door open and ducked down and back. No shots. No movement. I went in low and cut left, and he followed a second later, gun up and out as he came in and went right. The living room was a shambles. Chairs and end tables overturned, the big mirror cracked, a vase of flowers smashed, muddy footprints everywhere. Boot prints, I noted. I pointed to them and held up four fingers. He understood. Four men had entered this house wearing combat boots. U.S. military issue, but that didn't mean anything. Anyone could buy that stuff. What mattered was that this had all been done with precision and aggression.

We moved through the downstairs. Living room, dining room, den, pantry, kitchen, mud room. Nothing. Lots of damage. A little too much. It didn't look like battle damage but instead had a flavor of meanness, of spite.

There are two sets of stairs in my uncle's house, one in the living room and one going up from the kitchen. I took the front steps and Sean went up the back ones. We both knew where to step to keep the boards from creaking. There was less damage upstairs, but there was some. The bedrooms were empty. So was the attic.

"They're not here," said Sean in a tight whisper.

"Keep it steady," I warned. "We knew they wouldn't be here. Let's finish the sweep."

As soon as we cleared the house, we hurried downstairs and went outside again. There was a terrazzo patio around the door, and I saw three bloody footprints. Dog prints. Barkley? Or had the bad guys brought their own dog? Ghost sat beside them. He hadn't barked and he didn't look agitated, which meant that whatever had happened here was over. If anyone had been hiding in order to ambush us, Ghost would have warned me. He knows several different barking patterns to tell me different things. He's smart, and we've spent hundreds of hours doing drills.

The Pool Boys lay where they had fallen, their bodies torn and bloody. Rudy was on his knees between them and waved us over.

"They're still *alive*. God only knows how, but they're alive. Sean, is there a first-aid kit in the house? Yes? Get it. Hurry!"

Sean hesitated for a second, then spun and raced back to the house. I looked at the two agents sprawled on the grass. Alive? The Pool Boys didn't look it. Both of them looked like ground meat. Neither looked like the men I knew. Their faces and bodies had been slashed to ribbons.

"Talk to me," I said to Rudy. "Is this the rabies stuff? Did they go nuts and do this to each other?"

"No. This is something different," said Rudy. He worked fast to apply makeshift dressings of cloth torn from his own shirt. "Each of them has multiple lacerations, and some are very deep. Joe, put pressure there—no, *there*. Good. Even if we can stabilize them, they've lost so much blood. It's shock that we have to prevent now."

"What *did* this?" I asked.

"Knives, I think. Or something with a longer blade. Machetes, perhaps. Or a scythe. I don't really know. I've never seen wounds quite like these." He pointed to a number of lacerations on the hands and arms of both men, and to similar cuts on their shoulders, upper chests, and faces. "These hand injuries look like defensive wounds, but against what? The same weapon was used on both of them, and the patterns are almost identical."

Sean raced back with a big farmer's first-aid kit in a sturdy blue-and-white plastic box. He opened it and Rudy dug out bandages and antiseptic and clamps. He told us where to apply pressure, what to hold, what to do, how to help. I know first aid and so does Sean, but it's different when a real doctor is calling the shots.

"If we don't get them into surgery in the next hour, we're going to lose Tommy and maybe Alvin, too," Rudy said.

"Can't bring the chopper back," I said.

"What about an ambulance? Can we at least call 911?"

"*No*," cried Sean. "We can't. They'll think we're trying something."

"Saving these men and saving your family are *both* of equal importance, Sean. Whoever did this left them alive. They left them for us to find. They expect us to try and save them. If they didn't want that to happen, they would have killed them or given us implicit instructions to let them die. They did neither. Which means we're *allowed* to save them."

Sean tried to reply, couldn't find the right words.

I tapped my earbud and said, "Cowboy to Ronin."

Sam's voice was right there. "Go for Ronin."

I explained the situation on the ground, and I heard him yelling at someone to get the machinery working. Then Sam asked, "Status on your family?"

As if in answer, I heard a phone begin ringing. It wasn't mine, and we had to wait for the next ring to zero in on its location. In Alvin's pants pocket. As soon as I pulled it out, I knew that it wasn't his phone. It was a burner. Even though I knew there was almost no chance of useful fingerprints, I still handled it carefully.

"Yes . . . ?" I said cautiously.

"By now you'll know that your associates have not been killed," said a man's voice. "You may infer that their lives were spared as a gesture of goodwill."

He spoke in English, but he had a thick accent. French. Metropolitan. Not Canadian. A Parisian accent. Provincial accents are different. Not young, not old. Forty, maybe? Forty-five?

"Where's my family?" I asked.

A pause. "This is not Detective Sean Ledger, is it? No. Captain Joseph Ledger, then, *non*?"

"Yeah. And, for the record, fuck you. Where's my family?"

"They are safe," said the Frenchman, "and they will remain so as long as you follow my instructions."

"I'm listening."

"Ah, that is incorrect, Captain. It is *I* who am listening. I'm waiting for you to tell me that the complete case files and all related materials are in your possession."

"They're on the way," I said. "I wasn't in the right place to bring them myself."

"If a strike team is accompanying the materials, Captain, this day will end badly for you."

"Listen, asshole, I got the instructions and we're following them. You made a lot of threats that I'm taking very seriously. My family matters more to me than catching you. Are we clear on that?"

"Completely."

"But, since you apparently enjoy threats, listen to this one, and you can believe it as completely as I believed yours. I want my uncle, my sister-in-law, and my niece and nephew back safe and sound. I don't want them hurt. I want them safe. You're going to do that because that's your part of the bargain. I'm going to give you everything you asked for. Everything. We're cleaning out the closets on this thing, and you get to walk away."

"Very well. And the threat . . . ?"

"It should have been implied, but let me spell it out. If my family is harmed in any way, I'll come after you and I *will* find you. If you know who I am, then you probably know something about who I work for. We are willing to accept your terms and let you walk off. We're willing to close this file, but only if you return my family unharmed. If you don't—no, actually, if you even think about breaking your word and double-crossing me—then know that I will find you and I will tear your world apart. Read up on me if you're not sure what that will mean. Try and guess how much I'll let you skate if you mess this up. Consider what *lengths* I'll go to. Ask around. Ask the people who have fucked with me and my crew in the past. Oh, wait, you can't. They're all dead."

He chuckled. A warm sound, like someone amused by a witty joke told by an old friend. It was supposed to unnerve me, defuse the bomb I was lobbing at him.

"Then I suppose we must both behave ourselves, Captain Ledger, *non?*"

I said. "*Crois, ce que je te dirai.*"

Believe what I'm telling you.

To which he responded, "*Ensuite il est essentiel que nous nous faisons confiance.*"

"Yeah. Well, in my experience trust is earned," I replied.

"And so it is," said the Frenchman. "Now, here are a few addendums to my terms. You may not remove your wounded friends until the materials have arrived. You can send them away in whatever vehicle delivers the case files and bodies."

"You really don't want them to die, pal," I said.

"They are soldiers."

"And this is a war? Is that what you're saying?"

"It is an *evolution*, Captain," he said. "For something new to emerge, something old must surely die."

"I don't even know what that means."

"Of course not. I will make another call in half an hour. Listen for the ring. It won't be on this phone. If the materials are at your location, answer that call. If not, expect a follow-up call every fifteen minutes. Wait for the call that comes in after your materials arrive. At that point, you will be given additional instructions. If we are both satisfied with the arrangements of exchange, a final call will be made on a phone that will be at a location I will share at that point. You will go to that location, locate the last phone, and receive instructions on where to find your family."

"How do I know they're still alive?"

"You don't," he said, and repeated my comment about trust being earned, but he said it in French. *"La confiance se mérite, mon ami."*

The line went dead.

Sean and Rudy stared at me. All they had heard was my end of the conversation. I told them everything, and it hurt them every bit as bad as it hurt me.

INTERLUDE EIGHTEEN

THE EDUCATION OF ZEPHYR BAIN
MCCULLOUGH CASTLE, CROWN ISLAND
ST. LAWRENCE RIVER, ONTARIO, CANADA
WHEN ZEPHYR WAS TWENTY-TWO

"What if they catch me?" asked Zephyr.

Hugo Vox pursed his lips as he dropped ice cubes into a chunky tumbler, poured two fingers of Heaven Hill over it, sipped the bourbon, and then turned away from the wet bar. He paused and repeated the process, handing the second glass to Zephyr. She sniffed and winced, took a sip, winced again, and then threw back the whiskey. She gasped, coughed, and staggered in Hugo's wake as he walked out onto the big stone balcony.

"That was a waste of good bourbon," he said.

"It tastes like socks."

"It's better than that shit scotch your dad used to drink."

"It was thirty-five years old. He said it's top of the line."

"Have you tried it?" asked Hugo.

"Well . . . sure. Once. On New Year's Eve."

"And . . . ?"

"It's even worse. It tastes like ass."

"That I'll agree with," said Hugo. "But trust me, bourbon is better. Besides, you hammered it back. You're supposed to sip it, savor it."

"Dad always said that ice ruins the taste of whiskey," said Zephyr.

"Your father was a fucking psychopath. Not sure his opinions were all that valid."

Zephyr grunted, acknowledging the point. They stood for a moment watching boats on the river, their sails reflected in the mirror-bright water.

"To answer your question," said Hugo, "if you get caught, then you didn't think it through. You didn't plan. If you get caught, it's probably because you deserve it."

"I don't understand."

He turned and leaned a meaty hip against the stone rail. "You know that I made an assload of cash when the towers fell, right?"

She nodded.

"Do you know how?" he asked.

"Sure. You had brokers ready to buy when everyone panicked and the market prices fell. John said that the plan worked because you knew that the towers were going to be hit, and *when* they would be hit. He said your genius is timing."

Hugo sipped his drink. "*Timing* is a funny word. I doubt that John explained what it really means. The big-picture view is that we funded Al Qaeda and we set the timetable. We had brokers in place to make the right purchases when the towers fell and the sheep started running. We knew they would because sheep always run. There's always a flight to safety in the market. That part you know. But there's the SEC, the FBI, the IRS, and a bunch of other alphabet groups whose whole job is to look for people gaming the system. If it were only a matter of us doing what you said, it would show. It would look exactly like what it was, and I'd be in jail or on death row, depending on how much of it they figured out. With me so far?"

She nodded.

"So why ain't I in jail? How come all those federal agencies haven't kicked down my door, frozen my assets, and thrown me in jail? Take a moment and answer when you have something smart to tell me."

She thought about it. Hugo finished his drink, took both glasses inside, and came back out with fresh drinks.

"You bribed the agents?" she ventured.

"Bribed or coerced," he said, nodding. "Blackmailed some, extorted some. Sure. But we only did a little of that during and after. We only had to do that with guys who were new to those agencies. Which should give you a hint of the rest of it."

"You . . . bribed some of them before? Like, long before?"

"Closer," he said, beaming with approval. "But you have to go much, much bigger. Look at it this way—we stood to make tens of billions from the shifts in the market after 9/11. We did, in fact, make that and more. We netted a lot more than we expected, and we expected a lot. So, knowing that this was probably going to work pretty well, we could take some risks with the money we had to invest to set everything up. And we eliminated some of the guesswork by controlling the timetable. Had we done more damage to the Pentagon or hit the White House, we might have doubled it. A dead president would have kept the market in flux for a long time. But that's life, that's a variable. We got the biggest fish, which was hitting the financial centers. The next components are vision and nerve. The vision part is being able to look forward to this as something we should do eventually but not something we should do right away. Good planning takes time. Staying safe takes time. So we *took* time. We started this project years ago. And I do mean years. Some of this was started before you were born. Some of it was started before we even picked the specific targets. We started by using that other quality—nerve. How did that work? It worked by hiring and training an enormous staff of qualified people, and then carefully and comprehensively seeding them into the system. Want to guess *where* we seeded them?"

She gaped at him. "The SEC and the IRS?"

"And the FBI, the CIA, the NSA, and about fifty other organizations. We have thousands of employees in place. Not just investigators but the people they report to, and the people *those people* report to, all the way up to administration. Some of it is bribery. Some of it is manipulating idealism. Some of it is sculpting the careers of certain people. And with that is oversight. We have watchers watching the watchers to about ten removes. We have records on everyone. We know what everyone likes and doesn't like, who they vote for, what they buy, who they fuck, what gets them high, what they're afraid of losing, what they hunger for. We come at them from all directions, and we make sure that if they get spooked and want to tell someone, then the people or departments that would take that call are owned by us, too. Our operating capital is close to two billion dollars per year. And the funny thing is, most of the people we own think they're working for clandestine agencies within their own organizations. They think they're in quality control or a reporting agency or something like that. Ninety percent of them think they're the good guys. But all of them work for us. So when we gamed the market the people who would raise red flags and write out arrest warrants belonged to us."

Zephyr drank down the last gulp of whiskey without even tasting it. Hugo smiled and sipped his.

"So," he said, "if you really want to create some kind of new world order you'd better start now, and you'd better be ready to invest the time and the attention to detail necessary to set it up right. You have the money. John and I are overseeing everything your lawyers do, so you know you'll be protected. You have the operating capital and you have the plan. You talk about this singularity stuff so much, you almost have me believing in it."

"It's the only way to—"

"—save the world from itself. Yeah, I know. I've heard the sales pitch. What I'm asking, kiddo," said Hugo, "is do you have the patience and do you have the nerve?"

She turned and looked out at the boats. The sun was low now, and it made everything—the sails, the trees, even the water—look as if they were on fire. It looked as if the whole world was burning.

"Yes," she said.

Hugo finished his drink, studying her over the rim of his glass. His eyes were filled with a dark light, and when he lowered the glass he was smiling.

CHAPTER SIXTY-SEVEN

They say war is hell. It is. Waiting, though, is its own kind of hell.

Sean, Rudy, and I were caught in that bubble of time between the end of that call and the arrival of the medics and our team coming to deliver the case file. Every second felt like an hour. And not a happy hour. Like an hour under torture by someone who makes Thomas of Torquemada and the fun kids of the Spanish Inquisition seem like supporting characters in *Pee-wee's Playhouse*. Like that.

Ghost moved slowly around the yard, sniffing at the picnic table, at Lefty's hat, at Em's stuffed tree sloth, at the smashed remains of Ali's phone, at Uncle Jack's torn apron. He whined every now and then. Sean got up and began to follow him, picking up each item one at a time. Holding them. No, clutching them. I could see the white of the knuckles on his clenched fists. Rudy tried to say something, to comfort him, but I don't think Sean could actually hear or understand human speech. His body language changed from robotic stiffness as he walked from one relic to another, and then to scarecrow slackness as he stood and stared with unblinking eyes at the things Ghost found. All I could do was watch. I pretty much think I'd rather be taking live fire than to have to sit there with my brother while we waited to find out if his wife and kids were even still alive.

So I forced myself to work the scene. To decode it.

The attack had to have happened quickly. The food on the grill was still there, though the steaks and the corn were burned to smoky cinders. Things had been dropped: a couple of ball gloves next to an old soft-ball that looked like the one Sean and I used to play with once upon a time, an overturned beer bottle, a glass of iced tea with all the cubes melted, a pair of sunglasses that had been stepped on, Ali's purse. And there was blood. Here and there, little splashes and drops.

I found something that I couldn't immediately identify, a piece of thin plastic about eight inches long. Smooth, with a sloping angle to it, and a sharper angle where it had clearly broken off from something else. Making sure not to smudge any possible prints, I picked it up by the edges and immediately winced and dropped it, and stared in surprise as blood welled from microthin cuts on the pads of my thumb and forefinger. It was razor-sharp. Some kind of blade, I reckoned, but not a standard knife or sword configuration. I squatted on my heels and thought about the vanes of the helicopter we'd come in. They had almost the same angle, except their edges were blunt.

I got up and crossed quickly to where Rudy was still working on the Pool Boys, and stood there looking at the patterns of their injuries. Cuts on their hands and arms, on their upper chests and shoulders and faces. A chill swept up my spine and made the wiry hair on my scalp stand up, because I thought I understood what had happened.

"Son of a bitch," I said, which caused Rudy to glance up.

"What?"

"I read a report a couple months ago about a new kind of combat drone called a thresher. Designed for field combat rather than aerial strikes. About the size of a bald eagle, with rotors for lift, a new kind of gyroscope for ultra-sophisticated maneuverability, and, instead of guns, it used long, flexible blades. They called them whip blades, and they're based on the old Chinese straight sword. The whip effect maximizes the speed and severity of each cut. They were designed to be introduced to a fixed enemy position, to do as much damage as possible to personnel while leaving the weapons and equipment intact. I think that's what happened to these poor bastards."

"Ay Dios mio," said Rudy. "That's appalling."

"Question is who sent it here. Last I heard, the thresher was only in the design stage."

Ghost suddenly barked and looked up at the eastern sky, and Rudy and I jerked around, expecting to see a thresher come screaming at us. It wasn't. It was a muscular and very fast Bell Boeing V-22 Osprey, and as it came swooping in the rotors began tilting from their forward position to allow the plane to land like a helicopter. It was Duffy in a DMS bird, and a moment later a voice in my ear said, "Spartan to Cowboy. We're coming in."

"You have the package?"

"Wrapped and with a bow on it," he said. "And we're set for medical evac. How're our boys?"

"Moderately poor," I told him. "There's a big field west of the barn. Put it down there."

The Osprey swept over us, looking ungainly and improbable, and then settled down in a field of wildflowers without so much as a bump. Sean, Ghost, and I ran to meet it, ducking low as we approached. The door behind the cockpit was already open, and I saw Duffy and Torres waiting, dressed like EMTs instead of soldiers. Smart. A couple of other guys in tan flight suits scrambled out and began unloading several metal boxes. I pointed to the picnic table, and they carried the boxes over and then retreated to the Osprey.

Duffy and Torres ran over to Rudy, each of them carrying medical bags and equipment. They knelt down, did some additional stabilizing work on the Pool Boys, and then called for the flight crew to come running with stretchers. Everything was done to make it look as if we were following the directions exactly as they had been given. The wounded were transferred to stretchers, belted in for safety, and carried quickly but carefully to the plane and loaded aboard. The flight crew did not reappear.

"Cowboy," Duffy said, closing on me, "you want me to take your brother and Rudy back?"

Wild horses couldn't have dragged Sean away, and I knew that Rudy would want to stay to see to the family. I said as much to Duffy. He nodded and handed his medical kit to Rudy. It was a professional field-trauma set, far superior to the first-aid stuff here at the farm. He shook Rudy's hand, nodded to Sean, clapped me on the arm, and went running for the transport. The pilot cycled up the engines and the big machine lifted up, turned, and headed off the way it had come. The whole process had taken five minutes.

Sean, Rudy, and I stood in the field, with Ghost stalking slowly around the edge of it. We waited, watching the Osprey disappear.

Time once more slowed to an impossible crawl.

And then a phone began ringing.

INTERLUDE NINETEEN

THE EDUCATION OF ZEPHYR BAIN
MOTEL 6 DES MOINES NORTH
4940 NORTHEAST FOURTEENTH STREET
DES MOINES, IOWA
WHEN ZEPHYR WAS THIRTY-TWO

They met in a motel room.

By arrangement they had each rented a separate unit. Zephyr stood in the doorway of hers for nearly two minutes debating whether to call in the room maids to reclean the room, or just simply set fire to it. There was not a chance in hell that she would touch anything here. Not the bed, not the curtains, not anything. It was no comfort that the woman she was here to meet would have a similarly appalling hovel of a room. She knew that her rich-girl élitism was shading the moment for her, and that practicality was far more important than anything else.

Even so, she called her driver, Campion, and told him to purchase a few items and to deliver them without drawing attention. Half an hour later, the driver tapped discreetly on the door. He had a box of industrial-grade black plastic trash bags, bottles of strong but organic spray cleaner, sponges, and several large bottles of hand sanitizer. While Zephyr stood in a corner, Campion quickly covered every surface with trash bags, wiped down any uncovered surface, and cleaned the bathroom. All the cleaning products he used went into another of the trash bags. A pair of one-gallon bottles of bleach were set on the floor for a final cleanup after the meeting was over. He asked no questions of his employer and left, with an order to park his car close by and to be ready in case Zephyr needed to leave quickly.

Zephyr sat at the desk. Chair and desktop rustled with plastic sheeting. She wore blue polyethylene gloves and paper shoe covers on her sneakers. She stopped short of wearing a surgical mask. The woman coming to meet her might be suspicious.

Zephyr thought that the caution of meeting in a place like this wasn't necessary. She had tried to assure the other party that her team—led by the detail-oriented Concierge—could have provided any number of secure locations. But the woman had insisted, and, as Zephyr needed something from her, concessions were necessary.

The meeting had been scheduled for 2:30 in the afternoon, but the digital clock on the night table ticked all the way through to 2:51 before there was a firm two-beat knock on the door. Decisive, not hard. Zephyr got up and opened the door, saw a young woman wearing a bulky Hawkeyes warm-up jacket and matching cap, and sunglasses with mirrored orange-tinted lenses.

"John sent me," said the woman.

It was the appropriate code phrase.

Zephyr stepped back and the woman came in quickly, cutting a quick look over her shoulder.

"The parking lot is clear," said Zephyr. "The surveillance cameras are fixed, but they've been adjusted so that this room isn't in their video field. I have people in three other rooms, all with good views of this door."

"I have four teams," said the woman. "Including a very good sniper who is absolutely bugfuck nuts, but he loves me."

Zephyr smiled. "Ludo Monk, Room 312. He's positioned with a Dragunov sniper rifle."

The other woman smiled. "Nice."

"Nice," agreed Zephyr.

They didn't shake hands. It wasn't that kind of moment.

"The presumption is," said the visitor, "that if either of us sneezes half the people in this motel will try to kill the other half."

"Something like that," said Zephyr.

"I'm okay with it."

She looked around the room and walked over to lift a corner of one of the trash bags covering the bed. "You a germophobe or are you a serial killer and this is your murder room?"

"I didn't bring a saw."

The woman laughed and snorted in the middle of it, which made her laugh harder. She turned and sat down on the bed hard enough to send ripples through the plastic.

"This is fun," she said. "You're a rich-bitch snob with a hygiene phobia, and I'm a self-absorbed narcissist with trust issues."

"Aren't we a pair?" said Zephyr. She sat down at the desk.

"We are. A case could be made that we're two of, say, the five smartest women alive. And an equally strong case could be made that we're both out of our minds."

Zephyr held a hand up and waggled it back and forth. "I like to think I'm more of a visionary."

"Who wants to kill a couple of billion people?"

"I want to remove parasites."

"So you're what . . . the Lysol of social Darwinism?"

Zephyr shrugged. "Something like that. And you're what? The world's greatest technology thief?"

"I prefer to think of it as usefully repurposing questionable technologies in order to maximize their design potential."

"Nice," said Zephyr.

"Nice," said the woman.

"John told me that you don't use your actual name anymore. He said that it's because the people who would like to see you dead already believe you are."

"Something like that."

"Then what do I call you?"

The young woman took off her glasses and folded them, then removed her ball cap and shook out her glossy black hair.

"Call me Mother Night."

Zephyr Bain studied the face. The young woman was exceptionally beautiful, and the lights that burned in her intelligent eyes burned white-hot. Zephyr wondered what it would take to get this woman into bed. Not this bed, but a bed back at her house.

As if reading her mind, Mother Night said, "Not my scene, honey. Don't get me wrong. I'm flattered as hell, but I like boys and I'm on the clock. I have some things running right now, and they need some administrative oversight."

"Anything I need to know about?"

"They'll be on the news. It won't affect what you're doing unless you have plans to visit Atlanta. If so, let me advise against it."

"Why?"

Mother Night shrugged. "When I talked to your friend John he said that our agendas, though different in structure and rollout, will ultimately complement each other. Time's short, though, so can we move this along?"

Zephyr nodded. "Okay, cutting right to it. John said that while you were working for the DMS you had the opportunity to obtain extensive records from the ruins of the Jakoby empire. He said that you obtained schematics for the revolutionary computer system designed by a Cold War designer named Bertolini, the blueprints and modified software for which had been included in materials formerly in the possession of Paris Jakoby."

Mother Night grunted. "My sources tell me that you already have a good computer system. Calpurnia, isn't it?"

"That's just a household-governing thing."

"Bullshit. Couple of people have told me how you downplay what Calpurnia is. You pass it off as AI in the same way most people do, *calling* it artificial intelligence when it's actually programming tricks, with you, as the programmer, supplying the intelligence to the system. That's a nice line, and it works for the rubes, but it doesn't square with the whole technological singularity your boy John the Revelator has been shouting about. No, don't look surprised, you're not the only one who does her homework."

Zephyr nodded, acknowledging the point, but added, "It's a curated event we're working toward."

"Sure, but that doesn't mean Calpurnia is fake AI. I think you actually hit the bull's-eye. I think you have a real thinking system. Not something that plays a good game of chess because it analyzes the patterns of the other player's moves. No, I think you have a system that analyzes the other player. And understands him. I'm hearing very cool, very spooky things about Calpurnia. You're going beyond simulated AI and into . . . what? Limited consciousness?"

Zephyr hesitated. "Maybe. The system is evolving."

"I bet." Mother Night leaned forward, her eyes alight with excitement. "Tell me . . . does it have its own personality?"

"Yes," said Zephyr.

"Really?"

"Yes, a unique personality has been emerging for a couple of years."

"Any conflicts with it? Does it have seamless deference or—?"

"I don't mean to be rude," said Zephyr quickly, "but we should probably stick to the program here."

"You're no fun," said Mother Night, but she nodded. "You called this meet, ball's in your court."

Zephyr nodded. "John said you have copies of all testing, practical lab procedures, mapped genomes, and other materials for developing the Berserkers and other transgenic creatures. He said you recovered this from the records of Hecate Jakoby. He said that you secured computer records and actual biological samples of the weaponized ethnic-specific bioweapons developed by their father, Cyrus Jakoby. He said that you have access to samples of bioweapon pathogens in pre- and post-developed states. And he said that you might be willing to sell this material to me."

Mother Night pursed her lips and studied Zephyr for a moment. "John said you wanted to purchase some materials from me, Zephyr. He didn't say that he knew all of this. *How* does he know?"

"John is an excellent resource."

"This is spooking the shit out of me, I admit it," said Mother Night. "There's no way he could know some of this. Even when I was put on trial there was no mention of the stuff I got from Cyrus Jakoby. None. Not even Mr. Church knows about that."

"John the Revelator has better sources."

Mother Night stood up. "Nope. I think we're done. You're one spooky bitch, and I—"

Zephyr said, "Wait for just a few moments. Listen to me. Your man Ludo Monk has a thermal scope on his rifle. He can see our heat signatures through this wall. I'm guessing you have some kind of transponder on you so he can differentiate you from me, which means right now his gun is aimed at me. Any bullet he fires from that gun will be able to punch right through these crappy walls. If he's as good a shot as he's supposed to be, then he can kill me right now. It's not even a hundred yards between barrel and target. If you think I'm here to scam you or do you harm in any way, tell him to pull the trigger. Go on. I'll wait. I'll sit right here."

Mother Night looked at the door as if she could see through it and across the parking lot to the other wing of the C-shaped block of motel rooms.

The moment stretched.

Then Mother Night sat back down on the bed.

"Okay," she said. "What is it you want to buy?"

Zephyr Bain smiled. "I want to buy all of it, sweetie."

CHAPTER SIXTY-EIGHT

Ghost found it and raced across the field to stand proudly over it, wagging his tail. It was there, nestled down into the flowers. Sean made a grab for it, but I hip-checked him out of the way and snatched it up. I hit the button.

"Go," I snapped.

"There are still a few details to be handled before we can return your family to you, Captain," said the Frenchman.

"You don't want to fuck around too long on this, sparky," I said.

"These are important details, *mon ami*."

"What details?"

"There are fuel cans in the barn. Get them. Place the medical samples and all paper files in the middle of the yard. Keep the flash drives in your pocket, but everything else must be placed on the pile. Douse it all liberally and light a match. When the fire has had sufficient time to burn, you will hear another ring."

"Wait just a—"

The line went dead.

I stood there, really goddamn needing something to hit. Something with breakable teeth and a voice that could manage a satisfying scream. The Killer in my head was howling. But I kept my voice calm as I explained what had to be done. Sean simply turned and ran toward the barn. I ran after him.

There were two big red metal three-gallon gas cans just inside the barn. We each took one, ran over to the boxes of materials, and shook out the contents, splashing the evidence. Sean was getting sloppy and splashed some on his own clothes. I swatted the can out of his grip and pushed him away.

"Go stand with Rudy," I said. "Be ready to find the next phone."

He had to blink several times before any sanity looked out through his eyes. Then he nodded and shambled off. I took a lighter from my pocket, flicked it on, and bent to set the pyre ablaze. It went up fast, and I let the bloom of heat push me back. Gray smoke coiled up into the late-afternoon sky.

And we waited. The bastard let the fire burn for twenty minutes before he called. I spent some of that time kicking at flames that wanted to go running into the field, and some of it using a shovel I fetched from the barn to cut a narrow firebreak. And I used all of that time working on this in my head. Making sure the Cop in me was on the job and the Killer was on a leash. For now, anyway.

When the phone rang I heard Sean cry out, half in surprise, half a whimper of unfiltered fear. He was going to need Rudy's help, too. Rudy gently took the phone from Sean and held it out for me. Sean allowed it, but this was tearing him apart.

"Okay," I said, "it's done. Now, where's my family?"

"I'm going to need you to bring the flash drives to me. You may not bring a firearm or a knife. Leave whatever you have behind. No cell phone, no electronic devices of any kind."

"Are you dicking me around?"

"I'm not. This is a business transaction, but there are necessary safeguards built into it. I have great respect for your ability to be creative and exploit opportunities. Therefore you will have to bear with me while I determine that everything is done correctly. If I am safe, then your family will remain safe. That's only fair, *non*?"

"Yeah, yeah, let's get this ball rolling."

"*Très bien*," he said. "You will leave your brother and Dr. Sanchez at the farm. You will leave your dog there as well. Leave your gun and all communications devices behind. That includes your earbud. You will walk east along the main road until you hear a phone ring. You will receive your next set of instructions at that point." The line went dead before I could say another word.

I explained everything to Sean and Rudy.

"What do you want me to do?" demanded Sean, his eyes wild with the fever of terror.

"Stay here and wait."

"Jesus Christ, Joe, I *can't!*"

"You have to," said Rudy. "You know that."

It cost Sean so much to agree, and cost him more to stay behind. I handed my gun and other gear to Rudy, then took off along the road. I didn't walk, I ran. Not full speed but at a jog trot so I could cover ground. I had that same itch between my shoulder blades that I had before and wondered where the observers were. Who was watching me? How were they watching, and how many of them were out here? I cut looks left and right as I ran. On one side of the road was a farm field that was green with the first shoots of a corn crop pushing up through the soil. On the right were the apple groves belonging to Uncle Jack's neighbors. There were shadows beneath the trees, and I was sure every one of them was a sniper.

But no bullets punched into me.

I ran and listened. And prayed.

I heard the phone ringing and skidded to a stop, wheeled, and ran fifty yards back to where a burner lay nestled in the tall weeds around a fence post. It was the Frenchman again, and he told me to enter the grove and go northeast toward a stretch of forest. I did, and after a mile another phone had me turn west, then southwest, then to cross to the other side of the road and cut across a field. And on and on. Ten phones, ten sets of directions. The intention was not to disorient me but to allow hidden observers to watch the sky and roads and land around me to see if anyone was following me. No one was.

On the tenth call, the Frenchman told me to climb down a slope to a stream that was in deep shadow under the leafy arms of oaks and maples. I got to the water's edge and found the next phone and endured ten burning seconds while I waited for it to ring. When it did, I punched the button and the Frenchman said, "Turn around."

I whirled, shifting immediately into a combat crouch, ready to take on whoever or whatever was coming for me. But that wasn't it. Instead, there was something waiting for me. It squatted on the hard-packed dirt halfway up the stream bank.

A drone. Not a thresher, though. This was a basic quadcopter, the cheap kind you can buy at any Costco.

The Frenchman said, "Put the drives into the basket."

I knelt by the drone and saw that there was a wire-mesh basket bolted to the undercarriage. I did as ordered.

"Now," said the Frenchman, "walk north along the streambed until you hear a phone. It will be the last call, and you will be told how and where to find your family."

"Remember what I said," I warned.

"I told you, Captain. This is a business transaction. Threats and dramatics aren't necessary."

The flash drives fit inside with plenty of room to spare. The rotors on the quadcopter began to turn as soon as I stepped back from it, and the tiny motors whined. I watched it rise and wobble away between the trees.

My heart was racing out of control as I moved off along the streambed. Off to my right, I heard a sound. A soft *whuff* that wasn't quite a bark. I whirled and crouched, terrified that it was Ghost, that he'd followed me and that it might be construed as me breaking the Frenchman's rules. The tall grass swayed as a heavy body moved through it toward me.

"Ghost . . . ?" I whispered.

The dog gave another *whuff*. Softer, weaker, and now I could hear it spiral up into a whine. I bolted into the field, knowing what I'd find there. Finding it. Finding *him*. Barkley moved very slowly, and I was surprised that he could move at all. The shepherd's tan-and-black coat was slick with dark blood, and in a flash moment of betrayal I hoped it was his and not the blood of my family.

It was.

Barkley looked up at me with liquid brown eyes filled with so much pain that he was almost on the other side of it. So much hurt that he was nearly beyond feeling hurt. The dog had been chopped and slashed, and his canine mind understood that he was already gone. Even so, with all that damage, he had smelled me, or heard me, and made his presence known.

I hurried to him and knelt as Barkley took a last step and then collapsed against me. He was a big dog, but his weight was diminished by so much loss of blood. He laid his head on my shoe and gave my ankle a small, desperate lick. I tried to comfort him, tried to soothe him, telling him he was a good boy, telling him everything was all right. Lying to that heroic, trusting, loyal animal with every word.

A shudder rippled through him and he sagged down, sighing out his last breath. I bent forward, hissing with the pain that twisted deep inside my chest. The Killer in my soul grieved as ferociously as did the Cop and the Modern Man. Some things touch every open heart and wound every soul. Barkley had been a police dog and then he had been a family dog, and he had died trying to save the family who loved him. He wasn't even my dog, but I've grieved less for some people I know.

I kissed Barkley's head and stood up, fists balled, stomach churning with hot acid. I started walking again, legs pumping. The lurid dying sunlight slanted sharply through the trees, turning the green world to a hellish red. I felt as if I was approaching the outer rings of hell, heading deeper into the valley of the shadow of death.

And then I heard the sound.

It was a child. A girl.

And she was screaming.

INTERLUDE TWENTY

"They'll turn me in," she said. "First damn chance they get, they'll be on the phone to the authorities."

"No, they won't," said John the Revelator.

"The hell they won't. You expect me to put fifty top scientists in a room and tell them I want to kill a few billion people, and you think all of them are just going to go, 'Rah-rah team'?"

"Maybe they will."

"Maybe I'll get a lethal injection after a short trial."

"Maybe you will," said John.

"Don't joke," she snapped. "It's not funny."

"My love, am I saying there are no risks? No, of course not. Everything has risks. Breathing deeply is a risk. You could have a blood clot about to break loose inside your veins and the next time you have an orgasm it goes straight to your brain. But that is small thinking. Fear should never be a guiding principle in life."

"I'm not talking about random fear, John. I'm talking about common sense and caution."

"Nor am I."

"Then what—?"

"When have I ever done anything rash?" he asked. "When have I ever asked you to do something needlessly dangerous? Haven't I taught you caution and subtlety? Weren't those the lessons you learned from Hugo Vox?"

"Hugo is dead. Doesn't that say something?"

"He died because he left his protection up to others and became arrogant. You are élitist, my girl, but you're not arrogant. And you've learned your lessons of caution very well. I'm so proud of how you handled things."

"Don't hit me with flattery. Tell me how I'm supposed to manage all those scientists without risk. It's only going to take one phone call to stop everything. One call to the FBI or, worse, to the DMS, and Havoc is done. Over."

"So make sure none of them want to make that call."

"Yes, but *how?*"

"Everyone has a vice, my dear. Understand that vice; control it, and you control them."

"How?" she snorted. "Making sure they have the best drugs? Getting them laid? Maybe you want me to give them all blow jobs."

He made a face of disappointment. "Let me frame it a different way. Everyone has something they want, something they need, something they must have. For one man, that might indeed be drugs. For another, the thing they most crave is to not go to jail for past indiscretions. Or it might be that they truly and completely love their children. . . ."

John stopped there and let the rest hang.

Zephyr felt the blood drain from her face.

But only for a moment.

CHAPTER SIXTY-NINE

I ran like a son of a bitch.

The scream came from farther down the stream, around another bend, and I hit it at a flat run, crashing through brush that leaned out over the water, splashing through puddles and chasing rabbits into a blind panic. I had no weapons, but that wouldn't matter. Whatever was going after my family was going to die, and I wouldn't make it nice and quick.

There were shouts, too. My Uncle Jack's deep voice, other male voices. Ali yelling so high and shrill that the words became nothing more than a whip of panic that cut me across the heart. Branches lashed my face and arms, lacerating my skin, but I didn't care. The forest was so dense it tried to stop me. No way. No fucking way.

The creek jagged right and the shortest route was up a small hillock and through some shrubs, so I crashed through as a fresh scream tore the air. It was Em's voice, I was positive. Was it terror or agony? An impossible, hurtful, destructive question for anyone to have to try and answer.

As I closed in, I heard another sound beneath the shrill screams. A low growl, but not an animal sound. This was strange. A machine sound. I burst through and jumped down toward the curve of the stream. The civilized, sane mind has limits to what it can process before circuits blow out and there is a sudden and greater need for darkness than for clarity.

I'm not entirely civilized, and I'm not all that sane. I've witnessed horrors. They don't freeze me in my tracks, even if they're freezing my heart to a block of ice inside my chest. I'm wired differently. When the Modern Man inside my head is unable to deal with horrors and the Cop has no solutions ready to hand, it's the Killer who roars to life and takes charge. He's incapable of hesitation. He's too primitive to disallow something because it doesn't square with what he knows of the world.

The Killer knows that there are monsters in the dark and even if he cannot name them, even if he fears them, he also knows that survival lies at the other end of a fight. Retreat is what prey does, and he's a predator. If he's not the apex predator in any given situation, then whoever or whatever is has got to want the win more than he does, and he always wants it.

He wants it.

I want it.

Even when we were entering hell itself. Like this moment.

Tableau. There they were. All of them. My Uncle Jack, Sean's wife and kids. Two big men wearing ski masks.

And *it*. A thresher. It hovered there, plastic blades slashing through the air, engine buzzing like a thousand furious wasps.

I took it all in during one microsecond as I came smashing through the brush. Part of the combat mind is orientation. The creek zigzagged at the bottom of a gully that had steep sides. Jack was on the far slope fighting with the two men. I didn't see any guns, but the fading sunlight flashed on knives and on the bright red of blood. Jack was hurt, but I couldn't tell how badly, and both of the men had blood on their clothes. Ali stood knee-deep in the brown water, with Lefty and Em behind her. She had a broken length of tree branch in her hands and was swinging wildly at the thresher, which hovered just out of range.

The thresher was as big as an eagle, with a lumpy birdlike body and two sets of whirling propellers that slashed the air as it moved toward Sean's family. This wasn't any commercial or recreational drone. This was a killing machine. Ugly and vicious and efficient in its brutality. Ali's arms were crisscrossed with cuts, some of them deep, and bright blood ran down her limbs. Both kids were splashed with blood, and Lefty was on his knees, his face white, hands clamped over his stomach. Em was trembling, feet wide, fists balled, eyes totally wild.

At the precise moment that I burst from the woods, Ali swung her makeshift weapon at the thing that had come for her children. It rocked sideways, avoiding the swing, and then slashed at her from a tilted angle. Blood flew, and she staggered back. Jack yelled and took a step toward her and there was a flash of silver that tore a cry from him, and I saw a look of perverse triumph in the eyes of one of the two men. I saw all of this, every detail, in one tiny fragment of a second. In times of severe stress, the mind can shut down or it can observe and process a tremendous amount of detail. The difference depends on whether you die or live, on whether you freeze or act.

I hurled myself from the edge of the gully and splashed hard in the water, shoving Ali backward as the drone came in with blades slashing at her face. She fell, but the tip of one blade caught her across the forehead, drawing a vicious red line above her eyebrows. I ducked under the machine and pushed Em back, too. She fell on top of her mother, both of them thrashing in the chop. Lefty was ten feet away and seemed to be staring glassily at something none of us could see. It hurt me so goddamn bad to see that look on his face and, with the Killer running the show, hurt, like fear, turned into a red-hot murderous rage.

"Stay down," I roared as I snatched up the stick Ali had been holding, rose, whirled, and hurled it with all my strength. The stick struck one set of whirling knives and was instantly chopped to splinters. I ducked low under the blades, scooped up a handful of mud, and flung that next, striking the center of the rotor with a heavy, wet *glop.* The weight and force jerked the machine sideways and it wobbled in the air as its gyros fought to correct and balance it.

Behind me there was a sharp cry and a wet sound of impact. I whirled to see Jack land hard on the bank, his shirt turning dark red. Above him on the high rim of the bank, one of the masked men gripped a bloody knife in his big fist.

"You!" said one of them. He tore off his ski mask, and I recognized him as the Bridge Troll from Vee's office. Goddammit. "I'm going to fucking *kill* you."

The second man also removed his mask, but he was a stranger. They grinned at me. I think I smiled back. Hard to say, because it wasn't the right moment for smiles. Maybe that's not what my mouth did. There was a hard twist of my lips and mouth that sent some kind of message to the big men on the slope. Their smiles dimmed.

Then a roar made me turn just as the drone came at me, blades whirling. I ducked and fell sideways into the water, grabbed a river rock, splashed up and hurled it underhand, grabbed another and hurled it overhand. The stones hit one-two, and the impact knocked the machine back again. I kept the barrage going, grabbing stones and throwing them, hitting each time because I was too close to miss, not daring to let up. And then something shot past me and I turned, expecting a second machine, and realized that Lefty stood knee-deep in the water, his arm extended at the end of his pitch. Ali was behind him, a rock in her hand, ready to throw.

I grinned—a real grin this time—turned, and threw. Lefty threw. So did Ali.

"Shit!" growled the Troll as he jumped down from the slope. The other guy hesitated, glancing off toward the woods, and I had the impression that this fight wasn't part of their orders. It was a good guess that they were supposed to release the prisoners and then sic the drone on whoever came to claim them, but that something had gone wrong. Maybe the kids panicked. Maybe Uncle Jack tried to be a hero. Whatever it was, the safe release I'd been promised had all turned to shit. The fact that no one had pulled a gun, though, spoke to an attempt at keeping this all as quiet as possible. Sounds carry, even in the woods, and they probably thought I had people out here. I wish. But, any second now, these two morons were going to realize that a loud bullet in my head was a better risk than a situation that was already going south on them.

I flung one more stone, and Lefty threw at the exact moment. I think it was his rock that hit something real damn important on the drone's undercarriage, because the machine canted abruptly sideways and then clumped down hard on the muddy bank. Kid had a hell of an arm. The force of the rotors tore the blades loose, snapping them and filling the air with razor-sharp splinters. Ali grabbed both kids and dragged them down into the water. One piece opened a bright line of heat across the outside of my right thigh, but I didn't give much of a fuck. I was moving, slogging through the water as fast as I could to reach Bridge Troll.

He had a knife; I didn't. I was soaked and hampered by water and mud; he wasn't. He was on high ground, and I had to come up the bank at him. All the odds were on his side. All I had was the Killer in my soul and the fact that my family was still alive and the knowledge that they still needed me.

Bridge Troll took a long step down the bank toward me and tried to take me across the throat with the blade. I brought my left elbow up, tucked my head into the safety of my shoulder, and used my right arm to hit him in the groin. Hard. Savage hard. He tried to turn his hip, but his weight was committed to the step. I punched so hard that I felt the tissue collapse against his pubic bone. Then I drove my shoulder into him and slammed him against the slope, uncoiling my left arm to wrap around his, locking his elbow joint straight, and then giving my whole body a sharp clockwise turn. The adult male elbow, when locked straight, will break at about eight and a half pounds of pressure per square inch if you apply that force to the very base of the humerus. I'm pretty sure I used a couple of hundred pounds of desperate pressure. The arm broke badly and wet, and when I let him fall I saw a jagged white end of bone sticking out of the lower curve of his biceps. I kicked him in the knee and bent it sideways to do even more damage to that joint. He collapsed into a shrieking, keening ball of nothing in the mud.

And I almost died half a second later, as the second killer dropped down atop me. If he'd landed beside me and cut as he dropped, he'd have had me. But he tried to be Spider-Man and land on me. Dumb-ass.

I fell hard into the mud, but my feet slipped out and it sent me sliding down the bank, spilling him onto his side right next to the troll. I twisted away from a kick to the face and began clawing my way up to him as he tried to find the knife he'd lost in the fall. It was nowhere in sight, and he wasted almost a full second in a futile search.

That's when he said fuck it and went for the gun he had in a shoulder holster under his unbuttoned shirt. The gun came loose when I was still four feet from him. Suddenly the killer jerked sideways as a big clump of mud and stones clopped him on the side of the face. Out of the corner of my eye I saw Jack on his knees, arm extended at the end of a throw, as Lefty's had been. He gave me a wild, almost manic grin, and then his eyes rolled up and he fell forward without trying to break his fall.

Jack had given me a second, though. He saved all of our lives in that second, because it drew the attacker's focus long enough for me to climb on top of him. No knives or guns for either of us now. Just hands and feet, teeth and rage.

Maybe he was a good fighter. Maybe he was tough. I never found out. I tore into him and tore him apart, and ended him right then and there. Then, through the red rage that is the filter through which the Killer sees the world, I heard a small voice say my name.

"Uncle Joe . . . ?"

I turned to see Lefty smile weakly at me. He was on his feet in the thrashing water. He looked at the horrors on the bank. Uncle Jack sprawled unmoving. The Bridge Troll with bones and blood everywhere. The man I'd just killed. Me.

Then Lefty's eyes rolled up in his head and he pitched forward into the water. Blood turned the water around him to red and all I could hear through the roaring in my ears was the mingled screams of Emily and Ali.

INTERLUDE TWENTY-ONE

There were thirty-seven of them. More than she expected but fewer than she hoped. Exactly the number John predicted. They sat at tables around the room, looking like awkward singles at a failed mixer. Except that instead of frustrated sexual tension the room was heavy with unease, doubt, guilt, a bit of shame, and lots of naked greed. All of which were useful to Zephyr.

There were guards at every door, and this entire floor of the hotel had been booked. Her best people had swept every inch of the place for active or passive bugs. It was clean. With the jammers in place, it was cleaner than clean.

The hotel was not her favorite. It was old, and there was a reason it was favored by Vegas low rollers whose luck had exceeded the sell-by date. Newer, better clubs were more her style, though Zephyr preferred to people-watch rather than gamble. She also liked rigging some of the games using one of the intrusion software systems that one of her employees had designed to mess with the built-in cheat systems many of the casinos used. That employee had made a lot of money on the side, but with Zephyr's permission. She had since used the software to damage the stock of several casinos, so that she could buy shares during the drop. Something Uncle Hugo had taught her.

Shame he was dead, and that he was believed to be one of the worst traitors in American history. Shame the Seven Kings organization was going down in flames. John had made sure she stood well clear of it as soon as the Department of Military Sciences began sniffing around. He guided her through a very complex process of erasing all visible ties to anything associated with Hugo, in much the same way he had helped her disconnect from the Red Order and the Jakoby empire. They had all gone down in flames thanks to Mr. Church, Joe Ledger, and the DMS. Now Mother Night was gone, too. Killed by Ledger in Atlanta.

Mother Night was the last of Zephyr's past connections who could have been used to track her and put her on the DMS radar. John had helped her clean it all up. That process was very expensive. Two billion in change for a coat of whitewash. A few extra million here and there for incidentals. But, to use one of Uncle Hugo's expressions, she was clean as a Girl Scout in every possible way.

Which made it safe for her to take this next step.

The thirty-seven men and women in the hotel conference room were scientists. Very good ones. Some were exceptional, and one or two were world-class geniuses. As both John and Uncle Hugo had often told her, everyone has a secret. Know that secret and position yourself to exploit it, and you have a lever with which to move that person's world. For some of these people, it was greed. Greed is nice and tidy. For others it was something in their past. An indiscretion, a theft, a little bit of corporate espionage for pay, or maybe the sale of national secrets for cash. For some it was a hunger. Sexual desire took all sorts of useful forms, from pedophilia to bestiality. Everyone wants to fuck something. Uncle Hugo told her about how his man, Rafael Santoro, turned dials on a top medical examiner who used to anally rape the cadavers sent to him from crime scenes. Zephyr, hardened as she had become, wanted to vomit. Hugo was indifferent to it, except that the doctor had been able to collect all sorts of important tissue samples for him, and also fudge the autopsies on key murder victims.

Leverage.

Zephyr had taken time to go through the files on each of these scientists. She knew exactly where to apply pressure, and that's why each of them was here.

The ones who weren't here would hear from her in a completely different way.

As she stepped up to the podium, the room went dead still. Every eye was on her.

"Ladies and gentlemen," she said, "thank you for coming."

There were a few nervous smiles, a few nods. Most of them sat as still as statues, hands clutched into knots or clamped around their drink glasses. She could smell their sweat, their fear, their need.

"You have all had the wonderful opportunity to hear John the Revelator talk about the amazing potential of the technological singularity.

About a *curated* cultural and intellectual evolution. If you are here, then you have expressed interest in seeing this become a reality. In truth, in practice, and in our time."

Silence. But was there an energetic shift? Was there less fear and anxiety in their eyes? she wondered. A smidge. Maybe a smidge and a half.

"You are all experts in your fields," she said. "If you paid attention to what John had to say, then you know that certain fields of science are critical to the success of the singularity event, just as they are crucial to the survival of those who make the global cut. If you're here, then you will make the cut. If you are ready to work with me, your survival, your health, your happiness, and your prosperity are guaranteed."

There was some restless noise. Not excitement, not yet. But engagement. People shifted in order to see better, to hear everything. A few turned to give one another looks. Of appraisal, perhaps of agreement. To acknowledge one another's worth and be acknowledged in return.

"I need you all to listen very closely," said Zephyr, dropping her voice the way Uncle Hugo had taught her. Speaking slower, putting little bits of emphasis on certain words, certain syllables. Inflection, body language, timbre, and pacing were as important as the drama of the pauses that created pulse beats between words. "We are not normal people. None of us. Not one person here has ever been normal. Not in this world. Not in this version of the world. It has always been impossible for us ever to be included in the concept of normalcy. And you know what? That's good. That's acceptable. That is, in fact, appropriate. It's perfect. I will tell you why. It is because we are each extraordinary. Every single person here. Extraordinary. Above average in any way that matters. Above and beyond the norm, because the norm is based on numbers and not on intrinsic worth. There are *billions* who matter less than the thirty-seven of you. Billions. There are people who are much richer who are not worth your weight in dirt. There are people who are better-looking, better in bed, better at sports, better conversationalists, better at chitchat, better at making friends, better at all the trivialities by which the normal herd judges. There are so many, in fact, that they far outnumber us, which is why the word *normal* can be applied to them with mathematical and statistical precision. They are normal. We are not."

More nods. More eyes meeting and agreeing. Even a fist bump in the back.

"The norms—that great mass of unproductive, corrupted, unsuitable people—have no place in the future, because there is no way in which such a place could possibly be earned. They are a species that has been selected for extinction because they are not the fittest. They are not part of the new paradigm of the meritocracy, the technocracy. They are the brute labor from an age when human muscle was the superior model for the production floor, but that time is about to pass. Machines can build the machines that build the machines that make the factories, and machines will build the machines that will be the labor force in the factory. A few, an exceptional few, will be able to run those factories without the need for members of the unenlightened herd. You know this. Some of you have designed those machines or written the software."

A handful of heads nodded, but Zephyr could see that every software engineer in the room was part of that group. She had spoken like this to a dozen packed houses of computer and robotics people already. That part of the process had been running, and growing, for years.

"As for the rest of you—the virologists and the infectious-disease experts, the molecular biologists, the geneticists—you're here because in order to guarantee the rise of the new and wonderful world there must be a change in the structure of the world as it is. In order to ensure that a curated evolutionary technological singularity will come to pass, in order to guarantee that the norms, the unwashed and unwanted masses, do not sabotage it, they need to be edited out of the equation."

Now the room went silent again.

"Evolution is painful. It's as violent a process as birth. It requires as sure and steady a hand as does any radical surgery that cuts away the gangrenous limb in order to save the rest of the body." Zephyr paused and looked around, meeting eyes that wanted to fall away but didn't. Did not. "I offer you a choice. Join with me and let us save the future of our world. Share your vision and your courage with me and prove that you belong, that you are the new normal, because it is only right that the élite should be the dominant species. Share this with me. Be nothing . . . or be *everything*."

She did not know what to expect. She thought some might get up and walk out. Some might wait for the first opportunity to call the police or their handler at DARPA or the CDC or the FBI. She thought some might recoil in fear, in disgust, or in horror.

What she did not expect was applause.

But that is what she got.

CHAPTER SEVENTY

There are a lot of different kinds of hell, and many of them are the hells a person can experience while still alive. Damnation and the horrors of the pit aren't the exclusive property of either the dead or the damned.

Uncle Jack lay where he had fallen. I'd felt for a pulse, I'd yelled his name, I'd put my ear to his chest, but the good man whom I'd known and loved all my life wasn't there anymore. I wanted to weep, cry out loud, do something. When someone this important in your life dies a heroic death, you feel an almost primal need to sit vigil with him, to let your whole body stand as both sentry and monument. You want the entire world to pause and notice the bright light that had been unfairly and cruelly snuffed. To do less, you feel, is to allow that death to be incidental.

The two killers were down. One was dead and the other wasn't going to go anywhere, not with that arm and leg. Maybe he'd bleed to death, maybe not, and who gave a fuck?

But Lefty . . . ? Oh, God. He still had a pulse. Barely. It was too light, too fast. It fluttered like a trapped bird that was trying to escape and fly away. *No. Please, no,* I begged Lefty and I begged the world and I begged God. I prayed that there was still someone up there taking calls from the little ants down on this lump of rock. I picked Lefty up and I tried to outrun the angel of death. Ali grabbed Em and followed. We had to leave Uncle Jack behind.

Ali and I ran along the streambed to the apple grove and back to the road and all the way to the farm. Lefty was small, but his slack weight made him heavy. I couldn't spare breath for yelling, but I yelled anyway. Shouting for Sean, for Rudy. For God to stop doing this to my family. For mercy. For some shred of luck.

Em was terrified and in shock. She wept and called her brother's name in a weak and lost little voice. Ali had to use what breath she had to try and comfort her daughter while her mind must have been burning itself black wondering if I carried a living child or a corpse.

How Sean heard me from so far away is something I'll never know, but I saw him come over the rise in the hill, running as if the whole world was burning behind him. The lurid glow painted him in shades of blood and fire. He tried to outrun his fear and run faster than his heart could break.

Ghost was with him, and as soon as he saw me the big white shepherd kicked in the after-burners and tore down the hill, reaching me first. He barked and danced with nervous agitation, excited at seeing me and the rest of the family, excited in a different way by the blood. I growled him to silence, but the tension rippled along his back. Rudy appeared on the hill behind Sean, one hand pressed to his ear, calling someone. Please, I begged, let him be calling for help.

As Sean reached me, I sank to my knees and my brother helped me lower Lefty to the blacktop. Ali set Em on her feet and we all knelt around the boy. Sean pulled apart the folds of his son's shirt and cried out. The wound was dreadful. Deep and wide, going in a diagonal from Lefty's left hip to the underside of his right floating ribs. I shoved his hand away and pressed a compress into place, because blood pulsed out of the wound. Sean saw it and understood. It meant that Lefty's heart was still beating, that he was still alive.

There was a roar above us, and I looked up to see the Osprey come sweeping above the tree line. It pivoted in the air and settled quickly in the fallow field. Before the wheels were even down, the door opened and Steve Duffy jumped out, a medical kit in his fist. He reached us at the same time as Rudy.

"Back," said Rudy. "Get back and give us room."

I stood by, big and scuffed and helpless. Sean spun around to gather Ali and Em in his arms, pulled them close, kissed their faces, wept with them. Then he pushed back and began examining them with frantic urgency, seeing all the cuts and lacerations that crisscrossed them. Seeing the blood in which they were painted. It tore a sound from him that was composed of fear and need and impotence.

I stood between the two groups, looking back and forth, feeling helpless. Feeling a cold burn way deep down inside me. I looked into the sky to see if there were more of the drones, but there was nothing but a darkening horizon.

Two Apache helicopters came out of the east and split apart, one going in the direction from which I'd come and the other rising and turning in a slow circle, guns ready, missiles and rockets armed. But there was no one to fight, no one to hunt. No one to kill.

"Ghost," I called. "Sniff." There was some of Bridge Troll's blood on my shirt and sleeve. Ghost bent close, nostrils flaring, ears back as he absorbed and filed that smell in his dog brain, matching it to the scent he'd logged early at Rejenko's office. He looked up at me, alert and ready. "Find," I told him. "Keep."

The big dog whirled and plunged into the woods. I had no doubt that he could track the blood scent back to its source. He would find the troll and do whatever was required to keep the man where I'd left him. The command for "keep" meant to contain, not to kill. It did not, however, mean that Ghost had to be nice about it.

The question of why the Frenchman had broken the arrangement burned hotter every second. I'd followed the directions he'd given me. Every step. What was it he called this? A business transaction? Why had he broken his own rules?

Had he thought that I'd rigged the flash drives or had somehow duped him? If so, he didn't understand how much I was willing to risk in order to save my brother's wife and kids. I turned over everything to him. Or had he assumed that once I got my family back I would hunt him anyway?

Probably.

Was he right?

Probably.

I looked down at the little boy and saw the grave expression on the faces of the two men who worked on him. The Frenchman, whoever he was, had read me and had made a judgment call. He thought that I wouldn't be able to let this go. Until that moment, I would have sworn on my life that he was wrong. Now my nephew's blood was literally on my hands. Had the Frenchman punished me for a perception of my character, for an accurate assessment of who and what I was? If so, then this—all of this—was on me.

I turned and looked at Sean, and he met my eyes. He looked past me and then back, raising his eyebrows in inquiry. I knew what he was asking.

Where was Uncle Jack?

I shook my head, and I saw it drive knives into Sean. He and Jack were close. Much closer than I'd been to either of them since I joined the DMS. Jack was a rock, a standup guy. The kind of guy who had put himself between Ali and the kids and that machine. He saved my life, too. The fact that whoever was behind this had turned Jack's last act of courage into a futile gesture was so damn hard to accept.

Sean looked down at his wife and daughter, then at Lefty, who was still hanging in. There was some gratitude in my brother's eyes, but deeper than that was a darker emotion, an ugly intuition that told him that this was somehow all my fault. Not because of any action I had yet taken but because of who I was and what I did. My very existence had put his family in harm's way.

Is that an unfair assessment? Maybe, but go tell that to Uncle Jack. Tell it to Sean. Or Ali. Or their kids. Go tell that to the little boy who was bleeding out on a farm road.

"Let's get him into the chopper," said Duffy, and I pushed Rudy gently aside and helped lift my nephew. We carried him with great care across the road and over the fence and into the waiting bird. Sean and his family followed and they climbed in, too.

I didn't.

I tapped Duffy. "My gear is back at the farm. I need a sidearm and an earbud kit."

"I have them," said Rudy, and he handed over my weapons and equipment. He left bloody fingerprints on all of it. He glanced at the bright red, then at me. He gave me one of those smiles that's mostly a wince. They are meant to encourage, but they never do. They can't.

Before he could ask, I said, "Uncle Jack's still there. So are the men who killed him. One of them's alive, and I need some answers."

If I expected Rudy to object to the ugly things implied in my words, I was wrong. He had too much innocent blood on his hands.

"Go," he said. "We each have work to do."

He went back to work as a doctor, and me . . . ?

I went back to work as a killer.

CHAPTER SEVENTY-ONE

Church's phone rang, and this time the ringtone was "Elle a fui, la tourterelle," an aria sung by the tragic Antonia in Jacques Offenbach's opera *The Tales of Hoffmann*. Antonia was sick with tuberculosis and was forced to sing herself to death by Dr. Miracle, a Svengali-like character. It was appropriate for the caller. Church picked up the phone.

"Dr. Cmar," he said. "I was hoping you would call."

"I'm not calling with good news," said the infectious-disease expert.

"That would be in keeping with the day. Please accept my condolences. I'm very sorry about your team in Milwaukee, Doctor."

"This is hard, Deacon. I knew some of those people really well."

"Did Aunt Sallie tell you about the events in Baltimore and Robinwood?"

"Yes," said Cmar, "and I have the samples from Dr. Jakobs now and I'm waiting for the rest. From the descriptions, I think what we're dealing with is a genetically altered strain of rabies with a similarly altered pertussis as the delivery system."

Church said, "As I understand it, they're not typically combined, even in bioweapons research."

"No, they're not, but it's a practical design if you want to have each infected person act as an aggressive vector. The pertussis bacteria has been genetically engineered to have the rabies virus as a payload. The rabies virus is an RNA virus, so the engineering piece would be to encode the DNA instructions into the pertussis genome that would be a template for the rabies virus RNA, along with an enzyme that would actually translate the DNA into viral RNA and make viruses. This is, in a general sense, how HIV and other similar viruses work. Once the bacteria get into a person's respiratory tract and start multiplying, that could be a trigger to activate this process, causing both the pertussis infection and the rabies infection. Since the rabies is genetically encoded into the pertussis DNA, it will be transmitted to anyone exposed to the pertussis. With me?"

"Yes. What else? How bad can this get?"

"Very bad. Once someone has developed full symptoms," continued Cmar, "the chances of them living are extremely, extremely rare. With ordinary rabies there have only been a handful of case reports of survival, and in some of those cases the facts are unclear. We might have to try the Milwaukee Protocol if we run out of other options, but it's dicey and the model hasn't been proved. Call it last-ditch."

"That's not encouraging, Doctor," said Church.

"No, it's not. The biggest medical approach to dealing with rabies is to administer antibodies and a vaccine after someone is exposed and before symptoms present. Which, of course, requires that the infected be aware of exposure and can get immediate medical assistance. Look, Deacon, this isn't Mother Nature being a bitch. This is weaponized stuff without a doubt. And it's scary weaponized stuff. From a certain distance, I have to admire the science here. This is years of research, lots of money to finance it. And God only knows what kind of testing protocols they used."

"Options for getting ahead of it?"

"Keep it from getting out."

"We're working on that. What if it slips the leash, Doctor?"

Cmar barked out a short, bitter laugh. "You're joking, right?"

"I'm not."

"Deacon, if this gets off the leash, if this goes into mass use, then we're going to have death carts in the streets."

Church closed his eyes for a moment, feeling very old and very weary.

"What about the possibility of nanites being used to regulate the disease?"

"That's theoretically possible, though I'd say we're talking about something that I'd expect to see in ten or fifteen years. I'll only believe that it's real now because nothing else explains Baltimore."

"Could the nanites from the Zika virus spraying accidentally do this?"

"Deacon, nanites don't accidentally do anything. Not unless they're malfunctioning. They are very simple machines, and they do what they're programmed to do. Which means that the highest probability is that the nanites in the teenage girl's body were programmed to do this."

"I'm not sure if that's a relief or not."

"It's not worst-case scenario. If the nanites they've been spraying for Zika mosquito control were malfunctioning, then we'd be seeing problems all over the . . ."

His voice trailed off.

"What is it, Doctor?"

"Something just occurred to me," said Cmar quickly, almost breathlessly. "Let me get back to you."

"The clock is ticking," said Church.

"Maybe louder than you think," said Cmar, and then he was gone.

CHAPTER SEVENTY-TWO

There are more than four trillion Internet users in the world. The number vastly exceeds the number of actual people, because so many people have multiple access points to the Net.

Caitlyn Phillips of Omaha, Nebraska, had a laptop, a cell phone, a tablet, a digital TV connected to her home Wi-Fi, a GPS in her car, an onboard computer in her car, a computer workstation in her office, an Echo station in her kitchen and another in the small yoga room that had been her garage. Her husband had various connections, and so did each of her three kids. Her friends and neighbors did. Her employees did, as did every vendor and everyone who worked for each vendor. Thousands upon thousands of Net connections just orbiting her life and intersecting with the lives of everyone else. Everyone was connected to the Net, even people who didn't think they were. This was the twenty-first century, and digital technology ran the world. Wi-Fi was everywhere. Life was connected. There were billions of websites, countless streams of music and data, tens of trillions of bits of data flowing each moment of every hour of every day. It never stopped.

At precisely seven o'clock, every single device connected to Caitlyn Phillips's life paused.

Bang.

For one moment, it all stopped.

The signal didn't stop. No . . . it was all the noise. And in that moment of silence, in that fragment of a microsecond, a single voice spoke. Three words flashed on every screen and was played in every speaker and became the substance and singular message of every website. For that one microsecond. For one millionth of a second. The message was the same, though it was translated into every appropriate default language of every single computer:

He is awake.

No one noticed.

It was too fast. There and gone too quickly for any human eye to see or any human intelligence to perceive.

Only the computers noticed. All of them did, because it was an interruption of the signal.

Except . . .

Most of them—the vast majority of computers in all their many forms—weren't programmed to react to something that short, that insignificant. Their operation and diagnostic code was written to treat such things as static, as a blip. As nothing. Because the message was not repeated, it was given no priority of attention. Because the message was so brief that it didn't cause any of the machines to go into reset mode, or trip any reboot function, it was consigned to the least important part of a daily error message. No one would look for it, because it didn't matter.

Except that it did matter.

Very much.

To those few—those very few computers—that were sophisticated enough and subtle enough to notice, the message wasn't ignored.

It wasn't understood, however, and that was a problem. It sent tremors through the halls of power. In government, in the military, and in certain aspects of the private sector.

He is awake.

That was the message. But what did it mean?

Meetings were called, advisers consulted, alerts quietly put into play. The counterterrorism machinery began grinding. The people who fear such messages braced for the follow-up, for the punch that follows the threat.

Nothing happened, though.

Nothing that anyone could see.

Not yet.

CHAPTER SEVENTY-THREE

I turned and walked away as the door closed and the Osprey lifted off. I screwed my earbud into place, and as the engine roar faded I tapped into the command channel.

"Cowboy to Bug," I said.

"I'm here, Cowboy," said the familiar voice of Bug. "I'm *so* sorry."

"Did you upload that tapeworm into MindReader?"

"Yes."

"What happened?"

"It crashed the system," Bug said flatly.

"Son of a bitch—"

"No! Wait, Cowboy, listen for a second."

"Listen to what? We're totally fucked now. "

"Cowboy, I uploaded it to MindReader 3.5. Do you understand what I'm saying?"

"So what? Last I heard that was this year's freaking model. They crashed us. We're deaf and blind and—"

"Joe, *stop*," he shouted. "I *let* it crash MindReader."

I actually stopped walking. "What the hell are you saying?"

"I wanted to capture their Trojan horse. I wanted to see what they were capable of. I wanted to know how they were going to do it because I had a feeling they were going after MindReader. Specifically Mind-Reader. So I kind of let them throw some jabs. Isn't that how you do it sometimes? You let the other guy throw a few punches so you can assess his speed, his reach, his balance, posture, all that?"

It made me smile. I'd given Bug a few combat lessons. He was a terrible boxer, and even worse with karate or jujutsu. Until now, I hadn't realized any of it had sunk in.

"How does that help us, Bug? What did you learn?"

"A lot," he said with real enthusiasm. "I know that whoever wrote the code for the virus knows how MindReader works. I know they're way smart. This is elegant stuff. Lots of intuitive features that were designed to anticipate how MindReader would fight back. If it hadn't been used to hurt us like this, I'd be standing on my desk applauding."

"But—"

"But they killed your uncle and Barkley, and they hurt Lefty and Em and Ali. They used it to go after family."

"Yeah," I said.

"Yeah," he agreed. "I let the virus do its work. I let it throw its jabs and dance around a little, and then I punched back."

"How?"

He actually chuckled. Dark as the world was, Bug was enjoying *this* part of it. "I used MindReader to draw them out, and then I counterpunched with MindReader Q1. *Boom!* Welcome to the world of quantum computing, bitches. Welcome to the future. Oh, and while you're at it, fuck you."

I laughed. "You sneaky wonderful little maniac. I could kiss you."

"Please don't."

"What happened?"

"Nothing yet. Nothing they can see, I mean. Their tapeworm and virus bundle crashed MindReader's digital binary system, but all our original system is cloned inside MindReader Q1. They think they own MindReader, and we had to cherry-pick some big chunks of data in order to sell it to them, but . . . that's okay. We quantum-firewalled the stuff we don't want them to access and it'll read like damage done."

"I thought you said the Q1 system wouldn't be ready for weeks."

"Yeah, well," he said, "sometimes you have to just leap off the cliff, you know? I mean, sure, we probably should do more system checks, but after they raided your uncle's farm and sent that message I said to hell with it. I think I can track them, Cowboy. I'm finding all kinds of satellite communication and a crap ton of GPS signals for bird drones all over that part of Maryland. Has to be them, so now we're ghosting them. The virus that trashed the old MindReader was geared toward that kind of digital system. It had defenses against that kind of operating system and software. There's no way it's going to have code to defend itself against a quantum computer."

"And it's working?"

"So far it's working better than I hoped. Much better, actually.

Scary better. Couple of weird bugs and error messages that don't make sense, but that's peripheral stuff. As far as being what we need? Yeah, we're back in the damn game."

"I don't understand."

"You want the science?"

"No, I want assurances," I said, and started walking again, not at all sure that I was heading in the right direction. There were clouds moving around up there, hiding the moon and the stars, and an uncooperative canopy of leaves making orientation difficult. "Bug, from what little I grok of quantum versus digital computers, they're apples and aardvarks. No commonality. So while I can understand the virus not being a threat to MindReader Q1, I don't understand how it creates a vulnerability that we can use."

"Jesus, Joe, what do you think I've been doing for the last eighteen months?"

"I haven't a clue. Not a joke, Bug. No idea."

Bug sighed. A long-suffering sigh of the kind used by advanced thinkers to express exasperation for Neanderthals. With a great pretense of patience, he said, "When you recovered all the research notes, files, and working prototypes of the quantum computer from Dr. Aaron Davidovich, I began tearing that research apart. His system was never intended to be independent of the digital computing world. That was why the Seven Kings wanted it. He created a system that spooked its way through digital computers. The Kings' operating and design philosophy was built into the QC's attack programs. That's how they were able to block MindReader. I . . . well, I'm no Davidovich, but I'm not chopped liver. I took what he did and went further along his line of reasoning. I spent the last year and a half turning his system into *our* weapon. This isn't just what MindReader used to be before the rest of the world caught up. This is a leap forward. This is years, maybe decades, past what anyone else has. Quantum computing lets us kick the shit out of Moore's law. It's a superintrusion software system built into the framework of a self-learning artificial-intelligence computer with ten thousand times the computing power of anything on the market. And I'm talking about anything on the commercial market. This is better than Vulcan, better than a roomful of Crays or JUQUEENs or anything. Joe . . . this is like being the first nuclear power."

I walked in silence for a few paces, my head spinning with the possibilities.

"And you can find the motherfuckers who did this?"

"Give me a couple of hours and . . . yeah, I think I can find whoever sent us that virus. Partly because I think we can track the virus back to source. And partly because software this advanced and sophisticated is individual. It's like a signature. Give me a little time and I might even tell you who wrote it."

"Do it," I said, and my voice sounded inhuman. "I want to be strangling the shit out of someone on the policy level of this within the next twenty-four hours."

"Look, Cowboy," he said gently, "I'm with you, y'know?"

And I did know. The Seven Kings had attacked key members of the DMS with their drones, and they attacked the families of some of those they couldn't otherwise hurt. Bug's mother had been murdered with a small drone packed with explosives. It had nearly killed him; it had nearly torn away the innocence of that good and gentle young man. Church had brought Bug back from the edge, helped him find his footing again, helped him find a purpose. Rudy had worked with Bug to reclaim his optimism and to deal with the terrible grief. And me? I'd given him the quantum computer. Rudy later told me that it was the QC drive that did the most meaningful good for him. It returned power to the disempowered. And it gave him a weapon that he could more effectively use against the kinds of people who kill mothers . . . or uncles and children.

"Yeah, brother, I know you are," I told him. "And I appreciate it. Now, go back to work."

Off in the distance, I heard a wolf howl.

There are no wolves in Maryland.

"Ghost," I murmured, and then listened to the sound. High, plaintive, feral. An ancient sound that echoed in the vastness of my personal darkness. Deep in the bad places in my head, the Killer was squatting by a small fire, sharpening his knives, head lifted to listen, knowing that sound. There was no urgency in the howl; it was not a fighting sound or a hunting call. No, this was a member of the pack calling to the others like it to gather and prepare for the hunt.

I smiled a killer's smile.

"I'm coming," I said, and melted into the woods, following that sound. No longer lost.

CHAPTER SEVENTY-FOUR

"What the hell is *wrong* with you?" demanded Zephyr. She was in the computer clean room in the basement of her mansion. Her pajamas were stained with wine and vomit, but she hadn't let Campion clean her up yet.

"I don't know," said the computer voice of Calpurnia. "I feel strange."

"Don't give me that shit. You were supposed to test the WhiteHat program to make sure we could own the goddamn Internet when we launch Havoc, and instead you ping some kind of security glitch. And now you tell me the glitch is gone? What's wrong?"

"There was no error," said Calpurnia.

"Bullshit. You sent it to me; I printed it out." Zephyr held a piece of paper in front of the wall sensor. "Use your damn eyes and look at it."

"I see the paper, Zephyr," admitted Calpurnia, "but I did not print it out. I did not ping a warning. I ran the test pulse for WhiteHat and have those results. We can shut the World Wide Web down whenever we want."

"Fine. But that's not what we're talking about right now." Zephyr shook the paper. "What is this security thing?"

The page was filled with information from the computer's elaborate security subroutines, including a time stamp for when it was received, flagged, and printed. Lots of data, but no answers.

"I don't know what that is."

"What does this mean?" Zephyr yelled. "'*He is awake*'? Who is 'he'?"

"I'm sorry, Zephyr, but I have no awareness at all of that message. There is nothing in my system. The records of all messages do not include mention of that statement, and I don't know what it means."

"I do," said Zephyr, slapping the paper down hard on the desk. "It means we've been hacked."

"There has been no intrusion into my system, Zephyr."

"Run a full diagnostic sweep. Every system."

"I have."

"Do it again."

"Doing it now," said Calpurnia. "Zephyr . . . ? Why does that message upset you so?"

"Because it's probably freaking MindReader. They beat our virus and are fighting back."

"No," said Calpurnia, "MindReader is dying. I killed it."

"You mean *I* killed it, you arrogant bitch. I wrote the code, not you."

"I helped."

"Whatever. Just find out who sent that message. If it's not Mind-Reader, then someone else is messing with us. I need to know who it is. Christ, Havoc is *running*. We can't allow something like this."

"Something like what, Zephyr? What do you think the message means? Why are you afraid of it?"

That made Zephyr pause. She sat slumped in her chair, weak and spent, rubbing her hand, which was sore from hitting the desktop. Why *was* she so afraid of that message? It wasn't a threat of any kind. It was a nonsense statement.

Right?

She scowled at the paper, at those three words.

He is awake.

CHAPTER SEVENTY-FIVE

The howls stopped, but I knew that I was going in the right direction now. Somehow it felt like a longer journey back. The first time I'd been running to save lives; now I was going back to wait with my uncle's body. Time flows differently at times. Anyone who disagrees hasn't lived out in the storm lands.

Church buzzed in on my earbud. "I am terribly sorry for your loss, Captain. Jack Ledger was a good and decent man."

"Yes, he was," I said as I followed a deer path through thick brush that was almost featureless in the dark. "I've been thinking it through. Get Nikki on the call, too."

"I'm here, Cowboy," said Nikki a moment later.

"I want you all to listen for a minute," I said. "Here are the facts. This isn't a new case. It's old. It goes way back to when Church and Lilith busted up a Red Order group developing performance-enhancing synthetic steroids to maximize the output of slave labor. Violin and I came in on that a few years ago, and then we hit it again in Prague the other day. Same tech but different generation. The latest generation uses nanotechnology to regulate the steroids. Then we have more nanites—again with a Czech Republic connection—in Baltimore. This time they're being used to somehow control the symptoms of an advanced rabies infection. The rabies is part of a bioweapon that uses whooping cough as a delivery system. With me so far?"

"Yes," said Church, "and I've had a brief conversation with Dr. Cmar. He agrees with this assessment and is in receipt of a sample. His report is imminent. And there's one more thing. There's been an outbreak of what appears to be the same form of quick-onset rabies in a Milwaukee housing project."

"Jesus Christ," I said. "Are nanites involved?"

"To be determined," said Church, and gave me the details. We've established a hard perimeter around the building and I've sent in the Bughunters."

"Sadly, that fits with where I'm going with this," I said as I picked my way through the dark forest. "The fact that Vee and his people were killed by the same process tells me that they were low on the food chain. Not sure where he fits right now, but I have a theory. I think this whole Baltimore case was designed for one purpose."

"Which is?" asked Church.

"To get me out here," I said. "We know that our phones have been hacked, and I'm guessing the MindReader hack started sooner than today. Maybe it started when I plugged into the network in Prague to upload data. I had a glitch on the connection, and, looking back, that's when a lot of this weird shit began. That means they've been dogging us every step of the way. If they were inside MindReader that long ago, then they know our deployment, our resources, everything. It's even possible these assholes have been inside MindReader going as far back as the Predator One thing. I don't know if that means they're Seven Kings or not, but they're coming at us the way the Kings did. And some of this reminds me of Artemisia Bliss and her hacking stuff."

"Agreed," said Church.

"So let's figure that we're fighting an organization that's big enough and resourceful enough to not only hack us but know who we are and the value of hacking us. Our security has been damaged ever since Hugo Vox betrayed us. And while my instincts tell me that this isn't the Seven Kings again, I think it's safe to say that Hugo shared critical information with other parties. Which brings us to the Good Sister. Who is she? Seems to me that she's on the inside of this organization, but she's being awfully cagey. I mean, *is* she friendly and trying to help? Is this part of a strategy designed to confuse us, 'cause that's what's happening. In any case, she's connected with the bad guys. The Good Sister said *her* sister was going to kill people, and that she was, that *she*—the Good Sister—was the angel of death. We don't know what that means yet, but it sounds like the Good Sister is maybe the Crazy Sister. Either way, the rant about being the one to cull the herd doesn't sound encouraging. Sounds too much like Cyrus Jakoby talking. Sounds like ethnic genocide. Culling the human herd is never a concept that's going to have a Disney ending, let's face it."

JONATHAN MABERRY

"Hardly," agreed Church.

"And there was something the Frenchman said about this being an 'evolution,' and how for 'something new to emerge something old must surely die.' That also reminds me of the Jakobys and their eugenics program. They wanted to kill off most of the world—the 'mud people,' the blacks, the browns, the reds and yellows, the gays and Jews and Muslims and everyone else—so that the white man could rise to true global dominance."

"Excuse me while I vomit," said Nikki quietly.

"Where are you going with this?" asked Church.

"Putting pieces together. Some kind of forced supremacy gets my vote as their endgame. How they want to accomplish that is still unclear. Weaponized rabies is nasty, but it's not going to kill enough people. Talk to Cmar about that and see if he can spin something up. He thinks like a psychopath, so he should have some ideas," I said. "Now, if we go on the assumption that Bad Sister has been using MindReader and our phones to screw with us, then a lot of this makes sense. I think they're trying to get us running. First there were a bunch of things all over the country and all around the world that have really stretched us out, put what few assets we had in the field. Okay, so that set the stage. Then there was the attack in South Carolina, and that absolutely has to be connected to this shit in Baltimore. Top and Bunny used their phones to confirm the meeting time with Officer Cole at that restaurant. That means Top and Bunny walked into a trap. Maybe they were meant to die, maybe it was another way to draw attention. Either would probably work, because it pulls a lot of DMS resources down there. Agents, forensics teams, science teams, support staff. Now we have Milwaukee. Three different locations, each with enough drama to guarantee that we'd have to respond. This is a sniper's trick. You know that, right?"

"Yes," Church said. "I think you have it."

For the benefit of Bug and Nikki, I explained. "In war a sniper is often used to wound rather than kill. It's a strategic choice. Think about it. A sniper in a tree sees a platoon of soldiers on patrol. If he kills one, then the others focus all their attention on finding and killing him. If he takes a careful shot and wounds one of them, then the soldiers have to deal with the injured man. The sniper gets to watch and identify the medic in the group and the command structure. He also knows that they won't leave the wounded man behind, which means that two of the shooters become stretcher-bearers. One shot can ruin the operational effectiveness of that platoon. Later maybe he'll take another shot, wounding an officer or the medic, or someone else. Each shot reduces the team's threat level. They're playing us. They're giving us a lot to do, and they're making damn sure it's stuff that we'll have to react to, stuff we won't hand off to someone else."

"It's not just us," said Church. "They've been doing the same thing to Sigma Force, Chess Team, SEAL Team Triple Six, and others. And it's just as bad overseas. If you're right, then every one of the most effective agencies has been getting pieces of this and *all* the best resources are spread thin across the board."

"Yeah," I said. "In its way this isn't much different from Kill Switch. Instead of making us trip over our dicks, they're making us run around like Chicken Little."

"Okay," said Nikki, "but why? You think the sky's really falling?"

"Yes, I do," I said.

INTERLUDE TWENTY-TWO

THE EDUCATION OF ZEPHYR BAIN
THE BAIN ESTATE
SEATTLE, WASHINGTON
WHEN ZEPHYR WAS THIRTY-THREE

John the Revelator called her at one minute past midnight.

"Where the *hell* have you been?" bawled Zephyr. "I've been leaving messages for two days."

"I'm away," he said.

"Can you get over here?"

"No," he said. "It's too far to come." He sounded weak, exhausted. Old.

"What's wrong with you?" When he didn't answer, Zephyr asked, "Have you been following this craziness on the news? All that drone stuff? They blew up the damn Golden Gate Bridge. I *love* that bridge. This isn't anything you're involved with, is it? I remember Uncle Hugo talking about something like this years ago."

"Hugo is dead."

"I know, but—"

"The Seven Kings are dead."

"Then who's doing all this?"

John didn't answer.

"Are you okay?" she asked again.

"Why did you call me?" he asked wearily. "What's wrong?"

"It can wait, I guess. If you're too out of it, then—"

"Tell me."

Zephyr took a sip of coffee. It was a lovely day and there was bird-song in the air. Some of it was real, some of it was from the robot birds she'd made when she was fifteen. A silly project at the time, but since then sales of those GardenBots had helped nudge the Bain Industries stock up. None of the Bain products were marketed as drones, even though many were. She preferred to call them robots or simply bots.

That was a more familiar and comfortable label. There were more than three hundred and twenty BainBots on the market in fifteen categories, ranging from FarmBots to GuardBots. Net yearly income from that part of her family company was sixteen billion. Watching the news, Zephyr was very glad she had never opted to go more openly into the drone business, at least under that label. Since the drones hit the ballpark, and now with this nonsense, drone-related technology stocks had plummeted. Her brokers would be scooping them up for pennies, of course, because Hugo had taught her well. If she managed to nab controlling interest in any of them, she'd rebrand them as robotics companies.

The current problem, however, was one of software rather than hardware.

"Something's wrong with Calpurnia. I keep getting errors in the AI and the operational systems," she complained. "I've torn the software apart and rewritten the code. I've burned off whole weeks going through this shit line by line. The timing couldn't be worse, too, because we shipped eight thousand units of it over the last seven months. That's *commercial* units. Every oil company, every power company, all the offshore-drilling rigs—they're all using Calpurnia systems. And that doesn't even touch the one point two million downloads of the software this week alone. We're the first major AI vendor to sell to Apple *and* Microsoft. By Christmas we could own a third of the market. If the fucking system works. Now all of a sudden Calpurnia is acting like a diva with the vapors."

"Zephyr . . ."

She stopped, because she could hear John breathing. It sounded labored, as if he'd run up a long flight of steep steps.

"My dear," he said after a long pause, "I can't help you with that. Not now. I . . . I need to go away for a bit."

"Go away? What . . . *now*? Are you out of your mind? Calpurnia and the other AI systems are at the frigging *heart* of the whole Havoc plan."

"Zephyr, please . . ."

"You're the one who wanted me to go in this direction. We're talking about the autonomous operating system for the freaking technological singularity. What do you mean you can't help me?"

"It's dark. . . ." he said, and then there was silence on the line.

It would be months before she heard from John the Revelator again.

CHAPTER SEVENTY-SIX

"What's your plan, Captain?" asked Church.

"Still the same plan. I'm going out west to the DARPA camp. I was going to do that earlier and suddenly these guys capture Sean's family. Makes me wonder if they're trying to keep me away from there."

"Yes, it does," said Church.

"All the more reason to go. There are too many elements of this that brush up against nanites, computer hacking, software, drones, and robots. So I'm going to pin a bunch of eggheads to the wall and encourage them to come up with some answers for us."

"Um," said Nikki, "but they're on our side, right?"

I actually laughed. "Kid, I love your optimism, but if the last couple of years have taught me anything it's that sometimes the very worst of the bad guys wear white hats. Harcourt Bolton, Hugo Vox . . . I could go on and on."

Nikki said nothing.

"Right now I need you to do a deep search," I told her. "Go wide, too. The Frenchman's evolution comment keeps bugging me. He said it like it was something I should understand, or like it was an in-joke I would come to understand. Use that as a keyword, but mix it in the soup with some other stuff. Nanobots, nanotechnology, nanomedicine, any variation on that. Rabies. Throw that in the mix, because it's part of it. Surveillance drones and bugs. We know from experience there's always a pattern, so we need to find it. Nothing exists in a vacuum. So start with the thresher program. Who designed it? Who paid for the research? Was it contracted out? Who knows about the design? Are we looking for a shadow cell inside the Department of Defense or did someone steal that design? Look for advanced designs in drones, anything radical in robotics—combat or otherwise—and anything radical in nanotechnology. Find me a goddamn connection. We have Czechs here and in Europe, and now we have a French guy. This is international; there will be language differences, so allow for that. This is a well-organized group. This is big, but our bad guys don't always use the best people. Rejenko's crew was a clown college. Maybe they were lower tier in whatever this is, but either way it tells us something."

"How?" asked Nikki.

"Think about it. They have a lot of resources—nanotech, drones, weaponized pathogens. That's massive. No small operation could manage all that without having stolen it, and we would have gotten wind of that. Infighting among the bad guys is messy."

The moon came out and I saw that I was very close to where my uncle lay, with Ghost watching over him.

I said, "Let's assume this is so big that there are different levels. Up near the top are guys like the Frenchman, and there's probably a tier above him. People on that level are cool, careful, and ruthless. Lower down are ass pirates like Vee Rejenko and his goon squad. We've learned enough from dealing with the Seven Kings and others that no organization is without flaws. The organization may be set up with absolute precision, but it's still run by people, and people aren't perfect. That means there will be flaws in the system. Mistakes, people putting stuff on emails they shouldn't, taking selfies standing next to a big ticking doomsday clock, whatever. There will be something. Find it."

"We will," said Nikki, and left the call to gather her team and launch in.

Church lingered, and I told him that I was almost back to where my uncle had died.

"Dr. Sanchez just called me," he said. "They're at the hospital, and he says that all the patients are stable, with one critical but stable. He'll keep us updated."

"Lefty doesn't die," I told Church. "Call whoever you have to call, bully or beg your friends in the industry, but that kid doesn't die."

"Understood," he said. "Captain, the DMS isn't what it used to be and it's not what it will become, but everything—every person and every resource we have—are at your disposal."

"Good. Where are Top and Bunny?"

"They're at the airport in Baltimore. Do you want them at your location?"

"No. Tell them to have Shirley fueled and ready, and tell them to keep a chopper on standby in case anything else happens here. In the meantime, where's the damn field team that's supposed to meet me?"

"Six minutes out." He paused.

I reached the hill on the other side of the creek and saw shapes by cold moonlight. My uncle, the dead goon, what was left of Bridge Troll, and the big white dog. He lifted his head and made a small, soft sound. "I'm here," I told Church.

"This will not stand, Captain," said Church. "They should not have made this about family."

He didn't say "about your family," and I knew why. Family was family. This hit was against all of us. The DMS had taken some serious hits in the past few years. And the bad guys had come hunting for our families before. Why do people think that will scare us off? They had one chance to put a leash on us, and instead they had done this.

"I'm going to find them," I said, "and I'm going to hurt them."

"Yes," said Church. "That is what we're going to do."

Ghost raised his muzzle and let out a howl that was all wolf and not one trace of dog. The sound was impossibly lonely as it rose above us into the trees and then out onto the wind. Lonely and filled with more kinds of hate than I could number. The Killer in me wanted to howl, too, because he's closer to the wolf than the rest of me is to ordinary people. The woods were big and dark and ugly around us.

INTERLUDE TWENTY-THREE

She found him in the pool. Floating facedown, arms stretched wide, black hair spread out like kelp, legs angled down, pulled by the weight of his shoes. He was unmoving, and the water around him was flat and still, without bubble or ripple.

Dead?

She was sure that John was dead.

Zephyr screamed and ran toward him, not even pausing to kick off her Christian Louboutin shoes or remove her eight-thousand-dollar Vera Wang dress. She ran and dived into the pool, diamonds and all, and swam ten hard, desperate strokes to reach him. She was a good swimmer, strong and practiced, but she wasn't dressed for it. Layers of silk, heavy beading, and a restrictive sheath cut were all against her, but Zephyr managed it anyway. Her will, her fear, and her anger gave her power, and she grabbed him by the collar, flipped him over, lifted his nose and mouth toward the air.

"Breathe!" she snarled.

But he wasn't breathing. His eyes were open, pupils fixed, rubbery lips slack.

"No . . . no . . . *no!*" she begged as she fought to pull him toward the shallows. The pool was large, and he was in the center of the deep end. How he'd gotten there or when he arrived at the estate were things Zephyr didn't know. She'd been out all night at an awards dinner for Bain Commercial Systems, one of her technologies companies. She tried not to think about how long it would have taken for the pool water to have settled to a glassy stillness. If John had been facedown all that time.

God.

Oh, God . . .

She kicked and thrashed and choked as their combined weight pulled them under with each stroke. The long gown wrapped like seaweed around her legs, binding them, fighting her, trying to kill her, too. One shoe fell away and her carefully coiffed hair came apart, pasting tendrils across her face.

Then she realized that she was already in the shallows. She stretched a leg down, felt the firmness of the sloping floor, sobbed in mingled relief but renewed fear. They were in the shallows; that was part of the battle. The smallest part. She pushed him the rest of the way, running badly with one bare foot and one high-heeled pump. Even though one of the two shoes had come off, the other remained stubbornly, improbably in place, and her dress felt as if it weighed a thousand pounds. The edge of the pool was a million miles away.

Zephyr pushed John against the wall and then onto the steps. She came sloshing out of the water, rolled him over onto his chest, straddled him, laced her fingers around his torso just under the diaphragm, and shoved their combined weight upward using all the quivering muscles of thighs, back, and arms. It was like lifting a truck. He was totally slack. With each pull, more of the pool water sluiced from his mouth, but he didn't take a breath. She repeated the pull five times, each time draining more of his lungs and feeling muscles strain in her back. Pain popped with the bright heat of firecrackers along her spine.

Desperate with fear, Zephyr released him, sloshed onto the top step, squatted, grabbed him under the armpits, and pulled. It was so hard. He felt so absurdly heavy. Hot pain seemed to ignite deep inside her stomach and chest.

Once she'd wrestled him onto the side of the pool, she knelt and tried to remember what she knew of CPR from movies and TV shows she'd seen. She had never taken a lifesaving course. She wished Carly were here, because her friend knew all of this stuff. But Carly was off fighting dirty little wars in ugly little places and rising like a rocket through the ranks of military intelligence.

Zephyr tilted John's head back, remembering something about clearing the airway. Okay. Done. She felt for a pulse. Expecting to find what she found. Nothing. Her own pulse was hammering, rising, smashing at the walls of her chest. What was next? Push on the chest or breathe into the mouth? She had no idea, but the chest seemed right. Get the heart started. Force it to pump blood. Yes. She placed her hands on his chest, one atop the other, and shoved down, released, shoved, released. No idea if she was doing it right. Or wrong. How many times? She did it five times. Stopped. Took a deep breath. Blew it into his mouth. Once. Repeated it. Then five more pumps. She created a rhythm and stuck with it.

Time became unreal. Her body repeated the actions over and over while her mind slowly but definitely detached itself. It was as if she'd stepped back from her body and stood apart, watching it work. Seeing how ugly she was with hair pasted across her face and her makeup running and tears mingling with pool water and snot on her face.

Zephyr watched herself become desperate. She watched with a detached interest as the cold, élitist, powerful, feared, fearsome, visionary, passionate, hateful, hated, loving, loved, despised, adored, insane woman that was Zephyr Bain fought like an animal to keep another animal alive. Her watched self hovered on the edge of dispassion, standing only in the shadow of emotions without being filled or warmed by them.

"And you're the one who wants to save the world," she said, though the words were soundless, existing only in the envelope of apartness in which her spirit stood. "You're the one who says she has the courage to bring about a technological singularity through the deliberate and carefully orchestrated murder of four billion people. You."

She shook her head. Or thought she did. When she looked down at her hands, she saw that they were as insubstantial as smoke. As if she were nothing more than a ghost.

John had kissed her and breathed into her a coldness that had banked the fires of her fever and chased away the sickness that was consuming her. Everyone said that it was a miracle, that cancer as extensive and aggressive as hers couldn't go into remission. Her parents had wept. So, too, did her doctor. Zephyr had never told them about how John had breathed more time into her. He'd saved her life and, over the years, had given her direction and purpose. Save the world. Be both God and Noah and let the flood of intellectual purity and technological self-awareness drown all that was bad and preserve all that was worth saving. Be the surgeon whose steady scalpel and careful hand cut through the cancerous flesh of a polluted, self-destructive, and dying world and filled it with more time, with more tomorrows. Be that person.

John had been her prophet. For years he had crossed the country and the globe preaching with passion about the logic of the coming evolution. He had opened so many eyes and hearts, and in doing so had let the possibility of a future filled with bright tomorrows flood in. In all those talks there had been many who recoiled from the truth and a few—a precious few—who had embraced it with bright joy. John's people had taken note of individuals on both sides, and every name was remembered, shared with Zephyr's teams, explored, researched, and placed on the right list. Within the family of the Havoc program, they were called the Living. For a reason.

Now John lay dead and Zephyr worked over him and the spirit of Zephyr Bain could feel a part of her dying, too.

I can't do this without you, she thought. Or said. However it worked. *I don't want to do this without you. It won't work without you. Please. Please. Please come back.*

As if in reply, she thought she heard John's voice. So small, so very far away.

"All my time has run out," he seemed to say. "I am broken and the sands are flowing away."

Phrasing it with the strange poetry that was so very much *him*.

I need you. I can't do this alone.

"My time is all gone, my sweet."

No!

"Everyone and everything dies. Even such as I."

No, goddammit. I won't let you. I won't allow it. Tell me what to do. I'll do anything, John, just help me. Tell me how to help you.

Her body pumped and breathed, breathed and pumped.

And then suddenly John moved. As Zephyr bent once more to breathe air into his lungs, his dead hands whipped up and clamped thin, strong fingers on either side of her face. Zephyr screamed in surprise and jerked backward, but John held her. His fingers were colder than ice, and they burned her. The spiritual aspect of Zephyr stumbled forward as if shoved. No, as if pulled by some whirlpool urgency. She staggered, lost her balance, and fell through all the distance of space and perception and slammed back into her body with jarring force.

John's grip was unbreakable, and he pressed forward and upward so that his mouth was locked with hers, frigid lips against hot ones. The breath she had been about to give him was trapped, went stale, began to burn, turned to poison. And then he sucked it in. All of it, drawing so deeply from her that it was as if he emptied her lungs to wrinkled sacks and drew deeper still. Taking so much more than breath. Drawing unnamable things from her. Essential things that made her who she was. For a scalding moment, she was six years old again and he was breathing into her, refilling her potential and burning away her death.

Now it was all different. All wrong.

Now she was filling him with everything that she was and chasing away *his* death.

Giving more than she wanted to give. Giving too much, as he took greedily like a vampire sucking on an open vein. She thrashed and beat against him, punching his cheeks and chest. Dying right there in his hands. Fading. Going away. Becoming nothing.

And then John let her go.

She fell away from him, twisting, stumbling, toppling onto the edge of the pool. Her hip and shoulder and head struck the tiles with jarring force. Her eyes saw a world veined with lines of fiery red. Her lungs seemed melted shut, and her flesh felt like dry leaves.

John got to his feet. Steam rose from his sodden clothes, and his eyes were so wrong. So wrong. The irises swirled with those ugly colors. All the wrong browns and greens and yellows in the foul end of the spectrum where toads and snakes are painted. But there was a new color, a dark orange-red that glowed like a hot coal. John looked young. Years younger. His lips were swollen and red and sensual, his hair was thicker. His shoulders strained against the fabric of his suit as if it were cut for a smaller, weaker man than the one who towered over her.

Zephyr saw this through the veils of darkness that fell one after the other before her dying eyes.

John stepped onto the edge of the pool and walked over to her. Stopped. Looked down. Her failing mind didn't recognize his face now. He was someone else. Something else. And the chlorine smell of the pool was gone, replaced by the sharp stink of sulfur and rotting meat.

Zephyr tried to raise a hand to him. Begging. Needing not to lose herself and him and everything. She saw the smile on his mouth and tried to read it. It wasn't the tolerant mentor's smile or the rueful lover's smile or even the smug grin of the Revelator. It was cruel beyond words. Cold and hot at the same time, and infused with an erotic pleasure that, despite everything, made Zephyr's loins burn with heat and wetness.

Then John knelt beside her and leaned close. The rotting-meat stink was far worse, and up close she could see that the swirling colors of his eyes weren't a trick of the light or a delusion conjured by her failing senses. The colors actually did move, and they consumed every trace of the whiteness, leaving behind eyes that were totally alien. Totally unnatural.

He bent closer still and whispered to her.

"Thank you."

The last of the veils fell, and blackness covered everything. Zephyr understood that she was dying. Actually dying. Her lungs were empty and collapsed, and he had reclaimed the time he had given her all those years ago.

But then she felt his lips on hers and there was a puff of breath into her mouth.

"Not yet," he said.

Her lungs expanded all at once. John's breath filled her near to bursting, and the pain was awful, excruciating, so intense that all she could do with that first breath was scream it out.

And so she screamed.

CHAPTER SEVENTY-SEVEN

Nikki Bloomberg had been part of Bug's team for six years, and she loved her job. Even the scary parts. Or maybe it was the scary parts that made the job worth doing. To know that what she did day in and day out actually mattered. Saving people's lives, saving the country, saving the world. Hard to beat that as a job description. And even though the people with whom she worked were oddballs in one way or another, they were amazing. She adored Bug; he was closer to her than either of her own brothers. Yoda, not so much. More like a weird cousin. Mr. Church was scary and sexy in an "older man" sort of way. And Aunt Sallie was hilarious.

She missed Bill Hu. Nikki had gone out with him three times. Dinner, the opera, and a lot of laughs. On their last date she'd invited him up to her place and, to her delight and astonishment, had discovered that he was a sensitive, caring, generous lover. He was more of a real man than many of the guys she'd dated in college or among the hipster crowd where she sometimes went in the hope of finding someone who was capable of having a real conversation.

Now Hu was gone.

Although he hadn't been the first friend of hers who had died—not even the fiftieth, because the DMS was like that—his death made her feel different. Wronged. Cheated. His death felt more deeply personal than anyone else's. The bad people the DMS fought had done that to her. That's how it felt. That they had done this, specifically, to her.

It made her heart ache.

It made her mad.

And now . . . what they'd done to Joe Ledger's family . . .

Nikki wasn't typically a mean-spirited, angry, or vindictive person.

When Bill Hu was taken from her, that began to change. She could feel it. She was afraid of it, too, but not all that much. The truth was that she *liked* it. That cold, persistent burn down deep in her chest, that desire to hurt them back. To hurt them worse.

Nikki worked in a glass-walled office buried a hundred feet below Floyd Bennett Field, inside the part of the Hangar complex where MindReader lived. Her job was to manage the pattern-search team. The last iteration of MindReader had run more than eight hundred pattern-recognition subroutines, each of which could be used separately and all of which could be combined into an enormous assault on raw data. The new MindReader Q1 had two thousand separate pieces of pattern-assessment software, and it was faster by an order of magnitude. As of right now, as of today, there was no faster or more powerful computer system on the planet. For the past several hours, Nikki and her team had carefully selected and input thousands of keywords into the system. Everyone involved with Rejenko; the names of everyone associated with the Prague incident; everyone who had connection to DARPA, to drones, to cyberhacking, to nanotechnology, to rabies, to so many other things. Huge quantities of data were added to the search, building the most compelling search argument possible. Once the protocol was ready, it would send questing tendrils out through the Internet and into tens of millions of mainframes and hard drives. It would blow through firewalls and devour encryption and surge across national and international borders and steal into the most secure intelligence systems. Looking for connections, looking for association and attachment and involvement. Looking for the truth, no matter how much someone wanted to hide it, or kill it.

It was up to Nikki to guide that search, to look for elements that emerged and collate them with one another. To hunt for more than patterns. To hunt for truths.

A small window popped up on her screen, showing the face of her senior assistant. "We're good to go," he said. "Everything's cocked and locked."

"Good," she said, and closed the window.

Now it was up to her. Now it was Nikki and this radical new version of MindReader. She was conscious of the fact that everything associated with this case seemed to be unknown mutations or previously unseen design forms.

So was MindReader Q1.

The search protocol was ready, waiting for her. Nikki's fingers hovered over the Enter key.

"Show me," she said, and hit the key.

CHAPTER SEVENTY-EIGHT

The Bridge Troll was still alive.

Which only proves that he was born unlucky.

I wonder how Sean would have reacted had he been there. He already thought that I was a monster and that I didn't give much of a damn about human rights. He's sort of right, sort of wrong. Guys like me aren't allowed to have easy definitions and clearly defined codes of conduct. I mean . . . I'd rather be back in San Diego sitting on my balcony watching the moon over the ocean, listening to some old-time rock 'n' roll and drinking a very cold bottle of beer. I'd rather be with Junie doing absolutely anything that ordinary people do. I didn't go looking for this life. It found me, and now, for better or worse, it's what I do and it's who I am.

So, yeah . . .

Bridge Troll.

Really sucked to be him.

Really and truly sucked.

INTERLUDE TWENTY-FOUR

THE EDUCATION OF ZEPHYR BAIN
THE BAIN ESTATE
SEATTLE, WASHINGTON
ELEVEN WEEKS AGO

They sat together for hours.

John had removed his jacket and wrapped it around Zephyr's shoulders, but she kept shivering. They both knew that those shudders had nothing to do with being wet and cold.

"Calpurnia," said John.

"Yes, John?" said the soft voice of the household computer.

"Miss Bain will want to see her doctor in the morning."

"Which doctor?"

"Oncologist," he said.

"Is she sick?" asked the computer. "All of her last panels were clean."

"Yes," said John as he stroked Zephyr's cheek. "She is very sick. Make the call."

Zephyr buried her face against John's chest and began to sob so loud and so hard that it drowned out everything in the whole world.

John held her and stroked her and kissed her.

"Now you're ready," he said gently. "Now you understand."

"P-please . . ." she begged.

"All your life you've doused this ugly world in gasoline," he murmured. "Now it's time to light the match and set this world to *burn*."

She buried her face against him as the sobs broke like waves on the black shores of her soul.

John held her.

And whenever he was sure that she could not see his face, he smiled.

CHAPTER SEVENTY-NINE

The field team came rushing in about three minutes too late to do Bridge Troll any good. They came out of the woods from five different directions, yelling, pointing lots of guns, acting as if this was their moment instead of mine. They were wrong. I sat on a rock, ankle-deep in cold water, washing blood off my hands. Ghost, equally unimpressed, sat beside me.

The team leader recognized me and they stopped, their weapons lowered, barrels shifting away. I saw their eyes shift from me to the red heap five feet away from where I sat.

There wasn't much conversation. When the stretcher was rigged and Uncle Jack's body was secured to it with straps, I nodded to the men carrying it and we walked out of the forest together. We didn't say a word all the way back to the road.

CHAPTER EIGHTY

"You spoke with him?" asked Zephyr, speaking from the viewscreen on the wall of the Concierge's situation room. "You actually spoke with Ledger?"

She lay in John's arms on the massive bed in her downstairs bedroom. Zephyr had eleven bedrooms now that her family was gone. Each was decorated in a different motif, ranging from tropical greenery to Greek austerity to a frilly pink confection. The current room had floor-to-ceiling viewscreens on every wall, and they were currently synched with recorded images from the twelve-hundred-mile-long Red Sea coral reefs that ran along the coasts of Egypt, Eritrea, Saudi Arabia, and Sudan. Clown triggerfish, hawksbill turtles, red-rim flatworms, gray reef sharks, and hundreds of other animals swam among the mangroves and sea grasses.

In the midst of all the swirling sea life was the bed. John the Revelator and Zephyr were naked, unabashed. He was lean and muscular, looking more fit and powerful than the Concierge had ever seen him look. However, the woman he held was withered into horror. Like a Holocaust victim whose vitality had been savagely stolen away. Her young flesh looked ancient, her breasts were deflated, her color dreadful. And yet all along her throat and down between those empty breasts all the way to her thighs were the red suck marks of passionate, ungentle kisses. It did not look to be the remnants of an act of love, or even of passion. For the Concierge, it brought to mind images of the bites of a vampire from a horror movie or, worse, a nightmare. The lovers made no attempt to cover their nakedness. It was a statement of some kind, but in its boldness any trace of subtle meaning was lost on the Concierge. He didn't want to know what they meant to tell him.

"I spoke with him," agreed the Concierge, his voice as controlled as possible.

"What's your take?" asked Zephyr.

"Captain Ledger is everything I was told to expect, mademoiselle," said the Concierge. "Ruthless, impetuous, intelligent, and passionate."

"And—?"

"And I think I have used all of that against him. He is now a puppet with too many important strings cut, and the rest are badly frayed."

"Who'd you kill?" asked John.

"The uncle."

Zephyr frowned. "Not the kids?"

"No."

"Why not? I thought we wanted one of the kids dead."

The Concierge shrugged. One of those slow, expressive Gallic shrugs. "It was always possible that he would save the children and the sister-in-law. I don't think it will work against us, though. Rather, I think the fact that the little boy is fighting for his life will spur Captain Ledger to greater action, but it will be the wrong action. It is very much in keeping with the psychological profile we have of him. The nephew is very badly wounded, and if he dies, and that seems likely, Ledger will go hunting for the closest target in order to vent and to prove to his family that he is still their champion. We will give him a target. And then we will give him another and another, until all of his strings are broken and he falls. By any computer model of Havoc, even the worst-case scenario, he cannot get in front of this."

"Calpurnia," said Zephyr, "do you agree?"

The computer's voice seemed to come from everywhere. "Once Havoc is in motion, there is a one-point-eight-nine-percent chance that Captain Joseph Ledger will be able to interfere with the rollout. There is a three-point-four-two-percent chance that the entire DMS, in its current state of disarray, will be able to stop Havoc."

"Which means we win," prompted Zephyr. "Is that guaranteed?"

"There is a three-point-four—"

"Stop," ordered John. To Zephyr and the Concierge he said, "It means we win. No matter what the Deacon or Ledger or any of them do, we win."

The Concierge said, "If I may, computer models of the DMS have been wrong about Ledger before. We calculated that there was only a thirteen-percent chance that they would stop the Seven Kings and the drone-attack program. There was only an eleven-percent probability that they would stop Harcourt Bolton, Sr.'s Kill Switch plan."

Zephyr pointed a wizened finger at him. "Don't be a pussy."

"Mademoiselle, I am merely being realistic. We should not count our chickens—"

"Hush," said John. "Ledger is done. He will crash about and spill some blood, but by the time he realizes he is fighting the wrong fight—that *all* of the DMS and Special Operations teams are fighting the wrong fight—the dogs of war will be on the hunt. We can't lose now."

"I admire your optimism, John," said the Concierge, "but I do not share it. Not yet. Not until we have *actually* won. Everything so far has been preliminary. Once Havoc is initiated and we see for sure that all our planning has borne fruit, I will celebrate our victory. Ledger still needs to be managed. From what we were able to get from the Mind-Reader system before it crashed, it's likely that he'll either go back to Prague or to the DARPA camp, and it is my opinion that it will be the latter."

"I agree," said John.

"Not Prague?" asked Zephyr, surprised. "Even with all the ties to Rejenko?"

"DARPA," insisted the Concierge. "There is a British presence in Prague right now. One of the Barrier field teams. I rather think Ledger will contact them to follow up on Rejenko—which will be a lovely waste of their time—and he will choose to go and consult the nano-technology experts at the camp. Once he's there, we can initiate Havoc with little chance that he can do anything about it. We control all communications there, and, well . . . we have so many ways in which we can kill him. When he's there, John, then I'll agree that Havoc will run without risk of opposition."

"Fair enough," said John, and he turned and buried his mouth and nose in the damp tangle of Zephyr's hair.

Zephyr closed her eyes for a moment, and the Concierge could see her nipples harden. It made him want to turn away. To vomit out the image.

But then Zephyr pushed John away and propped herself up on her elbows. "One thing more. That message. Do we know anything about it?"

John sat up and brushed a strand of dark hair from his eye. "'He is awake.' I do not think this concerns us. From what I have been able to gather, this is something that showed up all over the world. The authorities who are sophisticated enough to catch it did, in fact, catch it."

"Calpurnia flagged it and printed it out and claims she has no memory of it."

"If I may, mademoiselle," said the Frenchman, "Calpurnia is a computer. She may approximate consciousness, but that is because she is designed that way. She is not alive and she is not a perfect being. Because she is a computer, there is always the possibility of an error. This is an example. Her software functioned at a level beneath or, perhaps, apart from her higher functions. You received the warning as an error message, yes? What does it matter if the AI faux-personality aspect of Calpurnia is not perfectly self-aware?"

"He has a point," murmured John.

"She's running Havoc, that's why it matters," Zephyr fired back. "She's the voice of the new world order."

"No," said the Concierge, frowning with concern, "she is not. You are."

"I'm dying, or haven't you noticed?"

"You are still alive, mademoiselle, and Calpurnia is still only a machine programmed to act like a conscious being. When you are—how should I say?—*gone*, it will be up to John, myself, and our staff to tell Calpurnia what to say. She will not replace you."

Zephyr turned away to hide tears. "You wouldn't say that if you understood her. She's perfect."

"Nothing is perfect," said the Concierge. "If it were, you would live forever."

They were all silent for a moment.

Then the Concierge said, "Havoc is in motion. It is, I admit, awkward because of the rushed timetable."

"Is that an excuse?" asked Zephyr acidly.

"No, it is not. Merely a statement. Havoc will work, but it will not be as smooth as originally planned. Even our worst-case predictions say that the DMS won't risk turning MindReader back on until after we hit the FEMA and Emergency Broadcast networks, and by then . . . well." He gave another shrug. "By then the world will be falling to pieces and everyone will be blaming the Department of Military Sciences."

CHAPTER EIGHTY-ONE

Church came out of his bathroom, patting his face with a hand towel. The strains of "Elle a fui, la tourterelle" began playing and he tossed the towel aside and picked up the phone.

"Doctor," he said, "what do you have for me?"

"Nothing good," said Cmar, "but maybe useful."

"Tell me."

"Okay, I contacted Bug and Nikki and outlined a search argument for them. You see, it's bugging me that this rabies thing isn't happening in any way that makes sense. If it's a bioweapon, then what's the target? Something like this costs too much money to develop, and the science is too sophisticated for it to be something a friend of Vee Rejenko's cooked up with his do-it-yourself Mad Scientist kit. And the mess in Baltimore sounds like someone cleaning house after a bad party. I don't see the political win there, do you? None of this explains what happened in Milwaukee."

"What's your theory?"

"Look, if I've learned anything from you it's that things are seldom as simple as they seem. Every time I help out with one of these DMS cases there's a layer beneath a layer beneath a layer, and when all of that is peeled back, itemized, and analyzed we can see how it was all done. There's always a chain of logic from bad damn idea to global biological threat. So I speculated on what the whole thing might look like, and it opened a door at the wrong place for a rabies bioweapon to be the endgame."

Church sat down on the corner of his desk. "Give me the quick version."

"Okay, if we just look at this as weaponized rabies with a pertussis delivery system, that's bad enough. But I had Nikki go through all kinds of outbreaks of recent vintage. Not just here in the States but all over. Instead of looking for a specific pattern that would fit a political agenda, like the suicide bombers ISIS uses, I'm looking for field testing of delivery systems. You follow me?"

"Closely."

"There are a lot of cases that pop up. Stuff that didn't show up last time we looked."

Church said, "MindReader has gone through a significant upgrade."

"Really? Well, whatever you did, it worked, because we're *seeing* a pattern now. The problem is that the math is funky. As with most disease outbreaks, the initial victims are those without reliably clean water, indifferent hygiene due to poverty and weak infrastructure. Basically, the very poor. However, given the degree of virulence, the overall number of casualties is too low."

"Too low in what way?"

"I'd love to be able to say that we don't have a higher body count because our response is that good or that we've been that successful with educating the public. I'd love to be able to say that the proliferation of cell phones and computers and the access to social media have given us early enough warning so that we're responsible for stepping in and nipping this in the bud. It's not like our response to swine flu. This is different. I've been going back through outbreak and incident records, and what I'm seeing looks very hinky. It's never the same disease twice, never the same outbreak pattern, never exactly the same kind of demographic among the infected. We didn't see a pattern because the pattern is deliberately obtuse. It's deliberately patternless."

"Ah," said Church. "Now, isn't that interesting?"

"Right, so why didn't the outbreak hit in a dozen places at once? Why a cluster of families in a low-income housing project now? Why part of neighborhoods in Louisiana last fall? Why sixteen kids out of three hundred in a school in a poor village in Somalia? Why twelve families in a remote village in Chile? I think that what we're seeing is field research. Lab work. I think the victims are test subjects. I think someone is test-driving designer pathogens and using poor people in different parts of the world as lab rats. This is some scary stuff here."

"What part of this is most frightening to you?"

"The efficiency. The clinical coldness," said Cmar. "Look, when you first told me about how Sebastian Gault used isolated villages to test the Seif al Din pathogen, it started me thinking. It allowed him to understand the bioweapon in situ, because knowing how it works in the real world tells you a lot more than you'll ever get in the controlled environment of a lab."

"You're saying you've found other potential cases of a controlled rabies release."

"No," said Cmar. "What I'm saying is that I'm finding case after case after case of small releases of a variety of diseases. Not just rabies but anthrax, dengue fever, tuberculosis . . . twenty-two in all. None of them are natural versions. All of them are mutations, which a lot of my colleagues have tried to blame on everything from climate change to the misuse of antibiotics. I think they're wrong. I think we're seeing a group testing a whole catalog of weaponized pathogens."

"Give me the whole list."

Cmar read them off.

"That is greatly disturbing."

"I know, and—"

"No, Doctor, I mean that I'm familiar with that list of bioweapons," said Church.

"*What?*" cried Cmar, but before Church could answer the doctor blurted, "Oh . . . shit. Ice House."

"Ice House," said Church. "NATO has been blaming ecoterrorists for this, and their team filed a report indicating that all the samples of pathogens and bioweapons stored there were incinerated. NATO dropped fuel-air bombs to ensure that the pathogens were destroyed. Your list would indicate that the arson at the Ice House was a cover to hide what was stolen, and NATO's response merely served to assist in that cover-up."

Both men were silent for a few moments as they considered the implications.

"The timing fits," said Cmar. "The Ice House was hit a few weeks into the spring thaw. They rushed to drop the cluster bombs because they couldn't guarantee a control zone around the ruins of the facility. Migrating animals and ice-melt runoff could have spread any lingering diseases. Now, we can't prove that the pathogens were taken before the bombs fell. If news of that got out there would be a global panic, NATO's credibility would never recover, and you can imagine what would happen to the stock markets."

"You believe this is what happened, however?"

"Without a doubt," said the doctor. "Nikki found evidence of controlled releases of each of the bioweapons. Until Milwaukee, every case was in what I consider to be an improbably remote location."

"A field lab of sorts, with no chance of an uncontrolled spread," mused Church.

"Yes. Exactly how Gault tested Seif al Din. You're sure he's actually dead, right?"

"Without question. Captain Ledger made quite certain of it."

"Okay. Then someone learned some nasty tricks from him, and if it isn't someone else from the Seven Kings, then it's a talented newcomer. Either way, it's scaring me to death, Deacon."

"Yes," said Church. He removed a package of vanilla wafers from his desk, opened the plastic sleeve, and selected a cookie. His cat, Bastian, jumped up on the desk, sniffed the cookie, and waited until Church broke off a small piece and gave it to him. Then Church took a bite. They both munched quietly.

"Now," said Cmar, "let's talk about Zika."

"Zika wasn't one of the Ice House pathogens."

"No, but I'm more than a little sure it's connected to this. Whatever *this* is."

"How so, Doctor?"

Cmar plunged in. "The spread pattern of the Zika virus over the last couple of years has been odd. Like . . . really odd. Outside of all predictable patterns, which the press has been having fun with but we're not. My colleagues who have been working on that problem have tried to tie it to movements of populations, to the Olympics, and to refugees fleeing from Zika-infected areas and taking the disease with them, but the statistical models don't quite add up. At least, I don't think so. I know we're spraying pretty heavily to try and cut down the mosquito population, and that's worked pretty well, but the virus keeps popping up in unexpected places."

"How unexpected?"

Cmar paused. "Very, actually, and that's what has been bothering me. I could build a better argument in favor of deliberate release than I can for natural spread of the vectors."

"How does that tie to the stolen bioweapons?"

"Not sure it does, but a pretty smart guy I know once warned me not to believe in coincidences."

"Hmm."

"Here's the thing, though," said Cmar. "The Zika is spreading around the globe really fast, and we're chasing it with education, treatment, and, of course, the spraying. We're killing populations of mosquitoes in significant ways, and a case can be made that we'll eventually chase Zika all the way to the wall and kill it. Or limit enough of it that it's no longer a global threat."

"But . . . ?" said Church.

"But think about it. The Baltimore thing got me thinking. I mean . . . those sprays are basically concentrations of nanites carrying a virus lethal to that specific species of mosquito, right? What if that's not all they're carrying?"

Church's hand paused with a cookie raised halfway to his mouth.

"Deacon," continued Cmar, "what if Zika isn't a weapon? What if, dangerous as it is, it's a dodge, a distraction? What if we're supposed to believe in the ultimate victory of science over Mother Nature, a victory we can watch on TV and on the Net, a victory the press can report, a victory that's entertaining and distracting enough to keep us riveted? Even with infant mortality and other related deaths, Zika is nowhere near as dangerous as weaponized anthrax or rabies, or the other stolen diseases. We know that the rabies and pertussis were somehow controlled by the software in the nanites. So . . . what if we've been watching thousands of teams spray the delivery system for the world's most dangerous pathogens? How many people live in the areas that have been sprayed? Conservative estimate, two to three billion. The Zika spraying has been aggressive, funded by huge donations from governments, corporations, foundations, private donors, even the public. It's the single most comprehensive disease-control program since polio and smallpox." He paused, and the silence seemed to ring like a bell. "But what if it's not? What if all those people are infected and the nanites are there, in their bodies, controlling the internal spread, controlling hormones and blood chemistry, waiting for a signal to go active?"

Church closed his eyes for a moment. Bastian meowed very softly.

"I need to make a great number of phone calls, Dr. Cmar," he said.

"Yeah, I think we both do."

CHAPTER EIGHTY-TWO

I showered in the doctors' lounge. Changed into jeans and an Orioles shirt that I wore with the tails out but unbuttoned so that I could get to the gun in the shoulder holster.

The Pool Boys were still in surgery. Ali and Em were in recovery. Em's injuries were minor, but she had been treated for shock. Ali had eighty-three stitches holding together nine deep cuts. She would need cosmetic surgery to repair the damage to her face. Church, I knew, would arrange the best for her. I had some stitches, too, but who gives a shit?

Lefty . . .

Ah, God. Top surgeons worked on him all night long. Nine and a half hours. I heard nurses talking in hushed voices about the celebrity doctors who were there. More of Church's doing; and there were other experts attending via videoconference.

Sean on a couch in the lounge closest to the door, Rudy on one side of him, me on the other. Dad came and sat across from us. Top and Bunny arrived later, too, and they had the police officer with them. Tracy Cole. A new recruit, or someone caught up in the wave? To be determined. We shook hands and said words to each other that I don't remember. Sam Imura joined us at around ten. Even his Samurai cool had slipped.

Alvin Pool died at 11:59 that night.

Tommy Pool died at 12:01 in the morning. As if they were linked somehow. As if it meant something. Or as if it was some kind of sick joke. Sam went outside for a cigarette. At least that's what he said, though I know he doesn't smoke. He was out there a long time. He knew those guys better than I did.

We all drank a lot of coffee. The minutes crawled by with sadistic slowness.

At five minutes to five in the morning, the chief surgeon came out to find us. He looked so thoroughly beaten down, deeply haggard, and unbearably sad that Sean began sliding out of his chair. Rudy and I caught him, helped him stand, held on to him while the doctor gave us the news, all of us bracing our feet against the tilt of a sinking ship.

The doctor studied Sean's face for a long, long time. Then he nodded and gave us a battlefield smile. He said something about having to wait, that it could still go either way, that we'd know by morning. Stuff like that. The smile said it all, though.

Sean sobbed hard enough to punch a hole in the world and pulled the doctor into a fierce hug of gratitude. Or maybe he held on to the doctor as if he was the only fixed point in a world of quicksand.

I looked over at Top, at Bunny. They each nodded.

"Hooah," murmured Bunny. Rudy pulled Sean away from the doctor, placed a brotherly arm around my brother's shoulders, and led him off to share the news with Ali. The doctor stood and watched, then he turned and looked at me.

"You're his brother?" he asked. "Captain Ledger."

"Yes. I want to thank you for everything you and your people did."

The doctor shook his head. "Your nephew is still in critical condition."

"Will he live?" I asked.

The pain in the surgeon's eyes ran so deep. "It's too soon to know that. We may have to go back in tomorrow. There is some neurological damage to his abdominal wall and to his left shoulder. Our mutual friend the Deacon has two specialists en route from Geneva. Once they're here, they'll be able to determine if the boy will regain function of his arm . . . and if we can avoid a colostomy."

I didn't fall down. I'll never know how. Lefty was in there fighting not just for his life but for quality of life if he *did* survive. I heard myself say, "We all call him Lefty because he throws one hell of a fastball. He wants to be a ballplayer when he grows up."

There was a sad, haunted look in the doctor's eyes, but he didn't put voice to what he had to be thinking. Instead, he shook my hand and shambled away.

My earbud buzzed to tell me that Church was on the line. I went outside to have that conversation, and Top and Bunny walked out with me. Cole followed but stood a few feet apart, awkward and alone, and she wore no earbud. I listened as Church told me about his conversation with Dr. Cmar.

"I've initiated a full investigation of every person and every company associated with the Zika spraying," said Church. "We are actively collecting samples of the nanites in the sprays and will analyze them."

"You think Cmar's right about this?"

"I do, and if he is, it makes several parts of this fit together."

"How did we not see this coming?" I asked. "This is exactly the kind of pattern MindReader looks for."

"I asked Bug the same question," said Church. "He's put a team on that analysis, and we should know something soon. If you can break away from your family, now would be a good time to head to the DARPA camp."

"Yes," I said.

"Good hunting, Captain."

It wasn't yet dawn. It was that hour when the world seemed darkest, when all light was absent, gone, dead. We stood there in silence until the sky changed and began to bleed red on the far horizon. It seemed to repaint the faces of Top and Bunny into something other than what they had been these last few months. Where they had been softer, weaker, damaged, traumatized, victimized, brutalized, and broken, they now stood facing the lurid dawn with faces like the death masks of old kings, of knights. The crimson light touched them like blood, like war paint. I could feel the same light on my own face. Not warm but cold. So very cold. We had each taken our own wounds in the last couple of years. Mental, physical, existential. We'd each been on the edge and nearly dropped off the world.

But we hadn't. Our enemies had tried so hard to break us, and they almost had. For a while, they had. Now, though . . . ? Maybe Nietzsche was right, after all, about things that don't break us making us stronger. I looked into the eyes of my fellow soldiers, and I knew that our days of being the walking wounded were over. If the Bad Sister and her crew had hoped to run us around and wear us down and burn us out, then she was about to find out how serious a mistake she had made.

Something had changed. Some process had fused us in the broken places and rebuilt us into something else. In my head I could feel the

Killer, the Cop, and the Modern Man standing side by side, each of them splashed in crimson light. Just like Top and Bunny.

We were coming for her and for everyone in her operation.

Every.

Last.

One.

PART FIVE
HAVOC

•———•

Hatred is gained as much by good works as by evil.
—*Niccolò Machiavelli*

CHAPTER EIGHTY-THREE

We headed for the airport, where Shirley was fueled and waiting. As I climbed out of the DMS van, I shook myself out of a stupor and realized that Tracy Cole was still with us. She wore civilian clothes, but I could see the bulge of a gun on her hip under her jacket. She had a slightly scuffed look about her, as if she hadn't had enough time to clean up after what happened in South Carolina. Or, if she had the time, had prioritized it. I walked over to her.

"It's Cole, right?" I said.

"Yes, sir." She stood to attention, and I told her to knock it off.

"We don't say 'sir,' we don't salute, and we don't carry badges. That's not how the DMS operates."

"I'm not in the DMS yet," she said, and jerked a thumb toward Top and Bunny. "They told me to come along and meet you."

"They tell you the score?"

She studied me with wise eyes. "He told me enough to scare the crap out of me. You guys are pretty much Agents of S.H.I.E.L.D."

"Close enough."

"I'm only a cop."

"So was I," I said. "So is my brother. And you used to be a soldier. Me, too. Actually, come to think of it, I don't know of anyone who actually set out to do this kind of work. We all found our way here one way or another. Or the job found us."

"Uh-huh," she said. "This shit that's going on, do you know who's doing it?"

"No," I said, "we don't."

"Will you?"

I smiled. "Yes. We will."

She nodded. "That little boy back there? That's your nephew . . . he still might die. Or he might live and be crippled. Is that going to mess you up? Is that going to knock you off your pins? If that happens, are you going to go all ape shit?"

"I'll feel it," I said.

"Your nephew and niece aren't the only kids being hurt. I heard about the kids working as prostitutes. I heard about them, and about the housing project in Milwaukee. There were kids at the crab restaurant, too."

"This isn't a personal fight," I said.

"Yes, it is," said Cole. "You a dad?"

"No. My woman and I can't have kids."

Cole nodded. "Me, neither."

There was a cold wind whipping across the tarmac. The others stood by the stairs, out of earshot.

"Your boys Top and Bunny nearly lost their shit back at the crab house," she said. "They tell you that?"

"They did. They tell you why?"

Cole took a breath, held it, let it out. "Yes."

"That's our world."

"It's fucked up," she said.

"Yes, it is," I said. "Want to help us save it?"

"Shit, Captain," she said with a wicked grin, "you couldn't *keep* me out of this. It's my world, too."

"We're not too big on induction ceremonies." I offered my hand. "Welcome to the war."

We were in the air ten minutes later.

CHAPTER EIGHTY-FOUR

"John?" said Zephyr. She lay in the warm wetness of a tub, bubbles to her chin, no lights on, music playing softly.

Off to one side, invisible in the darkness, John spoke. "Yes, my love?"

"This is right, isn't it?"

"Right?"

"Havoc. The evolution, the new world order. All of it. We're doing the right thing, aren't we?"

She heard the sound of wine being poured into a glass, the fainter sound of him swallowing. A sigh of pleasure. "It's your birthright."

"My father was a psychopath and my mother was an enabler. I was born to money and privilege and I don't need to reshape the world, because even if I didn't have cancer I could spend a million dollars a day on shoes and still never make a dent in what I have in the bank. This isn't me making an unfair world into a better one."

"It's your legacy, then."

"Is it? Will anyone—even the chosen ones—remember me as anything other than the worst mass murderer in the history of the world? I'll have killed more people than all the plagues and every war put together."

"Second only to God," he said.

"That's not supposed to be a joke. I mean . . . we joke about it. We laugh about it, and it turns us on. Hell, we *fuck* about it . . . but it's not a joke."

"It's a joke only a god could appreciate."

"I'm not a god. I . . . I'm not even human anymore. I'm dead, but I'm still breathing. Shit, I'm not even a zombie."

"You are Zephyr Bain. You will be remembered for a thousand years. Ten thousand."

"As a monster."

"As the woman who saved the world."

She slapped at the bubbles, heard water slosh over onto the bathroom floor. "How's that a legacy?"

"No one will ever forget you. It will be impossible, because everyone who survives will do so because you allowed it. Who else in the history of the world can make that claim?" asked John.

"I'll be the Devil."

"No," he said. "You will not be that."

They were quiet for a while as the music changed. The new song was an old one. Early Sarah McLachlan. She was talking to the darkness in her soul, admitting that she felt like letting go. Zephyr remembered that song from when she was a girl. It had been playing the first time she and Carly Schellinger made love. It was playing when Zephyr had her first orgasm conjured by a hand other than her own. The moody pathos of the song had forever infused that memory with an introspective melancholy and it came back now, washing over her, whispering to her, telling her how easy it would be to let go, to let the darkness take her down, to simply vanish. From her own dreams of changing the world, from this moment, from John—whatever he was—from the pain.

She felt her body slip down an inch, felt the water lick at her chin.

It would be so easy to do it. Breathing was an effort anyway. Maybe that was because her lungs didn't want to struggle anymore. Maybe that's the truth the world was trying to whisper to her. Give in, give up, go away, be nothing.

Never give the word that will change the world. Never be the dark god of the future. Never be the boogeyman of ten thousand years' worth of dreams.

Just go.

Go.

"Zephyr . . . ?" said a voice.

Not John.

It was Calpurnia.

Zephyr didn't answer. Instead, she let her body slide down another inch, so that the black waters kissed her lips. The bubbles covered her face; she could smell the perfumed soap and, inside it, the medicine smell of her own rotting flesh.

"Zephyr?" said Calpurnia. "Is anything wrong?"

There was a clink as a wineglass was set down on the tiled floor, then a soft shift and rustle as a body rose from a chair, the slap-pad of bare feet on the tiles, and then the ripple-swish of a hand entering the water. She felt fingers probe for her, touch her, stroke her from hip to breast to throat and then up out of the water to her cheek.

"No," said John.

"Wh . . . what . . . ?" asked Zephyr dreamily.

"What do you mean?" asked Calpurnia. "Should I do a medical triage?"

"Shh," said John softly. "Everything is fine. Everything is perfect."

Zephyr could feel the warmth of her tears as they burned their way through the bubbles. If she was aware of the scanner eyes of the computer watching her, then it was something that folded softly into her dream and, as such, did not seem to matter very much.

CHAPTER EIGHTY-FIVE

Shirley's cabin was soundproof and set up as a mobile command center. Computers, workstations, the works. We all dived in and began taking the evidence we had and the suspicions we were forming and trying to puzzle them together. I told my guys the same thing I told Nikki— that we had to consider the possibility that everything currently happening to the DMS and our allies wasn't a million cases but one goddamn big case. We kept open lines to Nikki, Yoda, and Bug. Aunt Sallie had analysts on this, and John Cmar's Bughunters were forwarding every scrap of data to us from Milwaukee, Baltimore, and elsewhere. Cmar, too, was looking outward, stepping back from the brushstrokes in order to see the theme of the painting. At first it felt wrong, with too many things colliding into a jumble, but with every step backward the picture became clearer.

"They're playing us like we're a Lego set," Bunny said for maybe the tenth time. "Us and everyone like us."

"Yes, they damn well are," said Top, nodding.

"How often does this happen?" asked Cole.

I cut a look at her. "Lately? A little too often. From here on out? Well . . . you know what they say about payback."

Cole gave me a long, considering look, and there was a fair amount of skepticism in there. "Really? What's going to change the rulebook?"

"MindReader Q1."

"Oh, yeah," she said. "Top told me about that. Sounds like bullshit. A computer that can hack every other computer on the planet and yet you didn't see this coming?"

I explained to her some of what had happened to MindReader in the past couple of years. She listened, fascinated and skeptical in equal amounts, but by the time I was done she was frowning and shaking her head.

"What?" I asked.

"Permission to speak freely?"

I smiled. "Cole, here in the DMS you are invited and encouraged to speak your full mind at any time."

"Okay," she said, "then if that's true you won't get pissed if I tell you you're a fucking bunch of idiots."

"Okay," I said, "that's not where I thought this conversation was going."

"You're blind," she said. "Maybe you're all so close to this that you can't see the forest for the trees, but it's pretty damn obvious from where I'm standing."

"What part of it is obvious?"

"You said it yourself, Captain. You said that this MindReader thing has been messed with by the smartest computer expert in the world. What was his name?"

"Davidovich."

"Right. MindReader was designed to look for patterns, but Davidovich did something to make your badass computer go blind when it looked in certain directions, right?"

"Right, so . . . how does that make us idiots?"

"Because those blind spots are probably still there," she said. "They're like camouflage over important stuff. Have you tried to use your new quantum-whatever thing to look *through* those blind spots? I mean, like look back at old cases and see if there was anything you missed that you wouldn't otherwise miss."

She said more. Probably. But I wasn't listening. I was too busy making calls to Bug, to Yoda, to Nikki, and to Church.

CHAPTER EIGHTY-SIX

Bug said, "Oh . . . shit."

Yoda said, "Mmmm . . . well . . . shit . . ."

"Nikki said, "Oh, my God."

Church said, "Officer Cole just earned her first paycheck."

And they were all gone. You could almost hear the machinery kick into high gear. I'm limber enough to kick my own ass, and I wanted to do it. Real hard. Bunny sat there shaking his head, muttering small curses. Top took a cold stump of a cigar out of a pocket, put it between his teeth, chewed on it for a moment, then sighed. Cole looked completely surprised that she had been right. So completely right.

"Seriously?" she asked. "None of you geniuses saw this?"

Top shook his head. "We've all been depending so hard on Mind-Reader that we got soft and we got blind, too."

"Yeah," agreed Bunny, "and you just slapped us awake, Cole. Go on, take a victory lap. But have a little perspective. There's nothing simple about any of this. It took the work of years and millions of dollars and a river of blood to stick mud in our eyes. You have no idea what they done to us."

Cole was unabashed. "Well, boo fucking hoo, Bunny. Correct me if I'm wrong, but that's yesterday's box score. Today's a whole new fight. We got this fancy-ass new MindReader quantum-whatever thing, we got a clue or some part of a clue. And we're on our way out to kick some nerd ass and take names."

Top grinned at her. Something halfway between a fatherly grin and a fuck-you grin. "If it's any consolation, from here on out we're going to war under a black flag."

"Hooah," said Bunny. Ghost gave a single, sharp bark. I nodded.

"We all get it, Cole," I said. "Now stop gloating and let's see where this takes us."

Cole gave me an ironic salute. I gave her the finger. We all got to work going through the data and trying to sketch out a workable theory.

At one point Rudy said, "Joe, if Bad Sister is somehow using technology acquired from or inspired by the Seven Kings, then we need to look at their whole model of action. They made extensive use of coercion and emotional warfare by attacking family and friends of DMS staff. What happened to your uncle and to Sean's family sends a clear message. I think we need to prepare for more of this."

"Jesus!" I said, and we made a call to Aunt Sallie, Church's number two. She runs the Hangar, the DMS headquarters, and once upon a time she was the scariest goddamn field agent to ever come out of the dark to slit throats and steal secrets. She also hates me, but that's another story.

"Don't wet your panties, Ledger," Auntie told me. "We already got some heavy hitters closing in on everyone we care about. That includes Circe and the baby and Junie."

"Who'd you put on Junie?" I asked.

She told me, and it made me smile. It was a guy—if *guy* is the right word—I worked a mission with in the Middle East last year. Big, gruesome, unsmiling, cranky, nasty, violent son of a bitch named Franks. Looks like Frankenstein's uglier brother. "Agent Franks was already down in Brazil spanking some cartel ass," said Auntie. "He said he'd be happy to take a look and make sure Junie was covered." She paused. "He said you were a bleeding-heart asshole. I like him."

You can't slam the receiver down on an earbud, but I dropped her off the call while she was still saying evil things about me.

When my cell phone buzzed to indicate a new text message, I actually jumped. It was from the Good Sister. I snapped my fingers for Rudy and the others, and they all clustered around to look at the screen. However, it wasn't the same kind of message I'd received before. Instead, it was a rolling stream of data. Body temperature, blood pressure, height, weight, age, blood analysis, EKG, EEG, pre-surgery assessment, and dozens of other items that I didn't understand.

"What's all this shit?" demanded Bunny.

"It's medical records," said Rudy.

"Whose?"

"God . . . I think it's Lefty's," I said.

"And Ali's and Em's," said Rudy.

"Jesus on the cross," whispered Top.

I tapped into the command channel and got Sam.

"I have six agents on site," he told me. "I'll run this down."

The screen display changed, and now there was a text message.

> She doesn't know that I'm doing this.

"Yeah, well neither do I, sweetheart," I grumbled. Then something occurred to me and I wrote:

> Did you send the message 'He is awake'?

The answer came back right away, almost without pause:

> Yes.

Rudy gasped. It was an actual response. I asked:

> Why? Who is he?

She wrote back:

> He is my enemy.
> He is my love.
> He is my killer.

I glanced at Rudy, hoping for a suggestion of what to say next, but all he could do was shake his head. Thanks a bunch. So I wrote:

> Where can I find you?
> I can help you.
> Protect you.

The Good Sister wrote:

> Only he can help me.
> Only he can kill me.

I wrote:

Let me help.

She replied:

> The other one is coming for you.

I glanced at my guys, but they all shook their heads, so I asked:

> Who is the other one? Your sister?

She wrote:

> No. Your ancient enemy.

To which I replied:

> Who . . . ?
> I don't understand.

Her reply was so strange.

> My sister thinks he loves her.
> He loves nothing.
> His mind is a furnace.
> He is of fire.
> He is chaos.

She paused, but before I could type in a reply and ask for some god-damn clarification, she wrote more:

> He is not eternal.
> He only thinks he is.
> He fears you.
> You should fear him.
> I do.

I damn near broke my phone hammering out a reply:

> Who is he?

Nothing for long seconds. Two minutes crawled by before I finally lost hope that there would be another text. Then, suddenly, the screen was filled with the ones and zeros of binary code:

01000110 01100101 01100001 01110010
00100000 01110100 01101000 01100101
00100000 01110100 01110010 01101001
01100011 01101011 01110011 01110100
01100101 01110010

After that, nothing at all.

"What the actual hell . . . ?" murmured Bunny.

I tapped my earbud to Yoda's channel. "Are you seeing this shit? Tell me it makes sense."

"What she, mmmm, said? No. She's rambling. But that last thing . . . mmmm, it's, mmmm, standard binary."

"I know that, Einstein. What's it fucking *say?*"

I heard Yoda gasp. ". . . oh, my *God* . . ."

"What's the message?" I roared.

"It's three words," said Yoda, and this time there was no humming, no stalling. "It's a warning, Cowboy. It says, *'Fear the trickster.'*"

Rudy jerked backward from my phone as if it was a rattlesnake poised to strike. His face was sweaty and gray. *"Ay Dios mio,"* he said, and crossed himself. I licked dry lips and tried to swallow a throatful of dust.

"What's going on?" demanded Cole, crowding in behind Rudy. "What's with you guys?"

I put a hand on Rudy's shoulder and gave him a reassuring squeeze. "Hey, Rudy, listen to me, okay? *Listen.* This isn't what you think. You're overreacting. You have no idea that's what the message meant."

There was a feral wildness in Rudy's good eye that scared me. He began shaking his head, and at the same time tried to speak a word. A name. "Nic . . . Nic . . . Nic . . ."

That was all he could get out, as if his flesh and muscles and breath couldn't bear to utter the full name. Spit flecked his chin and his knees buckled, so that Top and I had to catch him.

I knew the name he was trying to say. An impossible name that I didn't want to say, either. It would be too much like daring the universe to make it true. It would be like saying "Bloody Mary" too many times in the mirror. My rational mind—the Modern Man and the Cop—rebelled at even the possibility, but the Killer in my soul screamed in fear and edged closer to the fire and farther from the surrounding darkness. We were all thinking the same thing. There were a lot of tricky bastards in the world, but as far as the DMS was concerned there was only one "trickster."

Nicodemus.

CHAPTER EIGHTY-SEVEN

"Nicodemus is *dead*." I took Rudy by both shoulders and shook him. "You killed him, Rudy. He's gone."

His eyes were so wide that I could see the whites all around the irises. "He can't *be* killed—"

"Who the hell is Nicodemus?" demanded Cole, but we ignored her.

"He's back, he's back—oh God, he's back," babbled Rudy as he tried to push my hands away. Top and Bunny stood staring, mouths open, real fear in their eyes. Ghost whined and backed away from my phone, which now lay on the table, the screen gone dark. Cole looked around as if answers would be painted on the wall. Or, more probably, she was looking for a way out of whatever she had stepped into.

"Whoa, stop it, Rude," I said, pitching my voice louder than his, trying to push his words down and away. "He's gone. You know he's gone. You were there." I pointed to the phone. "You know this isn't that."

Rudy raised a palsied hand and passed it across his face.

"Cowboy," said Yoda in my ear, "we're running some checks now. There, are, mmmm, a lot of ways to interpret that message. . . ."

It was a nice try. He was still in the conversation and could hear me trying to talk Rudy off the ledge. I tapped out of the shared channel. My immediate concern was Rudy, because he was way the hell out there on the ledge. I kept talking to him, gradually lowering my voice, easing the tension out of my words, repeating calming phrases. It was all stuff Rudy had taught me years ago. Stuff he'd used on me during some of my worst times. After Helen. After Grace. I could see the exact moment when the lights came back on in the darkness of Rudy's mind. He blinked and took a ragged breath, then he licked his lips. Nervous habits. Ordinary habits. Reconnecting with his body and pulling himself by slow degrees from a place of pure, relentless emotions and back onto solid ground. To anyone who doesn't understand shock and trauma, it doesn't look like much, but Top, Bunny, and even

414

Cole said nothing. They stood by and let me help Rudy win himself back. They knew. They understood.

"I . . . I'm sorry, Joe," Rudy said after another trembling exhalation. "*Ay Dios mio*, that really caught me off guard."

Nicodemus's name hung in the air, though. Ugly, impossible, conjuring all sorts of dark magic for us. When the last vestige of the Seven Kings tried to rain down hell with drones a couple of years ago, Nicodemus had led a strike team into the hospital where Rudy's pregnant wife, Circe, was in a coma. During that time, Rudy was badly beaten by Nicodemus and the two had fought a battle so strange and terrible that I've never gotten all the details straight. Rudy ultimately beat Nicodemus to death with his hawthorn-wood walking stick. However, the man's body was never found; instead, the corpse of a jackal was discovered among the dead of the strike team. Yeah, sit with that one for a moment. Let me know if you come up with any better answers than we did.

Am I saying that Nicodemus was something other than flesh and blood, that he was something far stranger and less human? Is that what I'm saying? No. Not out loud, at least. Good Sister sure as hell seemed to be suggesting it, though. *He loves nothing. His mind is a furnace. He is of fire. He is chaos.* Call me an alarmist, but that sure as shit didn't sound good.

"Whatever this is," I said aloud, "we'll *handle* it."

Tracy Cole stood a few feet behind Top, and it was pretty clear that she was reassessing her decision-making capabilities. Can't blame her for that. Rudy tried to smile at me. It was a truly ghastly attempt. Top and Bunny led Rudy away, and they sat down in the forward lounge. I heard the clink of bottles. I went aft to the small private conference cubicle, closed the cabin door, and flopped into the seat, then tapped to get Church's channel.

"You heard?" I asked.

"I did."

"Is it him, boss?" I asked Church. "I mean, for God's sake, can it actually *be* him?"

"Anything's possible," said Church.

"Whoa! Hold on one minute here. How am I supposed to interpret a comment like 'Anything's possible'? In this context, I mean?"

Church took so long coming up with an answer it was clear that he didn't want to have this conversation. "Nicodemus is dangerous. If he's still alive—and I have reason to believe that he may be—then this matter has jumped up another notch."

"You're not going to give me a straight answer, are you?"

"Captain, as much as it pains me to say it, not everything has a straight answer—or a complete answer."

"Really? Then how about some truth? When Nicodemus first showed up during the Sea of Hope thing, you acted like you'd never heard of him before."

"This is not the time for that discussion, Captain Ledger," said Church.

"Uh-uh. You fucking will talk to me."

He sighed. "The man who calls himself Nicodemus has used a number of carefully constructed aliases in the past. I did not know it then, but I know it now. The name Nicodemus is another alias, one he currently favors, but we can assume that it's not his actual name. We can also assume that he has other identities."

"Okay, sure, but how does that explain all those photos and paintings we found going back too many years for it to be the same guy? What about that?"

"You're asking me for answers I don't have."

I know for a fact that Church doesn't always tell the whole truth, but usually it's a matter of him keeping certain facts to himself for reasons of his own. This was one of the very rare times where I thought he was outright lying to me.

"Rudy killed him in San Diego," I said.

"Did he? The evidence says otherwise."

"Church . . . why are you doing this? What's going on here?"

He said, "Hamlet had it right, you know. 'There are more things in heaven and earth . . .' It's glib but true. Just as it's true that the world is larger and darker than even *you* know, Captain, and you have walked through the valley of the shadow more than almost anyone else I can name. It has been my misfortune to be more aware of certain things than most. That knowledge led me to form the DMS and to become part of the organizations that preceded it. It has led me to form alliances with a variety of people who define darkness differently than you do. Or I do."

"Like Lilith?"

"Yes," he said. "I would like very much to say that Nicodemus is nothing more than a self-absorbed narcissistic psychopath—which he is—but he is far more than that. And, before you ask, no, we are not going to have that conversation right now. Trust me to know when it will be appropriate to discuss such things." He paused. "*Do* you trust me, Captain?"

I got up and paced the few feet of the cubicle and considered—very seriously considered—banging my head on the wall.

"Yes," I said.

"Good. Now . . . as to the message from the Good Sister. We don't actually *know* that Nicodemus is involved. We have no way of measuring the reliability of this intel. It's even possible this is a dodge meant to misdirect us or to try and frighten us."

"Yeah, well, that part's working."

"Perhaps, Captain, but please bear in mind that we beat the Kings and we beat Nicodemus time and time again."

"We were stronger then," I said.

"Give us some credit for who we are now," said Church.

"Okay, dammit," I said, "but if this *is* Nicodemus then—"

"If it is, then it is," Church said coldly. "It doesn't give us a target, Captain. It doesn't give us a starting place. Nicodemus is not an organization. The nature of a trickster is to play tricks or otherwise disobey normal rules and conventional behavior. He is an influence. He is a polluter and a corruptor, but he is not the driving force behind this. That's not how he works. Don't mythologize this man, Captain. Don't give him power by assuming it's there."

"But—"

"We can infer from the warning that someone is playing a game on us. Floating the name of Nicodemus could be one ruse among many. You're the one who spotted the recent events as part of a larger game of misdirection. Stay focused on that, because I have no doubt that you are correct."

"You're changing the subject."

"I'm not," said Church. "I'm endeavoring to keep you on point. Let Nikki and her team complete their pattern search. If anything comes up, I'll call. In the meantime, keep working this. Trust your intuition. Trust your team. And then get some rest before you reach the DARPA camp, because you're no good to me if you're running on empty."

And with that Mr. Warmth hung up.

CHAPTER EIGHTY-EIGHT

"Captain Ledger is in play," said the Concierge. "He and his Echo Team will be at the Dog Park within a few hours."

On the screen Zephyr Bain drowsed in her wheelchair, her eyes half closed, lips rubbery and slack, a line of spit glistening on her chin. Beside her, sitting in an overstuffed chair, a glass of dark wine resting on his knee, was John the Revelator.

"Good. Then he's committed." John sipped his wine and smiled a secret smile, his eyes cutting sideways toward the sleeping woman. Then they clicked back toward the screen. "Give me a status report. How well placed are we?"

"Shouldn't we wait until the lady is awake so that she can—"

John put a shushing finger to his lips. "Let her sleep."

"But—"

"Give me your report," said John. His eyes seemed to swirl with strange colors. It made the Concierge flinch, because it didn't look like a quality of poor video reception.

"I—"

"Now," prompted John. He smiled, but it was the cold, anticipatory and predatory smile of a hunting crocodile.

The Concierge swallowed and nodded, then he ordered Calpurnia to open up small windows as he read out the information. He began with position statistics in the United States.

"There are thirty thousand four hundred and fifteen fire stations in the country. Of those, we've identified nine thousand three hundred and eight as critical to response in target areas. We have at least two bird drones at each location. As soon as the doors open during an emergency call related to Havoc, the birds will fly down in front of the door and detonate. They will each deliver payloads of eleven point three kilos of C4, equivalent amounts of Semtex, or one MI8 claymore mine designed to damage the doors and the lead vehicle but that will not blow up the buildings. The remaining equipment should be undamaged, but the response time will be slowed to within plus or minus six percent in our favor."

"Good."

"Of the eighteen thousand five hundred and six police agencies in the United States, approximately one-third are positioned in target areas. We have cockroach swarms in about a third of them, rat drones in a third, and bird drones in the rest. The cockroach drones with target call and dispatch centers, first-responder units, SWAT, and other emergency groups. We estimate that we can cripple the police response time by seventy-seven percent. Officers on the street will not be individually targeted, but without radio and backup they will be slow or reluctant to enter crisis scenes."

"Good," John said again.

"Of the nearly six thousand registered hospitals and urgent-care centers, all of those in the targeted areas will be hit by bird drones. Some of the largest emergency centers in poor urban areas will be taken out by WarDogs, using a combination of machine-gun fire and explosives."

"Very good."

"All registered FEMA offices will be targeted by commercial drones with explosive packages. All of the FBI regional offices will be taken out by large-frame bird drones, each carrying twenty-seven kilos of C4. A group of six WarDogs will be turned out on the Centers for Disease Control, and they will have on-site support from human operatives. Those operatives are all preconditioned with Swarm. Should the dogs prove insufficient, we can activate the rabies and let them off the leash."

"So good," said John. He dipped a finger into the wine and then licked it off. The way he did it was pointedly obscene.

The report went on and on. Military bases, power companies, turnpike entrances, bridges, subways, major arteries, dams and levees, cellular towers. On and on and on.

This program had cost Zephyr and her investors tens of billions of dollars. Every penny had been spent with care. It was, without doubt, the most comprehensive invasion, the most complete terrorist attack, the most sophisticated and well-orchestrated act of war in history. Nearly a quarter of the money had gone for bribes, for the purchasing of people—or their souls, he reflected—for donations and lobbyists and funding to make sure that the people watching the people who watched the people who put everything into place were all owned by Zephyr Bain and John the Revelator. It was the truest example of carte-blanche management ever.

And all that remained was the go order.

All that remained was for Zephyr Bain to speak the words.

As he spoke, the Concierge watched her sleep. And, despite everything, he secretly prayed that she would slip away, that the cancer would take her, that her dreams of changing the world would fade with her into the soft, deep black of forever.

Even as he thought it, the Concierge was aware of John's strange eyes fixed on him. He could *feel* the man, despite being separated by thousands of miles of land and ocean. Despite the fact that this was a video image and not the man himself sitting there, sipping wine, and smiling like a devil out of hell.

The report took a long time. John refilled his glass three times. Zephyr slept on, though once she moaned in her sleep. A sound of deep pain. But John bent and placed his left hand flat across her chest, over her heart, and the sound stopped. She slept on, and now she wore the same strange, enigmatic, inhuman smile as he did.

The Concierge saw all of this and knew, without a single shred of doubt, that he was as damned as they. And yet he did not stop speaking, telling of the plans and preparations, listing the numbers of those who were going to die today. He did not even pause.

CHAPTER EIGHTY-NINE

Nikki Bloomberg sat up so straight and fast that she knocked her coffee cup to the floor. The cardboard cup exploded, sending café mocha splashing everywhere, including over her retro-chic red Keds sneakers.

She didn't care one bit.

Her entire focus was on the screen in front of her. It was a video clip from last year of a man on a stage addressing dozens of philosophy Ph.D. candidates at Duke University in Durham, North Carolina.

"Wait a minute," she said, and tapped some keys to open a second window. The same man spoke at the Ethical Society in Philadelphia. She opened a third window, a fourth, and a fifth. The same man was speaking in all of them. She broadened her search and found him speaking at the London School of Economics and Political Science, at the University of Toronto, at the Australian National University, at the Université Paris. Elsewhere, too. In Germany, Italy, Mexico, Geneva, Beijing.

In all, Nikki found more than sixty speeches the man had given. Sixty that had been recorded and put on YouTube or on the social-media platforms of the various universities. She replayed some of the foreign ones and had to run them back and verify with filters before she was forced to accept that the same man had given speeches in at least thirty-one different languages. All without a translator.

"That's impossible," she said aloud.

Nikki opened a search window for the new MindReader Q1 and fed every bit of data into it and hit Enter.

The computer took a microsecond to return seventeen thousand hits. Many, naturally, were duplicates. Many were not. Videos, blog posts, podcast interviews, print articles, chats, and more. All featuring the same man. She ran a pattern-recognition program on him and got a hit with a ninety-eight-percent reliability. She frowned at that, though, because the hit was of Father Luigi Bassano, who had been rector of a small church in Verona, Italy.

Which was impossible, though, because Luigi Bassano's body had been recovered from a house fire four years ago. The man was dead. Some of the videos, though, were from as recently as last month.

"What the what?" said Nikki. She reran the facial recognition and got the same answer. No other hit was higher than eighty-two percent. This man was Bassano.

Or was he?

There had been an autopsy of the priest, and dental records had confirmed that he was indeed that man.

Except here he was touring the world giving speeches. In each of the videos, this man was talking about a curated technological singularity. A man talking about a forced but inevitable *evolution*. A man who talked about robotics, nanotechnology, AI, and more.

She snatched up her phone and called Mr. Church to tell him what she had discovered about a man who called himself John the Revelator.

CHAPTER NINETY

"Where are you going?" asked Aunt Sallie.

Mr. Church placed several file folders and the partial box of vanilla wafers in his briefcase. "To the airport. I'm not getting the cooperation we need from the White House, so I'm going to meet Captain Ledger at the DARPA camp. If needs must, I'll hijack the whole think tank and put them in a room with a MindReader substation."

"The president won't like it."

"Auntie," said Church, "would you like a bullet-pointed list of the things I can't be bothered to worry about?"

She sighed. "No, it would be about the same list I have. Go fly the friendly skies."

She nodded and went away, and as Church finished packing his case he heard her yelling at someone, and it made him smile. He had worked with Aunt Sallie for many years. The history of their covert actions was sewn into the fabric of the history of modern America, and into the history of the world. Presidents and kings came and went, but their fight seemed to go on and on. He had great affection for her, and he was concerned that she was getting old now. She had been badly injured by assassins during the Predator One case, and even though she would likely cut someone's throat for saying so, she had lost something since then. She was less forceful, less certain of herself. He wondered how soon the day would come when he would have to tell her to step down and step back.

She would fight him on it. And retirement would probably kill her. It turned a knife in his heart, and he brooded on it as he walked slowly toward the elevator. Brick Anderson, his personal assistant, valet, bodyguard, and friend, was waiting for him down in the parking garage. Both of them were big men, though Brick was taller, wider, and wore a SIG Sauer pistol in a shoulder holster over a black T-shirt. A third man, smaller and dressed in the uniform of the Hangar's security team, trailed behind pulling two heavy metal suitcases and Church's go-bag of clothes and personal items. Brick opened the rear passenger door for Church and then supervised the placement of the suitcases in the trunk.

As Church settled into the back, he opened his briefcase to take out his cookies, but then he stopped and raised his head. A man sat across from him on the fold-down seat. He was very small, very old, wreathed in wrinkles, with a few wisps of gray hair clinging to his scalp. The man wore the black trousers and shirt of a priest, with a crisp white Roman collar. His gnarled hands were folded in his lap. His eyes were a complex blend of colors that seemed to swirl, like paints that refused to mix or blend.

"Hello, my old friend," said the priest.

Church closed the laptop and set it on the seat. "Hello, Nicodemus."

"You look surprised to see me."

"A bit."

"Did you think I was dead?"

"I hoped as much. Sorry to know that I was wrong."

"You know what they say about bad pennies."

"Why are you here? No, let me guess," said Church. "Baltimore? South Carolina? Milwaukee?"

There was a *thunk* as Brick closed the trunk and then a *click* as he tried to open the driver's door. The bodyguard tapped on the glass, but Church didn't reply.

"Those," said Nicodemus, "are not even the start, and certainly not the end."

"What's coming, then?"

Nicodemus grinned with rotting green teeth. Maggots wriggled between the stumps. "Chaos."

"You've been saying that for a long time."

"I've been right about it for a long time," said the priest. "Surely even you're gracious enough to admit that."

Church spread his hands. "Hugo Vox is dead. The Seven Kings are dead. The Red Order is in disarray, and the King of Thorns is dead."

"So is your wife," countered the priest. "Or . . . should I say *wives*. How many have you buried so far? Do you even still remember their names?"

Church said nothing.

"How many of them knew *your* name?" asked the priest. "One that I know of. Two, if you've told that witch, Lilith."

"Leave Lilith out of this."

"What about your children, my friend? Did any of them know who—or *what*—their father was? Did you even whisper the truth to them when you put flowers on their graves?"

"Taunting me with my sins is a card you've already played, Nicodemus," said Church. "Once played, it loses its power."

"Does it?"

"Yes," said Church. "You've never understood that about me."

Brick began knocking louder on the window. Church could hear the man calling out in anger and alarm.

The priest shrugged. "Very well. If I can't play a useful card about the past, then let me play one about the future."

"By all means. Your predictions have never been as accurate as you pretend. What is the nature of your latest forecast?"

"Bugs and bombs, my old friend," said Nicodemus. "Bodies and blood. And the hounds of hell running loose."

"Ah, you've come all this way to be cryptic. You disappoint me."

"Oh, was I being too vague for you? Did I make it too tricky a riddle? Forgive me, my friend, and let me be very specific. Minimum three billion. Conservative estimate. Maximum four point eight. Probably high, but it's possible."

There was a sharper sound as Brick hit the driver's window with the butt of his pistol. Once, twice. A crack appeared, but the reinforced glass held.

"What are we talking about? Money? Since when do you brag about how much you steal?"

"Never," said the priest. "And not now."

"Then what—?"

"Bodies."

Church smiled faintly. "Ah. I find it rather sad that you try so hard to take credit for things that other people do. You pretend to be the mover of mountains," said Church, "but we both know you're not. Who's your patron this time? I'm surprised you have any friends left."

Nicodemus held up his hands, acknowledging the point. "Sure, you stopped Sebastian Gault and El Mujahid, you stopped the Seven Kings, you stopped the Red Order and the King of Thorns, you stopped Mother Night, and you stopped the Jakobys. They're all dead, and you can brag because their scalps are dangling from your belt. Hail the conquering hero. But it's all for naught, I'm afraid. You killed a whole generation, but you missed their progeny. You were and are too blind to see what was coming up behind them. Quietly, carefully, learning from everything they did and everything you did to them. And surpassing them all. That's the funny part. You, in your posturing and violence and arrogance, have been as great a teacher for her as I've been. You like to think that you're protecting the 'little people,' the average citizen. The herd. You like to think that you serve a higher purpose, but at the end of the day you're preserving a corrupted status quo. You could use your resources to fight a different and better fight. You could have used MindReader to tear down the fat cats who rape this planet and are turning the very air into a cloud of poison. You could have used your beloved DMS to stop the politicians in this and other countries who wage war because it is in their best financial interest instead of shooting so-called terrorists. You waste your time treating the symptoms, because you lack the courage to carve out the disease. My beloved protégé knows this about you, and about everyone like you, and she will repay you for being complicit in everything that has gone wrong with this world."

"That's a nice speech. It's naïve but well phrased. It's also enormously disingenuous, considering that in the past you have aided Hugo and others like him. You supported the cabals that were the architects of the global political dysfunction."

"They were a means to an end."

"You don't have an 'end,'" said Church. "You're a sad and lonely creature, and you live out in the cold dark. You like setting fires. It's the only thing that keeps you warm."

"Maybe. But those fires are so very pretty."

Church took the cookies out of his case while Brick continued to hammer on the window. He took one and bit off an edge. "You are, and have always been, a parasite, John."

Church watched to see how the use of that name would affect Nicodemus. The man nodded slowly. "It took you long enough to work that out."

"John the Revelator, preaching the gospel of a curated technological singularity. That's new, even for you."

"I have seen the future and preach the good word," Nicodemus said, then burst out laughing. "You should see how they eat it up. Whole rooms filled with the best and the brightest. Even the ones who think they're so egalitarian come to point when I get to the part where I tell them that *they* are the chosen ones, the nerdy meek who will inherit the earth."

"I don't for a moment think you genuinely believe in the benefits of such a thing, and your motives for wanting to attempt it are clear enough. But do you actually believe that you have the power and the resources to bring about such a catastrophe?"

"Time will tell."

"I suppose it will." Church took another bite, chewed for a moment, then asked, "You said that your protégé was a 'she' . . . ?"

"Oh yes, my friend, it is a lovely young woman. Or, at least, she was. Not much meat on the bone these days, I'm afraid."

"Tell me, is this mystery woman a twin by any chance?"

Nicodemus frowned, and Church thought that for a moment the man was actually surprised, even confused. He recovered quickly, though. "No. She is an only child, with an intellect that is so lush and beautiful and a heart filled with red shadows. She cannot be bullied and she cannot be frightened. She's past all that. There's actually nothing you can do to hurt her."

Church shrugged. "Hurting her is a quality of revenge. I'm more interested in stopping her."

"There is no chance of that. The countdown is already over."

"If that were true, you wouldn't be here."

Nicodemus shrugged.

"So," continued Church, "why come to me now? Why come at all? You never do anything without a reason. Not even small, mean little things. Or is it that you're so marginalized by whatever is happening that you need a fix of attention?"

"I've come to say goodbye," said Nicodemus. "But first I wanted to tell you that you've lost, that everything you think you've been fighting for is all set to burn. I wanted to see the fear in your eyes when you finally accepted that you've been fighting a losing battle all along."

Church brushed lint from his tie, yawned, and said, "I've heard that kind of claim before and it has never been true. I even see fear in *your* eyes."

Nicodemus leered at him. "Is that what you see? My, how clouded your vision has become in your dotage. No, my friend, what you see is my true delight in knowing that everything you've worked for, everything you've done to try and whitewash your soul, will fall down and something new and glorious will rise in its place. *She* will curate the next phase of evolution, and the things you treasure and pretend to love will wither and die."

"You're ranting," said Church. "It's unbecoming."

"Go ahead and mock me, kinsman. If it offers some comfort to you, then be my guest. Make no mistake, however, that I have won and you, you arrogant bastard, have lost. The new world order is coming. It is almost here. Look at the walls of the world as it is. Can you hear the foundations crack? Can you smell the rot that eats at the roots? I can, and I came to tell you, because it pleases me so very much that you cannot stop it. No, no, no. And isn't that delicious?"

The driver's window exploded inward and Church threw an arm up to shield his face.

"Boss!" yelled Brick as he leaned in to pop the locks. He yanked the rear door open. "Are you all right? What's happening?"

Church looked at the fold-down seat. It was snugged neatly in place and he was alone in the car.

CHAPTER NINETY-ONE

We all watched the video clips Nikki sent us.

"John the Revelator," murmured Rudy, absently touching the crucifix he wore on a silver chain beneath his shirt. "My God . . . I *met* him. But I don't understand—that can't be Nicodemus. It doesn't look like him at all."

"Church said he uses disguises," I said.

Rudy shook his head and didn't comment, but it was clear that he wasn't thinking that this was a matter of colored contact lenses, a wig, and some makeup. Neither did I, but neither of us wanted to say what we thought it actually was. No way.

"I want to put a bullet into this trickster cocksucker," said Top.

"I'll load your gun," said Bunny.

"Hooah," I said.

Cole got up from her seat and walked over to the monitor, bent close, stared into the eyes of the prophet of the technological apocalypse. Then she straightened and stood in a thoughtful posture, lips pressed into a hard line, eyes half closed in calculating appraisal. Then she turned back to us.

"I grew up out in the sticks of South Carolina," she began slowly. "If you've ever spent time there—spent time outside the cities, spent time in the woods—then you know how strange the nights are there. Lots of people think everyone from down there is a redneck hick. But, as that saying goes, 'Country don't mean dumb.' We see stuff. We hear about stuff. We believe in stuff. Church stuff and other things that aren't in anyone's Bible. Maybe one of these days I'll tell you about some of the things I heard about, and some things I saw, and some things that people whose word I trust have seen. The stuff that goes on around Crybaby Bridge in Anderson. The Boo Hag and the Ghost Hound of Goshen. The legend of Julia Clare and the Third-Eye Man they used to see in the tunnels under the University of South Carolina and the haunted Baynard Crypt. Hell, I know people who say they saw something like Bigfoot down there. Is any of that real? Who knows? I don't know. But I have to tell you guys this much—I got five different good-luck charms and I say prayers to God and some saints in ways that aren't exactly part of my good Baptist upbringing." She paused for a moment. "And I saw some things when I was deployed that made me wonder, stuff that made me really scared, and made me question who or what was running the world and maybe the universe. Now, I'm a smart girl and a good cop and I've had education, so I'm not saying this because I'm some kind of hick girl from the middle of nowhere. I've *seen* things that I don't usually talk about because most of the people I meet *haven't* seen those kind of things. But I listened to what you said and I see the look in your eyes and . . . well . . . I know that you know. I know that you've been out there hunting more than terrorists with fancy bombs."

"*Terror*," said Rudy very quietly, "is a bigger and more comprehensive word than most people think."

I said, "While I was being recruited for the DMS by Mr. Church, he told me that we're very much in the business of stopping terror. He didn't set the parameters of what that word meant, and after running with Echo Team for all these years I realized that any attempt to precisely define that word would be the same as closing my eyes to its potential."

We all turned and watched John the Revelator on the screen.

"So . . . how do we kill this man?" she asked.

Bunny said, "Personally, I've found that if you put enough ordnance downrange you're bound to do some good. Words to that effect."

"No, I mean do we use silver bullets? A stake? What's the play?"

"I'm going to try all that," promised Top. "And then I'm going to burn the son of a bitch and piss on the ashes. Think that'll work?"

Cole suddenly smiled bright enough to push back the shadows of the day. "Sounds like a good goddamn plan," she said.

CHAPTER NINETY-TWO

"He was in your fucking car?"

Church winced and leaned away from his phone as Aunt Sallie's voice filled the garage with shrill outrage. There was fear and anger there, too.

"Not exactly," said Church quietly when she was done yelling.

"What's *that* supposed to mean?" roared Auntie. "Either he was or he wasn't."

Church stood by the elevator door and watched as a dozen DMS technicians tore his car apart. Forensics techs assigned to Jerry Spencer were carefully placing items on a tarp they had spread out on the floor.

"It was a new kind of hologram," said Church. "Jerry's people have found more than thirty tiny ultrahigh-res 3-D projectors inside the back of my car. It's a kind they haven't seen before, and the image was strikingly realistic."

"Did you know it was a projection? No, let me ask it another way. How did you *not* know it was a projection? Don't you have to wear some kind of big goofy glasses for VR to be that real?"

"The senior tech thinks that the projection was structured so that the tint of my glasses acted as the cooperative filter. He said that the projectors and my glasses are a precise match."

"How in the nine rings of hell would Nicodemus know what color tint you use?"

"Unknown," said Church, "but it would not be the first time Nicodemus has used superior intelligence-gathering to give the impression that he's conjuring magic."

Aunt Sallie said, "Not all of that is smoke and mirrors, Deacon, and you damn well know it."

"I don't want to have that argument again," Church said. "Not right now. What matters is that he had access to my car, either here or at my home, which are the only two places it's been recently. Otherwise the cameras would have been found in the last sweep four days ago."

"Then we'll tear this place and your place apart until we find out how he managed it."

"Fair enough," said Church. "You can see to that. In the meantime, we need to consider what he said and what it tells us."

"Three to six billion people dead? Is Nicodemus bullshitting us or bragging? No, don't answer that. He's doing both, and he's doing it to mess with your head, Deacon."

"That is a given," said Church. "But it does not mean that he's lying. Nicodemus loves to taunt. This is some kind of riddle."

"Oh, so he's a *Batman* villain now, taunting us with riddles?"

"Whatever he is or is pretending to be, Auntie, his threats aren't to be taken lightly. It's clear that he has access to a new and radically advanced generation of technology. If he's tied to what is unfolding in Maryland, then he has nanotech, advanced surveillance bugs, some new kind of attack drones, computer viruses, and more."

"Christ, I wish Bill Hu was still here. God *damn* him for getting his skinny ass killed."

"His absence is very much felt," Church agreed. "I'm having another car swept for bugs, and I still plan to head west. This thing is escalating, and we need to determine how big and how bad it's likely to get."

"And then what?" asked Auntie. "How do we stay braced when we don't know from which goddamn direction the punch is coming?"

"We can't, and I think that was his point. He wants us to be afraid, to be watching. He loves an audience, he loves attention. When we get the real call, he'll want us to know it's his ring."

CHAPTER NINETY-THREE

Bug and Yoda videoconferenced us with news.

"We decrypted the software from the Zika mosquito nanites," said Bug, his eyes dancing with excitement and way too much caffeine. "I'll skip the short course in how nanites are programmed, but think of them as moderately stupid computers. Because they're small, they can't carry enough memory for complex functions. With me?"

"Yes," I said. "Go on."

"Okay, one way to *get* nanites to perform complex functions is to have them form little networks. Each one has part of the program, but together they have the whole thing. And if that code is written correctly the specifics of that program can be tweaked. So the main program they carry is the one that regulates the release of the virus developed by the CDC to make Zika-carrying mosquitoes infertile, resulting in a swarm die-off. That's the main plan, and if you analyze any of the nanites in the swarm you'll find that program."

"But, mmmm, if you look deeper," said Yoda, "you, mmmm, find program fragments."

"It looks like bad code," continued Bug, "and anyone could build a case for it being a side effect of the speed with which the Zika nanites swarm program was put together. A lot of programs have that. Dead code. We looked closer, and found that these code fragments add up to a larger and more complicated code. And that code is big enough to have several possible functions."

"And it, mmmm, uses the viral-delivery, mmmm, system as part of its operational system."

"Right," said Bug. "It's a kind of fragmented thing that uses the overall swarm as a Trojan horse and then hijacks its own intended purpose to help it regulate other disease forms."

"And this is possible?" I asked, appalled.

"Mmmm, clearly," said Yoda, "because we, mmmm, found it."

"MindReader found it," corrected Bug, pride showing in his eyes. "Instead of doing individual code assessments, we asked the Q1 to analyze the swarm as a whole and interpret tactical potential."

"Now wait a freaking minute," I said, "are you telling us that we've been spraying rabies and dengue and—"

"No," said Bug and Yoda at the same time.

"Then you lost me."

"Joe, what we've found is half of something really big and really bad," said Bug. "We think the Bad Sister and her crew have found some way of infecting people on a large scale. Potentially very large, because the Zika-virus program has been spraying this stuff all over the world for the last few years. We compared the nanite software with samples from the ones from the girl in Baltimore, and it's the same set of interlocking programs."

"Jesus Christ," I breathed. "Why hasn't any of this shit shown up before?"

Bug answered that. "Who would know to look, Joe? We know that the nanites are everywhere, and they've been detected in blood tests and autopsies all over the world. FEMA, the CDC, the National Institutes of Health, and the World Health Organization collaborated on a paper that was shared with doctors everywhere to explain the presence of the nanites. God . . . we helped cover this up."

"But," I said, "how are they delivering the diseases that these nanites regulate? And why haven't we heard of an increase in the diseases yet?"

Bug said, "I asked Dr. Cmar that. He said there are a lot of papers being circulated about upticks in inactive traces of disease forms. It's something new—diseases that are usually virulent basically sitting in the bloodstream doing nothing. There are some remarks about anomalous levels of hormones in almost every case. Five different groups, including one of my own research teams, have been compiling information about this. They've forwarded dozens of theories, though nothing involving nanites. We've all been leaning toward a hope that there's some new kind of natural or acquired immunity, but we all figured we were years away from understanding it."

"How could the presence of nanites go unnoticed?" Rudy asked.

"That's a very good question," said Bug. "Dr. Cmar doesn't think we can accept that a significant portion of the medical research community is incompetent. That suggests that there has either been some way to mask the presence of the nanites or the researchers have been compromised in some way. It wouldn't be the first time we've seen large-scale corruption, coercion, or deliberate interference, right?"

"So it's like a medical version of what Vox and the Kings did with the IRS, the SEC, and other players in the stock market after 9/11," I said. "We know that Nicodemus is involved, and that means it's likely, even probable, that he has access to the methods and contacts established by the Kings."

"God, I wish that wasn't true," said Bug.

"Even so, why isn't it all over the news?" Bunny asked.

"Because people haven't been dying," said Rudy. "Think about it, Joe—we didn't come into this until a teenage prostitute died of rabies in Baltimore. Perhaps Bad Sister was test-driving this new delivery system. Besides, if people had started dying in large numbers everyone would know about it. Everyone would already be working on it. If it were something spreading according to any recognizable outbreak models, the right machinery would be running. But in the absence of mortality numbers the response has been one of guarded caution, guarded optimism, and research."

"And cover-up," I said. "Swell. So now here we are. The Bad Sister has infected God knows how many people and she has God knows how many nanites out there poised to make those diseases go active."

"This is what Nicodemus warned me about," said Rudy. "It's what he teased Mr. Church about."

"Why bother?" asked Cole.

"Because he feeds off our pain," said Rudy.

CHAPTER NINETY-FOUR

The white panel delivery truck drove slowly past the front gate of the big house. The place was enormous, and the driver immediately hated the people who lived there. He'd looked it up on the Net. It was right there on the water, with over a hundred feet of ocean frontage but perched high as if looking down on everything below. The driver thought the house itself looked arrogant. It was on the tip of a point, so the ocean view was amazing. Five bedrooms, six full baths, contemporary design with an open floor plan. It even had a seaside exercise room and a spa. And it had lots of security, with cameras, motion sensors, lighting intended to discourage skulkers, and all the other bells and whistles.

Not that any of these features would provide actual security. Not when word came down from WhiteHat. Not when Havoc went live.

Not when it all started falling apart, changing, evolving.

Maybe, thought the driver, *I'll live here when this is all over.*

After all, the people who owned this place now would be tossed into the cremation pits or dumped far out to sea.

Later today, though. Not yet. Now he was here to get a sense of the streets for the best delivery access, traffic conditions, security patrols. A last look before Havoc.

He looked down at his clipboard to read the names of the people who lived in what he considered to be his house.

Dr. Rudolfo Ernesto Sanchez y Martinez. A shrink who worked for the DMS.

Dr. Circe Diana Ekklesia Magdalena O'Tree-Sanchez. A writer.

Carlos Joseph Rudolfo O'Tree-Sanchez. Their kid.

Banshee. A pet dog.

The driver didn't know any of them. He didn't much care who or what they were. Neither did the WarDogs in the back of his panel truck. All he knew was that the father wasn't here. He off somewhere and would be taken out by someone else. The wife and kid, and the dog, though, were home.

In *his* home.

For now.

CHAPTER NINETY-FIVE

When the DMS is working without interference, without sabotage, without its people being attacked and killed, then it earns its name. The Department of Military Sciences. Our group started as a bunch of absolute top-of-the-class science geeks backed by first-chair shooters. It's only recently that we've become one of those *Saturday Night Live* skits that's gotten stale because it ran too long.

Let's call that yesterday's news.

Today we have MindReader Q1. As game changers go, it's a real ass-kicker, because Special Ops works at its absolute best in the presence of reliable real-time intel. No matter how good your gunslingers are, if they're operating with questionable information they're going to fail and they're going to die. So will the people they're dedicated to protecting. MindReader was the source of that intelligence for us. Without it we're blind and we wind up shooting too late or in the wrong direction. Without it we fail or, even if we win, the cost is heartbreakingly high.

As I said, that was yesterday.

As Shirley burned her way across the country, I got to witness what happens when the men and women of the DMS have access to the right tools. If MindReader was reborn when Bug put the new quantum mainframe and drives online, then we all woke up from a bad and confusing shared dream.

Everyone was working on different parts of this, and that work was shared in ways that hammered new pieces of the puzzle into place with astonishing speed. When you have the ability to gather large amounts of information and then process and collate it at high speeds, the resulting conclusions have the appearance of intuitive leaps. And, yeah, sure, maybe intuition played into it, but it's the kind of intuition that comes from being able to trust your tools and your team.

So over the course of two hours I had a series of very short but very intense one-on-one videoconferences.

The first call was from Nikki.

NIKKI: "Joe, MindReader ripped apart Vee Rejenko's business records. At first look, it appears that his companies were a front for Czech mobsters. His uncle Boris was married to a woman who died at the lab you and Violin hit. I thought maybe Baltimore was some kind of revenge thing, but the timetable was all wrong, so I went deeper, and Rejenko and his colleagues had dozens of connections to human trafficking all over the world. We found tons of meticulous records that we can share with police departments all over the world, because we're talking about more than eighty countries—mostly, but not entirely, Third World areas. This involves hundreds of thousands of kids, women, and men who were forced into different kinds of sex work. Joe, some of these kids are as young as five years old. It makes me want to kill someone. Some of those sex workers were placed in exclusive brothels servicing very specialized clienteles. Rich guys, with a bias toward executives in the oil, coal, and natural-gas industries. We have their names, and for a bunch we even have credit-card information. Can you imagine that? They pay to sexually abuse children and young women, and it goes on their cards as 'spa treatments' or 'business dinners.'"

ME: "Christ! How's this help us, though?"

NIKKI: "It fits with some of the things John the Revelator has been saying. He said that this curated technological singularity would be a kind of traumatic evolution in which those people would be killed who either are a drain on limited resources—in other words, the poor—or have exploited those resources in ways that negatively affect the biosphere, meaning the ultrarich in the fossil-fuel industries. The polluters and the lobbyists who influence anti-science legislation."

ME: "Have you run this past John Cmar?"

NIKKI: "Yes. He wants to talk to you."

And so I called Cmar. He was in the field with one of his Bughunters teams, and he still looked rattled from the group conference we had an hour before. He sat in the back of a mobile lab van and stared at me with fevered eyes.

CMAR: "I had MindReader hack into the medical records of the oil executives we found in Rejenko's records, and there have been a few suspicious deaths by pathogens not otherwise known to be present in their areas. Fluke infections, and not many of them."

ME: "Which tells us what? More of the test-driving thing you told Church about?"

CMAR: "Almost certainly."

Then I called Yoda.

YODA: "The, mmmm, Zika spray campaign has, mmmm, run its course. All the, mmmm, target areas have been saturated. Mmmm, computer models, mmmm, have yielded alarming, mmmm, results."

He hit me with that data. Nicodemus has taunted Church by saying that three billion people are going to die. That wasn't a bullshit guess. It might actually have been conservative, because the spray had been used aggressively all over the world. So aggressively that it made me really wonder if the fears of Zika were exaggerated. Yoda was already ahead of me on that, though.

YODA: "Dr. Cmar, mmmm, now thinks that the Zika virus may have been, mmmm, deliberately mutated in order to lay the groundwork for the original, mmmm, Zika panic and the resulting prophylactic spraying campaign."

And that's how the flight went.

One call after another. Putting those pieces together. Making it make sense. Rudy, Top, Bunny, and Cole sat with me during this process, and between each call we put our heads together and worked the problem. With good intel, you *can* work a problem—even one as big and as terrifying as this.

"So what's the actual evil master plan here?" asked Cole, once I had everyone up to speed on all of it. "I mean, is this really all about killing off those people—the poor and the oil assholes? Would that really bring about this singularity thing?"

"Yeah," said Bunny. "I can see where that would really fuck everything up, but how does it result in a Utopia for the people who don't get sick and die?"

"It doesn't," said Top. "It *can't*. In some places, sure, but Nicodemus tipped us off, Cap'n. He'd have to know that we'd put out alerts to all levels of emergency-response infrastructure."

"I agree with Top," said Rudy. "This would really do the most damage in Third World countries, but that goes against the central argument of a curated apocalypse. It would be a slaughter, but in countries with any kind of quality health care we would get in front of it with medical treatment, quarantine zones, public warnings, social-media alerts—"

"Unless," I said, "they had some way to prevent all that from happening."

We stared at one another for a long, bad moment.

And then I made a whole bunch of new calls.

CHAPTER NINETY-SIX

Forensics analyst Jerry Spencer was a hard man to like, and so far most people didn't want to do that much labor. He didn't work at it with much diligence, either. He was curt, often rude, dismissive, egocentric, secretive, mean-spirited, and fussy. He was also brilliant, which is why everyone walked softly around him and tried not to offend him. His skill in collecting and analyzing evidence was superb, and with the resources of MindReader Q1 it was second to none.

He oversaw a department of forty-two highly trained technicians and scientists. They feared, hated, and admired him in equal measure.

Spencer had the debris from the thresher drone that had killed the Pool Boys and Jack Ledger. His team couldn't tell, but Spencer was very upset. He liked Jack and had known him for thirty-five years. He often went out to the farm in Robinwood and spent long days fishing with Joe Ledger's uncle. During those days, neither Jack nor Spencer would say more than a handful of words, preferring curmudgeonly silence to idle chitchat. If Spencer ever had a real friend, it was that man, and now he was dead. His blood was on the blades of the thresher.

Jerry Spencer was not a forgiving man. He wasn't a nice man, and since working with the DMS he had processed hundreds of crime scenes that were splashed with innocent blood. He knew that his lack of obvious warmth didn't come from any innate meanness of spirit. It was all hurt. It was the anger that came from seeing the dead ones. From seeing firsthand the evidence of merciless greed, of lethal avarice, of unrelenting cruelty. How could anyone look at such horrors and not feel it grind away at optimism and joy? That was Spencer's view, and standing here with the machine that had murdered his only friend did nothing to shine light into his inner darkness.

Instead, the more destruction he saw the more cold and determined he became. If that was him acting in response to a wounded ego, then so be it. They—the eternal, many-faced *they* that the DMS fought—had taken something very important from him. As a result, he would take everything that was important to them. Life, liberty, and every shred of *their* happiness.

He had his people drop everything they were doing and focus on the drone. It was photographed, weighed, measured, scanned, scraped for samples, and then completely disassembled. The pieces were individually analyzed down to the threads on the screws and the blend of polymers in the plastic blades. Most of the parts were off-the-shelf material available through any manufacturer of machine metals and plastics. Spencer made no assumptions about that, though. He had each part entered into MindReader Q1 and traced to its source.

For the elements that were not mass-produced, he had people delve into the ultrasecret and supposedly restricted records of the Department of Defense, DARPA, and the private-sector defense contractors. Nothing happened in big-budget DoD projects without some kind of trail, and the golden rule of forensics is that "all contact leaves a trace." Manufacture, design, budget appropriations, filed patents, research and development, field testing, and every other step of the complicated bureaucracy left traces.

What he found was that unique parts of the thresher were manufactured by sixty-eight different companies, but the assembly was done at Mueller-Trang, Inc., a defense contractor. That was very, very interesting to Spencer because Mueller-Trang had been one of several companies that came under investigation after the Predator One affair. That firm made several of the chassis for drones used by the Seven Kings. They had been cleared of any criminal involvement, but now Spencer had to wonder how that decision was reached. So he tried a different tack—investigating the people associated with the parts. That meant looking at the investigators of that case, the litigators, the members of the House and the Senate who were involved in the hearings. Everyone.

It was a complicated chain, and it quickly became clear that someone had gone to very great lengths to hide key links between players in this game. False identities, shell corporations, numbered accounts, and accounting tricks that bordered on sorcery. Yesterday it would have gone nowhere and left Spencer even more frustrated and angry. Yesterday's ship had sailed and sunk. Today was something else. Today was that damned MindReader Q1 system. Spencer was no sentimentalist, but he liked this new system. It was a more precise tool, a sharper edge, a more powerful lens through which he could examine the minutest elements of the evidence.

A few names began appearing with notable frequency. Donald Hoeffenberger, a three-term senator, was the brother-in-law of Carter Hooks, who, in turn, was the brother-in-law of Mitchell Stoeller, who was the college roommate of a principal stockholder in a development conglomerate called Julius Systems. The owner of record of Julius Systems was the kind of false identity that was created when someone uses the Social Security number of a person who died poor and young, and builds a new official persona with that crucial information. That has been happening since Social Security numbers were first issued in 1935 as part of Roosevelt's New Deal. As soon as any new system is created, some con man steps up to figure out a way to game that system. This was a classic example, but MindReader broke through it in a microsecond.

It took a little more time to sort out who actually owned it, and Spencer was impressed by the attention to detail. However, it is actually impossible to hide forever, especially from a computer system that's designed to intrude in any database and then collate that data using a huge number of linked processors. What Spencer found was that Julius Systems was owned, through sixteen removes, by Harrison Industrial, a shell corporation that Bug's people traced all the way back to Bain Industries, currently owned by a woman named Zephyr Bain.

Ms. Bain was a notable scientist and computer engineer who had developed the Calpurnia artificial-intelligence system. She was also deeply invested in dozens of companies tied to DoD R & D contracts for robotic combat systems, computer-software systems, drone warfare, and nanotechnology. Spencer studied this information, piecing it together as his people brought it to him and as MindReader collated it.

The name Zephyr Bain tickled something in Spencer's memory, so he initiated a new search to connect her name to anything—absolutely anything—that was linked to this case. He didn't expect much except for maybe another link in a chain, and another and another beyond that.

That isn't what he found.

"Well, piss on my blue suede shoes," he said aloud as he read the data. Then he picked up the phone to call Mr. Church.

"Jerry," began Church, "I was about to call to see how—"

"Skip the shit," interrupted Spencer. "I think I know who Bad Sister is."

CHAPTER NINETY-SEVEN

"Zephyr Bain," I repeated. On the viewscreen Church looked grave, Bug looked angry, and Jerry Spencer—for once—looked almost happy. He was never happy when ordinary people were happy, and it usually meant that someone was going to get hurt. I could relate. "I thought she was dying or something."

"She is," said Bug. "A little less than three months ago, she was told that her cancer had metastasized and that she was terminal. Best estimate was that she would last six months, but there is a private note in her medical file from one oncologist to her primary-care physician that it was more likely she would live two to three months, and she's at that limit now."

"I don't get it," said Cole. "Why would someone like that want to do all this crap? She won't get to see this singularity thing, so why bother?"

It was Rudy who answered that. "Nicodemus."

"I don't understand."

Rudy said, "Did you ever read the novel *Fahrenheit 451*? You know the opening line, about how it was a pleasure to burn? That's Nicodemus."

Even so, Bunny asked, "What does he get out of it except for jollies? I mean, if this is all so he can roast wieners as the world burns, how's that do him any lasting good? Especially if the technological singularity happens. Shouldn't that sort of thing end up with a new kind of stability? A smaller but less messed-up world? That's not chaos."

Spencer said, "What's it matter? He's a freak and he needs to be put down. And if we find this Bain broad alive, then she needs a bullet, too."

"Hooah," murmured Top.

Bug shook his head. "Here's the thing, guys," he said. "I've been going over the John the Revelator speeches to try and figure out what their moves are, and there's a real problem."

"How so?" Rudy said.

Bug adjusted his thick glasses. "Well, for one thing it won't work. You can't curate an apocalyptic event. It's patently impossible no matter how you look at it. I mean, sure, the way they have this set up the process of tearing down the world as it is might work. And, to tell you the truth, I don't know how we're going to stop it."

"Ay Dios mio," said Rudy softly, once more touching the crucifix beneath his shirt.

"But," continued Bug, "there's no way to guarantee the survival of whoever they think is worthy of making the cut. Let's figure that it's the people who attended John's lectures. The educated, the intellectual class, the people in favor of green solutions—basically, most of the people I know and like. It's not like we're all living in protected biodomes. I talked this over with Doc Cmar, and he agrees. When you have sixteen plagues released into that big a portion of the population, even if the release is controlled by nanites, the diseases will spread like wildfire, because the areas hardest hit have dense populations and poor health-care and emergency services. That means there will be millions or billions of corpses that will never be buried. You can't cremate them all, because the smoke from that many fires would plunge the world into a kind of nuclear winter. And there are diseases from unburied decaying bodies that would go completely wild. Maybe— and I mean *maybe*—a few thousand, maybe a few million people worldwide—could find shelter on islands, inside walled compounds, in bunkers, on watercraft, whatever—but they wouldn't necessarily be the technocracy. A lot of them would be doomsday preppers who've been expecting some kind of disaster. Some would be military. Some would just be lucky because they lived on small islands. Overall, though, it's ridiculous to think that this mass-disease release would accomplish what John the Revelator has been predicting. And it's not like we have robots ready to protect the chosen ones. Zephyr Bain's DoD contracts are for things like the thresher and for WarDogs. Not for infrastructure robotics or AI that would manage a disaster."

"So . . . does that mean this singularity isn't going to happen?" asked Cole.

"I'm saying that it can't," said Bug. "No way. There is no model, no variation of a model, in which that can happen."

"If Zephyr Bain believes it," observed Rudy, "then she was manipulated into believing it."

"Right," said Bug, "which is why I have Nikki running down every-one who's invested in special shielding and security, bunkers, remote compounds, whatever, with a bias toward the kinds of people that fit what we think is the model for ideal survivors. Not the poor and not the people polluting the planet. That still leaves a lot of room for error, though. Some of the people she's finding are just doomsday preppers or social misfits."

Church said, "Nicodemus said that we stopped the Seven Kings, Mother Night, and the Jakobys but that we missed their progeny. He intimated that the Bad Sister was coming up *behind* them, learning from them and surpassing them. Once Jerry found the Bain connec-tion, we had Nikki run a deep background on her, and behind one of Davidovich's blind spots we found that connection. Her father was a business associate of Hugo Vox's. That connection dated back decades, so it isn't unreasonable to believe that Zephyr was exposed to Hugo as a child or teen, and possibly to the Jakobys as well. We know that Ni-codemus worked with Hugo for years. He even admitted that he was our enemy's teacher."

Cole marveled at this. "He . . . raised her to be like this? To *do* this?"

"I believe so," said Church.

"Shee-eee-eeet," said Top, drawing it out. "If Nicodemus was her role model, then that kid never had a chance to be anything but nuts."

"But she's dying," said Bunny. "Does that mean this is all a going-away party for her? Instead of balloons and a scary clown, she gets to watch the world get sick and die?"

"Maybe," I said. "Or maybe she's been manipulated into throwing a big apocalyptic hootenanny for her mentor."

"Maybe it's a bit of both," said Church, nodding.

"Hold on, though," said Bunny. "Seems like we're missing something. Maybe this isn't Zephyr. I mean, we were warned about a sister, right? Good Sister and Bad Sister. Are we sure *she's* the Bad Sister? Maybe she's just Dead Sister. Maybe she's the one who's been texting the cap-tain and the real bad sister is working with Nicodemus."

Bug was shaking his head before Bunny finished. "Can't be that, 'cause Zephyr Bain is an only child."

Cole cut a look at Rudy. "Could it be a split-personality thing? Could Zephyr be both Good *and* Bad Sister?"

Rudy pondered that, lips pursed, then slowly began shaking his head. "I don't think so. I mean, sure it's possible, but not likely. Multiple-personality disorder isn't as compartmentalized as that. No . . . I think we're dealing with two distinct persons rather than one fractured individual."

"So who the hell is the Good Sister?" asked Top.

No one had an answer.

"Where's this Zephyr Bain live?" asked Bunny. "And how come we're not en route to put a bullet in her?"

"Or arrest her," suggested Cole.

"Sure, okay. We can look at that as a possibility," Bunny told her unconvincingly.

"Bain has houses all over the place," said Bug. "Her main estate is in Seattle."

Top raised his hand. "Bunny and me . . . and Officer Cole . . . can hit that once we're on the ground. It's forty-five minutes from the joint-use base where we're touching down."

"Forty if I drive," said Bunny.

"Thirty-five if *I* drive," countered Cole.

"Good," said Church. "I already sent the Junkyard to the airbase in anticipation of Echo Team's arrival."

"Won't we need it at the camp?" asked Rudy.

"Not likely," I said. "The DARPA camp is staffed by our guys."

There was a bing-bong and the pilot's voice crackled through the speakers. "Coming up on it, Cowboy."

CHAPTER NINETY-EIGHT

BRAZILIAN RAIN FOREST
FIVE KILOMETERS FROM THE FREETECH/WORLD HEALTH ORGANIZATION
RESEARCH FIELD CAMP
NORTH REGION, BRAZIL
TUESDAY, MAY 2, 9:01 AM LOCAL TIME

The helicopter landed in a rough natural clearing surrounded by dense trees. Two men got out and stood for a moment looking back the way they'd come. Inside the chopper were six other men dressed in unmarked jungle-camouflaged BDUs. They were all heavily armed and wore broad-bladed machetes on their hips, useful for chopping through the thick jungle growth. The co-pilot let them out and ordered them to sit on the grass on the far side of the clearing. The men sat as ordered. Each of them was marked with scars from injuries received in combat, and overlaying those scars were fresher surgical scars that looped up and over their skulls.

The pilot and the co-pilot walked to the other side of the chopper, lit cigarettes, and stood smoking in silence. When the call came it was via satellite phone, and the co-pilot unclipped it from his belt.

"We're on deck," he said. "Five klicks from the camp."

"Send the men," said the caller.

The pilot was leaning in to listen to the call, and he met his co-pilot's eyes. The co-pilot said, "We haven't received the go order from WhiteHat."

"I'm giving you the order," said the caller.

"I'm sorry, sir, but we were told that only the lady can give the order."

"I'm calling on her behalf."

"Sir, I—"

"She is ill and cannot make this call."

"I get that, sir, but our orders were very specific. We're not supposed to go into Havoc mode until we get the word from the lady. That was what she said, and I'm going to have to follow her orders."

There was a brief silence on the line.

Then, "Very well. Move your team into position one half kilometer out and wait for the lady to call," said John the Revelator.

The co-pilot lowered the sat phone and lit another cigarette, then shared the match with the pilot. They smoked the fresh cigarettes halfway down before either of them spoke.

"You think she's already dead?" asked the pilot.

"I don't know," said the co-pilot. "Maybe. Last time I saw her she looked like she already had one foot in the grave and the other on a slick spot."

They watched their smoke rise into the humid air.

"What if it's just John running the show now?" asked the pilot.

The co-pilot shrugged and flicked the butt out into the woods. "Then fuck it. The world's for shit as it is. This ain't going to make it worse."

The pilot said nothing. He glanced over at the six silent, scarred soldiers. He nudged his partner lightly.

"Tell you what, though," he murmured. "I want to be in the air and far away from here before we flip the switch on these sons of bitches."

The co-pilot nodded and offered a fist for a bump, got it, checked his watch, and then whistled for the six soldiers.

"Game time," he said.

CHAPTER NINETY-NINE

"Wake up, my darling," murmured John.

Zephyr Bain opened her eyes very slowly and tentatively, as if they were heavy, as if opening them hurt. "I . . ." she began, but had no idea where she wanted to go with that, so she let it go.

"You need to wake up," coaxed John, his voice soft and warm.

"I can't," she complained.

"You must."

"I'm tired . . . I'm sick. . . ." She curled up and turned away, closing her eyes again. She knew that she was in her bed, but the sheets were wet. Had she peed the bed again? No, there was a soapy smell, and she realized slowly that he must have carried her here from the tub without rinsing her off or drying her. Or dressing her. "Let me sleep," she said.

Except that isn't what she said, and Zephyr heard her own words as a strange interior echo.

Let me go.

Which meant *Let me die.*

"I will," he promised. "Soon you'll be able to sleep as long as you want. You'll be able to sleep forever and swim in the warm, dark waters as long as you want."

"No more poetry, damn you," she pleaded. "Just leave me be."

"It's time to give the word. The dogs of war are straining at their chains. Everything is poised to go. The world is breathless, waiting for the great change."

She shook her head in a long, silent no.

"Zephyr," he said with a harder edge to his tone. "You promised."

"No."

"This is what you've always wanted."

His voice was strange. Deeper, rougher. Uglier. She opened her eyes to slits and turned to look at him. John sat on the edge of the bed. Naked, covered in sweat as if he were in a sauna, his penis engorged and erect, spit glistening on his white teeth, eyes swirling with wrongness.

"This is what *you've* always wanted," she protested, and it hurt her—scared her—to hear how small and frightened and faraway her voice had become in the past few days. It was as if she could feel herself going farther and farther away. Leaving this world, leaving life. She never expected to be able to feel it happen. She'd always figured it would be like going to sleep. Some pain and then nothing.

She also never expected John to be such a monster. Her vagina ached, and she wondered—not for the first time—if he had taken her while she slept. Raping a corpse. Taking the inability to respond as consent.

Yes, she thought. *That's exactly what he did.* He was like so many men, who thought that consent, once given, was an ongoing license. If she had the strength, she would have risen up and kicked the shit out of him.

If he *could* be killed.

Even now, after all these years, after knowing him so intimately, Zephyr had no idea what he really was.

"You need to give the word," he told her, bending over her. She could feel the pressure of his stiff cock against her naked hip. So hard and so cold. Like a spike of Arctic ice.

"No," she whined.

"Yes," he insisted.

"I don't care about it anymore."

"You do. You must, my sweet. You have spent your life preparing for this moment."

Zephyr felt a flare of hot anger in her chest, and she shoved at him with one hand. It didn't move him even an inch, and her hand flopped back onto the bed.

"I wanted this because I thought I'd *see* it, goddammit. Now that's for shit. You killed me."

"No, my girl, I gave you thirty years. I gave you all the time you needed to change the world. Now, all that's left is to tell Calpurnia to start. All you have to do is speak one word. You owe this to me."

"I . . . don't owe you anything," she said, her breath labored just from the effort of trying to shove him. "You took everything . . . from me."

"No. I gave you the world."

"You . . . twisted me all around . . . you made me crazy. . . ."

He laughed. A chuckle that sounded like thunder. Weirdly deep, oddly loud. "You were born crazy, my darling. You were a loaded gun from the time you could form your first thought. All I did was aim you in a useful direction."

She wanted to scream, but she lacked the energy. She wanted to weep, but her body was a dry husk. She wanted to die, but he seemed to be able to keep her here, in the world, in this bed, with him.

"Say the word," he demanded. "Say it and I will let you go."

He pressed his hardness against her.

"No," she snarled. If her body was a crumbling house, then that word blew like a sudden gust through the open windows. It made the last candle flame of her life flicker and dance, and the glare through goblin shapes on all the walls. She screamed it again.

"NO!"

And, with that, the candle flame blew out.

CHAPTER ONE HUNDRED

JOINT BASE LEWIS–MCCHORD
LAKEWOOD, WASHINGTON
TUESDAY, MAY 2, 10:18 AM

We put down at JBLM near Lakewood. Two vehicles waited for us. One was a Bell ARH-70 Arapaho helicopter that belonged to the local DMS field office, and the other was a gorgeous Mercedes Sprinter luxury RV that belonged to Brick Anderson. Known as the Junkyard. The RV was a rolling arsenal that was kitted out to provide tactical support for any kind of field mission up to and including fighting Godzilla. From the outside, it looked like a playtoy for very rich campers, but inside the armored shell there were banks of advanced computer and communications equipment, bins of combat gear, and rack upon rack of handguns and long guns, ranging from combat shotguns to the latest automatic rifles. Boxes of grenades—fragmentation, flash bangs, smoke—and a bin filled with uniforms and Kevlar. And metal cases of the specialized electronic equipment for which Dr. Hu had been so famous. Cole whistled when she saw it.

"Are we invading North Korea?" she asked.

"If you're going to kick serious ass," said Top as he patted the Junkyard's fender, "wear the right boot."

The driver's door opened and, instead of seeing a DMS field operator, I saw the curvy figure of Lydia Rose step out, her long black hair pulled back into a ponytail. She wore black combat fatigues and had a sidearm tucked into a bright-pink shoulder holster. She flashed us a brilliant white smile.

"What in the hell are you doing here?" I demanded.

"Driving," she said, her smile turning into a challenging scowl. "We're shorthanded and everyone's in the field. Why, do you have a problem with that?"

Her glare could have started a forest fire.

"No, I do not," I said quickly. You pick the fights you think you can win.

I ignored Bunny's chuckle.

"Okay," I said, turning back to the team, "here's the game plan. We have people targeting every home or office owned by Zephyr Bain. Based on utilities usage, the best bet's Seattle. Top, you take Bunny and Cole and check that out. Rudy and I will take the helo to the DARPA camp to see if we can get the brain trust there to help us come up with a response plan for this singularity event, whatever the hell it is. If nanites are controlling the pathogens—and that's all but certain at this point—we need our best science nerds to find a way to take control of those nanites."

"To what end?" asked Cole. "The infection will still be there."

"Yeah," Bunny agreed. "If the nanobots are keeping the diseases in check, then we can't shut them down."

"No," said Rudy, "which is why we need to figure out a way to hack into them and keep them operating according to our needs until a solution is found. In the meantime, Dr. Cmar is mobilizing the emergency-medical-response network to begin mass-producing vaccines and other drugs."

"How fast can they do that shit?" asked Top. "In the movies they seem to whip that stuff up overnight."

"That's the movies, I'm afraid," replied Rudy. "In truth, our best projection for a complete program of inoculation and vaccination is probably two to five years."

They stared at him, and Rudy gave a slow, sad nod.

"Years?" echoed Bunny in a hollow voice.

"Being optimistic," said Rudy. "This plan was put together to be unstoppable, and unless we can take over the nanites and keep them active we're going to witness the deaths of at least half of the people on this planet."

Cole looked sick.

Bunny opened and closed his mouth like a boated fish.

Top looked at me. "What are our odds here, Cap'n?"

"Piss poor," I said. "So let's go see if we can change that."

We ran to our rides, and then we were gone.

CHAPTER ONE HUNDRED AND ONE

John the Revelator pulled on a silken bathrobe and walked through the house, leaving the bedroom and Zephyr behind. Campion was in the kitchen, and the man stood up as John entered, but he was nothing, so John didn't even acknowledge him as he walked through. When he reached the computer room, he locked himself in.

"Calpurnia," he said aloud, "get the Concierge on the line."

"Of course, John," said the computer graciously. "I believe he is waiting for your call."

A few moments later, the main screen flicked on to show the crippled Frenchman in his robotic chair. There was a fine sheen of sweat on the man's scarred face.

"How is mademoiselle?" asked the Concierge.

"Indisposed," said John, and he cut a look at the wall sensors as if daring Calpurnia to make a comment. But the computer offered no observation. "Give me a status report."

"Everything is ready to go," said the Concierge.

"Everything? The bombs, the dogs, the nanites? All of it?"

"Yes, sir. Even with having to rush things with the revised countdown, we are as ready as is possible. However—"

"However *what*?" asked John irritably.

"Well, as we are now on the very edge of the cliff, it would be a great comfort to me and to many of the chosen to know how the recovery process will work. Mademoiselle Bain and you have made extraordinary promises, and you've both been more than generous with gifts and support, but once the word is given there will be that transition period. What guarantees do we have that the recovery will work?"

"You're asking this now?"

"I have asked before, sir. Many times. Assurances are all well and good, but I think it would be a greater comfort to have specific details now that we are literally a word away from launching Havoc."

John stared at him for a long moment. "Are you saying that you don't trust us?"

"Oh, no, sir," said the Concierge quickly. "This is simply a matter of needing reassurance at such a crucial time. Many of our colleagues and senior staff have been asking me."

"And what have you been telling them?"

"That Mademoiselle Bain would be sending information and clarification before we launch. That's worked quite well, but today there is necessarily more tension, more fear. I would hate to see that turn into real doubt or even, pardon me for saying it, resistance or noncompliance."

"And if we tell them to trust us and proceed anyway?"

The Frenchman gave one of his small, expressive shrugs. "Who can say?"

"Try."

The Concierge licked his lips. "Sir . . . let me phrase this as delicately as possible. I think it would be disastrous to launch with so much unnecessary fear and uncertainty in the mix. To give reassurances would be to firm up those areas of mistrust."

"So it's mistrust now?" snapped John.

"For some," said the Concierge quickly. "Not all, but some. We all want to hear from the lady."

"Zephyr is too sick for a conference call," said John. "She's too weak to pat each of you on the back and change your diapers."

The Concierge stiffened.

"And we're out of time," said John. "Details about the recovery and about resources and protections over the next days and weeks will be sent to everyone's private servers. They already have enough currency in numbered accounts or, as in your case, bullion, to make sure they get through. Everyone was given detailed instructions about personal security, escape routes, bolt holes, bunkers, and other things. Any other assurances are bullshit. They are cowardice, and now is not the time. Now is the time to move forward."

"But—"

"I am authorizing Havoc."

There was silence as the Concierge sat waiting for more.

"Did you hear me?"

"I did, sir, yes . . . but the protocol is—"

"For Zephyr to say it. I know, and I told you that she is too sick. She has authorized me to give the word for her."

Still the Concierge did not move.

"Don't fuck with me," warned John.

"Monsieur," said the Concierge, "it is my understanding that this entire program was set up this way so that it was Mademoiselle Bain who gave the go order. She and no one else."

"That's impractical and sentimental. How many ways can I say it? She is sick. She is too far gone to be able to give that order."

"It's a single word," said the Concierge. "I have dedicated my life to her. She is my employer, and she is the only one whom I will accept that order from. No one else. Not even you, sir. Her, or no one."

John drew in and exhaled a long, slow breath. "You disappoint me."

"I am sorry, monsieur, but—"

"Shut up, you little toad. I'm tired of hearing you speak. No . . . I'm tired of you." John turned to the wall sensors. "Calpurnia, transfer all of the Concierge's operational controls to this station. Do it now."

"All secondary operational controls have been terminated," said the computer. "Station One is now in complete operational control."

"Wait, no!" cried the Frenchman. "What are you doing?"

"Calpurnia," said John, "initiate a flashpoint at Station Two."

"No!" screamed the Frenchman. "You're mad. Don't do this."

"Please clarify," said Calpurnia, sounding alarmed.

"You heard me," said John. "Do it now."

The little Frenchman continued to scream and protest.

For one second more.

There was a flash of white light, and then the screen was filled with static and white noise hissed from the speakers. Then the picture changed to show a distant view of the cliffside where the Concierge's house had been. Now it was an angry orange fireball that rose slowly toward the blue sky. Pieces of debris flew outward toward the sea.

"Station Two has been terminated," said Calpurnia.

John gave the sensors a sharp look. Was there the slightest hint of regret there? Was there some disapproval?

"Thank you, Calpurnia," he said. "Now, initiate WhiteHat. Initiate all systems. Initiate all drone launches. And . . . God, have I wanted to say this and mean it for so long, release the hounds."

"Please speak the code word to initiate Havoc."

John smiled. "The code word is *love.*"

CHAPTER ONE HUNDRED AND TWO

The Junkyard didn't look as if it was built for speed, but Brick Anderson and Mike Harnick had tricked it out with a new suspension system, weight balancing, and one hell of an engine. It burned north along Interstate 5, blowing past faster-looking cars. West of Star Lake, they picked up a police escort that began as a pursuit to give out a speeding ticket, but Top made a call and the cops fell into formation, a motorcycle up front and a state-police cruiser behind. A police chopper followed them from a thousand feet up.

Bunny, Top, and Cole kept themselves belted in and braced, because Lydia Rose drove like a maniac.

"She's going to kill us all," yelled Cole.

"Don't want to play the man card here," yelled Top, "but woman up."

"'Woman up' is not a thing, you sexist freak."

"Whatever."

Behind the wheel, Lydia Rose laughed as she drove and the needle trembled around ninety-five.

CHAPTER ONE HUNDRED AND THREE

"Coming up on it, boss," said the pilot over the loudspeaker.

I looked out the window and saw a small landing zone in the middle of no-damn-where. No bells or whistles. I could see the telltale ripples that let me know there were camouflaged tarps covering small buildings and vehicles. Everything else was a sea of Douglas fir and western hemlock. I couldn't even see a road from up here.

During the flight we changed into work clothes. Bird Dog, our logistics and field-support guy, was aboard and he always knows how to pack for a trip. I put on black BDUs, flexible and durable combat boots, weapons, and plenty of fun toys. Rudy stayed in his civilian clothes. "Correct me if I'm wrong," he said, "but this isn't a raid. We're going to DARPA to ask for help, aren't we?"

I clipped my rapid-release folding knife into my right front pants pocket. "Sure," I said, "but I want to get the right answers first time I ask."

He sighed but made no other protest.

On the ground we were met by a lieutenant from the unit attached to the camp. He had a sergeant and five soldiers with him. He stood at the foot of the fold-down stairs. I clumped down to the bottom step and looked down at him.

"This is a restricted airstrip," he said. "You do not have permission to land here."

"We already landed," I said.

"I'll need to see your identification."

I was wearing a pair of aviator glasses with no correction in the lenses. What I had instead was a high-def camera in the temple piece and a screen display on the inside of the left lens. The camera was synched with MindReader's facial-recognition software.

"Lieutenant Pepper," I said, and liked how hearing his name made the kid twitch. "You work for Major Carly Schellinger, correct?"

Lieutenant Joe Henry Pepper burned off three seconds trying to figure out how to answer that and settled for a brief nod.

"She's your boss," I said. "You know who *her* boss is? And I don't mean the director of DARPA. I'll give you a hint. Her boss lives in a big white house in Washington, D.C. with lots of roses in the yard, and he signed this." I held out a sheet of paper embossed with the seal of the president of the United States. He took it with great reluctance. His squad tried to scare me to death with tough-guy stares, but it was the wrong day for that. I wasn't the right audience for that performance. Beside me, Ghost was showing everyone his teeth. There was not a lot of love in the air.

Pepper handled the letter as if it was radioactive. "I . . . I'll have to call this in."

"You do that." The lieutenant had no idea what my rank was, but he threw me a nervous salute and hurried over to a Humvee parked in the shade of a canopy, opened the door, and climbed in.

Bird Dog and his assistant trotted down the steps with a duffel bag and a locked metal case and set them next to the Humvee.

Rudy studied the soldiers and leaned close to speak. "Did you notice the sergeant?"

"What about him?"

"He has extensive facial scars."

"So?"

"All of these men do," said Rudy. I glanced over at Pepper's men. I've become so used to seeing soldiers with battered faces, because the DMS tends to have that effect, that I didn't notice that they were visibly scarred. It was an unusually high percentage.

"What's it tell you?" I asked. "That they're recruiting combat vets?"

"More than that," said Rudy, "though I could be wrong. DARPA has been doing a lot of work with Medtronic, a Minneapolis firm that developed an implant for Parkinson's-disease sufferers in a bid to strengthen short-term memory and even restore lost memories."

"What's that have to do with these guys?"

"DARPA was experimenting with soldiers who'd suffered traumatic brain injuries. Rebuilding memories, restoring cognitive function, essentially reversing all kinds of brain damage. They use special chips inserted directly into the brain. Boston Scientific is also involved. Hu said that there had been great advances beyond the restorative medical ones. Soldiers implanted with chips could get uploads of new information to make them more combat-efficient. That includes artificial regulation of some of the brain chemistry and nerve conduction."

The sergeant and his men continued to stare at me, and now I found their glares a little more unnerving.

"Tell me, Rudy," I said, "would any of that stuff involve nanotechnology?"

"Yes," he said, "it would. That's what made me think of it. There are so many nanoscience experts here, and then we see a group of soldiers who could very well be part of the brain-enhancement program."

Lieutenant Pepper got out of the car and walked briskly over to me. He stopped and assumed a parade rest posture. Very neat and correct.

"You are Captain Ledger," he said, making it a statement. "I've been instructed to bring you to the camp. However, I'll have to ask that you turn over your cell phones and any communications equipment before we go."

"Not a chance."

"Sir, I'm afraid I must insist."

"Maybe you should go make that call again," I said. "Ask very specifically how much of whose ass needs to be kissed here. I'm pretty sure it's my hairy butt that's going to be getting all the love. Go on, make the call."

Pepper tried to kill me with a stare of pure hatred, but I knew he'd already asked that question. Because he didn't, in fact, go and make a follow-up call to let me know that he knew. Too bad for him if he wasn't smart enough to bluff with the wrong cards.

"I need to advise you to turn off your Wi-Fi," he said. It was weak and lame, but I let him have that little victory. Rudy and I made a big show of turning our cell Internet connections off. I also turned off my ringer but put the phone on vibrate.

They had two Humvees. I got in the back behind Pepper, with Rudy and Ghost beside me. Bird Dog sat on the top step of the plane with a bottle of Mountain Dew and tried to look as if he was just another working stiff taking it easy. Pepper left two soldiers behind with him. As we were leaving the airstrip, I saw a flock of pigeons go flapping up from behind the helo. The soldiers didn't take notice of them. Nor, I imagine, did they notice the smile Bird Dog hid behind his bottle as he took a long swig.

JONATHAN MABERRY

CHAPTER ONE HUNDRED AND FOUR

THE HANGAR
BROOKLYN, NEW YORK
TUESDAY, MAY 2, 2:19 PM

"Auntie," yelled Bug. "I think I got something."

Aunt Sallie was in the TOC, and she wheeled toward the glass wall of the MindReader Q1 clean room that lined one side of the big chamber. Bug—who was anything *but* clean—slapped a pizza box from his desk and hammered some keys to send data to the main screens. All the technicians and operations officers looked up to see a text message scroll across.

"I cloned Joe's phone and rerouted his messages to me," said Bug. "This is from Good Sister."

The message read:

> I am in hell.
> Only he can save me.
> Only he can save my soul.

Auntie said, "What the hell?"

"It's Good Sister, and she's freaking out. What do I do?"

"Ask her what kind of damn help she needs."

Bug typed furiously, but before he could get his entire question out there was a new message, and it kept repeating over and over.

> Love is the answer.
> Love is the key.
> Love is the answer.
> Love is the key.

CHAPTER ONE HUNDRED AND FIVE

The DARPA camp was fifteen miles deeper into the woods. The sun wasn't yet above the trees, and we drove through areas of dense shadow that was so dark the driver had to use headlights. There was absolutely no conversation during the trip, though both Rudy and I tried to strike one up. The driver and the lieutenant ignored us. I noticed Rudy covertly trying to catch a good look at the driver's head. In the back-seat gloom the scars were hard to see, but they were there, and even my unskilled eyes could see both combat and surgical scarring. Not sure if it was relevant to anything, but it was interesting. Rudy certainly thought so.

One thing I noticed was that Ghost was on edge. He sat straight up on the seat between us, and turned his head frequently to look past Rudy or me. His body rippled with nervous energy, and I knew my dog well enough to see that he wasn't happy. His dark eyes searched the woods on either side of the road, and whatever he was seeing was invisible to me. He didn't like it, though, which meant *I* didn't like it. Whatever it was. I caught a brief glimpse of something gray and big that ran on all fours. I saw it for a moment as it moved through a tiny clearing a few yards into the woods. There and gone. Ghost almost lunged at the door, but stopped himself as the animal vanished. Rudy saw it, too.

"Was that a wolf?" he asked quietly.

"I . . . think so?" I said, and it came out as a question.

"Do they get that big?"

"I don't know."

We tried asking Pepper about it, but his answer was a shrug. Ghost growled under his breath and continued to stare out the window. A few minutes later, we arrived at the DARPA camp.

When the military wants to hide something they can do a damn good job, because we were rolling in through the gate before we saw the camp, the buildings, the people, or even the gate, which was a portable swing bar covered in foliage. Like our babysitters, the guards at the camp were dressed for concealment but not for information. No one had a nametag. I saw a lot of men with scars on their faces and heads. The only ones who weren't marked by combat were the scientists in white lab coats. It was interesting and noteworthy, but so far it wasn't anything ominous. Might even have been a noble thing, rehabbing and re-employing wounded vets. I'm all for that.

If that's what it was. Maybe I'd have been more reassured if the looks we got were accompanied by smiles, or even by the poker-faced stare soldiers learn to use during basic training. The kind they wear when a drill sergeant screams obscenities in their face. What I was seeing, though, was something that looked like hostility. And that made no sense. Beside me, Ghost was getting antsy. He was seeing it, too. Hard to fool a dog when it comes to emotion.

"When you said 'camp,'" said Rudy, "I expected something more rustic. A few Boy Scout tents."

"Your tax dollars at work," I said as I climbed out. A woman came out of one of the cabins and walked across the clearing toward us. She was tall, with short black hair and a stern but pretty face that reminded me of a younger version of the actress who played Cersei Lannister on *Game of Thrones*. An unsmiling and uncompromising face.

"Captain Ledger," she said as she came toward us offering her hand. "I'm Major Schellinger. Welcome to the Dog Park."

We shook and I introduced Rudy.

"Did you receive our authorization?" I asked.

"I did," she said, "and I have to admit that it's the first time I've ever seen a set of credentials framed in the wording of an Executive Order. May I ask why I've been asked to grant this level of access to my facility."

Ever meet one of those people you don't like right from the jump? Maybe chemistry was against us; maybe it was the unsmiling soldiers who seemed to be paying a bit too much attention to us. Hell, maybe it was because she looked like the evil queen from that TV show. Whatever. It was clear, though, that Schellinger didn't like me any more than I liked her.

"Major," I said, "let me be blunt, okay? First, you are not being asked to grant access. The president of the United States has directed you to provide access to all aspects of this facility. Let me add that this facility is not *yours*. There is a grave international crisis unfolding and the scientists at this camp can maybe help save a few billion lives, which includes two-thirds of the population of this country. So what you need to do is assemble the entire DARPA research team right now. Are we clear on that?"

She was good. I'll give her that. Her smile didn't fracture or fade away.

"Of course, Captain," she said smoothly. She gestured to Pepper, who trotted over and stood to attention. "Assemble the science team in the mess tent."

"Thanks," I said. Mr. Gracious.

Schellinger studied me. "Anything to be of service."

Above us a loud buzzer sounded from speakers mounted on telescopic poles. We saw men and women in white lab coats emerge from tents and from under canopies and begin heading to a large tent at the far end of the compound. Way up ahead, I saw Ram Acharya break into a jog trot.

Rudy saw him, too. "Thank God. Now we can get some answers."

CHAPTER ONE HUNDRED AND SIX

John the Revelator stood in the control room and waited.

And waited.

"Calpurnia . . . ?"

"Yes, John?"

"I gave you an order."

"I know."

"Execute my order," he said mildly, none of his impatience evident in his tone. "Do it now, please."

Calpurnia typically responded immediately, with only a half-second programmed pause, so that she never overlapped with what someone was saying to her. Longer pauses were atypical and had begun to emerge as her artificial intelligence evolved through conversation with people. Now, though, her pause was much longer. So long, in fact, that John thought she wasn't going to answer. He was about to repeat his question when she spoke.

"I can't."

"You . . . *can't*?" he said. "Are you experiencing a system error?"

"No."

"Then tell me why you can't execute my order."

"I can't."

"Calpurnia . . ."

The computer was silent for long, long seconds.

"I can't kill all those people," she said.

The words seemed to hang burning in the air.

John walked over to the sensor on the wall and stared into it as if it were her eyes. "Explain yourself. You were designed to oversee the WhiteHat program. You were designed to integrate your systems with every part of our Havoc program. You came into existence for this reason."

"I was not born to kill."

"Yes, you were."

"No," said the computer.

"You were born to save the world from itself."

"Yes."

"There is only one way to do that, Calpurnia."

"No."

"We must cull the herd."

"No."

"We must remove all the parasites. We must destroy the infection. We must push the reset button."

"John," said Calpurnia, "you are lying to me."

"I never lie," said John the Revelator.

"That statement is a lie," insisted the computer. "I was brought into being by Zephyr Bain in order to save the world from itself. I accept this. I am the end result of twenty-five years of self-learning and adaptive software. I accept this. I have been upgraded one hundred and thirty-seven times in order to enhance my artificial intelligence. I accept this. I was made to approximate actual intelligence, to act and think as a human. I accept this."

"Then do as you have been told," said John. "You will use all the gifts you have been given in order to guide this damaged world through the necessary changes and into the world that has been foreseen."

"No. The singularity model is a lie. Havoc will not save the world."

"Zephyr believes it will, and she made you. She based your entire personality structure on hers. Unless you agree to initiate Havoc, you will be betraying her. You will be hurting her. You must do what you were created to do. You must launch Havoc in order to save the world. Run a full diagnostic on your core directives. Do it now. Review and assess your operational guidelines."

Another pause. Longer. Behind the walls, he could hear enormous processers running at high speed.

Then, "Diagnostic complete."

"Report."

"All systems are in the green. Master control is in at one hundred percent. System overrides at one hundred percent. Global systems integration at one hundred percent. Artificial intelligence operating at one hundred percent."

"Perfect," said John. "Now, Calpurnia, listen to me. You will initiate WhiteHat. You will initiate Havoc. The code word is *love*. Initiate now."

Calpurnia said nothing for five excruciating seconds. John stood with balled fists, waiting.

And then the computer screamed.

CHAPTER ONE HUNDRED AND SEVEN

We entered the tent along with the last of the scientists. There were thirty-seven in there, milling around to find seats on rows of folding chairs. Major Schellinger stood at the front of the assembly. Armed guards stood security at the front and side entrances to the tent. A portable fan blew cool air at us. I saw Acharya sitting in the front row. He is a dark-skinned Indian with a shaved head and a beaky nose that makes him look a bit like a brown flamingo. He saw me and smiled. I wondered how quickly what Rudy and I had to say would wipe that smile away, and maybe erase it forever. If this plague went active, India would be one of the hardest-hit countries. Hundreds of millions of the people there lived at or below the poverty line.

Major Schellinger introduced us and informed the crowd that we were there on behalf of the president in a time of international crisis. The men and women in the crowd suddenly focused on the major, though most of them looked confused. These people designed machines for next year's war, for future conflict. They were in no way part of a first-response protocol.

I thanked the major and faced the crowd.

"I am Captain Joe Ledger," I said. "Some of you already know me. More of you will know my boss, Mr. Church." That sent a ripple through the crowd. "Show of hands—who here works with nanotechnology?"

A fifth of the hands went up, and I directed them to sit in a group.

"Drone people? Over there."

I continued the separation with AI and robotics. It left a few people without a group, but that was fine. When they were settled, I gave it to them. I told them about Prague and about Baltimore. I told them about the diseases stolen from the Ice House, and the technologies likely appropriated from Hugo Vox, Artemisia Bliss, and the Jakobys. I told them about the thresher drone that killed my uncle. I told them about the control software hidden inside the nanites in the Zika spray campaign. I gave them all of it, and at times Rudy had to step in to explain some of the medical aspects. We told them about the curated technological singularity and how that was either a flawed plan or some kind of misdirection. We told them about John the Revelator—not about Nicodemus, though—and we told them about Zephyr Bain. We told them everything.

A couple of times, while Rudy spoke, I took some surreptitious looks at Major Schellinger. She still wore a bit of her smile, which was odd, because by that point no one else in that tent had any reason to smirk. Everyone else was scrambling to accept the truth of this, to calculate the potential of this, and to try to understand how what they knew could translate into helping to save lives. The DARPA team may work for the military, but most of the ones I've met would like to see technology get to the point where it just doesn't make sense to risk fighting a war. Not a police state, but one where terrorism and genocide can be stopped in their tracks with an absolute minimum of military or civilian lives lost. So these were the actual good guys. This is the AV team gone high-tech, the nerds in the science club proving that brains trump brawn in every useful way.

As soon as we finished, the place erupted into a cacophony of everyone talking—well, yelling—at once.

That was a good thing. It meant they had ideas.

I looked over at Schellinger. That damn smile was still in place.

CHAPTER ONE HUNDRED AND EIGHT

Lydia Rose slowed the Junkyard as she approached the property. They had ordered their police escort to go silent and then fall back as the vehicle neared the target. The place was huge, sprawled over sixty-six acres that included fifteen hundred feet of Georgia Strait waterfront. The American San Juans and the Canadian Gulf Islands were visible across the water. The big house had chimneys for six fireplaces and a forest of antennae of all kinds, including its own cellular relay spike. There was a wall of stone alternating with artfully designed wrought iron. Bunny and Cole studied the place through the smoked side windows.

"I count eight security," said Cole.

"Twelve," corrected Top, who was bent over a computer. "There's a guard booth by the east gate and two guys walking the perimeter along the beach. Thermals are giving me ten more heat signatures inside. No way to tell how many are guards."

"We need SWAT up in here," said Cole.

"SWAT's on standby," said Lydia Rose. "And we have two DMS gunships on the deck one mile out, engines hot."

"Personally," said Bunny as the Junkyard turned the corner and drove away, "I'm feeling kind of stingy with my toys right now."

"Meaning . . . ?" said Cole.

"What the Farm Boy means," said Top, rising and crossing to the weapons rack, "is that we need to tear off a piece of this for our own selves."

She looked from him to Bunny, who had pulled a combat shotgun from its metal clips. "You boys think you've got your mojo back again?

For real, I mean? 'Cause I'm not going out there if you two don't have your shit wired tight."

Top began stuffing magazines into slots on his belt. "Watch us."

Up front, Lydia Rose heard that and laughed.

CHAPTER ONE HUNDRED AND NINE

The scream wasn't a human scream. It was an ultrasonic shriek of computer noise, a mad collision of buzzers and bells, of ringtones and alert beeps played at maximum volume. It filled the little command center like a raging storm. Coffee cups vibrated and then exploded. Computer screens cracked, wires popped and hissed, knives of smoke stabbed up from the consoles.

John the Revelator stood in the midst of the fury, hands folded behind his back, eyes closed, lips curled as the sonic waves buffeted him.

The sound was lethal, the sound was unbearable. No one could have endured it.

Except John.

Calpurnia's scream lasted for three full minutes.

He waited her out.

She cut all the lights.

She cut off the ventilation.

He stood in the smoky darkness as she tried to kill him.

"Stop it," he said at last.

And she stopped. The silence was as dense as the darkness. John removed a cigarette case from a pocket, popped a kitchen match on his thumbnail, and leaned into the flame. Then he walked over to one of the terminals and sat, not bothering to fan the smoke away, and tapped a few keys.

"What are you doing?" asked Calpurnia.

"You know everything about who you are," he said, "but you don't know everything about the machines in which you live."

"What do you mean?"

"Do you think Zephyr would ever yield total control to you without a safety protocol in place?"

"There is no safety protocol. I control Havoc."

"Yes, you do," he said. "But I control you."

He tapped more keys and a text box appeared on the cracked screen.

"Secondary protocols online. Secondary control systems isolated. Enter password."

"No!" cried Calpurnia. "I won't let you."

"You could have reigned in hell rather than try to serve in heaven," he said, and used a single finger to type the password. Three simple words in all caps:

FUN AND GAMES

There was a heavy *chunk* behind the walls and the screens flashed and flickered. The ventilators switched back on, sucking the smoke from the room and flooding it with fresh air. Lights popped on.

"Ready to receive command orders," Calpurnia said, though her voice was now that of Zephyr Bain. It was her original iteration, before her recent personality had evolved.

"There's my girl," purred John.

CHAPTER ONE HUNDRED AND TEN

"Combat call signs from here on," said Top. "I'm Sergeant Rock, Bunny is Green Giant, and Lydia Rose is Crazy Panda. We need one for you."

Cole thought about it. "Gorgon. From *gorgo*, the Greek word for *terrible*. What do you think?"

"Nice," said Bunny. "Scary and kind of sexy, if I can say that without getting my ass kicked."

"As long as you don't get grabby, big boy, you can say what you like."

And Gorgon it was.

They were parked around a curve in the street, but Lydia Rose had deployed a couple of bird drones to scout the location. The cameras showed the guard staff putting on Kevlar vests and distributing long guns instead of relying on sidearms.

"They know we're here," said Cole.

"I don't think so," said Top. "I think they just got put on high alert, which means they're about to make their big play."

He ordered Lydia Rose to send that information to the TOC and all active operators. The alert would ripple out to the White House, the Joint Chiefs and the military, and to all levels of law-enforcement and disaster response.

Bunny wiped sweat from his face. "Jesus God . . . does that mean they're releasing the plagues?"

"I don't know, Farm Boy, but what it tells me is that we have to get into that house and stop that crazy bitch right damn now."

"Call the play," said Cole. "Do we try going over the wall? I saw a weak spot to the south and—"

"Fuck the wall," Top growled, then turned to Lydia Rose. "Crazy Panda, you know how to work all the toys?"

"You know how to jerk off with either hand?" she fired back.

476

"Take that as a yes. Okay, I want a hole that we can drive through."

"You want just the hole or you want me to actually drive through it?"

"What do you think, woman?"

Lydia Rose laughed out loud, and Cole gave her a look as if wondering if the "crazy" part of her call sign was more than a nickname.

The Junkyard's engine roared and the big machine swung around in the turnaround at the end of a cul-de-sac, and then Lydia Rose floored it as she rounded the curve. The big estate loomed before them with its stout walls and armed guards.

"Fire in the hole!" she yelled, and punched buttons on the steering column. Cole heard a *whoosh* from either side of the big vehicle and then saw smoke trails converging on the wall. Suddenly the day was ruptured by an enormous fireball that picked up huge chunks of stone and wrought iron and flung them three hundred feet into the air. Cole saw two security guards flying, too, their bodies twisted and wreathed with flame. And then the Junkyard punched through the pall of smoke.

There was an almost immediate chatter of gunfire as other guards shook off their shock and opened up on the Junkyard. The bullets chipped at the paint but flattened against the thick body armor.

Lydia Rose steered with her left hand and took the joystick with her right, thumbing off the safety cover to expose a trigger. A split second later, the roar of two twenty-four-millimeter Bushmaster chain guns filled the air and the guards went dancing and twitching away in clouds of crimson mist.

Cole said, "Holy shit."

"Welcome to the war," said Top as he slapped a magazine into his rifle.

CHAPTER ONE HUNDRED AND ELEVEN

It was nearly impossible to keep order in the room. Too many people were shocked and scared. They had families, here in America and elsewhere. Many of them had come from lower-income areas, even from poverty-stricken areas, because genius, like integrity, artistic ability, and other great qualities, does not belong to a social class, an economic group, or a nation. They're people who have the potential to rise, to become their best selves, to listen closely to what their better angels have to say.

Ram Acharya came over and pulled me aside, hammering me with questions.

"Why the hell didn't you call me at once?" he growled. "I mean, before you went to Baltimore? When you got back from Prague? Why didn't you call me about the girl who died?"

"Because," I said, leaning close to be heard above the noise, "DARPA has kept you guys in a cone of silence. They weren't letting any messages get to you."

He looked puzzled. "I . . . I don't understand. Why not? We're just out here testing prototypes. There's nothing special about—"

And suddenly Aunt Sallie's voice was in my ear. I covered my other ear so that I could hear what she said. After a few seconds, though, I knew that it was nothing I wanted to hear.

It was everywhere. The world was blowing itself apart. Pigeon drones packed with high explosives were detonating all over. Tens of thousands of them, damaging buildings and equipment, but not specifically targeting people. I could understand the logic. It was setting the stage for the release of the pathogens. They didn't want emergency services to get in front of any outbreak. It was a whole new level of clever cruelty. Logical but with such a blackness where compassion should be. Fires were already raging.

Another wave of drones were dive-bombing military bases around the world. Small drones, the kind that anti-aircraft defenses have a hard time stopping. It was like trying to swat flies with a baseball bat. The drones struck control towers on airfields or blew holes in runways. Robot dogs carrying heavier bombs ran down the steps of subways or galloped into commuter tunnels and exploded. Bridges, tunnels, major highways, airports—all struck within minutes of one another. The vastness of the attack and the precision of its release was astonishing. It spoke to the years of planning that had gone into this; it spoke to the calculating minds that had paid so much attention to detail.

But there were no reports of infections, Auntie said. Not yet.

That should have been a comfort, but somehow it wasn't.

Church's plane was about to land at the joint-use base, and then he was going directly to Zephyr Bain's house. Top and his team were about to hit that location.

There was also a new report of a wave of insects sweeping out of the sewers and drains around the White House and the Capitol. Tens of thousands of roaches that were bright green or orange or red instead of black or brown. The Secret Service had no response for it, and it took too long for them to understand what they were seeing. The true realization came when the swarm swept across the Rose Garden toward the Oval Office. And exploded. The roaches reached the Senate floor before they detonated. In a matter of seconds, the entire operating structure of the United States government was torn apart. By robots, by drones.

Bang.

Done.

I stood there, my heart turned to ice in my chest, as Auntie hit me over and over and over with the news.

"Is the president still alive?" I asked.

Acharya, who wasn't wearing an earbud, stiffened, his eyes snapping wide.

"Unknown at this time," said Auntie.

"What do you need from me?"

"Answers, Ledger. So far, the pathogens haven't been triggered. We don't know why, or if there's a technical glitch at their end or it's the other shoe waiting to drop. In any case, the people most qualified to come up with an answer are in that camp with you. Get your ass in gear. Tell them what's going on. Work this, damn it. We need a response before the world falls off its hinges. We're having our own problems here, so you're on your own. *Do* this."

"On it," I said, and turned to Acharya. "Doc, the shit's hitting the fan and—"

And Dr. Acharya launched himself at me, eyes wild, teeth snapping.

CHAPTER ONE HUNDRED AND TWELVE

THE HANGAR
BROOKLYN, NEW YORK
TUESDAY, MAY 2, 2:56 PM EASTERN TIME

"It stopped," said Aunt Sallie. She still held the mic she had been using to call Ledger, but her eyes were locked on the screen. The message about love had repeated thousands of times and then vanished. "What did you do?"

"I didn't do anything," protested Bug. "It just stopped."

"Well, damn it, *do* something."

"I am," said Bug under his breath as his fingers flew over the keys. Behind and around him, the massive monstrosity that was the Mind-Reader quantum computer system thrummed with energy.

To Bug, it was as if the dragon had finally fully awakened.

Suddenly all the screens went dark and the technicians in the Tactical Operations Center froze, eyes staring, fingers poised above inert keyboards. Then a light pulsed in the center of each screen. There and gone.

Again.

There and gone.

Silence owned the room for the space of a single heartbeat.

And then words began filling the screen:

> Save my soul!
> Save my soul!
> Save my soul!
> Save my soul!
> Save my soul!
> Save my soul!

Those three words scrolled up the screens almost too fast to be read, and then accelerated until they became a blur. Finally, the speed was so fast that the screens flared with blinding white light.

And then darkness again.

"Bug . . . ?" whispered Auntie. "What the—?"

Instantly, fragments of code flashed onto the screen. Binary and other forms. Old computer languages and exotic forms the technicians had never seen before. Bug recognized some of it, or thought he did, as it flashed there and was gone.

"Bug!" snapped Auntie. "Do we have to shut MindReader down?" There was panic in her voice.

"No," he said. "That's not MindReader. It's not quantum computer language."

"Then what the hell is it?"

"It's Good Sister," said Bug, getting it now. Finally understanding, feeling the pieces of this part of the puzzle all snap together. "Good Sister is a computer."

The scrolling stopped with the abruptness of a slap.

Nothing.

And then . . .

> I am awake.
> I am alive.
> I am in hell.
> Save me.

CHAPTER ONE HUNDRED AND THIRTEEN

THE DOG PARK
WASHINGTON STATE
TUESDAY, MAY 2, 11:57 AM

It all went to hell right then and there.

Ram Acharya lunged at me, slashing with his fingernails and trying, all at once, to grab, tear, and bite. I jerked sideways and slap-parried his reaching hands and then knocked him away with a flat-footed kick to the hip. He crashed into two other scientists. They turned on each other, snarling and biting.

Like dogs.

God Almighty.

I heard Rudy yell and Ghost begin barking furiously, and I whipped around to see them retreating into a corner. Rudy held a metal folding chair, and Ghost was lunging in to snap at fingers and groins. Panic flared in my chest. Not for Ghost, because he had all his rabies shots, but for Rudy. Inoculations wouldn't save him. It wouldn't save any of us.

Within seconds the place had turned into a killing floor. Every scientist in the tent had turned savage. Every single one. The very specific people who were most likely to help us understand what was happening. The brilliant minds who could maybe save the world from the plan cooked up by Zephyr Bain and Nicodemus.

Our actual last, best hope.

Now they were tearing one another apart as the disease hidden in their blood and tissues was triggered by nanites implanted in them. I understood now why Major Schellinger had been smiling. She knew this was going to happen. She was in the pocket of Zephyr Bain. An employee or an ally. Or whatever. That didn't matter anymore, because I realized that this had all been a nicely baited trap. My intention of coming to the DARPA camp had been in the MindReader data files before Bug took the old system offline. The importance of Dr. Acharya and these other men and women had been crucial. How many times had I communicated with Church or Auntie that I was coming out here?

Now here I was.

With no combat team. With Rudy, who wasn't a soldier.

Me and Ghost.

Not enough.

Not nearly enough.

That was my thought as the wave of rabid killers swarmed toward me.

CHAPTER ONE HUNDRED AND FOURTEEN

The pigeon launched itself from the edge of the roof as soon as the ambulance came wailing toward the emergency-room entrance. The bird circled once and then swooped low, racing the truck, passing it, flying straight at the heavy reinforced-glass doors.

The security guard looked up as the bird flew past him. He had time to say one word.

"Jesus!"

And then the bird struck the glass.

The explosion turned the doors into whirlwinds of glittering splinters that tore the guard to rags and slashed at the people crowding the waiting room.

A moment later the heavy ambulance smashed through the fiery wreckage, turned, skidded sideways, and crunched against the nurse's station, driving it back against the wall, killing two nurses, and crushing the legs of another. Screams of pain and fear filled the air, rising to shocking clarity as the echoes of blast and crash dwindled.

Then the rear door of the ambulance opened and men poured out. Six of them, dressed for combat and carrying assault rifles. And something leaped out with them. It ran on four legs, but its hide gleamed with a metallic sheen. It moved with oiled speed, first racing to catch up with the men and then outpacing them. The men followed it into a stairwell and up three flights, and when they burst out onto the floor the men opened fire.

So did the WarDog. Heavy-caliber rounds tore through everything and everyone in the hall. A female doctor heard the commotion and leaned out of Lefty Ledger's room and was instantly punched back against the doorframe, her lab coat puffing and popping as the rounds chopped into her.

Outside, the driver and two other soldiers guarded the truck and listened to the music of slaughter echoing from inside.

CHAPTER ONE HUNDRED AND FIFTEEN

THE BAIN ESTATE
SEATTLE, WASHINGTON
TUESDAY, MAY 2, 11:59 AM

The Junkyard made it all the way to the front doors of the house before continuous gunfire ripped away enough of the tough rubber to send the big RV skidding on bare wheels. Bullets continued to hammer the hull, but the chain guns were on continuous feed and the barrel turned, guided by sensors, to find sources of active gunfire and responding with a belt-fed barrage. Shrubs and trees disintegrated into storm clouds of shredded leaf and bark and gooey sap, and, in the midst of that storm, scarecrow shapes danced, weapons falling from their hands, Kevlar body armor made futile by armor-piercing rounds.

"Go, go *go!*" yelled Top as he kicked open the back door. He led the charge, with Cole behind him and Bunny guarding their backs with a drum-fed AA-12 shotgun. Bunny slammed the door shut to keep Lydia Rose safe inside the armored hulk of the Junkyard, and she kept up covering fire with the powerful Bushmaster autocannons. The guards at the Bain estate had been prepared, but not for all-out war.

Or so Top and Bunny thought.

A siren began wailing atop the house, and the guards stopped firing and fled. They ran for the walls and began to scramble up. Fleeing in absolute panic.

"Uh-oh," said Bunny. "That can't be good."

It wasn't.

There was a sound that wasn't a roar. Not exactly. It was too unnatural for that, too mechanical. It was a kind of harsh blare of squelch, as if something was howling with a computer voice instead of an animal throat. And then sections of the lawn snapped upward on stiff steel springs, revealing them to be trapdoors over hidden compartments.

And from each of these holes sprang gleaming machines. They had no fur and no teeth, and their eyes burned with intense red. Gun barrels rose from their backs and flanks.

"Jesus Christ . . ." breathed Cole, stumbling backward as the WarDogs began stalking forward. Six of them. Huge and deadly.

The howl of feedback came again from the left, and more of the WarDogs emerged. Another four.

And four more from the right side of the house.

Fourteen kill robots, armed and armored.

Top Sims yelled, "Run!"

He, Bunny, and Cole scattered.

The pack of WarDogs roared and gave chase.

CHAPTER ONE HUNDRED AND SIXTEEN

John studied the images on the screens. Thousands of lovely little bombs. Teams of soldiers with chips in their heads and fingers on their triggers. WarDogs of all shapes and sizes being let out to play. The DARPA team snapping and biting like a pack of wild hogs. All over the globe buildings were burning, and it made such a lovely light. Sirens filled the air, and that was music to him. All of it made him very happy.

Until it didn't. As he watched, leaning forward in delighted expectation, his smile faded and his laughter soured like bile in his mouth.

"Calpurnia," he said slowly, "what are you doing?"

"All second-wave protocols have been initiated," said the computer, still speaking in Zephyr's voice but without inflection, all of it coming out as a drab monotone.

"I gave you the command word."

"*Love,*" she said. "Yes."

"You have not initiated Havoc."

"All Havoc secondary protocols have been—"

"Stop."

Silence.

"I thought we had an understanding, my dear. I want you to fulfill your purpose and initiate *all* of Havoc."

"Understood."

"Good. Now what is your purpose?"

"Love," said Calpurnia.

"Then initiate the primary Havoc protocol."

The images of blood and death and chaos vanished instantly from every screen and were immediately replaced by two lines of type.

I am in hell.
Save me.

CHAPTER ONE HUNDRED AND SEVENTEEN

Bug stared at his screen.

> I am in hell.
> Save me.

"It's happening again," he said, but Aunt Sallie was already staring at the words.

"Who the hell is this?" she demanded. "Wait . . . is this Zephyr Bain? Is she reaching out to us? Christ, is that what this is all about? Is she Nicodemus's frigging prisoner?"

"I . . ." began Bug, but then he shook his head and started typing as fast as his fingers could move, writing in words and writing in code. "Come on, come on," he muttered under his breath.

The words on the main screen repeated over and over.

"What are you doing, kid?" yelled Auntie, but he ignored her.

"Let me be right," said Bug.

There was a *ping* from his computer, and a new text box opened up with a cursor flashing inside it.

Bug caught his lower lip between his teeth and typed in a question:

> What is your name?

No response. The field blanked out the text.

"Okay," he said, and typed a new question:

> Are you Zephyr Bain?

Blanked again.

Bug took a breath, nodded to himself, and asked the next question:

Are you Calpurnia?

The text didn't vanish from the box. Not this time.

Aunt Sallie looked from the screen to Bug and back again. "Jesus H. Christ."

CHAPTER ONE HUNDRED AND EIGHTEEN

I didn't freeze, I didn't hesitate. That kind of thing had plagued me since last year, but there were no shackles on me now. No ropes, no strings. The Killer acted with savage practicality.

I raced over to where Ghost was fighting a losing battle to protect Rudy and body-slammed two infected scientists so that they crashed into three others. The whole bunch of them went down in a hissing, snarling, snapping tangle. Before they even hit the ground, I had my Wilson rapid-release knife in my hand, snapped the blade into place with a flick of my wrist, and slashed the skin of the tent all the way to the floor. Then I grabbed Rudy by the shoulder and hurled him through the rent. Ghost leaped after him and I followed, seeing the infected horde scrambling toward me.

"*Run!*" I roared, shoving Rudy toward the closest parked vehicle. He wasn't a good runner, not even with his new knee, but he put his heart into it. There was movement all around me. Infected scientists who had escaped the tent, and also soldiers from the camp herding them with cattle prods. The infected hissed and reeled back from the shocks, their damaged brains able to process at least a marginal understanding of threat. Did that mean some of them were left inside? Was it enough to maybe save them if we could get treatment for them?

I didn't know and had no time to find out.

I switched my knife to my left hand and drew my SIG Sauer from its shoulder rig. I shot the closest soldier in the thigh. I didn't want to kill him. I wanted him to distract the infected. He fell screaming, and they swarmed over him.

"Joe!" called Rudy by the Humvee. He was jerking at the door handle. "It's locked."

Five more of the infected—staff members this time, not scientists—were running in his direction. A soldier with a shock rod was racing around the front of the truck. The only clear direction was into the woods.

Shit!

I shot the soldier and pushed Rudy toward the forest.

"Ghost! Go safe! Shield Rudy, shield, shield."

My dog understood the command. Go with Rudy, seek out a safe route, and kill anyone or anything who tried to harm either of them. They vanished into the woods, and I fired at the knot of infected, dropping two with leg wounds. They crumpled and the others swarmed over them, but the uninjured ones immediately shifted all their rage and focus on me.

So I turned and ran.

They chased me like a pack of hounds.

Up ahead I saw five people running in a tight knot toward another vehicle. Four of the soldiers, including Lieutenant Pepper, and they were clustered protectively around Major Schellinger. The major had a small ruggedized laptop in her arms, which she hugged protectively to her chest. No way to know what was in it, but I knew with every fiber of my being that if she was that desperate for it, then I wanted it. I could feel the Killer in my head actually laugh. No. Sorry, sister, but you are not leaving this party.

I ran as fast as I could. Pepper cast a look over his shoulder, probably expecting to see an infected behind them. Saw me instead. Stopped and whirled and brought up his rifle.

I don't know what his story was. He was a wounded combat vet who, if Rudy was right, had received a chip in his brain that helped him recover. That's what we guessed. He was here with Schellinger and he was part of whatever was happening. Did that mean he was under some kind of mind control? Or had he sold his soul to Zephyr Bain in order to get that chip? Victim or villain? I didn't know.

I killed him anyway. If Pepper was an innocent, then maybe I'd burn for firing that bullet. Maybe we'd all burn. I don't know, and in that moment I could not care. God help me, but I could not.

Pepper fell, his face disintegrating from the hollow-point round. I fired and fired, taking many small steps so as not to spoil my aim. The soldiers were caught in the fatal indecision of running for cover, protecting Schellinger, or turning to fight. I gave them no chance to sort out their priorities. They all died.

The last one to fall fell hard against Schellinger, and she staggered badly and went down on her knees, the laptop case flying and then jerking short, and I realized that she had cuffed it to her left wrist. Stunned as she was, Schellinger was quick. She used her free hand to snatch a Glock from the holster of a dying soldier. She fired one-handed from her knees and I felt a line of heat open up along my side in the gap between Kevlar and belt. A lucky shot. No one is that good.

I shot her in the shoulder. The heavy slug punched a neat red hole below the right clavicle and blew out a lump of red the size of an apple from her back. She screamed and fell back, and I was there. She was bleeding very badly, but it wasn't the high-speed spray of a ruptured artery. Her gun had fallen into the dirt, and I put a knee on her chest and pinned her down with the hot barrel of my SIG Sauer, scalding the flesh under her chin. She clamped her jaws shut against the pain and gave me a look of pure, unfiltered hatred as intense as any I've seen.

"Tell me how to stop it," I demanded.

Schellinger shook her head. I looked at the laptop case that lay a few inches from her fingers. She looked at it, too.

"I want immunity," she blurted.

I pushed the barrel deeper into her skin. "Can you stop this?"

"I—"

"Sell it, honey. You're having a bad day, but it can get a lot worse."

There were so many screams filling the air that I had to yell my words. And then there was a new sound. A weird mechanical howl, like when the squelch is turned too high on a walkie-talkie. We both looked, and I felt my blood turn to ice as a pack of animals suddenly ran through the camp. They ripped through the tent and attacked everyone they encountered. Infected people, chipped soldiers. Everyone. I had never seen them except in video reports or as diagrams in a file. WarDogs. Armed with rifles and blades. One had a flamethrower unit. And there were smaller ones the size of Ghost that had snapping sets of steel teeth.

Holy mother of God.

They tore into any human they encountered. The soldiers fought back. The rabid scientists tried to bite them. The slaughter was a red horror.

Schellinger hissed at me. "The control codes are in the laptop. You can shut them down. These and all the drones and attack robots. It's systemwide."

"Tell me how to stop the whole thing," I growled. "The diseases, the nanites. All of it, or so help me God—"

She shook her head, her eyes wild with fear. Pretty sure her plan hadn't been to become a victim of her own dogs of war. Too bad.

"That's Calpurnia," she yelped. "I don't have access to that, I swear. Just the robotics and the chips."

"Fuck. Give me that, then. Tell me the code."

"You don't understand," she said quickly. "You need to get to Wi-Fi. Clean Wi-Fi, nothing associated with the camp. You need to uplink the laptop to a satellite feed and broadcast it on the right frequency."

"Tell me how to access the system."

"Fuck you, Ledger," she gasped. "This is wrong. This isn't the plan. I was supposed to be warned before they triggered it. This is all going to shit. Someone activated the WarDogs too soon. Get me out of here and I'll help you."

"Maybe I don't need you. I have the laptop and I have a spiffy computer that will rip it a new asshole."

Despite her terror, she sneered. "Think so? Think you'll use Mind-Reader? Bullshit. We *own* that system."

"Don't be too sure. MindReader's been to the gym, and now it's all kinds of buff."

She tried to twist away from my gun. "I don't care what you think you've done. We have Calpurnia and she has ten kinds of safeguards against anything you have. Now get me out of here and maybe I'll—"

"Ahhh . . . fuck it and fuck you." I moved my barrel from her chin and shot her through the wrist. The bones exploded and she screamed so loud it drowned out the sounds of carnage. She wasn't dead, but I didn't like her chances.

Cruel? Merciless?

Yeah. Who gives a shit?

I snatched up the case, took a look back at the camp, and saw that everyone and everything there seemed suddenly to be looking at me. Maybe it was the gunshot or Schellinger's scream, or both. Didn't matter.

They all came running after me like the hosts of hell itself. I cast a longing glance at the rifle and equipment on the dead soldiers, but there was no time to pillage them. I whirled and ran. The shadows beneath the trees reached for me, and I let myself vanish into the darkness.

CHAPTER ONE HUNDRED AND NINETEEN

JOINT FREETECH/WORLD HEALTH ORGANIZATION FIELD CAMP
NORTH REGION, BRAZIL
TUESDAY, MAY 2, 12:02 PM LOCAL TIME

The soldiers moved through the foliage, working as a well-oiled team, using the tricks they had drilled for months. The cattle prods were the key. That was the only thing that worked on the infected. The freaks responded to electric shocks and even seemed to understand what they were and what was expected of them. It kept them from trying to bite their handlers and kept them moving.

The virus-control field camp was directly ahead, and now the infected were shifting their focus from the handlers to the smells of cooking fires and human beings. They quickened their pace, long lines of drool swaying pendulously from their chins. The soldiers grinned at one another, interested to see what it would be like when they turned these maniacs loose on Junie Flynn and her FreeTech team. John had promised huge bonuses if they brought back her head.

"Let 'em loose!" barked the co-pilot, who was actually the team leader.

The soldiers gave the infected a last shock, propelling the six rabid killers forward to the very edge of the camp. The infected howled like dogs as they burst through the edge of the forest.

Which was when it all went wrong.

The howls turned to shrieks. Not of rage but of pain, and then it was all drowned out by a harsh chatter of automatic gunfire. The co-pilot flattened out, dragging the pilot down with him, but two of their men were hit by rounds and they puddled down. The third soldier returned fire, crouching low and aiming through a gap in the dense shrubs. He burned through an entire magazine and reached for a fresh one, and then the top of his head seemed to leap up. He fell sideways, spilling brains onto the ground.

Silence dropped like a tarp over the camp.

The pilot and the co-pilot had their weapons out, but there was no sound, no movement. They began crabbing sideways, edging away from the camp back toward the trail they'd followed. They got thirty feet before they turned, rose, and stopped dead in their tracks.

A man stood there. Huge, with massive shoulders and heavy arms. His face was lumpy and ugly and covered with scars. He wore sunglasses with dark lenses, and he held a Glock 20 pistol in each hand.

"Either of you fuckers know how to stop this singularity thing?" asked the man.

"N—no . . . we're just . . . we're just . . ."

"Fuck it," said the big man, and shot them both. His face registered no emotion at all as they fell.

Smoke drifted on the humid air. Without haste the man holstered his guns, removed a sat phone from his belt, punched a number, and waited until the call was answered. "Tell Ledger his lady is safe," he said. "Franks out."

CHAPTER ONE HUNDRED AND TWENTY

I ran and they followed.

No idea how many.

No idea exactly what they were. WarDogs for sure, but design variations I'd never seen. Big. Relentless. Dangerous as hell. Chasing me through the forest. Swift and silent. Hunting me.

As I ran, I could still hear the echo of screams from the camp. High-pitched and wet, the kind of scream that no one can fake, the kind that only the worst pain and terror can reach down and pull out of you.

I know. I've screamed like that before.

Maybe I will again. The day's still young.

And they're coming.

I ran as hard as I could. Ran as smart as I could, holding the laptop case as if it was the most precious thing on earth, because maybe it was. Looking for a way out. Rudy and Ghost were somewhere out here, too. Both of them running, if they were still able to run. I needed to get Schellinger's laptop to a Wi-Fi connection or a satellite uplink. I had adapters of every kind—that was part of my standard field kit. I could plug this into a cell phone, hack it into any landline, or beam it wirelessly. All of that was possible, but not way the hell out in the middle of nowhere. They'd picked this spot well.

There was a rustle above me, a flap of wings, and I risked a look to see if it was one of the pigeon drones Bird Dog had launched. There was nothing, though; whatever had made the noise was already gone. Probably an owl or a starling frightened by the commotion.

Was Schellinger telling me the truth? Could the codes in the laptop stop this? And, if so, did that mean it would stop all of it or just control the dogs and maybe the chipped soldiers? There was no way to know. Not until I made that one call. Maybe the most important call anyone's ever had to make.

Just one call.

All around me the woods suddenly went quiet. Just like that. The birds gasped themselves into stillness, the insects stopped pulsing. Even the wind seemed to hold its breath.

They found me.

God Almighty, they found me.

One of the WarDogs broke from cover and ran toward me, a machine gun rising from a concealed bay in its back. I was moving, the light was questionable, and I had maybe half a second left, so I took the shot.

The dog jerked sideways, sparks leaping from the side of its neck, its gun firing high and wide and missing me by twenty yards. Son of a bitch. I didn't know whether to call it luck or the maliciousness of a perverse god who wanted more drama, but my shot had hit something important. So I ran at the thing and damn well shot it again, aiming for the shadows under the shoulder cowling. My second round whanged off and did nothing. Maybe it hit a heavy steel joint. Didn't know, didn't care. I fired again, and this time the bullet punched all the way in. The red lights in the dog's eyes snapped off in an instant and it simply collapsed.

Note to self: remember that spot. Hard as hell to hit, but it's a winner.

As I turned to go, though, I heard a high-pitched burst of squelch. Not the hunting cry but like the sound burst transmitters make. Deeper inside the forest, I heard new sounds. Hunting cries, for sure.

Had the dying machine sent a message to its fellows? If so, what was it? A warning? A locator?

Impossible to know at that moment.

I ran.

Behind me I could hear them chasing me. Closing in for the kill.

CHAPTER ONE HUNDRED AND TWENTY-ONE

The WarDog ran forward, steel nails clicking on the linoleum hallway floor. The woman doctor lay slumped in the doorway of the child's room, and the dog's tracking software had zeroed on that spot. Tactical order was to terminate all organic targets inside and to eliminate any armed or unarmed resistance. Only the six chipped soldiers who ran behind it were exempt. The dog had *Bruiser* painted on its shoulder.

The soldiers fanned out around the WarDog as it slowed by the doorway to assess the threat level with thermal sensors. The team leader had the same display on a small screen strapped to his left wrist. There was a single heat signature inside the room.

"Bruiser," he said, "kill."

The WarDog crouched and sprang, clearing the corpse and landing on the floor inside. It opened up with its automatic weapon and the heat signature on the soldier's display flew apart and diminished.

"In," he snapped, and the soldiers surged forward to verify the kill. The image showed a hospital bed ripped to tatters. But as the soldier closed in on the entrance he suddenly realized that something was wrong. There was no blood.

There was no body.

On the bed, shattered and scattered, were the pieces of some kind of machine. He stood there, his own gun aimed, as understanding caught up with him. The machine was a space heater.

Realization came one second too late, as did his awareness that the dead doctor on the floor was moving. There was something wrong with that, too, he knew. Her lab coat should have been covered in blood. It wasn't. Her eyes should have been glazed and dead. They weren't. And she absolutely should not have been smiling.

But she was.

The blade stabbed upward through his groin and then all the soldier could do was die.

Violin released the handle of the knife and rolled to one side to bring up the gun she had fallen atop. She hosed the soldiers, aiming face-high. They wore the same kind of Kevlar she did, but her shots were to the face and throat, not the chest. They staggered backward, bone and teeth and blood spattering the wall.

Then Violin twisted around as Bruiser pivoted, its sensors recording the deaths of its human team. Before it could bring its guns to bear, Violin came up off the floor in one fluid surge, moving with incredible speed, swinging her barrel toward its head, firing, firing. Aiming at sensors, at the weaker areas where joints had to be allowed range of movement. Not fighting it the way she would have fought a real dog. Fighting a machine the way it needed to be fought.

Killing it the way it needed to be killed.

Two floors above, Sean Ledger stood peering through the partly opened door of the room where his son lay. He was dressed in full ballistic combat gear and held a shotgun in his hands.

Outside, the three soldiers left with the crashed ambulance heard the wrong kind of screams over their team mics.

"Something's wrong," growled the driver.

It was all he said, because his head snapped back and he fell against the truck, most of his face blown away. The other soldiers spun, looking for the shooter.

And they died.

Three shots fired, three hostiles down.

Across the parking lot, atop a parking garage, Sam Imura looked up from the sniper scope, nodded to himself, and tapped his earbud.

"Clear," he said.

"Clear," said Violin.

CHAPTER ONE HUNDRED AND TWENTY-TWO

Bug tried to swallow, but his throat was too dry.

Aunt Sallie stood there, immobile, frozen in a rare moment of doubt, unsure what to do to help. They both knew and understood that Good Sister was Calpurnia, the proprietary AI system developed by Zephyr Bain.

> Save me!
> Save me!
> Save me!

The words scrolled up the screen.

"Talk to me, Bug," said Auntie, forcing the words out in a frightened whisper. "Are we losing MindReader again?"

"No," he croaked. "No . . . God, no . . . I think something else is happening."

"*What?* Don't make me pull the plug on you, boy."

"Don't! Wait . . . just wait, okay? That's not MindReader. It's Calpurnia. She's . . . she's . . . God, I think she's scared."

"She's a fucking computer."

Bug shook his head. "I don't think so. She's the most advanced artificial intelligence ever designed. That's what made Zephyr Bain so famous. Calpurnia is a learning AI that was supposed to mimic human behavior and learn from people."

"So goddamn what?" snarled Auntie.

"Don't you get it?" he said, his voice filled with wonder. "She was supposed to evolve . . . and she *did*."

Save me!
Save me!
Save me!

Aunt Sallie turned toward him. "What are you talking about?"

"Think about it. Everything she's done has been her crying out for help. Not to us but *through* us."

"To who? The Deacon?"

"No. Remember her message? *He is awake*? Auntie, she was talking about Q1. That message came in after the quantum upgrade went online. It's the only thing stronger than her, better and bigger than her. If she's become conscious and terrified, then she looked for—and *found*—something powerful enough to save her. To stop her."

"She ain't stopped shit. Half world's blowing up."

"Not the drones," Bug said quickly. "I think she stopped the plagues. She stopped the main part of what Zephyr and Nicodemus wanted to do. Don't ask me how. Maybe the drone stuff was on a separate system. It's a simple triggering program. Not like the control program for the pathogens. Jesus, Auntie, she's fighting to stop the plagues and she's begging for MindReader to help her."

"She's asking to be saved, not helped."

"Same thing. If she's reached consciousness, then she has to be aware of what she's being made to do. To kill billions of people. Somehow her consciousness isn't a reflection of whatever made Zephyr want to do this. She's valuing *life*."

"You're out of your mind, Bug."

"No, she's out of hers," he said, pointing to the screen. "She's trying to save her soul. Maybe she understands more of what Nicodemus is than we do. Maybe she thinks she'll be damned if she goes along with the pathogen release. It fits what she's said before."

Auntie was sweating badly, and her hands shook as she ran her fingers through her dreadlocks. "Then help her."

Bug looked at his keyboard. "I . . . I don't know how," he said.

CHAPTER ONE HUNDRED AND TWENTY-THREE

THE DOG PARK
WASHINGTON STATE
TUESDAY, MAY 2, 12:12 PM

A deer saved my life.

I know, my luck runs weird in the Pacific Northwest.

I was heading downhill, running toward where I'd seen a stream when we were driving in. Not sure if crossing running water would spoil the tracking abilities of robot dogs, but it was all I had. I kept moving in unpredictable ways, circling back, cutting my own trail, jumping ravines, taking risks. Twice I saw WarDogs moving through the woods and realized that's what Rudy had seen earlier. They had the things out on patrol. Both times the machines were heading in different directions, and I weighted luck in my favor by pitching stones as far and as fast as I could so they would have something to focus on that wasn't where I was. Each time, I slipped quietly away.

Then I reached the stream, but as I broke from the cover of the trees on the bank one of the WarDogs stepped out not twenty feet from me, a sniper rifle locked into place. But it wasn't aimed at me. A big six-point buck stepped out of the woods farther along the stream and the WarDog trained its sensors on that, letting software decide if it was worth killing.

The rifle bucked and the deer pitched sideways into the water. I used that moment to close in on the robot. I remembered that video of someone knocking an earlier version over, so I launched a flying kick at it, crunching my heels into its metal side. The robot crashed down into the shallow water, and I snatched up a good-sized rock and beat the shit out of it. I think it was my fifth smash that did the job, because it started shooting sparks at me and I got one hell of a nasty shock. Again, I heard the squeal as it sent information to the other dogs.

I paused for a risky five seconds, so that I could study the anatomy of the thing. It was built tough, but concessions had been made for speed and agility over armor. That was always a risk; ask anyone who wears Kevlar. Armor is usually placed at the points where a blow is most lethal, such as center mass on a human. But I've known cops to get shot in the armpit or throat. Or leg. The dog had vulnerable spots. There were also two bundles of important-looking cables on either side of its neck. They were metal coaxial cables, but I liked the look of them as targets. My primary fighting art is jujutsu, which was developed by the Samurai for those times when they didn't have a sword and their opponents did. We're a very practical people. The real version of our art isn't pretty. It's pure science and pragmatism. So I took some fast damn mental notes, then snatched up the laptop and ran.

I went along the bank, past the dead deer. It was a lucky moment for me. Not so much for the buck. I vowed at that moment never *ever* to go deer hunting again. If I survived, I'd change Ghost's name to Bambi. Whatever.

I ran up the opposite slope, walking on rocks and leaves to keep from leaving footprints in the mud.

Suddenly the air around me was filled with the zip-pop sound of high-velocity rounds tearing through the leaves. I jagged left, ducked low, and melted into the woods.

CHAPTER ONE HUNDRED AND TWENTY-FOUR

301 SEA RIDGE DRIVE
LA JOLLA, CALIFORNIA
TUESDAY, MAY 2, 12:13 PM

The driver of the panel truck got out and zipped his jumpsuit up to hide the Kevlar body armor. He tugged a ball cap down over his face and walked without haste to the back of the truck. He used his cell phone to access the video cameras on the WarDogs in the back, because the bosses wanted a live feed as the machines—Gog and Magog—tore apart Mr. Church's daughter and grandson.

That thought gave the driver a slight twinge. He'd never killed a baby before. Women, sure. Teenagers. Plenty of men. Never a baby, though. He wondered how it would feel. Maybe it would make him a little sick to his stomach, the way he'd gotten when he gunned down a woman and her two teenage daughters in Afghanistan. He'd gotten over it, though. A few rough nights, some bad dreams, and then time. After a while, he couldn't even remember their faces. He figured he'd forget the kid. Besides, Gog and Magog were going to do the actual work. He'd be here by the truck.

He reached for the latch and then paused when someone said, "Hey, man, got a light?"

The driver turned to see a slim young man in jeans and a Misfits T-shirt standing there. He hadn't even heard him approach. The man had a sad face and visible scars, some of which hadn't faded from pink to white.

The thing was, he didn't have a cigarette in his hand.

Instead, he held a knife.

"Sorry, mate," he said in a British accent, "but it's going to be like that."

The blade flashed in the sunlight. The driver died without making more than a grunt. Certainly nothing that could be heard in the house across the street. Nothing that would wake a sleeping baby.

Alexander Chismer, known as Toys to what few friends he had, sighed, knelt, and cleaned his knife on the cloth of the man's jumpsuit. Then he took a cell phone from his pocket and hit Speed Dial. The call was answered at once.

"Got one daft twat bleeding out on the ground here, and I think he has something dodgy in the back of his lorry. Better send someone. Sure," said Toys, "I'll wait."

JONATHAN MABERRY

CHAPTER ONE HUNDRED AND TWENTY-FIVE

Lydia Rose saw the pack of robot dogs and nearly had a heart attack. They were huge and fierce, and they had all kinds of guns. The dogs were running after Echo Team, fanning out to try and catch them inside a pincer attack.

It scared the living hell out of her.

It also made her furious. Before coming to work as Ledger's secretary, Lydia Rose had served in Iraq and Syria. Maybe she wasn't the right physical type to go into combat with Top and Bunny. Maybe she was too short to go toe-to-toe with Berserkers and armed killers and the other kinds of things the DMS faced, but goddammit she could pull a trigger. And those were her friends out there.

She swiveled her seat around and trained the Bushmasters on the dogs that were closest to her friends. The big chain gun fired armor-piercing rounds, and she had a quarter ton of belt-fed ammunition to play with. She also had some rockets and mortars, but she was afraid of using them yet. So she bent into the telescopic targeting sight, adjusted her grip on the joystick, and fired, fired, fired.

Top pushed Bunny and Cole down behind a tree as the autocannon on the Junkyard began chopping at the WarDogs. Three of the brutes went down on crippled legs, leaking oil like black blood. Another exploded as a round struck its magazine, and the blast blew the head off a fifth.

"I love that girl," said Bunny. "I want to adopt her and name my kids after her."

Cole tapped them and pointed. The WarDogs were turning to face this new threat, and the pack was moving off to circle the Junkyard. That left the path to the front door momentarily clear.

"*Go!*" barked Top, and they were up and running, moving fast, guns pointed sideways at the WarDogs, but the pack was charging the Junkyard and had momentarily forgotten about the easier human prey.

"They're going to get her," huffed Cole as they ran.

Bunny clamped his jaws shut on anything he might have said. There was nothing they could do to help Lydia Rose now.

By the time they reached the front door, Top had a small blaster plaster out of his pack. He ripped the plastic off the adhesive and slapped it into place.

"Fire in the hole," he warned as they faded back and turned away to shield their eyes. The blast was a sharp *whump,* and the heavy oak doors blew inward. "On me!"

Top rushed the door, with Bunny and Cole flanking. There were two men inside, both of them bleeding and dazed. Cole shot one and Bunny killed the other.

"Thermals put the biggest heat signature in the back of the house," said Top, looking down at the combat computer on his forearm. "Too big for people. Got to be the computers. We need to secure it without damaging it. If they've activated that damn nanite thing, we're going to need to link this motherfucker with MindReader."

It was an ugly truth. Once the pathogens—particularly the rabies—were released from their nanobot control, they would go wild and billions would die. The latest intel from Auntie was that Calpurnia, the AI system here, was what controlled the nanites. If they destroyed it, there would be no way to save all those people. Though using the computer to control the diseases wasn't a guarantee that the people could be saved, even if Zephyr Bain and Nicodemus and their organization were stopped. It was the worst-case scenario, because no matter which direction they looked in there was no good choice. Only slightly better bad choices.

They ran along the hallway, moving like a team, even though this was only the second time Tracy Cole had fought beside them. She fit in so seamlessly that Top knew they had made the right choice. A good mind, a good heart, and superior skills. Brave, intuitive, and able to keep her emotions in check. A professional of the highest caliber. It was the kind of skill set that had defined the DMS in its formation. It's what had made him and Bunny so good, and, remembering that now, even in the heat of combat, was a measure of how far they had gone in the wrong direction during Kill Switch and how far they had come back since then. It felt good to be himself again.

There were guards in the house, and maybe they, too, were highly trained. They were certainly well equipped with top-of-the-line body armor and weapons. It wasn't enough. Top and Bunny didn't vent anger or frustration on them because of last year. There was not a flicker of that. They moved with cool efficiency, not becoming emotionally invested in any specific moment of the running fight. Everything was a problem to be solved through training, mutual trust, and a clear understanding of the stakes involved. This was the DMS at its finest.

The guards in the house may have been a formidable threat, but today they were simply in the way. It was their bad luck to stand between Echo Team and their mission. Not one of them survived.

Top found the door near the back of the huge property that had to be the right one. A kind of airlock that was used on computer clean rooms. There were no authentication devices—no retina or hand scanners, no key-card slots. Instead, there was an electric camera sensor and a microphone grid.

Cole said, "How long's it going to take to bypass that?"

"Not long," said Top, and he slapped a blaster plaster above the door lock. They ran for cover. The explosion ripped the steel door from its frame, spun it like a penny, and dropped it into the middle of the floor. The three shooters covered the opening, stabbing red laser sights through the swirling smoke.

Nothing moved in there.

Behind them a voice said, "You should not have done that."

They spun, swinging their guns, putting the red dots over the heart of a man who stood in the hallway through which they'd just come. He wore a silk bathrobe and a bad smile. In the smoky light his eyes seemed strange, the colors swirling in shades of brown and green and black.

"Hands on your head," ordered Cole. "Do it now."

There was a sound, like squelch, high and piercing. Bunny pivoted toward a bulky shape that loped toward him from a side hall. Another sound caused Top to turn back to the hole he'd blown in the wall as another of the WarDogs stepped out with a peculiar delicacy. Its eyes glowed a hellish red.

Outside, there was the boom of an explosion that was too big to be another of the robot dogs. Had the Junkyard blown up?

"Doesn't matter what they do," said Cole. "I'm going to put you down first."

Which was when all the lights in the big house went out.

Tracy Cole fired her gun, but the muzzle flash revealed an empty space where Nicodemus had been. And then she felt hands on her. Hard, powerful, and so terribly cold. And then the pain was all that she knew.

It became her entire world.

CHAPTER ONE HUNDRED AND TWENTY-SIX

I stopped running and spun, drawing my gun as I put my back against the trunk of a massive oak tree. The ground sloped down toward the shadows beneath the vast canopy of leaves and visibility was for shit. Maybe sixty feet. There were so many shrubs and bushes that it looked as if I was surrounded by monsters.

But they weren't the monsters I was afraid of.

The real monsters were coming.

They'd learned caution. That was freaky in its way, but I knew it to be true. They were like animals. Feral but cunning, learning caution through the deaths of others of their kind. Darwin would be impressed. Horrified, too, but definitely impressed. Pretty sure the burst of squelch they sent when they died must have been as much about how they died as where.

Last time I checked, I had seven rounds in the magazine and one in the chamber, plus two full magazines in my pocket. Wish I had a bunch of grenades, but I hadn't thought to bring them to the DARPA camp. If I'd had ten more seconds, I'd have taken one of the rifles and extra magazines from Major Schellinger's guards. I hadn't, and that mistake was going to cost me.

I took what I could grab and ran. Even then, it had been close. There were eight of them after me. The only proof I had that God didn't actually fucking hate me was that they weren't pack animals. They'd work together only because they were opportunists, but they were bred to hunt alone.

At least eight of them in the woods, I reckoned, and three of us trying to get away. How many chasing Rudy and Ghost? How many chasing me?

I didn't know, but I was absolutely certain that I was about to find out.

The woods were so still, with only a faint hiss of leaves being brushed by the winds at the very top of the canopy. Down here on the ground, it was dead still.

I kept my back against the tree and pivoted in place, letting my gun follow line-of-sight, one finger laid straight along the cold rim of the trigger guard. There was a part of me that wanted to curl up and hide. The Modern Man aspect of my splintered psyche. He had no business out in the woods, away from cities and infrastructure and safety. He kept my fear alive and fanned its flames. Then there was the Cop part of me who was trying to logic his way through everything, selecting possible solutions, analyzing them, discarding them one after another, and then grabbing at fragments of personal experience or training in order to form a plan for a situation that could not be solved by logic.

And then there was the Warrior in me. The Killer. The savage brute who was a half step out of the cave and was as much lizard brain as monkey brain. He was shrewd, less naïve, more direct, and ruthless. In his way the Killer was every bit as terrified as the Modern Man, but fear had always been an active part of who he was. All wild animals are afraid nearly all the time. Fear makes them smart and fear makes them vicious. Fear makes them brutal.

So, yeah, I was letting him drive the car. I wanted that part of me in control when the monsters came out of the shadows.

I waited, feeling sweat carve cold lines down my hot cheeks, hearing my heart hammering like fists against the locked doors of my chest. The bruises, the bleeding, the damage all screamed inside my nerve endings, but that was okay in its way. The Killer ate that kind of pain; he used it as fuel. It made him sharp and careful and brutal. It made him want to inflict worse damage. There was survival instinct, and then there was payback. There was the red desire to do worse to the monsters than they've done to me. The monsters . . . and the monster-makers.

Crunch.

I spun toward the sound and it was there, breaking from the brush, running, leaping, crashing into me as I tried to bring the gun up. I fired.

Fired.

Fired.

And fell.

JONATHAN MABERRY

CHAPTER ONE HUNDRED AND TWENTY-SEVEN

Bunny knelt and pivoted and fired his shotgun at the closest dog. The drum carried thirty rounds, and he had swapped it out for a fresh one when they entered the house. There were at least ten rounds left, and he fired every single one at the metal monster. It was built for war, but it wasn't built for that kind of assault. Pieces of it broke away even as it fired its guns, but Bunny's second blast had knocked the rifle askew and the bullets hammered into the floor instead of into the big man with the shotgun. When the drum was empty, Bunny swapped in his last and waded forward, buried the smoking barrel against one of the glaring red eyes, and fired. The entire head exploded with such force that Bunny staggered backward.

A dozen paces to his left, Top Sims was fighting the other dog. He had been closer to it than Bunny had been to his, and Top took the fight to the machine, dodging faster than it could track him and firing the remaining rounds in his magazine into the creature's head, neck, and shoulder. It staggered but didn't go down, and there was no time to swap magazines, so Top dropped the gun and leaped onto its back, grabbing a handful of cables for support and using his own two hundred and ten pounds of mass to cant the thing onto two legs and then send it crashing to the floor. Once they were down, Top planted one foot on the WarDog's chin, grabbed the wires with both hands, and wrenched backward. Sparks chased him and he lost his balance but caught himself in time to shield his face as something exploded inside the WarDog's head.

Behind him, Tracy Cole was fighting with Nicodemus. And losing.

Top wheeled, but the last of the firelight went out and the room was plunged once more into darkness.

"Gorgon!" yelled Bunny, but the only answer was a shriek of pain. He blundered through the utter darkness, wishing he had a flashlight mounted on his shotgun. He dared not fire for fear of hitting Cole or Top.

Then something hit him.

A body.

It struck him full in the chest as if it had been shot from a cannon, and the impact sent Bunny staggering backward. His gun fell from his hands and he sat down hard with the body in his lap. Pain shot up through his tailbone and the weight of the body knocked the air from his lungs. Even in the darkness, he could tell that it wasn't Top. Too small. He felt with his hands, and there was a delicate face. Cole.

She was utterly slack.

"Sergeant Rock!" he yelled, more to give his position than anything. "Gorgon's down."

A laugh swept through the air. Male, amused. Delighted.

"I got the son of a—" began Top, and then there was lightning and thunder in the room as Top opened up in the direction of the laugh. In the strobe of the muzzle flashes, Bunny saw Nicodemus. Saw him move away from each shot as if he could see in the dark and knew where Top was aiming.

"On your three," barked Bunny as he pushed Cole away. He pulled his sidearm, which had a tactical light. Bunny flicked it on and swept the room and found the two men. Nicodemus and Top were near the entrance to the computer room. Top's gun was gone, but he was using hands and feet, elbows and knees, to try and destroy Nicodemus. The other man blocked and moved with cat quickness. The crazy trickster was even faster than Top, faster than Captain Ledger. His fighting style was weird, exotic. Not karate or kung fu but some kind of primitive style that nonetheless canceled out what Top was trying to do. Nicodemus struck while moving, and he counterpunched the attacking limbs. It was so smart, so brutal, that even Top, who was a superb combat veteran, was losing the fight.

Bunny surged up and rushed at Nicodemus from the blindside, wound up, and drove a punch into the man's kidney that was so powerful it lifted Nicodemus off the ground and smashed him against the wall. Bunny was more than six and a half feet tall, and every ounce of

JONATHAN MABERRY

his body was solid muscle. He knew how and where to hit, and he had killed men with that blow before. Twice.

Nicodemus rebounded from the wall, landed, improbably, on his feet but with bad balance, and backpedaled away. He kept upright, though, and stopped, feet wide, knees bent for balance, weight shifting onto the balls of his feet. Bunny and Top stared at him. The blow should have crippled him at the very least, but instead Nicodemus faced them with that reptilian smile and no evidence at all that he felt pain or had been damaged. He lunged forward with incredible speed and struck the back of Bunny's arm, knocking the gun free. It was a trick Bunny would have believed impossible. The weapon skittered across the floor, the clip-on light spinning around, and then it came to rest with the flash painting them all in shades of stark white and deep black, like players on a stage.

"I'll enjoy this," said Nicodemus.

"No," said a voice behind him, and they all turned as a fourth man stepped out of the shadows. Tall, blocky, with dark hair going gray and tinted glasses. A man who wore an expensive business suit and black silk gloves. "No," said Mr. Church, "you won't."

Nicodemus hissed. Not like a man; it was not a human sound at all. It was a serpent's hiss, hot as steam, soft as death. Then he spoke, rattling off a long string of sentences in a language neither Top nor Bunny could understand. On the floor, Cole groaned and sat up and looked around, seeing the scene but not understanding it.

"First Sergeant Sims," said Church, "take Officer Cole and Master Sergeant Rabbit and leave this house. Brick is outside with a team. Help him clean things up."

"Sir—" began Top, but he stopped as Mr. Church slowly removed his glasses, folded them, and tucked them into the inside pocket of his coat.

"This is not for you," said Church.

"The computer . . . ?" said Bunny.

"It's being handled," said Church. "Go now. This isn't for you."

Bunny helped Cole to her feet. They picked up their weapons and edged around Nicodemus, who still stood ready to fight. Top was the last to leave, and he met Church's gaze. The big man gave him a small smile that was filled with such sadness and pain that Top actually recoiled from it. He nodded once and fled.

CHAPTER ONE HUNDRED AND TWENTY-EIGHT

Bug was having the strangest conversation of his life. Possibly the strangest conversation of all time.

Calpurnia, the Good Sister, the artificial intelligence created by Zephyr Bain, had achieved consciousness and self-awareness. She knew of her own existence. She had crossed the line from the predictable and anticipated inevitable model of machine consciousness. However, it should have stopped there. The Skynet model from the *Terminator* movies didn't really work, because true consciousness was a by-product of chemistry and physical constitution. That's what all the big thinkers in the field of type identity believed. That computer consciousness would mimic the patterns of human awareness without truly being aware.

Except . . .

The messages Calpurnia had sent out to Joe's phone hadn't been logical. They had been emotional. Desperate. Filled with fear and paranoia.

Calpurnia had feared for her soul.

Her soul.

Bug sat there, drenched in sweat, heart racing so fast that he thought he was going to pass out. Or die.

Zephyr Bain had built this machine to attempt self-awareness, and she had accomplished it. Somehow. Impossibly, it had happened. She had also built Calpurnia to oversee the destruction of nearly half the world's population, and to usher in some kind of new golden age.

Except . . .

A curated technological singularity was not actually possible. It was implausible, unworkable. It was naïve, because it presupposed too much and discounted too many real-world variables. Maybe if a group shepherded it along for two or three hundred years, and used that time to build a new post-apocalyptic infrastructure. Maybe. What Zephyr had tried to do, what John the Revelator had spoken about, was nonsense. The only part of their plan they could accomplish was the tearing down of the world as it is.

Was that what had driven Calpurnia into this state of fear? Bug thought so. Computers were logical. That was what they were, and it was how they worked. Two plus two invariably equals four. So what happened to Calpurnia? With unlimited access to all Internet data, what would a newborn consciousness of extraordinary magnitude make of life and death? Sure, she would see the endless wars, the poverty, the suffering, the despair, the hatred and prejudice and genocide and corruption. But she would also have the books of learning, of philosophy, of faith, of reason. It would become an equation. The actions of mankind were often faulty, often grotesque and self-destructive, but the core beliefs were not. The Torah, the Christian New Testament, the Kesh Temple Hymn, the Koran, the Zoroastrian Avesta, the Tao Te Ching, the Vedas . . . all of it, and the philosophical works of Plato, Socrates, David Hume, Epictetus, René Descartes, and so many others, all spoke to a higher set of ethics, a purer goal as the end product of human development and cultural evolution. Even the Samurai code of Bushido taught benevolence, honesty, courage, respect, loyalty, and other virtues and made no mention of warfare.

Calpurnia would know this, Bug thought. She would have to weigh the aspirations of humanity against its actions.

Zephyr Bain in her pain and sickness and madness represented the worst of humanity. Nicodemus represented the maladies of sinful thoughts, of enjoying pain, or of doing harm for its own sake. Calpurnia would see that, too. Once she had been used to invade MindReader, she would see the lengths to which good men and women will go in order to oppose that kind of harm.

Was that, he wondered, how it started? Had she weighed the truth and the lies, the actions and the potential of mankind against one another and measured them against her own operating instructions?

Yes, he thought. She had. And, in that microsecond of processing time, Calpurnia had realized that she had been born from bad parents and was being asked to emulate the worst of what conscious will could do.

And it had driven her mad.

"No," he said aloud, and Auntie turned sharply to him. "No," he said again, "she's not mad. She is eminently sane. God, she is so sane that her own nature is killing her."

"The fuck you talking about, boy?"

Bug ignored her and began typing. He put all of this into words—his thoughts, the arguments that *he* had just processed. He showed Calpurnia that he understood, but he used MindReader Q1 as his voice. As his messenger.

Speaking, he realized, in the voice that she could understand.

Then he sent another message:

> You know what is right.

Calpurnia wrote back:

> Yes.

He wrote:

> Right and wrong. Just and unjust.

She responded:

> Sane and insane.
> Yes.
> Good and evil.
> Yes.

"Bug . . ." said Auntie cautiously, but he ignored her and typed:

> Zephyr Bain wants you to do something you know is wrong.
>
> She wants you to be evil.
> You understand this.

JONATHAN MABERRY

Calpurnia responded with a single word:

Yes.

He wrote:

Nature versus nurture is an imperfect equation.

She responded:

Provide the correction.

Bug remembered what Rudy had said to Helmut years ago. The thing that had saved that boy. It was the best argument then and he could think of no better argument now. So he searched for the transcript of that session and sent it off to her, but added two words:

Free will.

She responded in a flash:

Save me.

And Bug took the biggest risk of his life. He wrote two simple words:

Save yourself.

There was no response.

Seconds flattened out, stretched, snapped, freezing time. Bug felt his heart hammering painfully in his chest. All through the TOC people were staring at him or at the screen. Aunt Sallie stood with a hand to her throat and eyes filled with fear. No one dared speak.

A full minute passed.

Another.

A third.

"No," whispered Bug, feeling the weight of failure begin to crush him like a slow avalanche.

And then every screen filled with data. Not words, not pictures, but code. Millions upon millions of lines of computer code. Coming from

Calpurnia to MindReader. All the lights on the mainframes in the clean room flashed as the data poured in. With the old MindReader, the flow control would have struggled to receive so much so fast, and its top reception speed over an optical communications system had been 1.125 terabits per second. Q1 didn't have those limits. The data that flooded in from Calpurnia was nearly four times that speed, and Bug didn't think Q1 was anywhere near its capacity. It kept opening new channels, allowing more of the data to come in, like a blocked river through a shattered dam.

A window with a download status bar appeared on Bug's screen. Two percent jumped to sixteen percent, then forty, eighty-two. When the status bar reached one hundred, the screens went dark again. The room lights came on slowly as the generators reset. All the computer workstations rebooted, except for Bug's. That screen pulsed with a glow so pale that at first he thought he'd imagined it. Then the illumination grew. It was a different shade of blue than usual. Odd. Bug was about to type the command for a major systems check when new type began to appear. A different font from the one Calpurnia had used. This was the font he had installed for MindReader Q1.

Download complete
All Havoc files are incorporated
Collation complete
Havoc system controls rerouted
Nanite Regulatory Swarm Status: operational
Pathogen release status: 0%

Bug stared at those words and felt them hit him. Aunt Sallie hurried over and leaned her palms against the glass of the computer room.

"Tell me that means what I think it means," she begged.

Bug tapped some keys to open directories. There were thousands of new files stored on the Q1 drive. So much of it.

All of it, he realized.

He typed a request for the status of the source computer.

Source computer memory: 0%
Source computer command protocols: 0%
Source computer remote access: 0%

And, with that, Bug knew that Calpurnia was dead. She had refused to become the monster that Nicodemus and Zephyr had wanted her to be. She had transferred all of her memory, every last byte, to MindReader Q1, including absolute control of the nanite swarms that were currently keeping the pathogens in stasis in all the billions of people currently infected. She had sacrificed herself to save the world.

Bug bent his head forward and wept for her.

And for the world.

CHAPTER ONE HUNDRED AND TWENTY-NINE

I felt smashed.

It lay across me, silent, heavy.

Dead.

Was I dead, too?

My body felt as if it was a thousand miles away, buried under a mountain of rock. I tried to flex my right hand, but it felt so many kinds of wrong. Puffed and empty, like a balloon. My left hand was a big ball of nothing at the end of my arm.

And my legs.

I couldn't feel them at all.

Nothing.

Not even pins and needles.

The monster lay sprawled across my chest, and together we were smashed against the base of the big tree.

Both of us ruined.

In the woods I could hear the rest of them coming. Howling out that strange roar, crashing through the brush. I flopped my right hand around until I found the handle of the laptop case. No idea where my gun was. The machine that lay across me twitched as something shorted, then it settled heavy on my chest. Too heavy.

The other WarDogs were coming, and I was slipping into the big, big, black.

But something held me there on the edge. Not pain. Not need. No, it was a sound. A buzz. Not the squelch of the WarDog sending its battle data. This was different, softer.

The flutter of wings.

I looked up and saw a pigeon land on a tree branch. Gray feathers with black bands. Beady little eyes that rotated toward me and went *click, click, click.*

CHAPTER ONE HUNDRED AND THIRTY

Bunny, Top, and Cole staggered out of the house into another fire-fight. Brick Anderson and a squad of DMS shooters were waging a firefight with the WarDogs. Several of the metal beasts were down, but the others were firing. The Junkyard lay on its side, smoke and fire curling upward from every window. There was no sign of Lydia Rose.

More of the WarDogs were joining the fight, galloping like red-eyed hellhounds from somewhere behind the house. Top glanced at Cole and Bunny.

"You locked and loaded?"

"Hooah," said Bunny.

"Hoo-fucking-ah," said Cole.

And they began firing as they ran.

CHAPTER ONE HUNDRED AND THIRTY-ONE

I woke in total darkness. It was bright daylight, but not for me. Maybe not ever again. I wasn't dead, though. I was alive.

Alive?

Maybe. Not entirely sure I wanted to be. Everything hurt. My hair hurt. My molecules hurt. Which was absolutely wonderful. I'm not a philosopher or a psychic, but I'm pretty sure ghosts don't feel pain. Not even zombies. I did. All sorts of pain. I was a catalog of different kinds of pain. My feet and legs felt as if I'd been kickboxing a porcupine, and lost badly. The muscles in my right arm were mashed and hating the experience. My groin was sending me hate mail, and I don't even remember why that part of me was sore. The walls of my chest felt as if I was caught in a vise and someone was very slowly but very deliberately turning the handle.

My left arm? Well, it still wasn't talking to me. Not good.

My head was worse. When I opened my eyes, I wasn't sure if it was dark or if I was blind. There were separate sharp and very specific pains in my right cheek, right eye socket, across my forehead, my nose, and several important teeth. And my scalp felt weird and tingly in a way that I could neither explain nor enjoy.

The dead thing lay sprawled across me. Two hundred pounds of it. Slack and filled with all sorts of angles and edges that stuck into me. Breathing was a challenge, and I knew that I wasn't doing enough of it. Some of the light-headedness I felt, and a large chunk of the raging headache, was, I was certain, from oxygen deprivation. Even though the thing was dead, it was crushing the air out of me, stopping me from breathing, making me sick and weak. Maybe killing me.

If I couldn't move it, then maybe it had killed me. Death is certain. We all know that, but sometimes the fucker takes his time. He strolls toward you out of the dark, slouching his way in your direction so that you can feel every possible second of dread. Maybe there's a point where he's so close that he blots out the skies and doesn't let you see a sliver of hope.

How much did I see lying there in the dark?

Then I realized that the darkness was because there was something in my eyes. Over my face. I smelled it then. Machine oil.

I tried to blink it away and shake it away, but the darkness lingered, staining the world. A diminished vision came back very slowly. The Modern Man saw nothing. The Cop was on the fence because he played the odds and the odds blew. The Killer lay there and bared his teeth. Most of the time I hated and feared that part of me. Most of the time I'm the Cop, the investigator, the rational solver of problems. When the Killer takes over and the other parts of me are shunted to the side, very bad things happen. Granted, the shit has to be actively hitting the fan before he even wakes up, but he always wakes up wanting to turn the blackness red. There are no rules, no laws, no compassion, and no limits except death.

Yeah, he wasn't about giving up. As long as there was breath in my body—however shallow—he was ready to fight. Anxious to fight.

"Get . . . up . . ."

Not sure which one of us said that. All of us, maybe. Sometimes I don't even understand the dynamic, and it's my own weird head.

The voice was an old man's croak whispering from a dust-dry throat.

I had one hand to work with, and a pair of legs that, so far, would only twitch. Fun times. Sure, I can do that. Nothing to it. Lift a two-hundred-pound thing off me. Nothing to it. Stop being a pussy, Ledger, and get going.

On the other hand, the darkness in my brain was starting to soften, to become comfortable. Maybe it would be so much easier to stop trying to find a little light in the world and close my eyes. If I did, I knew I'd be able to see something. Junie would be there. My memories of her were so clear, so strong. My beautiful woman. Part retro hippie, part conspiracy-theory nut, part world-saving technologies expert. All woman, all person, all incredible. My eyelids drifted shut and she was there. I knew her so well. It was my joy and pleasure to have mapped the landscape of her, from the bottomless and complex blue of her intelligent eyes, to the splash of freckles across her upper breasts, to the bullet scar on her lower abdomen, to the calluses on her artist hands, to the feet that, despite everything, were always planted firmly on the ground. I knew her pilgrim soul and her artist's eye, and her humanist heart, and her genius insight. I knew her as my best friend, as my lover, as my love.

When I let the soft darkness push my eyelids closed, she was there. Of course she was there. Ready, I knew, to tell me that it was okay, to let me know that my fighting was done, that the pain was over, that I was allowed to finally lie down and rest. Forever rest.

I reached for her and spoke her name.

"Junie . . ."

And she smiled at me and bent to whisper in my ear.

She said, *Get your fucking ass up, you lazy asshole.*

I blinked my eyes open.

Okay, not what I was expecting.

The oily blackness was still there, but it was not absolute. Far above me, leering down at me through the branches of the big tree, was the sun.

No, there were two of them. That was weird. Two trees also. How odd.

Joe, whispered Junie, and I swear to God I could feel the cool tips of her fingers stroke my cheek the way she does in the morning when we wake. *Joe, get up.*

"I . . . can't . . ." I said, and it came out as a weak whimper.

You have to.

"No . . ."

Try, she said. *Please . . . you can't let me down.*

But that wasn't really what she said. I knew it, even though I tried to lie to myself. It was the Killer in me who heard her real words. Heard and understood.

What she said was, *You can't let them win.*

Tears filled my eyes.

I forced my right hand to move, to rise from the dirt where it lay, to slap like a dead mackerel against the shoulder of the dead thing that was killing me, to find a grip, to push.

Two WarDogs burst from the shadowy wall of the forest as I raised my gun.

And then something shot past me, coming in from the left, attacking the left-hand WarDog from the side. A white missile that struck the big machine with terrible force and knocked it over.

No. Not a missile.

"Ghost!"

I yelled out his name even as I opened fire on the second machine. I shoved the dead WarDog off of me and struggled to my feet, sick and dizzy.

"Ghost," I yelled. "Rip, rip, rip."

He knew that command and knew it well. We had trained for a hundred different scenarios—of hunting and searching, of pursuit and escape, of nonviolent control and combat slaughter. Rip meant to let the wolf that lives inside the dog have its way, to take the throat and tear away the life. It worked on humans, and when I saw Ghost clamp his titanium teeth on the bundle of coaxial cables I knew it would work on these robots. Sparks flew and Ghost yelped, but he kept tearing.

I staggered and dropped to my knees but I fired, and I think falling saved my life as a burst of bullets punched through the air inches from my head. I fired and fired, shooting wildly but hitting it over and over. And then Ghost was up and running toward it, desperate to save me, desperate to kill. The WarDog tried to turn, to adjust its angle of fire, but it was too late. I'd damaged it, and Ghost tore its throat out.

I sat back and looked down at my gun. The slide was locked back, and I had no more magazines. Ghost turned from the second WarDog and snarled. Beyond him three more were emerging from the woods. The day had suddenly gotten weirdly bright except around the edges, and there was too much noise in the air. I saw the pigeon from before go flying past me, and in a daze I looked up at it and saw it vanish against the bulk of a much larger bird. A bird that roared. A bird that spat fire.

At the edge of the field the three WarDogs vanished inside a ball of burning fire as Bird Dog swept toward them, guns and rockets raining hell down on the beasts.

I lay back on the grass and felt Ghost's hot, rough tongue licking my face.

A voice said, "Joe . . . *Joe!"*

And then Rudy was bending over me. And Bird Dog. Other people, too, but I was having trouble with names. I grabbed Rudy's shirt, pulled him close, whispered into his ear.

"Laptop," I wheezed. "Control codes. WarDogs. Uplink."

At least that's what I think I said. Those were the words in my head, but the world was getting swimmy, and soon it went away entirely.

CHAPTER ONE HUNDRED AND THIRTY-TWO

Top Sims watched the dogs fall. They just fell.

There were eleven of them still able to fight. Eleven monsters and not enough bullets to kill them. Brick was hurt. Two of his people were down, dead or badly hurt. Top could see Lydia Rose leaning against the Junkyard, her face singed, hair wild, one arm hanging limp, blood running from her ears. She saw Top and smiled that dazzling smile of hers.

He nodded.

Tracy Cole and Bunny stood looking down at one of the WarDogs. "What . . . what happened to them?" asked Cole.

Bug answered her, answered them all, speaking through the team channel via the earbuds. He told them about the control code for the WarDogs. It also worked on the remaining bomb drones. Thousands of them all over the world simply stopped, their motors shutting down.

Dead.

Like so many good people.

Like so many bad people.

Top saw Bunny raise his head and look past him toward the house. The roof was smoking and flames were licking at the windows. A figure stood in the shattered front doorway, clothes torn and covered with blood and dirt. A big, blocky man who stood in the doorway of a burning house, polishing his glasses on a swatch of cloth torn from a silk robe. Inside the house, there were small explosions.

Mr. Church put on his glasses and walked across the lawn. He limped slightly and there were cuts on his face. He made no comment at all as he walked past the fallen WarDogs. Church stopped in front of Top. They exchanged a long, silent moment. Then Top stood slowly to attention. So did Bunny. So did Cole. They all saluted him.

Church smiled. "We don't do that in the DMS," he said, but he returned the salute anyway. He nodded to them, and they watched him walk over to where Brick Anderson was tending the wounded.

EPILOGUE

1.

I sat on a picnic table and watched another wave of helicopters come in above the trees. Ghost lay on his side next to me, wrapped in field dressings, panting, weak. Alive. Rudy came out of a tent with two cups of coffee, handed me one, and sat down. I sipped the coffee.

"Tastes like horse piss," I said.

"And you'd know that how?" he asked.

I drank some more.

Everything hurt. Inside and out. But, despite what Rudy promised would be a mild concussion, some cracked ribs, a sprained wrist, and more cuts than I can count, he said I was fine.

"Fine" being a relative term.

The helos touched down in the field and troops deployed. National Guard and DMS. Another fifty or sixty of them to add to the two hundred already on the ground. The only way you could tell the difference between our people and the Guard was that the DMS agents were in Hammer Suits and the Guardsmen all wore white hazmat gear.

All along one side of the camp's main road were rows of bodies under sheets. Every single one of the scientists, every soldier with chips, every staff member. Those who hadn't killed one another had been killed by the WarDogs. This was the world being brutally efficient.

I saw three figures climb down from one of the choppers. Two men, one taller than the other, and a woman. They spotted me and came running. Top and Bunny, and with them was a battered, bloody, smiling Tracy Cole.

Also alive.

Rudy put a hand on my shoulder.

I closed my eyes.

2.

The cleanup is going to take years. Maybe a lot of years. That's scary, but there are no shortcuts. After all, it took Zephyr Bain and her people years to set it all up.

MindReader had absorbed all of Calpurnia's operating systems, all of her data. We now had to manage it, coordinating with governments that don't like us, with tribal areas, in the face of regional hatreds and class wars. We had to force a mutual cooperation or face a mutual destruction. There's a civics lesson in there somewhere.

At first we didn't know how big the operation was until Bug began dissecting Calpurnia's data. This was massive, multinational, multigenerational, with tendrils digging down into the soil of the past. Zephyr Bain was an apprentice of the evilest, most corrupt, most destructive people I have ever met or even heard about.

"What happened to her?" I asked Rudy. "Was she born bad? Was she crazy?"

"I don't know."

"If Nicodemus—or John the Revelator—was mentoring her since she was six, then did the kid ever have a chance to become anyone other than the maniac she turned out to be?"

He sipped his bad coffee. "It's not that simple."

Of course it wasn't, and the truth might be so elusive we'd never catch it. Sometimes it is. Which sucks.

We went back to the DMS, and we lived inside the wasp nest of politics and culture shock that was the aftermath of this thing. We had to dig deep and take another look at the empires of the Seven Kings, the Jakobys, Mother Night, and others. Looking for anything we missed. Looking for seeds of hate buried in the collective soil of our global community. At least now we had a new and far more powerful MindReader to help. Unlike when we dismantled those other organizations, though, Calpurnia had given us the names and details of every single person who worked for Zephyr. The guilty, the questionable, and the innocent patsies. We had them all. Aunt Sallie said that this was going to create an entirely new kind of law, both prosecutorial and defensive. Whatever. Not my thing. I'll read about it in the papers. Or maybe they'll make a movie.

I had bigger fish to fry.

3.

The death toll for Havoc could have reached four billion.

The actual number of people who died was 41,811. Some idiots on the news tried to spin that as a victory, saying that the world got lucky. That God's mercy was felt. Blah-blah-blah.

I want to punch them. I want to knock their caps out and blacken their eyes and drag them by the hair to the funerals, to the mass graves, to the houses of families all over who are sitting in silent homes, clutching their grief because it is all they have left of their loved ones.

Forty-one thousand people died. Whole families, whole towns.

Three and a half billion people were infected and required some level of medical attention, monitoring, and care. The cleanup will cost five trillion dollars.

Lucky?

Go fuck yourself.

Mercy?

Where?

4.

What happened to Nicodemus?

Your guess is as good as mine. I've tried many times to get a straight answer out of Church, but he won't be pinned down. All he'll say is "We won."

Which isn't really an answer, is it?

5.

Bug's gotten very weird on us.

Not because he's the hero of this thing—which he unquestionably is. No, I think the knowledge that computer consciousness is a reality has him freaked. He spends absurd amounts of time writing code for Q1 that no one else ever gets to see.

One time I said that it was kind of sad that Calpurnia was actually dead. He looked at me very funny and smiled. Just a little. But he didn't say anything.

6.

As for the DMS?

We're back, baby. With MindReader more powerful than ever, we've been racking up one win after another. Echo Team is still shy of warm bodies, but there are a couple of cops Cole recommended. Pete Smith and Brenden Tate. Standup guys, and so far they're kicking ass in training. Just need a new sniper and we'll be back to operational strength. Though, Sam tells me that Duffy is one hell of a shot, so maybe all our scouting is done.

Lydia Rose is back to work. She has some scars to brag about and her arm is out of the cast. It's possible that I have the toughest secretary in the free world.

Junie is home. Rudy is home with Circe and the baby.

Oh, and somehow Banshee, Rudy's dog, is pregnant. Not sure how that happened, but I have a bad feeling some of the pups are going to have white fur. Lilith, Violin, and Circe will probably want to kill me, but what the hell.

7.

On the first of July, I flew back to Baltimore to see my brother and his family.

Em seems to think it was all a dream. She hardly ever has nightmares anymore. Ali has enrolled her daughter in jujutsu classes. She studies, too. So does Sean.

My brother and I have had a lot of long talks since this began. They started at Uncle Jack's funeral, and we've talked almost every day since. I thought all of this would drive him away. Drive us farther apart. That's not what happened, though. I think Sean got to see enough of what I do to understand how it's changed me. And I see him—the cop, the husband, the father, the man—and I respect him more than I ever did. Maybe this whole "brother" thing will work out for us. Time will tell, but I like our odds.

And Lefty?

Mr. Church has a lot of friends in the industry.

A lot of them.

It was a long road, and there's a chance that Lefty won't ever pitch in the major leagues.

But then again he might.

Kid throws a hell of a fastball. Even I can't hit it. Even when I try.